The (Im)Perfect Girlfriend

♥

Lucy-Anne Holmes is an actress living in London. This is her second book. Her first novel, *50 Ways to Find a Lover*, had its genesis in Lucy's blog, www.spinstersquest.com, cataloguing Lucy's real-life love woes.

By the same author

50 Ways to Find a Lover

Lucy-Anne Holmes

♥

The (Im)Perfect Girlfriend

PAN BOOKS

First published 2010 by Pan Books
an imprint of Pan Macmillan, a division of Macmillan Publishers Limited
Pan Macmillan, 20 New Wharf Road, London N1 9RR
Basingstoke and Oxford
Associated companies throughout the world
www.panmacmillan.com

ISBN 978-0-330-45840-5

Typeset by Susie Bell, www.f-12.co.uk
Printed in the UK by CPI Mackays, Chatham ME5 8TD

Visit www.panmacmillan.com to read more about all our books
and to buy them. You will also find features, author interviews and
news of any author events, and you can sign up for e-newsletters
so that you're always first to hear about our new releases.

For Paul,
a wonderful man,
with love

♥ *one* ♥

I used to be in a wonderful relationship with a bloke called
Simon. We were supposed to live happily ever after. But
we didn't. Our wonderful relationship followed the other
oft-trod path.

It went tits up.

♥

I wish I knew when the tits started turning upward. Was
there one moment between us that activated a throbbing red
panic button marked 'DOOM!'? Or was the relationship
always wrong? Was it kaput from the start but we were so
drunk on sex, three-for-the-price-of-two wine offers and foot
massages that we didn't notice?

Or did I just cock it all up?

I bet it was the latter. I've always been particularly brilliant at cocking things up.

I wish I had protected the relationship. I wish I'd nur-
tured it like a child. Instead I said, 'Where do you want to
play? The building site or the road? And would you like a

gun or a knife, or how about both and some solvents?' So off my relationship toddled into the middle of the M25 with a Pritt Stick up its nose.

♥

But it was perfect to begin with. I remember the first of December last year. London was just settling into the season of goodwill, otherwise known as fraught hell. The weather had turned its usual off-white-knicker-grey and it was church-before-breakfast cold. The papers were flooded with stories of global warming and Simon and I had taken them very seriously. We'd decided not to touch the thermostat but use our body heat for warmth and share baths. We were eco-warriors, treating our one-bedroom flat in Camden as though it was a honeymoon suite in the Maldives.

Simon and I had been going out for a little over two months but we'd been great friends for twelve years and flatmates for one year before that. Simon said he waited patiently for me to wake up to the fact that the love of my life was sleeping in the next room. In my defence, I've always found it hard to wake up. Anyway, we were in love. We were in a bubble of love floating over the seasonal mayhem. I didn't think there could be a pin in the world sharp enough to pop it. And I definitely wasn't aware that someone was sharpening an axe with the intention of hacking our love bubble to pieces.

I'd always hated Christmas before. Each year I tried to

copy the gleeful expressions that women have in Boots adverts. But it's hard to experience glee when you've been queuing in Topshop for forty-five minutes, you're sweating out an office party hangover, you're just about to hand over all your credit cards knowing at least two will be declined and you're feeling obese because you've just tried on a dress that made you look like a papier mâché Christmas bauble. Historically, I'd endured the Christmas process by drinking through the pain and asking anyone who'd listen why we couldn't just chip in and buy Jesus a card. However, last year it was the happiest time of my life. I'd even bought an advent calendar. That was how much I wasn't hating Christmas last year.

'You have the first chocolate, babe,' Simon said when we opened the window marked '1'. We were post-bath, swaddled in a duvet, lying on the sofa. 'I'm going to massage your feet.' He wiggled himself around in the quilt so my feet were on his lap and I bit the milk chocolate snowman's head off.

'I love you, Sarah,' he said, but even if he hadn't said it I would have known. The fact that he was prepared to go within ten yards of my feet told me.

I've always had smelly feet. This is because I am a diehard supporter of cheap, high-heeled shoes. My family has called me Fungus Foot for most of my life. My response to this has been to tie shoes up in plastic bags, leave them outside rooms and then douse my honky hoofs in strong man deodorant. Simon had a far more radical response to my feet. He thought they needed some loving. He would wash them in the bath and then rub cream into them as we lay on the sofa.

'I love you, Simon Gussett,' I told him dreamily. I didn't even flinch as I said his surname. I just looked at his beautiful face with those blue eyes and that sexy brown stubble and the top of his muscly shoulders as they worked on my feet and I smiled. Then he smiled back, and the act of looking into each other's eyes and smiling always triggered the same reaction. We had to kiss. Kissing Simon was perfect. There was neither tooth-bashing nor dribble. We kissed until it became necessary to stop so that we could breathe, by which time my lips were so swollen it looked like I'd been pleasuring a brillo pad. We grinned at each other again and I felt the urge to utter something brilliantly intellectual.

'Have I mentioned that I'm hopelessly in love with you?'

He sighed contentedly and resumed work on my feet. Then he started a deep and meaningful discussion about a very important issue.

'Do you know who my favourite actress is?'

'Um . . . Angelina Jolie?'

'Nah . . . minger.'

'Penélope Cruz.'

'Munter chops? Hardly.'

'I give up.'

'Sarah Sargeant.'

I beamed because I'm Sarah Sargeant. And I'm an actress. And in just two days' time, I was going to fly to LA to play a role in my first Hollywood movie. Not just any Hollywood movie. An Eamonn Nigels psychological thriller. With seventeen lines I was going to immortalize a stripper called Taylor who got murdered in a hedge. This wasn't just the next rung on my career ladder. It was my leg-up into the loft. I'd been in a Pizza Hut ad. I'd done *The Bill* and *Midsomer Murders*. I'd performed on stage in the West End. Now I was going to Hollywood. It was the start of my dream. (My apologies. It was *X Factor* season.) Everything I'd worked, acted and extensively waitressed for my entire adult life had been granted. And I had a beautiful boyfriend who was proud of me. I'm surprised I didn't explode with bliss.

'Sarah Sargeant. I've heard she's up and coming,' I opined, as though I was on *Newsnight*.

'She keeps me up and coming,' he smirked, as though he was on a building site.

I sniggered dirtily.

'And do you know who my most favourite charity-setter-upper is?'

This was the cherry on the Bakewell. Simon's career was cooking perfectly too. He had made a lot of money as the sole importer of a drink you might have heard of, Cockalada. It's a tequila-based beverage served in a realistically shaped plastic willy. But he's so kind he didn't just want to make money and spend it on himself. So he'd set up a charity that offered adventure holidays to teenagers who couldn't afford them. The first trip had been to Brazil. I went with him. It was a huge success and now Eamonn Nigels, the famous film director, had not only given me seventeen lines in his film, he had also backed Simon's charity financially.

'No, no, I don't know who your favourite charity-setter-upper is. Bono?'

'Pah!'

'Geldof?'

'Don't be ridiculous.'

'Who, then?'

'Elton John.'

I thought I was very funny. Simon forgot my feet and lurched at me. I ended up squealing into his armpit as he tickled me. I wish time hadn't galloped away so carelessly from that armpit moment. The following day things started to change. A series of ominous phone calls were about to slyly wreck our elegant equilibrium.

♥ *two* ♥

The first phone call came when we were buying a Christmas tree. We weren't comically struggling through snow-covered streets in leafy Hampstead with a real evergreen held above our heads. Far from it. We were in Argos in Camden High Street. Argos had for a long time been on my list of most unpleasant things. It was wedged quite high up there between eating offal and thrush. So I should have known.

I suppose Argos deserves to be congratulated for making the simple process of shopping hard. Why go into a shop, pick up the item you want and pay for it when you can follow this nifty little process?

1 Locate a catalogue with all its pages in
2 Find the code of the item you want
3 Find a pen and an order slip
4 Write code on order slip
5 Queue at a till
6 Eventually talk to a man who will either tell you the item isn't in stock (in which case return to 1 now) or

take your money and give you a receipt with a code
on it
7   Wait for your code to appear on a screen
8   Go up to a counter and queue with all the other
people whose codes have appeared on the screen
9   Collect the item, which may or may not be the item
you want

On the day in question Simon and I were stuck on 3 because
someone had nicked all the little pens that the store
provided.

'Would my movie-star girlfriend mind staying here while
I whiz across the road to the bookies and pinch one of
theirs?' Simon asked.

'Your movie-star girlfriend wouldn't mind at all.' I
smiled. I loved it when he called me his movie-star girlfriend.
'As long as she can have a small kiss with a tiny amount of
tongue before her charity-setter-upper boyfriend leaves her
for a whole minute,' I replied, because love makes you feel
like a god but talk like a pillock.

We had a little snog while an eight-year-old boy shouted,
'Urgh!' and then Simon ran off, leaving me holding the
page. My finger was on the three foot Fibre-Optic Starburst
Christmas Tree that we liked because it had cascading lights
and was only twenty quid. My phone rang. It was Eamonn
Nigels.

'Oh my God!' I womanly whooped when I answered.
'Guess what! Simon and I are just buying a Christmas tree

and we've decided that rather than placing an angel on the top, we're going to put a picture of you there! Because you are like an angel to us.'

Now, Eamonn Nigels is a successful film director with gravitas and understated style. It was fairly obvious that he'd abhor the thought of us cutting out his head, placing it on cardboard and circling it with fairy lights. But I wanted him to know how grateful we both were to him.

'Sarah, where are you? Sounds like a riot!'

'Pretty much. Argos.'

'You poor thing.'

'Hmmm. Anyway, not for long! I'm seeing you in a few days,' I screeched. 'What's the weather like in LA? I mean, I know it's warmer than here. I've bought a lot of summer clothes. Like credit-card-abuse amounts of summer clothes.' I cackled. 'But does it get chilly in the evenings? My mum keeps going on about it. Now I'm sure you don't go out at night and your fingers and toes drop off, but, what I'm trying to say, not very succinctly is, do I need a jacket?' I have a habit of speaking incessant bollocks when I'm excited.

'Oh, Sarah. I don't know how to say this. But we've lost the film. It's off. The studio's gone bust.'

'What?' I said quietly, and I stepped away from the fibre-optic tree, past the Christmas shoppers and into the chilly outside air. I saw Simon darting out of the betting office and sprinting across the busy street. He spotted me and grinned as he waved a blue biro and narrowly avoided the front of a

134 bus. It was the first time since we'd been going out that I couldn't smile back at him.

'The studio's gone bust, Sarah,' Eamonn repeated. 'I'm so terribly sorry. I'll speak to you soon.'

I sat down sadly on the pile of Argos catalogues by the entrance. Simon arrived.

'I'm not going to LA any more,' I whispered.

'Oh shit, babe,' he said, standing in front of me and pulling my head to his chest.

'Bollocks and wank,' I groaned into his jumper as the disappointment descended. This left me with no job and no money. All I had was a dream in smithereens and a pile of vest tops that I didn't need and couldn't afford. It was like I'd been so close to success that I could smell it, but just before I could get my fingers on it some bastard had whisked it away.

'Come on, babe. Think positive.'

Simon was a big ambassador for positive thinking. He was the only bloke I'd ever met who bought books from the Mind Body Spirit section of bookshops. His latest purchase was *The Passage To Enlightenment*. But these books made him so chilled out he hadn't even minded when I wrote 'Back' in biro on the front cover before the word 'Passage'. I didn't read those books. I was much happier with a Jilly Cooper.

'Oh, not the positive, babe. Can't I just wallow?' I protested.

'No, Sare! Where focus goes energy flows! If you focus

on not having a job, then you'll never get a job. Come on, visualize getting another job.'

I moaned dramatically like a child who'd been told to pick up their toys.

'Close your eyes,' he ordered.

I obeyed, unwillingly and with a huff.

'Now, visualize!'

'Si!'

'Visualize. Come on. You're on stage. A big theatre. A huge audience. They're all cheering. Can you hear them?'

'Hmmm,' I said, even though all I could hear was traffic and the sound of the Argos automatic doors.

'Yeah!' he burst loudly, and he spoke with such enthusiasm that I opened one of my eyes to sneak a look at him. Simon still had his eyes closed. His face was scrunched up. He was taking powerful breaths as though he could smell summer dew, not flue. And he smiled contentedly like he really was imagining me in a great theatre job. I sat looking at him, thinking that he was the loveliest man on earth. Then a small boy approached and offered to sell us a tiny Argos pen for 20p.

❤ *three* ❤

Now, that wasn't exactly the beginning of the end between me and Simon. Nothing had really changed. We were still in love. The only thing that was different was that I felt a bit crap. I had gone from being a movie-star girlfriend to an unemployed girlfriend.

If I was to be honest, I felt a bit worthless. If our relationship was a shiny new car, then a dent had appeared on my side that I was ashamed of. But I was trying to fix it. I was trying to bash the panel straight. Simon prescribed that I use the disappointment to my advantage. So I spent three days sending out letters to theatre and television companies that said:

> *Dear Potential Employer,*
>
> *I was due to fly out to LA this week to film the new Eamonn Nigels film. However, the studio responsible for the film has gone bust.*
>
> *Hence I am writing to you cheekily today on the off chance that you might have a job going for a talented actress in her twenties*. Hollywood's loss could be your gain.*

I would be so very much obliged if you would consider me for any roles you might have.
Kind regards
Sarah Sargeant

* I was actually thirty, so that was just a small white lie.

I attached my CV to the letter. I was proud of my CV, although it did contain one or two more small white lies. Not that I am a liar by nature. I have hardly ever lied in my life. This is because:

1 I went to a convent. Catholic Guilt featured rampantly on the curriculum
2 The few times I have lied, the lie has been uncovered in a hugely embarrassing and public manner. (Most notably when I made up a sex story on a blog and the *Evening Standard* wrote a feature on it. Long story)

But, in my defence, everyone lies on their CV. A CV is a piece of promotional material. And we all know that pieces of promotional material are pretty lies fabricated to sell stuff.

Generally, an actor's CV is much more fictitious than a normal person's CV though. We have whole sections that are fun to embellish. I would like to meet a person strong enough not to have a crack at creative writing when faced with the heading 'Skills'. Personally, I am rendered dangerously weak in the face of a 'Skills' section. Here are a few of my skills:

Skills
Windsurfing (been once)
Ice skating (used to go when I was seven)
Flamenco (sure I could pick it up)
Conversational German (*Ja! Danke!*)
Yoga (Simon does it, so have watched it a lot)

There are also two other horrible sections that we have on our CVs that beg equivocation:

Weight
It says on my CV that I weigh eight and a half stone. Now, six years ago when I weighed nine stone five, that wasn't such a lie. But by the fifth of December last year when I'd reached ten and a half stone, it probably was.

Singing
Most actors can sing, so they must state what key they can sing in. My key is off-key. But you can't write that, or 'Tone deaf – only when drunk', because having a sense of humour isn't encouraged when writing CVs. So I wrote, 'Alto', which means 'can't do high notes' and is what I thought actors wrote if they weren't very good at singing.

So I admit my CV harboured a few little fibs, but it hardly made me Bill Clinton. And it had been this way for years. When my agent called that day, I just was eating the fifth chocolate from my advent calendar. It was a star.

'Sarah!'

'Is that my lovely agent?'

'It certainly is, Sarah.'

My agent is indeed lovely. He is a jolly, posh man somewhere in the upper end of his forties. I've only met him twice in the flesh. Our relationship tends to consist of him telephoning to tell me I have a commercial audition and me calling him afterwards so that he can tell me that I didn't get the commercial audition. I would like to see him more often though. He has a fine and generous portion of ginger hair. Many men would keep such ginger hair short. Not Geoff; he's gone for the full Mick Hucknall. But he's raised Mick . . . a beard. In case people don't recognize his eccentricity, he also smokes a pipe.

'I've been thinking.'

'You do surprise me.'

'I've been thinking of a role I'd be perfect for.'

'Oh marvellous, Sarah.'

'George Clooney's masseuse.'

'Wonderful, Sarah, I'll let his people know right away. I wish all my clients were as focused as you. Now then, you've been offered a job.'

'What?'

'A job.'

'Me?'

'Yes.'

'Is this a piss take?'

'I hardly have time to call you up to take the Michael, Sarah.'

'But . . .'

'In a panto.'

'A panto!'

'The role of the Princess.'

'Me? A princess!'

I'd never done panto. But I had an image of hundreds of children, their faces beaming at me in a pretty dress with a tiara, as they experienced the magic of theatre for the first time. It was a lovely image. So was that of a figure under the 'Money In' column on my bank statement.

'Do you want to take it? They're desperate.'

'Yes! So am I.'

'Marvellous.'

'Hang about. Why are they offering it to me?'

'It's Dominic, the director you worked with last summer. Apparently you wrote him a letter telling him you were out of work. Well, his leading lady dropped out. It's all been a bit dramatic by the sound of it. Anyway, he said he doesn't need you to audition. If you want it, it's yours. You're the same height and weight as the girl who pulled out, so the costume will fit. And they might even throw you in a flamenco solo if there's time to choreograph it.'

Now, perhaps I should have come clean at that point. But I opted to wing it instead. In hindsight that was a big mistake.

♥ *four* ♥

Dominic the Director was one disaster away from a nervous breakdown. And then I arrived at the theatre.

He beamed when he saw me.

'Nightmare doesn't begin to describe it!' he whispered with feeling in my ear.

It certainly had been quite exciting in Pantoland. The twenty-two-year-old *Hollyoaks* star who had been playing the Princess had eloped with the married retired cricketer playing the King yesterday during the dress rehearsal. The rest of the cast had understandably gone out last night and got drunk, and unfortunately one of the dancers had been arrested for indecently exposing himself in the local KFC. The young man was currently being questioned, although he was expected to rejoin the company when he was released on police bail. In the meantime, Dominic was trying to field calls from local and national press and the actors' respective families. No one knew where the lovebirds had flown to, although there were rumours circulating of a sighting in a Travelodge near the M5. It was better than an issue of *Heat*.

'Now then, here's your script,' Dominic the Director said,

handing me the jumbo script of *Jack and the Beanstalk* and steering me onto the stage.

'We're going to walk slowly through the whole show, incorporating you and Dennis in.'

'Dennis?'

'Dennis Waterman, he's replacing our errant cricketer. He's not in it until the second half. So let's get going.'

My mum will be pleased, I thought. She's a huge fan of Dennis Waterman and Piers Morgan. Weird.

'Dominic, let me just assure you that this Princess will be able to control herself around the King,' I promised, in a stage whisper.

'It's good to have you, Sarah Sargeant.'

'It's very good to be here.'

He smiled and for the first time that day started to look less like Gordon Ramsay before he had the surgical work done and more like the talented director in his early thirties that he was.

The rehearsal started brilliantly. I've always loved the dress rehearsal period of a show. Not that I was dressed in costume at that point, although the costume lady was expected to come and see me at any second. Everybody else was arrayed for the show though. There was even some poor girl stuck inside a cardboard beanstalk with her face painted brown. Hoards of dancers appeared on stage one moment dressed as farmyard animals, did an exhausting number and then reappeared twenty seconds later dressed as snowflakes and did another. All the offstage drama had created a frenetic energy that made everyone fire on all cylinders.

I quickly became very excited by my role as the Princess. I modelled her on Zara Phillips and Prince Harry. I played her *über* posh with a penchant for horses and late-night drinking. I even changed the line 'I've been on a shopping spree,' to 'I've been clubbing at Boujis,' and said it as though I had a hangover and couldn't open one eye. It got a huge laugh and Dominic clapped. This was what it was all about. Simon had been right. I was being applauded in a huge theatre. I suddenly felt overwhelmingly grateful for the chaotic series of events that had led me to that experience. I loved my job. It didn't matter whether I did it in Hollywood or Cricklewood. I loved acting and I would do it wherever and whenever I got the chance. Visualization rocked.

But then I turned a page and I suddenly froze. My stomach lurched. My throat went instantly dry. My hands started bizarrely sweating and I stumbled as I tried to dry them on my combat trousers. I didn't know what to do. But the script clearly stated:

PRINCESS SINGS SOLO

I closed my eyes, hoping it was an acid flashback from the one time I tried acid years ago. I reopened them. Bollocks. No such luck. The words were still there and, as if to highlight them with a fluorescent marker, a piano began playing some remarkably high notes and ten dancers dressed like pet chihuahuas crawled playfully onto the stage behind me.

'Oh, this is your first song, Sarah,' Dominic explained, climbing onto the stage next to me. *FIRST!*

'Can we play it through once so Sarah can get a handle on the tune?' *I'VE NEVER HAD A HANDLE ON A TUNE IN MY LIFE!*

The pianist nodded. I concentrated fiercely as I listened. Perhaps it was the atmosphere or the chihuahuas or the fact that I really wanted this role, but I convinced myself that I could sing. I remembered Simon's words about visualization. I imagined myself singing the high notes perfectly. I felt powerful and capable of anything. This was my moment. How I understood Martine McCutcheon then. When the pianist started playing the song again I took a deep breath. Then I opened my mouth.

I have never heard the sound that a duck makes when it's being attacked by a fox but I imagine it's similar to the noise I made that day. It was definitely the sound of a bird in torment. Dominic, the chihuahuas and the pianist all laughed cheerfully.

'Great, but go for it seriously, Sarah!' Dominic told me merrily.

'OK,' I whispered as I weakly smiled back at him.

The pianist commenced the song again. This time I produced the same sound, just MUCH louder. The pianist stopped playing. The chihuahuas stopped crawling and Dominic stopped smiling.

The silence was terrifyingly loud. My ears rang as it yelled to me that I couldn't sing and no amount of visualization would ever make me tuneful.

'Um, I didn't know I was going to sing, I, er, can't sing,' I mumbled to Dominic. He glared back, hungrily eating the inside of his lip, and then, after a long time, he said the word 'fuck'.

'Fuck' is the word he repeated ten seconds later when a lady appeared. She was holding a tiny piece of white material that looked like a napkin, and she too glared at me when she painfully screeched, 'YOU SAID SHE WAS THE SAME SIZE AS THE *HOLLYOAKS* SLAPPER!'

♥ *five* ♥

That was how I came to play the Beanstalk in *Jack and the Beanstalk* last Christmas. Two shows a day, six days a week, with only Christmas Day off, I stood on stage, sweating inside a cardboard tree, with my face painted brown and a fixed grin as I waited to say my fourteen lines.

Simon, on the other hand, had a great December. His charity had been chosen along with five other London charities to be part of a huge fundraising concert at the Albert Hall in the New Year. I didn't feel jealous of him. Far from it. But I had started to feel that perhaps I wasn't good enough for him. It was a feeling that had taken root. Looking back on it now, that probably did have something to do with our first tiff.

It was Christmas Eve. Simon was watching the evening show with my mum and dad, after which I was going to drive their car, with all of us in it, down to Eastbourne so that we could have Christmas Day there, with them.

I've had small roles in theatre productions before. And I've always loved them. Mainly due to these benefits:

1 A lot of time to read *Heat, Grazia* and books about star signs, and talk about boys and shopping in the dressing room
2 A lot of time to borrow other actresses' make-up so that you can go to the bar after the show looking like you work in Mac

Playing the Beanstalk allowed me neither of these benefits. I was on stage for the duration of the show so got no chance to do any cast bonding. That was a shame because I could have used some bonding. I had no good friends in the cast. I don't know whether that was because everyone considered me to be a freak after my squawk at the piano that day, or because I assumed they did and kept away. Also, the brown paint that covered my face each show was stubborn as a curry stain to remove. Every night, nearly a whole pack of facial cleansing wipes was needed to return me to skin colour. By which time my face look liked it had just been squeezed out of a vagina while everyone else was in the bar looking like Cheryl Cole.

Hence, I wasn't feeling hot when I joined them all in the bar after the Christmas Eve show. I just wanted to get in the car and leave. Sadly, that wasn't to be.

Now it was Christmas, and I realize that everyone likes a drink at Christmas. However, I was surprised to find that my partner and family had managed to get completely Bertie Bollocksed during live family entertainment where 70 per cent of the audience was under the age of eight.

I emerged from the dressing room alone and scampered to the pub next door where we had agreed to meet. I immediately saw my father. My dad's natural habitats are golf courses and pubs, so he looked very happily ensconced in the melee. He had befriended one of the gay male dancers from my show, who appeared to be teaching him a pirouette complete with jazz-hand finish. My father wasn't built for jazz dance. He has a dodgy leg and dad girth and he would have managed the turn better had he put his pint glass down. My mother was next to him trying to take a photo with the lens cap on. I felt it best to leave them to it and round up Simon first. So, I left Michael Flatley and Annie Leibovitz and wandered about the crowded, low-ceilinged pub trying to find Si.

'Oh my God!' one of the female dancers shouted as she charged past me in the opposite direction. 'Your boyfriend's gorgeous!'

She sounded so flabbergasted by this fact that it stopped me in my tracks for a moment. But then I smiled and nodded and headed towards the direction she had come from. When I eventually saw my Simon I didn't rush immediately to him. I stood watching him instead. He did look gorgeous. He was wearing a hooded top that I'd bought him when I was doing my Hollywood shopping. It was the colour of theatre curtains. It suited him. He looked relaxed and he was smiling. But he was also talking to the pretty, petite nineteen-year-old who had taken over my role as the Princess. His hand was on her tiny fishnetted thigh and he

was obviously saying something funny because she was giggling. I stood fixed to the ground like the tree I was. I didn't
want to go over to them. I knew I'd feel winch-me-out-of-
the-window-fat next to the girl. I tried to think of something
funny to say to approach them with but it's hard when
you're holding your bottom in. With my wit clocked off for
Christmas, I stood loon-like in this way for about a minute
until Simon looked up and caught my eye. He jumped off
the bar stool and ran to greet me. He hugged me.

'I'm a tree hugger!' he whooped loudly. The girl who was
playing the Princess laughed. But I didn't laugh. I felt embarrassed. I thought they were laughing at me because I was
playing the Beanstalk.

'Can we go, babe? I'm knackered and I've got to drive,'
I said quietly.

'Oh, babe. Stay and have a drink!' he said. But again it
was fortissimo. Everyone looked at me. And I floated out of
myself and I saw what they saw: the party pooper with the
massive arse, the face that had suffered an extreme facial,
who couldn't sing or act but who had somehow managed to
bag the good-looking funny bloke. I hated myself at that
moment and I resented Simon for making me feel like
that. I'm not proud to admit it. But that's how I felt.

'Babe, I'm driving!' I snapped. I sounded premenstrual.
I wasn't.

'Oh yeah,' he said without any oomph.

He circled the group, shaking hands with the cast members he'd just met. Then with a lot of persuasion and more

jazz hands than a middle-school musical we managed to lead Mum and Dad out of the pub and into the car, where they promptly fell asleep.

We (I) drove in silence for ages. The only time words came out of mouths was when Radio 2 played that Will Young song, 'Leave Right Now'. Simon turned it up and we sang along. For the rest of the journey the radio was turned down to protect us from Slade and Simon hummed tunes from the panto.

The real weirdness of the night started when we were on the M25. Bloody awful road.

'Sare?'

'Hmmm.'

'Do you know what I fancy?'

'Ah, babe. I'm not stopping,' I said.

He was a drunk man. I assumed he was referring to the purchase of fried chicken. I was wrong.

'You don't have to stop,' he said, suggestively.

'Si. No rude stuff while I'm driving!'

I was understandably shocked. I'm not the safest driver at the best of times.

'Babe, I'm not talking about that either.'

'Well, what do you fancy, then?'

'A baby.'

'Weurgh!'

'All those kids at the panto got me thinking . . .'

I quickly pulled my eyes away from the road and fixed them momentarily on Simon. It was supposed to be a 'you're drunk, you freak' type of look. But it turned into an 'OH MY GOD! HE'S SERIOUS!' expression of alarm when I captured his face and the soft look upon it. What was happening? His head was cocked to one side. There was a wet smile upon it. It was the sort of face that women get when they see men holding babies in Marks & Spencer. I didn't mean to scrunch my face up in disgust. In fact I didn't even know I had.

'Sare! Why are you giving me your tax face?'

'I'm not.'

'You are.'

Pause.

'Shit, I'll need to do my tax soon.'

Pause.

'Babe.'

'What?'

'Why did you change the subject?'

'Because you're drunk.'

'I'm not.'

'You are.'

'I'm not.'

'Ahhhh! It's like being back in panto! He's behind you! You are bloody drunk. You had your hands all over that girl. It was embarrassing. Now you're being all . . . weird.'

'Sare! What's up with you?'

'ME? Si, you're the one who's being a nightmare.'

And that was how I started a repetitive argument about Simon's drunkenness while all the time I was thinking, BABIES! HE'S BROODY! BOLLOCKS!

You see, I'd never been big on babies before. Everyone always said, 'Oh, isn't he or she beautiful?' and I was always stood there thinking, 'No! It looks like it's just been squeezed through a very small hole.' And the thought of squeezing something that was the same size as a Highland Terrier through my very small hole, getting a fanny like a bucket and being given a crying thing that demanded constant attention never really appealed.

I did want to have one with Si at some point. I admit that the thought of a little piece of us was appealing. But not then! Not for years. Not until I felt that I'd achieved something professionally. Or at least until I felt that I had the wisdom to raise a little person. Now was the time for practising. At some point I was sure I'd get broody and then I would grab him and say, 'Bang me up, big boy!' But not yet. I couldn't believe he had even suggested it.

We drove on in silence.

♥ *six* ♥

The next day we didn't mention the argument or the baby comment. The only clue a skilled sleuth might have picked up was my vehement forwarding of the track 'When a Child Is Born' on Mum's dreadful Christmas carol CD.

And we had a lovely day. It included some of my all-time favourite Christmas pastimes:

1   Eating a Crunchie and a Curly-Wurly before getting out of bed
2   Drinking champagne in my dressing gown before midday
3   Crispy roast potatoes and turkey skin
4   Two sleeps on the best sofa

'Val, that was delicious!' Simon said to my mum after Christmas dinner. The four of us were sitting around the dining room table. We were full of festive fodder. All the belts at the table had been loosened and in my case the zip of my trousers was undone as well. Not that we'd stopped eating. The cheese was still on the table, as was the Bailey's

29

ice cream. Actually, that was in my hand. I was scraping the carton. Dad was polishing off the brandy butter while reading Paul McKenna's book *I Can Make You Thin*. Each year I buy my father a diet book. He enjoys the season of indulgence more when he's reading about the diet and fitness regime he intends to start in the New Year.

'You're a pleasure to feed, Simon,' my mum smiled back. I think my mum and dad might have loved Simon more than I did. And he loved them back. He really did.

I did very well when God dispensed parents. Mine are lovely. They have been married for nearly forty years. I think their success lies in the fact that they are each slightly mad in a way that thoroughly complements the other. For instance, you might think that my father's unbridled crushes on Selina Scott and Katherine Jenkins were odd until you heard my mother's pornographic squeals whenever Piers Morgan comes on the telly. And for some, my father's obsession with his daily golf might grate. But my mum just calls him Golden Balls and dozes on the sofa with the paper when he's gone. They still have fun together and hold hands. They do smoochy dancing to The Drifters after every Sunday roast. I thought Simon and I were going to be like that. I thought we'd make each other laugh as we took on the world together. I imagined us soaring through life having fun and adventures and then growing old in a little bungalow somewhere with a vegetable garden.

'God, it's nice not having a brown face and the ring of two

thousand screaming children in my ears,' I sighed, after I'd given the Bailey's ice-cream container a little lick.

'Oh, Simon was wonderful with those children who sat behind us last night, Sarah,' said my mother in a tone that hinted of 'HE'LL BE A BRILLIANT DAD, DARLING. GET KNOCKED UP QUICKLY TO KEEP THIS ONE.'

'Was he?' I said, because she was talking to me and you're supposed to answer when that happens.

'They were good kids,' said Simon. 'They just weren't being disciplined, that's all.'

My mother clucked like she might lay an egg.

'Needed a good whack if you ask me,' snorted my father. 'Kept kicking me in the back.'

'You'll make a lovely daddy,' my mother said to Simon with another clucking sound. Simon beamed. I froze. Dad coughed but I think it might have been the brandy butter.

'How's the book, Dad?' I said, brilliantly changing the subject.

'Do you want to have children, Simon?' my mother asked, ignoring my efforts.

'Er, yes, Val. I can't wait.'

I didn't say anything. I just poured another glass of wine because I was suddenly feeling far too sober, and jumped up to change the CD because, by some divine joke, 'When a Child Is Born' had started to play.

'Put on Katherine Jenkins,' said my dad, perking up at the thought of Katherine Jenkins. I obliged. I stood by the CD player leafing through the flawless pictures of the Welsh singer in the CD booklet. I bet no one expected bloody Katherine Jenkins to pop children out, I thought. The most annoying thing about this baby issue was the assumption that I would have one. I felt sure that if I'd gone to Hollywood and done the Eamonn Nigels film everyone would have supported my career rather than expected me to start breeding.

I'd always loved being a woman. We're much prettier and cleverer than men and our clothes shops wee all over theirs. But suddenly, being a woman felt problematic. I didn't say any of this aloud though. I should have just said, 'Woah! Hang about, keen beans! Can't we wait a bit? I may be playing a tree but I haven't given up on more substantial roles in the future! So less of these conversations, please, for a year or five!'

I wonder what would have happened if I'd said something like that. Something at all. But instead I just avoided the subject. And I think that was because I loved Mum and Simon so much. No one wants to disappoint the people they love.

Anyway, it didn't matter because my father was about to do something glorious. He sprang up from the table. Actually, that's a falsehood. He groaned, moaned and belched a slow move from seated to standing.

'Time to watch *Top Gear*,' he said, and he left the dining room to traverse to the living room to settle down in front of the telly. But as he moved through the hall he called, 'Sarah, I think that's your phone.'

Now, normally I would have left the call. Sudden movement after Christmas consumption can only lead to injury. But as the conversation was liable to plunge perilously into babies, I darted out of the room and snatched my phone. I am so superlatively glad I did.

'Sarah! Eamonn! Merry Christmas!'

'Eamonn, you sound wankered!' I said, proving that I was also wankered otherwise I wouldn't have dared suggest that a world-famous film director was wankered.

'Pissed as a newt!' he replied, which I thought was rather brilliant.

'Isn't it pissed as a parrot?'

'I had a fax from my friend at Universal last night. Anyway. The film's going ahead! I shouldn't really be calling you but I thought it might be a nice Christmas present for you. That and I'm pissed as a toad as we discussed. Send my kind regards to Simon. I'd better be off.'

He hung up.

'I'm going to Hollywood, baby!' I screeched, and as I said the word 'baby' I felt pleasantly relieved. That was one issue that could safely be put on hold for the time being.

♥ *seven* ♥

The issue of babies wasn't discussed between me and Simon or Mum again. But I did think about it. It became like a small virus on my hard drive. Every so often as I stood in my cardboard tree my brain would find itself prodding the issue of procreation. My brain tended to prod the issue until it was septic. I kept imagining that I would tell Simon that I wasn't ready for babies and he would dump me. But also I felt guilty for not being honest with him. If he really wanted sprogs now, maybe I should let him be free so he could grow some with someone else. But the thought of someone else having Simon's baby was too awful. The day I stood in my tree thinking of Simon leaving me and having a baby with someone else I got in a right state. It made me feel like invisible hands were strangling me. Having morbid thoughts about your boyfriend impregnating someone else isn't conducive to panto. My face would set in its 'thinking unpleasant thoughts' expression. Unfortunately my 'thinking unpleasant thoughts' expression makes me look like I am trying to pass a difficult stool.

I didn't discuss my fears with anyone. I just let them

breed inside me, until the last day of panto, when my friend
Julia came to see the show. She was going to drive me and all
my bags home in her unreliable BMW, Big Daddy.

Julia arrived early, before the evening show. We had
planned to go out together and have supper in the break
between shows. Julia is my best friend in the entire world,
but I felt I'd hardly seen her while I'd been doing panto, and
when I had, Simon and her boyfriend Carlos had always
been there. I was looking forward to a proper girl chat,
unedited for the boy market. I ran down the theatre steps
whooping when I saw her waiting for me.

'Ah!' I screamed when I reached her, because I am a
woman and that's what we do. She looked lovely. Julia has
always been very attractive, with big pouty lips and cleavage
that things could get lost in. But since she started going out
with Carlos she'd developed a Ready Brek-type glow about
her. That day, wrapped in her new Christmas coat, with
high-heeled boots and rosy cheeks, she looked gorgeous.
'You look wow!' I told her admiringly.

'Oh my God, Sare, look at you,' she cried as soon as she
saw me. But not in a good 'Oh my God, Sare, look at you'
way. I hadn't seen her for ages. She must have noticed how
much Christmas pudding I'd put on.

'Oh, I know, Fatty Bum Woman, aren't I?' I said, worried.
'Do I look much fatter to you?' I was off to Hollywood in
two days. I had tried to slim down after Christmas but
there's only so much you can do in two weeks with so much
Christmas chocolate around.

'No, you look the same,' she said.

I bounded in for a hug. She pulled away.

'What's up?'

'Sare, you're brown!' she said, referring to the fact that I still had my face painted like a tree.

'Oh, that. I couldn't be arsed to get rid of it. It takes forever and I'd have to put it back on again for tonight's show anyway. Do you mind?'

'You've got a brown painted face. It's not very politically correct,' she whispered.

'They're used to it round here. I'm a local fixture. We'll probably get the odd "your performance was wooden" jibe.'

'Mental,' she muttered and she took my arm.

We ended up in a bustling, cosy bistro, where they did a too-good-not-to offer on dinner with wine. It was one of those times with friends when there was so much to catch up on that conversation was explosive.

'Oh my God! Did I tell you about Carlos and that producer?'

'No.'

'Well, we were at that Pacha night.'

'Oh yeah, how did it go? What did you wear?'

'That red dress. But I washed it after and shrunk it.'

'Wank. That happened to my black off-the-shoulder jumper.'

'No way, I loved that.'

'Is there garlic in this?'

'Loads.'

'At least I don't have much to say in the show.'

'What's Dennis Waterman like?'

'OK.'

'What was I saying?'

'Um, something about Carlos. Has he ever mentioned babies?'

This was the first time we stopped for breath in our dialogue. She looked at me seriously and leant forward.

'What, like baby babies?' she said, pointing towards a high chair next to us.

I was pleased that she mouthed the word babies as though it was toxic.

'Yeah.'

'No. Thank God. Why?'

'Simon's broody.'

'Urgh.'

'Exactly.'

'But you're my superstar actress friend. You can't have a baby at the moment.'

'Jules,' I said, and I meant it, 'Thank you.'

'That's cool. Although he is, like, really, really good with kids.'

'I know.'

That was another problem my sadistic brain had been flirting with. Simon was terrific with kids. He was like the Pied Piper of Camden. They always appeared from nowhere when he was around and started following him.

'God, remember that time he made that kid laugh so much it was sick?'

'But kids hate me!' I wailed.

'No!' she said immediately. But then she thought for a moment. 'Well, I wouldn't say "hate" . . .'

I looked at the high chair next to us. A tiny person whose gender I wasn't sure of was throwing chips onto the floor. I hesitated. Then I smiled at the child.

'Hello, there,' I said in a voice like Yogi Bear.

The baby stared at me and smiled back. And I found myself thinking how cute it looked, even though it could do with a good wipe with a baby wipe or seven. I was so relieved that a child seemed to like me. Obviously, it didn't like me as much as it would have liked Simon. But I could make a child smile and that was a nice thing. However, as I was experiencing this warm glow of infant affection I realized that the child wasn't actually smiling at all. It was grimacing. Because it was starting to cry. Actually to bawl. I looked at Julia. She had started laughing. Very supportive.

'Fuck, Jules. That baby hates me,' I hissed at her.

'Don't swear in front of the baby,' she sang primly.

'Fuck off,' I whispered back.

'It's your face.'

'I can't do anything about my face!'

Julia snorted into her pasta.

'It's my face!'

'Oh, I know what I was going to tell you. This American producer wants to work with Carlos on a dance track.'

'Oh my God. That's so cool!'

'I know.'

'Wowzers.'

'Oh, and Sare?'

'What?'

'That baby's crying because you've got a brown face, you knobhead.'

♥ *eight* ♥

Talking to Julia helped. Relieved not to be the only baby-phobe, I became king-size excited about finally going to Hollywood to make a film.

'I'm flying to LA to do a movie,' I sang repeatedly. And I think if I had been a man that sentence would have given me a small semi.

I finished all my packing the night before my early flight. I had packed for all weather conditions, plus unforeseen eventualities such as headaches, period pain, tummy upset and thrush. It was a feat of organizational dexterity for Sarah Sargeant. I didn't want anything to spoil my enjoyment of the trip.

'What's that?' Simon said, looking at the small *Apprentice*-sized carry-along case that I had found in the hallway cupboard and was using for my hand luggage.

'It's a carry-along case.'

'Genius. No. Whose is it?'

'Is it not yours?'

'Nah.'

'Oh.'

He stood looking at the carry-along case. It was quite a smart one.

'Oh, maybe it is,' he shrugged. 'Must have forgotten I had it.'

Simon had done a lot of travelling, so I didn't think anything of the fact that he bought luggage and then forgot all about it.

'Can I use it?' I asked politely.

'What's mine is yours, baby.'

'Thanks, sexy.'

And he was sexy, phenomenally sexy that day. He was also naked. We'd given up on the environment by this point and the radiators were back to boiling. It was much more fun than the thermostat embargo because Simon had taken to walking round the flat full-on, lumber out, starkers. Although it was quite distracting and I frequently forgot what I was doing.

'Have you got the camera?'

'Yep.'

Simon had given me his old digital camera to go away with.

'Is the suitcase all packed?'

'Yep,' I said, proudly pointing at my big old battered suitcase full of at least two choices of what to wear per day. I was going to be away for six weeks. I hoped it wouldn't explode.

'Pants.'

'What's up?'

'No, pants. Have you packed pants?'

'Oh fuck, bollocks, no!' I exclaimed.

'That's my girl,' he said, shaking his head and smiling.

'It was intentional. I wasn't going to wear any there,' I joked.

'Oh, Sare, don't say that.'

'What?'

'I don't like the thought of you with all those blokes out there. And that actor you do that sex scene with.'

'Baby,' I cooed, 'it's a rape scene and he kills me. It's hardly hot monkey sex.'

'I don't like thinking about it.'

'Baby,' I said, and I walked towards him. I wasn't starkers. I was fully clothed. I didn't like wandering around naked on account of me being the shape of a not particularly pretty pear. I preferred my nakedness to be done under a duvet with the lights off with a man with dodgy eyesight who'd had at least two drinks. But I loved seeing Simon bare because he had the lovely firm body of a man who finds the gym fun(!).

I put my arms around his waist and stood close to him. I rubbed my nose along his stubbled cheek and then I kissed him on the lips.

'Oooh, do we have take-off?' I said, feeling something against my thigh.

'Yes, we do. We have a semi!'

But before I got involved with Simon's aviation equipment, I looked into his eyes and said these words: 'I only want you, forever, Simon Gussett. You know you can trust me.'

And he kept our gaze and didn't flinch.

'It's you for me forever, Sarah Sargeant. And it goes without saying you can trust me too.'

What a load of old bollocks that turned out to be. But we didn't know that at the time, so we lunged at each other and had amazing sex on the suitcase and then I christened my new camera by taking naughty photos of the two of us.

♥ *nine* ♥

How soon excitement turned to panic. I speedily discovered a problem with the sentence 'I'm flying to LA to do a movie.' It was the bit about doing a movie: a proper movie that was going to be shown in cinemas all over the world.

I was at Heathrow, the start of my journey to Hollywood, and my nerves felt as though they'd been doused in petrol and thrown a lighter.

'Ahhhh,' I whimpered, as a familiar feeling of terror gatecrashed my stomach. It was the sort of feeling that made me worry about the contents of my tummy landing on my shoes.

Simon smiled sympathetically at me.

'Baby girl. Don't be scared. It'll be fine. Your accent's great.'

'Urgh! The accent!' I cried, clenching my bottom furiously. That was another problem with flying to LA to do a movie. The fact it was in LA and I was supposed to be Californian in the film. But I wasn't Californian; I was born in a small district to the south of Croydon. And although I was born in Croydon, I don't look like Kate Moss. More like Lorraine Kelly. And the camera puts ten pounds on you.

'Si, I think I need the loo.'

'Come on, baby, you're all right, you just need to breathe and think of the positive!' He started to stroke my back. 'You are brilliant. Brilliant. Brilliant at acting, at the accent. And you're brilliant at blow jobs.'

I punched him in the stomach at the mention of blow jobs. It was becoming an unfortunately long-running gag. Excuse the pun. When I got together with Simon, I had been single for a long, long time and I hadn't had sex for over a year. Our sex was a little bit odd at first. The first time we undressed each other we were quite uncomfortable. I'd say I behaved the same as I did when I entered a sex shop for the first time. I kept giggling and making bad jokes. It was such a shame because I so wanted to be demure.

I wanted to give him a blow job that would eclipse all others. But when I felt the girth of his penis, I found myself tapping the top of it and saying, 'Testing, testing, one, two, three.' Then I sang a verse of 'Sweet Child o' Mine'. Including the guitar bits. It was the nerves, you see. I don't even like Guns N' Roses.

'Now then, I want to give you this.' Simon took a wad of dollars from his back pocket. 'So you don't have to worry about money and can get a cab at the airport.'

'Baby, you don't have to give me money.'

'Come on, Sare, take the money.'

'I'm fine. I don't need it.'

'Buy something nice for yourself.'

'You sound like a boss who's boffing his secretary.'

'Yeah,' he said, sounding bizarrely pleased. 'Treat yourself, sweet-cheeks.'

'Si, put it away! You look like you're trying to solicit me.'

'How much for one of those amazing blow jobs?'

'Si!'

'I don't want them. Filthy fifties, look at them.' He tossed the money onto the floor.

'I'm not getting it,' I said. But it's not nice to see good money go to waste, so within about two and a quarter seconds I was on my hands and knees. I had to apologize to the petite girl behind me. She was holding a crucifix and murmuring something.

I stood upright, clutching the money. Simon was waiting for me. He was holding his Filofax and a biro.

'Babe, just put your hotel address down in here for me, will you?'

'Hmmm,' I said, taking them. But he looked so gorgeous that I just had to give him a little kiss on the lips first. 'You're the most wonderful man in the entire world,' I told him.

'I'm the luckiest man in the entire world,' he said. He put his arms around my waist and gave me a kiss on the lips with a cheeky bit of tongue.

'I am so going to miss you.'

'Ohhh, baby.'

We were talking in baby voices because that's what you do when you're in love.

I took the Filofax and pen from him and flicked to the back page. There was a photo there. It was lying face-down.

'Do you keep a photo of me in your Filofax?' I squeaked, using my baby voice.

I turned the photo over and stared at it.

'What the fuck's this?' I whispered. I definitely wasn't using the baby voice then.

'Just a photo,' he shrugged. I still can't believe he said that.

'Just a photo!' I repeated.

The photo in Simon's Filofax wasn't of me. It wasn't of his mum. It wasn't a still of Kylie from the 'Can't Get You Out of My Head' video. It was a photograph of a girl called Ruth. She was in her underwear, demonstrating a suggestive yoga move.

Simon may have claimed he waited patiently for me to wake up to the fact that the love of my life had been sleeping in the next room. He forgot to mention that he whiled away most of that time having mind-blowing sex with a flexible girl called Ruth. And she wasn't just any woman. She was a woman with no visible cellulite who could touch her toes. And it wasn't just any old mind-blowing sex, it was sex that I heard because we were flatmates and she howled and the walls were thin. They went out together for a year and they only split up a month or two before Simon and I got together. Up until that moment I had barely thought of her. It was about to become impossible for me to forget her.

Finding that photo affected me badly. To put it plainly,

finding that photo made me go a bit mental. All right, quite a lot mental. If I had to pinpoint the moment I began to turn into a nightmare nutter woman, it was probably then. Not that it happened straight away. It wasn't an instant Superman-like transformation. It was a slow metamorphosis.

But what was I supposed to say when I saw it? 'Oh lovely, darling, you've got a picture of your semi-naked ex-girlfriend in your Filofax. Those are pretty pants, aren't they? Why don't we frame it and put it up in the lounge!'

As it was, I didn't say anything at all.

'Sare, what's the matter?' he asked. 'It's a beautiful picture. You're not jealous, are you?'

I just shook my head and, luckily, the heavily made-up woman at the flight desk nodded me over to her at that moment.

♥ ten ♥

I was understandably very perplexed before take-off. Aside from the hideous photo I had just seen, and the embarrassing incident at the luggage screening when a lady held up my Canesten cream and Imodium and asked me to put them in a clear plastic bag, I had also discovered another problem with flying to LA to do a movie: the flying.

Am I the only person who's noticed it's not right? An aeroplane weighs eight hundred and seventy-five thousand pounds. (Why do I Wikipedia these facts?) Eight hundred and seventy-five thousand pounds is quite heavy. In my experience heavy things don't stay in the air. I find they tend to plummet downwards at great speed before landing with a thud. I rest my case.

The flying angle of the whole LA job felt like a massive spanner in the works or, more realistically, a pigeon in the engine. This actually happens. Wikipedia told me. Pigeons do sometimes fly into the engine. And when they do, the engine breaks down. The intoxicated pilot doesn't realize. He's drunkenly squinting into the fog. The air stewardesses are trying to put out the small cigarette-started-fire in the toilets. The passengers are sneezing, having picked up swine flu. Then the hijackers stand up.

I probably should have done a Simon and thought of the positive, rather than sat on an aeroplane, before take-off, worrying about the logistics of commercial aviation. But I was so furious with him about the photo that I was refusing to look on the bloody bright side out of spite for him. I had a lot of time to stew because our flight was delayed taking off. We had to wait for a passenger who had checked in but gone AWOL. Now, buses don't wait. They rarely even stop. Trains don't just hold on for a few minutes while you get a Costa coffee to take on board. Yet there we were, waiting for someone to finish his or her duty-free shopping! The praying girl from the queue was sat in the seat next to me. She looked terrified too. She had been clutching that little crucifix round her neck since we boarded. She probably knew about the pigeons.

At least I was in First Class with a glass of champagne. I love champagne. I can't imagine meeting a sane woman who doesn't. It makes me feel giddy and light and lovely, like I've been put through a Soda Stream. Although on that occasion the effects were taking longer than usual to manifest. I valiantly believed they would come eventually, so I kept knocking it back. After a big gassy gulp I put down my glass. It was a glass-glass as opposed to a plastic-glass. I pinged it with my fingernail just to check. As I did, the good-looking air steward sprinted up the aisle towards me, holding an open bottle of champagne. 'State of emergency,' he panted when he got to me.

I glanced at the girl with the crucifix. She looked like she might wet herself.

'You need a top-up.' He smiled and filled up my glass.

'I love First Class,' I sang, to the tune of 'I Love Paris'.

'I'm Brian,' he told me. He was tall with dark hair, a huge, unrestrainable grin and very nice teeth.

'Sarah.'

I turned to smile at the girl next to me but she'd resumed the fervent praying. I would have been better suited to sit next to someone with man-hating and alcoholic tendencies. This girl was a funny little thing. She had a beautiful face, tiny features and sparkling blue eyes but she was wearing a French pleat and a high-necked white blouse. An interesting look to go for. Very Church of Latter-day Saints, especially with the praying.

I picked up my digital camera and flicked through the photos we had taken the previous night. They were basically a tangle of limbs. But there was one where my legs were round Simon's neck. That was one of my favourites. Simon looked gorgeous and my legs looked almost thin from that angle. Then there was the one of Simon standing naked with a banana covering his bits. And one of Simon eating the banana and showing his bits. I had been so excited about my digital camera. I lay there deleting everything until it looked like I had only one chin. Digital cameras had gone straight in between support tights and crackling on my list of favourite things. But now it just reminded me of that disgusting picture, which he probably took with it.

'Now then, another glass of fizz? Or perhaps you'd like to move on to something stronger? A gin and tonic or a Bloody Mary?' Brian asked, kneeling on the floor beside me.

'Oooh.' Not an easy question. I pulled my 'thinking' face.

'Well, I'll top you up with champagne for now, then I'll do you a nice Bloody Mary before dinn . . . ' He trailed off here. It was obvious that his attention had been stolen by the arrival of the late passenger.

'Oh, they've finally finished their shopping, have they?' I trilled to Brian.

I had meant to be conspiratorial but it came out quite loud. All right, very loud. So loud the Christian girl looked up from her praying and giggled. I mentioned that champagne made me giddy, light and lovely. I forgot the word 'loud'. In fact the word 'loud' should have gone before the other three. In capitals. With a hazard sign. I fought the urge to apologize to everyone. I was overwrought. First Class is unnerving for the first-timer. I kept thinking that someone was going to tap me on the shoulder and say, 'Get back to your own seat.'

I was secretly hoping that, after all the waiting, the new arrival would be Anne Robinson or Simon Cowell. The only disappointment with First Class was that it appeared to be bereft of famous people but bursting with buxom balding businessmen.

I leant into the aisle hoping to get a close-up view of reality TV cosmetic dentistry and surgery. But as soon as I saw who the late arrival was I threw my head back against my seat and noticed I had started to breathe more quickly. He was gorgeous. I wasn't surprised the plane waited for him. I bet the airport staff were saying, 'Take your time, why don't you get a croque-monsieur and chill out before you have a look round Ted Baker?'

He was the best-looking person I'd seen in the flesh. This guy had to be a model. Or a surfer. Or an actor whose ideal casting was Greek God. He was at least six foot. His shoulders were wide and his legs were long. He had a big dishevelled mass of blond, unbrushed hair that nearly reached his shoulders and a real not-out-of-a-squeezy-tube tan. He was wearing a faded tight T-shirt emblazoned with the word 'suck' and to this day I've never seen a pair of jeans worn so well. He looked familiar but I suspected that was because I recognized him from fantasies I had in puberty. He might have been gorgeous but I wasn't happy about the situation. I had wanted a famous person. Not a beautiful person. I hate being around good-looking people. I'm crap at it. I always act like a pillock.

I looked at Brian, the air steward. He was no help. He was frozen. I had suspected that he was too lovely to be straight. The Greek God lifted the overhead locker above me. His groin was slightly above my eye level. I quickly diverted my gaze and looked down at the in-flight entertainment guide on my lap. However, I was still very much aware of his groin, as it didn't seem to be moving and it really was very close to my head. I snuck a look up to see what his problem was. He was reaching into the overhead compartment but he had stopped, was stood statue-still and was staring at me. It looked like there was a ripe orange of muscle under the skin on his upper arm. I tried to peel my eyes off it. I looked back down at my lap. I could sense that he was still looking at me though. Quite a few people had stared at me at the airport. I think it was because I was wearing pyjamas. I seemed to be the only person in the whole of Heathrow who had realized the comfort and flexibility afforded by wearing pyjamas on a flight. After years of trying to look smart in the hope of being able to wangle an upgrade I had been elated that I didn't need to bother. So I was travelling in the comfiest clothes that Primark provided.

I heard him say, 'Hey.' He had a deep, masculine, slow American drawl. I assumed he was talking to Brian. I couldn't bring myself to look at him again so I studied my lap hard. The in-flight entertainment magazine was riveting.

'Hey,' he said, louder this time. 'What's your name?'

Now obviously I knew that he wouldn't be talking to me but I decided to look up anyway, in a very casual manner though. I lifted my head and flicked my hair back, cunningly using the hair flick to look at him. He was staring at me! He was talking to me! He was waiting for an answer. Bugger! What was my name? There was a bemused smile at the corner of his mouth and his eyes were looking straight into mine.

'Oh, Sarah Sarah, Sarah, S-S-S-S-Sarah Sargeant,' I replied. I was trying to sound cool, which obviously meant I sounded like a young-looking twelve-year-old boy whose voice hadn't dropped, trying to buy fags.

'Hi,' he nodded. 'I'm Leo. Leo Clement.'

I didn't say, 'Fuck me, that's a cool name,' which I think was impressive under the circumstances. Not that saying, 'Excuse me, I just need to go the loo,' and running away was a reaction I was proud of.

I was almost at the toilet when I heard him drawl, 'Sarah Sargeant, you dropped this.'

'Oh, what's that?' I turned round. I was much cooler now. I had finally got the hang of it.

He was proffering something in his outstretched hand. I squinted at it. It was a tube of Canesten. It must have fallen out of my handbag. I snatched it and forgot about needing the toilet and rushed back to my seat. 'The whole of First Class thinks I've got thrush!' was all I could think. Somehow it wouldn't have felt so bad in Economy.

There was a very hot feeling in my cheeks when I sat down. Christian Girl reached over to me and gently touched my arm.

'Did you say your name was Sarah Sargeant?' she said, in another American accent.

'Yes,' I smiled, hoping she wouldn't ask me about the thrush. I was shaking with embarrassment.

'We'll be working together. My name's Erin Schneider. I'm in the film too.'

55

'No way! It's so nice to meet you! Are you excited?'

'Well, yes, and a little nervous.'

'Oh my God, me too. I'm proper like shit-scared about being in an Eamonn Nigels film!' I realized I was gushing, but we were about to share a big adventure together.

'I've got that camera too.' She smiled, nodding towards my poisonous Panasonic. 'Great camera.'

'Hmmm. Well, I'm not so sure about that at the moment . . .'

Finally the plane started gliding across the runway. Erin took a deep breath and grabbed her cross again.

'Oh sorry, sweetheart, I'm wittering. You get back to your pessary,' I said with what I hoped was a kind, understanding smile and turned around.

'Rosary, Erin, is what I meant!'

❤

Brian took my champagne away for take-off. It was very upsetting. I sat back in my seat and closed my eyes and tried to tell myself I was on a very safe train. I'm not sure how long I'd been tensely sitting there like that, when I heard, 'Hey.' I knew it was Leo Clement because I recognized his deep, cowboy voice. I opened one eye. He was leaning over the back of his seat, which was very naughty because the seatbelt light was still on.

'We're in the clouds,' he said, and took his gaze towards

the aeroplane window. We were. We were just entering the clouds.

'People tell me I'm always in the clouds,' I said and smiled.

We didn't say anything else. Brian told him to sit down.

♥ *eleven* ♥

When I have a bad thought, my mind has always been able to take that one bad thought and give it an intense course of rampant IVF until it has bred a thousand bad-thought offspring.

For example, I might think, Shit, I'm skint. In roughly four and half seconds other thoughts will also have appeared in my head. I can't pay my rent, I'll get evicted, I'll have to get a proper job to get me out of debt, I have no skills, I'll end up in King's Cross giving blow jobs for money, I'm not even very good at those. Then I will start to cry.

I learned an important lesson on that flight. Alcohol makes bad thoughts breed quicker. Much as I bonded with Brian, I shouldn't have had the dessert wine with the chocolate ambrosia. And I really hadn't needed the port he'd insisted on fetching me to go with my cheese and biscuits. I was desperately trying not to let my mind get horny with Simon and Ruth thoughts. They were too awful.

'Here we go, angel,' Brian said as he put my fourth or possibly fifth course in front of me. 'Oh ho ho, what's with the face ache, petal?'

'Nothing,' I smiled. 'Thanks.'

'Tell me, darling, tell all. A problem shared.'

'No, you're all right, Brian. You don't want me to bore you.'

'Oh, for God's sake! You won't bore me. Now, get it off your chest.'

I sighed and looked at him.

'No, it's too awful.'

'Man trouble?'

'Hmmm.'

'Who's the man?'

'His name's Simon.'

'Is he a brute?' he asked dramatically.

'No,' I chuckled. 'He's lovely.'

I grabbed my digital camera and showed him a photo of Simon. It was the one with the banana as that was the least explicit. Brian was rightly impressed.

'Well, then. The problem?'

I took a deep breath. I didn't want to say it but I did.

'I found a photo in his Filofax.'

Brian nodded in a lovely concerned way. I took another deep breath before I continued.

'It was of his ex-girlfriend.' I paused and tried to keep calm. 'She was doing a downward dog.'

I think Brian was trying to suppress a smile. I noticed he had to suck his cheeks in before he spoke.

'What's a downward dog?'

I wouldn't normally demonstrate yoga moves on a plane

after a heavy dinner but Brian's candid lack of sympathy forced me to do so. I checked my neighbours. Erin was fast asleep and Leo Clement was reclined in his seat wearing his eye mask. He looked like a bat (if you were kind) or a twat (if you were not). I lowered myself onto the gangway floor. I placed my hands out in front of me and then I stuck my bum in the air.

'Ouch, bollocks,' I muttered, unused to intense Indian postures. 'Ah, ah, fuck me!'

'Darling, you're not my type,' said Brian, like Julian Clary. 'Oh, I'm so sorry, sir.' His tone quickly switched to peerless professional. 'I was just giving Sarah here some stretches to do. Very good to stretch on a long-haul flight. Would you like me to show you how?'

I peeked in between my legs and saw one of the overweight businessmen shake his head and quickly turn around to find an alternative route back to his seat.

'So, what was she wearing in the photo?'

'Pants and a bra,' I spat.

'Oh.'

'Exactly! It's yoga porn.'

I collapsed on the floor and looked up at Brian, who was standing over me and shaking his head.

'What did he say about the photo?'

'He said it was a beautiful picture and that's why he kept it.'

'Was it a beautiful picture?'

'Well, there is a sunset behind her and stuff,' I said, thinking for a moment. 'But it's still a picture of HER with her bloody arse in the air!'

'What else did he say?'

'He said I was being . . .' I huffed. It was so ridiculous that he should have said it.

'What?'

'Jealous,' I said with a venomous laugh.

I noticed Brian was doing that thing with his cheeks again. I chose to ignore it.

'I've got an idea.'

'Yes.'

'I'll take a photo of you doing a downward dog. Get it developed and put it in his Filofax. He'll think it's sweet and funny.'

'OK,' I said, handing him the camera. 'Oh, and here, take one on my phone as well, would you?'

'Good girl,' he said proudly when I was back on the floor with my bottom in the air. 'See, this is much healthier than taking the photo and burning it on top of her hair.'

'Brian?'

'Hmmm.'

'I feel like I've known you for a billion years.'

'Strange that, isn't it?'

'Brian?'

'Hmmm?'

'You know that second option with the hair burning?'

'Hmmm.'

'I liked the sound of that too.'

♥ *twelve* ♥

So I landed in Los Angeles Airport, or LAX as the Americans call it. A ludicrous nickname. There was absolutely nothing lax about it, as I found out when I was led through the airport by a member of Airport Police.

'S'cuse me, but could you loosen your grip on my arm, please?' I cried, because the security guard had a grip like a crab.

'I'm under orders to escort you out of LAX, ma'am,' he responded, not very warmly.

'I was only taking a photo.'

'We don't allow photos to be taken in the airport, ma'am.'

I didn't like being called 'ma'am' as I'm not the bloody Queen.

'I didn't see any signs,' I mumbled.

All I did was take a photo of Erin going through immigration control. It was very arty. I got her little face with its 'I've just escaped from a cult' expression and the back of the immigration man's head and you could see her passport. It was the sort of photo you'd see in those magazines you get in trendy hairdressers. Anyway, the sight of my digital camera got everyone acting official. It just went to show that the camera was evil. Still, it was a quick way to exit the airport.

We walked through the exit sign and the first person I saw was Rachel Bird, Eamonn Nigels's girlfriend, who had come to pick me up. I went to the same school as Rachel, although we didn't really know each other because she was two years above me. We bumped into each other again last year and it was I who inadvertently introduced her to Eamonn. (In a S&M club. Another long story.)

She was at LAX waiting for me, wearing the shortest pair of shorts that I had ever seen. I'd seen more fabric on a pair of Marks & Spencer's mini briefs. She must have waxed her bikini line in order to wear them. She looked sensational. The cow. Long tanned legs, frayed non-existent shorts and a white vest over a floral bikini top over a very good boob job.

The security guard tightened his grip on me and he pulled in his burger belly when he saw her.

'Sarah,' Rachel Bird gasped, looking at me.

'Oh, I had a load of dr . . . ' I was about to say 'drugs up my fanny,' but I stopped myself. Thankfully. I don't think that LAX would have left anything to chance and I would have ended up with an intimate examination and a charge for wasting police time.

'Is that your friend, ma'am?'

'Yep. The one who forgot to put her shorts on.'

The security guard checked his breath on his hand. Unbelievable.

'Sarah! What's going on?'

Rachel was really concerned. Everyone was looking. I so wanted to say that thing about the drugs up my fanny. The man's grip on me loosened as we reached Rachel.

'Please may I have my camera back?'

'I just need to check what you've got on there.'

He turned my camera on and flicked through my photos. When he got to the one that made my legs look thin he turned the camera upside down very slowly and said, 'Mamma mia.' Eventually he got to the end, deleted the last one and handed it back to me with a wink. Rachel and I started to walk towards the exit.

'Sarah, you've just been led through LAX by security and you're wearing pyjamas.'

'Yes, I was aware, Rachel. How are you, by the way?'

'Good, yeah.'

We stepped out of the airport and there it was. That thing you forget that the rest of the world has on a daily basis. The sun. The glorious sun. It was midday and there it was, shining proudly in the cloudless sky. I opened my arms wide, closed my eyes and basked for a moment.

'Sarah. Get in the car. You look like a wino.'

'Oh, Rachel, listen, Erin Schneider was on the plane. She's in the film as well. Shouldn't we offer her a lift?'

'There's no way I'm taking that Christian imp anywhere,' she spat, and quickened her step. Then she unlocked the door to a cream convertible the likes of which I had only ever seen in hip-hop videos.

'Living the dream! I'm living the dream,' I muttered as I stroked the bodywork.

I'd barely got in the car before Rachel was in fourth gear and overtaking someone using the hard shoulder.

'Fucking shitbags! Rachel!' I shrieked, head stapled to the headrest.

'I love this car!' she yelled, smiling back.

'I love my life!' I whimpered next to her. I wanted to take in my first glimpse of LA but so far all I was seeing was tangled hair in my face. We pulled up at some traffic lights.

'Did we win?' I asked.

'What?'

'The Grand Prix.'

Rachel smiled.

'It's slow from here in. Traffic.'

'Phew. How do you know Erin then?'

'Urgh.' Rachel shuddered.

'Tell me, Rachel.'

'It was in my previous life.'

'Oooh, goodie. The rampant convent-girl past life?'

'That's the one. Her dad's a vicar, pastor, whatever they call them over here. In New York. And he caught me having sex in his church.'

'I can't believe you did that,' I whispered, shocked. Rachel and I didn't go to normal school. We went to convent school. We were taught by nuns. I definitely don't remember them saying anything about nooky in sacred places.

'I was seeing this bloke who lived there. We were bored.

Erin's dad is like this celebrity preacher and we thought it might be fun to have a quickie in his church.'

'R-i-i-i-ght.'

'Generally the best time of day to have sex in a church is dinner time. Clergy love eating so you normally get time for more than just a quickie.'

'Good life tip.'

'Not Erin's dad. Erin's dad sensed that some souls needed saving in his church. He came out, made us get dressed and insisted we had dinner with him. So we sit there having a family dinner like the Brady Bunch.'

'But the vicar had seen your bits!' I choked.

'Hmmm. Then Erin looks at me and smiles this "you're going to rot in hell" smile and says, "It's not too late to find God, you know, he's always listening." Or something like that. Anyway, I said back, "We were just trying to find my G-spot." But it wasn't a great answer to give a vicar's fifteen-year-old daughter at dinner. So they asked us to leave. You know, they insist we have dinner against our will and then tell us to leave. We weren't even hungry. We'd been snorting coke all day.'

'I thought she seemed quite sweet.'

'That's good, because you're sharing a hotel with her.'

'Will it not be a bit weird when you see her again?'

'I doubt she'll recognize me. I had a black French bob that summer. I, on the other hand, will know exactly who she is.'

'So, tell me how it's going with Eamonn.'

'Oh, Sarah, terrible.'

'Why?'

'I never see him. He works all day.'

'He is here to direct a movie, Rachel!'

'Yes, yes, but we had so much time together in London. It was heaven. Now I just get tired Eamonn flopping into bed next to me at night.'

'Oh well, it's not for ever.'

'Hmmm,' she agreed sadly.

We were silent for a while. I thought about Simon and that hideous photo.

'What's the secret?'

'It's a self-help book.'

'No! The secret of a good relationship.'

'Dunno.' She thought for a moment. 'Oh, Eamonn quite likes it when I touch the bit between his balls an . . .'

'Rach! That's not what I meant.'

'Well, what did you mean?'

'I, um, I don't actually know, but I don't think the answer lies in a sex act.'

Rachel raised an eyebrow at me. 'You'd be surprised.'

We had turned onto a busy dual carriageway coast road. I was in *Baywatch*, *Beverly Hills 90210*, and *The Lost Boys*. I felt as though I knew the place, but it was just because I'd seen it so many times on the telly. The most dazzling aspect of LA was not the sun or the ocean but the fact that everyone looked like Rachel Bird. There wasn't a minger in sight. No one would have got less than eight out of ten if they were marked for attractiveness. The women were all even tans and long slim legs, wandering along carrying yoga mats or, wait for it, it's very cool, surfboards. And the men. The men! They were either cycling topless or wandering along in half-pulled-up wetsuits. Everyone was shiny and bronzed and looked unimaginably healthy. It was nothing like Britain. I wondered how I'd ever fit in.

Rachel suddenly did an emergency stop outside a beautiful white building.

'Here we go,' she said, jumping out of the car and striding towards the boot. I just sat there, mesmerized, all open mouth and bulging eyes. The big white building was my hotel. It was on the beach. Literally walk out of hotel door, walk across golden sand, dive into the Pacific Ocean. I exited the car and Rachel handed me my cases.

'Living the dream! Living the dream,' I sang.

'Calm down, Sarah,' she reminded me flatly.

Then she gave me a surprisingly heartfelt hug.

'I'm so glad you're here. Now I'm going to head off for a yoga class. You're welcome to come. No? No. I take it by your face you're not a yoga fan. Now, right, very important. Try not to sleep or the jet lag will do you. Stay awake as long as you can. I'll see you tomorrow at the welcome party.'

'Thanks for the lift, Rachel,' I said, standing on the pavement to wave her off.

'Sarah, get in bloody side. Have you seen the state of you?' she hissed.

'I think LA needs a bit of mank,' I told her, because clearly it did. I wiggled my hips as I said it.

Rachel responded with a look that said, 'You are deranged and there are very few places I shall feel comfortable being in public with you.' But I didn't care.

'Oooh, Rach, what was it? The bit between the balls and the . . . ?'

But she was already revving the poor engine and couldn't hear me. I watched her do nought to seventy in under half a second as she drove away. 'Hi, I'm Sarah Sargeant, I'm doing a movie in LA, I'm staying in a hotel on the beach,' I said to myself in a sophisticated voice.

Under my pyjamas I was wearing a pair of big black knickers and a small vest top with boob support. It was my most comfortable underwear. I didn't want wires and thong wedgies on an eleven-hour flight. My comfortable underwear could also be used as a bikini without any embarrassment at all. I decided to go for a paddle, or even a small swim. The last time I swam in the sea it was in Eastbourne and it was a dare and I needed a double brandy after. I wanted a tan that wasn't Rimmel.

Sod checking in and unpacking. I wanted the sun and the sea. I altered my course. I walked around the hotel. In thirty seconds I was walking on sand. Bloody hot sand, actually. I started to run towards the sea to cool my hot feet off. I picked a spot that was mine and no one else's. I stripped off. I left all my belongings in a messy pile. I stood with waves lapping at my feet and I raised my arms over my head.

It was hotter than a sauna but there was a slight breeze gently whipping my body. I felt sublime.

'This is the start of my dream!' I whispered. And then I uttered the sound 'weurgh' with a jolt. I vowed to cut down on *The X Factor*.

♥ *thirteen* ♥

Julia, as my best friend, had insisted I Skype her whenever something important happened during my time in LA, for example after I met the cast for the first time, or after I shot my first scene, or after I bumped into George Clooney and he took me to Mexico for a cocktail. She hadn't expected me to Skype her as soon as I got into my hotel room.

'Jesus, Sarah!' she shrieked as soon as she saw me. 'What happened to your face?'

'Is it that bad?' I croaked.

'Carlos, baby, come and have a look at Sarah's face.'

Bloody Skype. Carlos's fuzzy face appeared next to Julia's on the screen. Carlos and Julia had been seeing each other for a few months. Carlos is a big beefy Latin-looking DJ. He's not Latin at all, despite his exotic name. He's from Southgate. His mum named him after a Spanish waiter from the tapas restaurant by the station. Carlos has my rarely seen 'best friend nod of approval'. I'd defy anyone not to like him, as he's so easy-going and agreeable. He smiles through life like a charmed cherub. And he's a proper DJ. Julia has snogged DJs before but they were generally just blokes with a box full of records who played in friends' flats. But Carlos plays in big clubs and gets paid to go to Ibiza. He is probably the coolest person Julia and I have ever even spoken to. But he's not intimidating. He likes dance music with lyrics and he talks bollocks like we do. It's brilliant.

They peered silently at their computer in England. I cringed to think what my face must have looked like in digital.

'So, what happened?' Julia asked eventually.

'I fell asleep in the sun.'

'For how long?'

'Ages.'

'Did you have any sun cream on at all?'

'Nope.'

'Is it sore?' asked Carlos.

'Agony.' I tried to smile at Carlos in thanks for his considerate question but the pain involved created more of a stroke-victim grimace.

I lay down after my swim to dry off and the next thing I knew someone's hand was on my breast. I opened my eyes to see Erin groping me. Not because she was moved by my physique. She'd seen me from her balcony and was concerned. She was trying to put sun cream on me. Unfortunately she was about four hours too late.

'But it's not all red, Sare, that bit is still white.'

Julia was squinting and pointing at half of my right cheek. Whereas my left cheek was pure roast tomato, the right was half roast tomato, half Best of British white. Put something blue next to me and I could have been the French flag. I must have put an arm over my head while I was asleep because the underside of my right arm was burnt as well.

'It's a look I'm going for.'

Julia started to laugh. Perhaps I should have felt grateful that the laughter took so long to come when I had expected it instantly. But there was little consolation in the fact that I was not just a laughing stock. I was a stunned silence that preceded it as well.

'Jules, it's not actually funny,' I pointed out.

Julia laughs like no one else I've ever met. She once got asked to leave a cinema because she was laughing so hard. I could understand it though. The popcorn she was eating at the time was going everywhere.

On this occasion, she was already laughing so much her nose had started to run. So she reached off-screen and returned with a tissue and she had just about composed herself when Carlos leant towards her and whispered something in her ear. Whatever he said set her off again.

'What did he say?'

Julia laughed and shook her head.

'What?'

'Nothing.'

'Julia!' I was getting cross now. There's a limit to how much ridicule a sunburnt person should be exposed to. 'What did he say?'

'He said . . .' She had to stop. She was laughing so violently.

'Jules!'

'He just said that . . . oh sorry, Sare, you know what it's like when you start and can't . . . stop . . . OK. Right. All it was . . .' She nearly gave up, but like a trouper she persevered. She took a deep breath. 'You're the same colour as the chicken tikka we had for dinner!'

I mentally withdrew my 'best friend nod of approval' as I watched them erupt. I started to close my laptop on their laughing faces.

'Oh, bubba, I'm sorry,' Julia shrieked.

'Jules, I've got a read-through in twenty-four hours with the whole cast and then a party in the evening. An LA film party. And it hurts. Look how slitty and swollen my eyes are. That's because I'm in pain just opening my eyes. And look how I'm speaking with my lips closed. That's because I'm in agony. And, AND, guess what I bloody well found in Simon's Filofax at the airport?'

'What?'

'A photo of Ruth in her underwear.'

'Huh!' they gasped.

'What, like a dirty sex photo?' said Julia with a bit too much relish.

'No, she was doing yoga. Her bum was in the air. No cellulite. Like none. Like she was airbrushed. The bitch.'

Now, I regret saying that because Ruth wasn't really a bitch. She wasn't the warmest of characters. She had a job in finance and was very career-driven and organized. But she wasn't a bitch. And I shouldn't have said it. Especially because the 'bitch' term proved very moreish.

'Hmmm. Bendy bitch,' agreed Julia.

'Why did he split up with her?' asked Carlos.

Julia and I looked at each other with wide eyes. It was another long story. But the gist involved a wedding at which Julia had jumped on Simon. They had a little snog. A very quick, drunken snog. But Ruth found out about it. Neither of us wanted to volunteer that information to Carlos though.

'Oh, dunno really, they just weren't right together,' I mumbled.

'Yeah,' agreed Julia. 'And she couldn't have kids and he really wanted a family. So he said it was never going to be a long-term thing. They were both just having a bit of fun.'

Carlos said, 'Oh, right,' and I just stared at the screen.

'She couldn't have kids?' I repeated eventually.

'Did you not know?' asked Julia, surprised.

'No. When did he tell you?'

'At that, um, wedding. Just before he told me how much he liked you.'

'Why didn't you tell me?'

'I thought you knew.'

'I didn't know.'

'Did he say anything else that night?'

'Just that he liked you and you'd make a really good mum.'

Skype obviously doesn't understand the concept of juicy relationship gossip because their faces froze on the screen at that moment and the connection was lost.

The news that Ruth couldn't conceive rattled me. It made me wonder whether Simon and Ruth would still be together otherwise. It made me nervous that Simon might want a baby more than he wanted me. But I am relieved to say that I responded in a very positive and mature manner. I suddenly faced the fact that having children was very important to my Si and I made a vow to discuss the issue with him as soon as I was back in England.

However, just seconds before I had that mature epiphany, I sent him an accusatory text with no kisses:

Why didn't you tell me that Ruth couldn't have kids?

To which he instantly replied:

Weird question. No reason. Glad you landed safely. Xxx

Julia and Carlos called me back and we didn't mention Ruth or babies again. The conversation took a completely different turn.

'How was the flight?' asked Carlos.

'Cool,' I nodded. We stared at each other's images in silence for a few moments. Then for some reason I said, 'Have you ever heard of a bloke called Leo Clement?'

They both scrunched their faces up.

'Name rings a bell, but I don't know where from,' shrugged Carlos.

'Why? Who is he?' asked Jules.

'Just some bloke who was on my flight. But he was like proper gorgeous. So I thought he must be famous.'

'Did you chat to him?'

'No,' I shook my head. Then I gave them an alternative subject to laugh at me about. 'He picked up my Canesten. It fell out of my see-through bag thing when I got up to go to the loo.' Julia gasped. 'Oh, hang on guys, there's a knock at my door.'

I heard Carlos say, 'What's Canesten?' but Julia was cackling so hard she couldn't answer.

I got up slowly and walked to the door. Obviously it wasn't just my face that was puce, but the entire front of my body, with the exception of where my big knickers and top were. I hobbled, winced and groaned my way there. I stood behind it and shouted, 'Hello?'

I should have turned the computer off. It sounded like Julia was having some sort of seizure in the background. I could barely hear who it was.

'Hello.' It was an American girl's voice. I thought she wanted to turn down the bed or something.

'I'm fine. Thank you.'

'Sarah, it's Erin. How are you feeling?'

I opened the door a touch and then I took a step back. I was giving off a lot of heat. I didn't want to stand too close.

'I went to the pharmacist and spoke to him. He strongly

recommends these products for you.' She held up a carrier bag that was nearly full. 'There's a lot. You need to take two lots of tablets and then there's a medicated cream as well, for extreme burns.'

'Erin, I don't know what to say.'

'Don't say anything. I was pleased to help. You could hardly walk there yourself.'

'Come in, Erin, I'll just get my purse. It must have cost you a fortune.'

'Sarah, it's a gift, please.'

Normally I do forceful wrestling, only stopping short of murdering the other party, in order to pay for something. That wasn't an option with the sunburn. I stood speechless instead.

'You're an angel,' I said eventually. I considered hugging her, then remembered that the gesture would be completely eclipsed by the intense pain on my entire surface area. I offered what I could manage of a smile. She smiled back. It was an oddly touching moment between two near strangers.

'Tell us about that bloke on the plane!' It was Julia at full volume.

I looked at Erin. She looked at me.

'My friend on Skype.'

Erin nodded.

'She's a sweetie,' I said emphatically.

'Sweetie' isn't the first word I would use to describe Julia. It would be there, however it would follow other words that had sprung to mind sooner, like 'nutter', 'mentalist' and 'hardcore'. I must have said 'sweetie' because Erin is religious. Not that it was a lie; it just wasn't a fully realized truth. As though to prove this fact, Julia took that moment to try out a new one from her own encyclopaedia of inventive expletives.

'SARAH! WHERE IN GOD'S BOLLOCKS HAVE YOU GONE?'

I winced, which hurt.

'I'd better go,' Erin said.

'I am so, so sorry.' I thought I'd sullied whatever Rachel Bird had left of Erin's innocence. 'Thank you, thank you. I'll have to take you for a drink some time.'

'Oh, I don't.'

'No, no, sorry, yes. But how about a milkshake, like they do in *Grease*?'

Erin looked blank.

'The movie, not the place,' I explained.

'Sure,' she smiled. 'I hope that works,' she said, nodding at the bag of creams I was holding.

Me too, I thought sadly, looking at it and willing it to perform a miracle in twenty-four hours.

❤ *fourteen* ❤

The miracle was unforthcoming. The creams did ease my sunburn very slightly but I was still the colour of ketchup the following morning. I didn't know what to do. And I definitely didn't know what to wear.

I'd bought two beautiful outfits especially for my first day. Julia and I had spent a whole day in Covent Garden with my credit card. I'd bought this lovely pink tea dress for the read-through and a strapless black dress for the party. The look was serious-yet-sexy-actress-about-to-be-discovered-in-LA-before-going-global. I was going to be a British style icon. The Sienna Miller for larger women. Julia was going to give up work and become my stylist. We had it all sorted. But, that morning, I tried on the pink dress. It looked like Miss Piggy had been put on a barbeque and someone had forgotten to turn her. And just the thought of the tight black dress next to my sunburnt flesh brought tears of acute agony to my eyes.

In the midst of this dermatological dilemma, I surprised myself by calling Rachel Bird for advice. And she surprised me again by getting straight in her car and coming to help me.

'OK, I've got this,' she said.

She held up a black polo neck. It looked like it would be tight on a Peperami.

I shook my head sadly.

'Whose is it? Barbie's?'

'Well then, this is the only other thing I could find.' She brandished a massive cloth with some sort of orange ethnic pattern on it. I stared at it.

'It looks like a wall hanging.'

She looked uncomfortable for a moment.

'It is a wall hanging.'

Rachel Bird suggesting that I wear a wall hanging was the last spliff before the whitey.

'I thought it would look like a sarong.'

I let my face crumple even though it hurt.

'Don't cry, Sarah, don't.' Rachel stood there, unsure of what to do. Then she suddenly lurched towards me with her arms open. She was aiming for a hug. A look of horror must have crossed my face.

'Oh, sorry, no touching,' she remembered, jumping back.

'I'm just going to have a little weep, Rachel. I'm OK, I just need a little cry.'

I was honestly trying not to feel sorry for myself. But no amount of positive thinking could dispute these facts:

1   I was about to do a read-through of a movie in which
    I would have to imitate an American accent, where
    most people in the room were actually American
2   There was a scene where I got killed. It involved
    crying, screaming, having sex and dying and I was
    used to playing comedy maids and bit-part shop
    assistants
3   I reminded people of chicken tikka
4   My entire front was excruciating
5   My boyfriend was obsessed by babies and his
    ex-girlfriend

While I was crying, Rachel Bird wandered around my hotel
room. She glanced at a ketchup-smeared plate that was left
over from my room-service binge last night.

'What was that?'

'A burger.'

'You didn't?' Rachel gasped in horror.

'Yeah, it was amazing.'

I'd always thought that placing some beef between two
slices of bread was a lame contribution to global cuisine on
America's part. But that burger was a sensation. It was a
thing of beauty and love and I was planning on ordering
another one later that night. But I didn't tell Rachel that.

'I've got it!' gasped Rachel. 'There's a gift shop downstairs. They sell hooded tops. I'll get you one. You can wear
that on the top and the wall hanging on the bottom.'

I would normally protest at the thought of teaming

home decor with sportswear in a tropical climate, but under the circumstances it was a very good idea. I handed Rachel my purse. She left the room and I slumped on the bed and picked up my script. I read the first line that I would say. My stomach made a familiar nervous gurgle and within twenty seconds I was on the loo for the sixth time that morning. I wondered whether Kate Winslet prepared like that. I finished emptying my system and I heard the phone ring. Please, God, I thought, let it be someone telling me they've cancelled the read-through.

'Baby?'

'Simon.'

'I just wanted to wish you good luck.'

'Thank you.'

'I just wanted to say you'll be amazing. I thought you'd be so nervous you'd be shitting for England.'

'I was.' I laughed.

We didn't say anything for a moment. It was just so nice to hear him there, even if 'there' was thousands of miles away.

'I love you, Sarah.'

'I love you too.'

'Even when you are a dickhead,' he said, obviously referring to my reaction to the Ruth photo.

'Si,' I replied, getting riled. 'I really don't want to think about that at the moment.' I sighed. 'I can't believe you just said that.'

There was a tense pause.

'How's it going over there?'

'I fell asleep in the sun, I look like a rare side of beef and I've got to wear a wall hanging to the read-through.'

I let him laugh.

'I've always thought you'd look hot in a wall hanging.'

'Thanks.' I softened. 'I wish you were here.'

'I had a dream about you when I went to sleep.'

'Yeah?'

'You were wearing football socks and nothing else.'

'Really? I'd like to see you in a half-pulled-up wetsuit.'

'Sare, I'm going to try and hold it in before you get back, but I can't guarantee.'

I smiled for a moment but then the thought of what I was about to do gripped me again.

'Si, I don't think I can go down there and do it. I mean it. You should see me!' my voice had gone up three octaves. I was near the panic place.

'You're brilliant, Sare, I mean it,' he said in such a calm voice that I almost believed him. 'I've heard you practise this about eight thousand times. I should know.'

We were silent again. His breathing was so comforting. 'I'd better let you go,' he said eventually. 'See ya, superstar.'

'Bye, baby.'

It'll be all right, it will, I thought as I put the phone down. And I managed to cling on to the edge of that thought with my fingernails, even when Rachel Bird returned with a XL red hooded top with 'I Love California' emblazoned across the front.

♥ *fifteen* ♥

The read-through was held in one of the basement function rooms at my hotel. As we waited to get started everyone looked at me. I would have blushed had that not already been my permanent state at the time. When I say everyone, I mean the forty-two actors sitting around the big table and the fifty-something other people with notebooks who sat on chairs around the sides of the room. Owing to the fact that we were sitting in a palatial meeting space with mirrors on all walls, even the people who were sitting behind me could see me. And I could see myself. Only I didn't look like myself. I looked like a giant baked bean. My mother would have said that I was being self-conscious and silly but for once my mother would have been wrong. I knew that people were looking at me because every time I glanced up I caught eyes staring at me, like I was a breakfast menu, before they subtly looked away.

Eamonn Nigels, the director, walked towards me. Eamonn is a very much younger-looking fifty-nine-year-old. Rachel Bird said that when she met him she was struck by his gravitas. He's certainly got an air of confidence and success about him. He's not flashy or arrogant though. He's unassuming, apart from a laugh that sounds like a large metal object has got stuck down a waste disposal. He is tall with a lot of thick grey hair, something of a Russian ballet dancer's chiselled features and a focused look in the eyes.

He was smiling. A friendly face.

'I won't kiss you, darling,' he said kindly.

I was grateful for his sensitivity to my pain.

'I might melt,' he added. Then he guffawed.

'Hysterical,' I said flatly.

'I've done it myself. British skin,' he pronounced, giving me an affectionate half cuddle.

'Ahhhh!'

'Oops. There's a wall hanging in our rental house like that,' he said, looking at my skirt.

'That's nice.'

'How was the flight?'

'Amazing. I could get used to First Class.'

'Rachel picked you up all right?'

'I wouldn't say that. Have you ever been in a car with her?'

'Yeaaas.' Eamonn looked around him and then started to speak with over-acted nonchalance, 'Was she OK?'

'Fine.'

'Really?'

'Eamonn.'

'Yes?'

'Are you quizzing me about your lady?' I whispered.

'She's not herself at the moment.'

I always ended up playing Relate advisor with Rachel and Eamonn. I did want to help. But I was hardly qualified. It was like someone coming to me for sunbathing tips.

'She's just feeling a bit neglected,' I told him.

'I am here to direct a film,' he puffed up.

'That's what I said.'

'I thought she was happy doing her yoga.'

'Eamonn, if she gets any bendier she'll be able to tie her hair up with her feet.'

Eamonn studied me thoughtfully. Then he straightened up and looked at the door impatiently.

'Where IS he?'

'Who?'

'Your murderer,' he told me with a freakish glint in his eye.

'Oh,' I said, surprised. 'I thought it was that guy.' I pointed out a man with a warm-looking if unconventional face who I had decided I could let touch my breast in an acting capacity.

'No,' Eamonn scoffed. 'That's the private investigator. We've got a great guy to play opposite you.'

'Oh.'

'Here he bloody well is. Finally.' Eamonn moved towards his own seat.

I looked towards the door just as the sweatiest human being I have ever seen in my life bounded through it. He was tall and he was wearing tracksuit trouser shorts and a soaking wet T-shirt. I stared at the T-shirt. It was familiar.

It had the word 'suck' on it. My heart plummeted. It was Canesten Man from the plane.

'Eamonn, man, sorry, no car came,' Leo Clement panted. He lifted the bottom of his T-shirt up and wiped his forehead with it. The gesture revealed his whole tummy to just under his nipples. It was tanned and toned and there was a line of glistening dark blond hair up to his navel. The sight caused drool in my mouth. So much so that I could have done with one of those spit suckers dentists use. 'I had to run here.'

'From where?'

'Malibu.'

There was a wave of taken-in breath. I deduced that was quite far.

'That's Sarah over there, she's playing Taylor. Sit next to her.'

Everyone now had licence to look at me. They took it. I did what I could by way of a smile.

He was coming towards me. I didn't think he'd recognize me as I'd been marinated in Indian spices since I last saw him on the flight.

'Hey,' he smiled.

I nodded and tried to look like a professional actress instead of someone with thrush who'd been boiled.

'We met on the plane.' Some of his sweat landed on my hand when he sat down. I watched my hot skin instantly absorb it, as it did half a tub of Nivea earlier that morning.

'Hi,' I said, feigning vague recognition terribly.

'You love California?'

It took me a moment to work out that he was talking about my hoodie.

'Oh yeah, I love California. The sunbathing is great.'

He gave me one of those direct eye-to-eye looks again. His eyes were baby-boy-gift blue. He said something. It sounded like, 'How's your little problem?' but I couldn't be sure. I opened my mouth to say, 'Pardon?' but Eamonn spoke first.

'Right, let's get going.'

Everyone opened their scripts. I clenched my bottom cheeks fiercely.

❦ *sixteen* ❦

I clenched like I was touching cloth for the entire thing. I was terrified but it went quite well . . . considering. I had two laughs. I'd been hoping to get some laughs. I wanted the audience to be sorry when I was strangled rather than pulling their fists down in front of their faces and going, 'Yesssss'. So laughs were good. But I was trying not to be too pleased about them because they could also be bad. The problem with laughs is that once you've had them, you always want them. If you say a line one day and it gets a laugh and then you say it another time and it doesn't . . . oh dear.

It's like going out one night and pulling Brad Pitt and then going out the next and only being able to pull a one-eyed drunken Irish man whom the barman calls Pirate. What do you do the next time you get out there? You put on too much make-up and try too hard and even Pirate doesn't look twice. Any natural allure you once had rots in your own neediness to be loved. I managed to concentrate even though I was very aware of Leo Clement next to me throughout. I could smell his fresh man sweat. It's my favourite smell after bacon frying.

We all realized how stonking the film was going to be. Eamonn Nigels is one of the most successful British directors in Hollywood. He is known for assembling casts of largely unknown actors in his films. He doesn't like, or to put it more accurately, 'Can't-fucking-stand, excuse my French,' working with the egos that can surround Hollywood superstars. His films have launched a lot of superstar careers though. Not that I was expecting to get lobbed into loopy fame land. I only had seventeen lines, three of which were two 'yes'es and a 'hmmm'. I was just amazed to find myself part of such an accomplished group. Had touching skin been possible, I definitely would have pinched myself.

As soon as the read-through was over people relaxed and smiled and walked around. Other people, that is. I just sat there. My heart was still pounding. I so wanted to do the job well. Erin came over to me.

'Well done, Sarah.'

'Oh, thanks, Erin.'

'I was real scared for you in that last scene.'

'You made me cry. You were so perfect, Erin.'

She looked uncomfortable with being praised.

'Your face looks much better.'

'Hmmm.'

'There's definitely an improvement.'

That was like saying Mr Bobbitt's second wife was an improvement. But I didn't tell Erin that because she was trying to be kind.

'I laughed when Eamonn said breast.'

'Did you? I didn't notice,' she smiled politely.

When Eamonn read out the stage directions as I was doing my scene with Leo, he said, 'His hand reaches out for her breast. Her nipple hardens at his touch.' I giggled like I was seven. Then because it's a rape scene I tried to make my giggle into a scream. It ended up sounding as though I'd sat on a cat.

Leo jumped up from the table as soon as it was finished. He didn't say a word to me. I assumed he was on the phone to his agent trying to get me recast.

Eamonn appeared and enveloped Erin in a hug.

'Wonderful. I'm so excited to be working with you.'

I looked down in the way one does when a director is praising another actress.

'And you!' he exclaimed, clamping his hand on my shoulder.

'EAMONN!' I hollered.

'I loved it! Sarah, you made her so warm. And she was so funny. Terrific!' BOLLOCKS.

'Now then, there was something else you did that I liked. What was it? Oh yes! You did this ridiculous girlish giggle at the start of the murder scene.' His eyes started to glisten as he spoke. 'I'd seen it as horrific because obviously it is. But you're right. The horror comes later. At first he woos you. He wants you. Here's a man in a hedge with you. It's night. He's a good-looking man. It's sexy. THEN it turns nasty,' he shuddered. 'Terrific!'

I noticed that Leo was standing behind Eamonn holding a plate. He must have been starving after his run.

'Ah, Leo. Great. I was just talking to Sarah about the rape scene. I want it to start like a tender love scene that gets darker. We don't know whether it's arousing, whether he's playing rough or whether . . . my apologies, I'm thinking aloud. I do that when I'm excited.' He stopped and smiled. 'It'll be great. Well done, Leo. Welcome aboard.'

Eamonn and Leo shook hands. I looked at the plate. It looked like it was full of wet flannels.

'What you eating?'

'Oh, oh,' he almost stammered. 'These are for you.'

'Um.'

'They're cold milk patties.'

I wondered whether Leo was mentally ill.

'My mom used to say it was the best thing to soothe sunburn.'

I touched the top of one of the flannels. They were chilly and divine. He placed the plate in front of me on the table. I looked down. Then like someone killed in a murder mystery, I leant forward in slow motion and lowered my face into it.

'I'll leave them with you,' he said.

I couldn't currently thank him because my face was in flannel heaven. The reading was over and my face was cool.

Bliss. The only thing that could have made that moment better was a gin and tonic.

I felt a hand on my back. But I couldn't bring myself to surrender my flannel heaven. Not yet. I heard a stern male voice.

'Sarah, I'm Miles Mavers, the voice coach. We need to talk.'

♥ *seventeen* ♥

And Miles Mavers certainly did want to talk to me. At length. About how dreadful my American accent was. And I must admit this surprised me. I'd worked phenomenally hard on my American accent for months. So fearful was I of doing the American equivalent of a 'cor blimey' Dick Van Dyke that I had even spent quite a lot of money going to see a voice coach in London.

In spite of this, Miles Mavers had spotted so many mistakes he requested that I have a private coaching session with him the following day. Now, call me British, but I would have thought that a good time of day to do a voice class would be late afternoon or late morning or after lunch or after brunch. So I was surprised when Miles confirmed our lesson for marginally after dawn. On a Sunday! He wanted to meet me at 8 a.m. on a Sunday. I will repeat that. AT 8 A.M. ON A SUNDAY. You'd never get that in Britain. You'd be lucky to get a roll over and a small fart at 8 a.m. on a Sunday morning in Britain. AND, it wasn't even any 8 a.m. on a Sunday. It was an 8 a.m. on a Sunday after a party. And not just any old party. A martini party for the cast and crew to get to know each other. Luckily for Miles Mavers I wasn't planning on going to said party. There were to be no glamorous LA film parties for the solar afflicted, so I had been happy, well, relatively happy, to accept his proposal.

I wonder now whether I had a sixth sense about Miles Mavers, because try as I did, I couldn't warm to him and I definitely wasn't looking forward to his class. As I lay on my bed that Saturday afternoon thinking about why that was, I came to these conclusions:

1 He was a squat little man with a tan. If I was being honest I would say that his face looked as though it had been made with Plasticine and then squashed by something angry. However, despite the somewhat challenging landscape of his visage, he had the aura and swagger of a man who believed he looked like Brad Pitt. It was curious.

2 He wasn't in any way encouraging about my accent. He didn't say, 'Gee, you've so nearly nailed it, just a little bit of work on your vowels and girl, you'll be giving Sandra Bullock a run for her money.' He didn't even say, 'Not bad.' He just went, 'This needs work,' and 'This, this and this need a LOT of work.' Now, I prefer 'stroke then poke' people. People who say, 'Darling, you really do have a rare gift for the stage, but shall we just have a little go without the windmill hands and the bit where you said the other person's lines?' Miles Mavers clearly didn't stroke before he

poked. He poked, poked, and then poked REALLY hard.

In many ways it was fortuitous that I didn't like Miles Mavers because it meant that for a short period I'd stopped worrying about Simon and Ruth. Sadly, it was to be just that: a short period.

'Knock, knock,' I heard a tap and a man's voice at my door.

'Knock, knock,' I imitated back. I listened to how I sounded. I was sure I sounded American. I assumed it was my room service burger at the door. Although I was a bit surprised because I'd only ordered it five minutes ago.

'Won't be a minute,' I shouted in my American accent. It was a lie. I was moving so slowly a dribble of syrup would have beaten me. I removed the milk patties from my naked body and slid off the bed, trying to keep sunburnt skin from touching other sunburnt skin on my body. I put on the giant-size towelling dressing gown that the hotel provided and shuffled to the door. Please, God, I thought, can the burger be cooked so I don't get E.coli and can they have remembered the ketchup, mayonnaise and mustard and have got really carried away when dishing up my chips.

'Come on burger, come to Mummy,' I cooed in American as I opened the door.

'A fax for you, ma'am.'

'Gee, thanks,' I said in my American accent, demonstrating that Miles Mavers was mistaken and I could actually be a native.

The man squinted at me.

'Australian?'

Bugger.

'Um, no, British.'

'I have a cousin in Chester.'

'Lovely place,' I said, having never been there.

I opened the envelope. It was bound to be a list of all my accent mistakes from Miles Mavers, which, in light of that Antipodean attack, I needed. But it wasn't from him. It was a whole page with Simon's illegible scrawl all over it. Bless him! I thought foolishly. I assumed he was wondering how the read-through went.

'I have the best boyfriend in the world,' I told the man, who was still in front of me. I didn't mention the fact that my perfect boyfriend was unfeasibly broody and sexually obsessed with his ex-girlfriend. I felt it best we should keep it on a need-to-know basis.

He stood there smiling at me until I finally fathomed that I was supposed to give him a tip. I shuffled back into the room to get my wallet and he waited patiently for me to return. I had no idea about this tipping thing. I gave him $10, which I took by his departing smile was too much. I settled onto the bed to enjoy Simon on paper.

Sarah, I need to say some stuff before I see you again.

   Its to do with Ruth.

   I love Ruth.

   She's a great girl and I spent a good deal of happy time with her. *I will always love her and she will allways be part of my life.*

I don't see why I should have told you that she couldn't have kids. Its not really the sort of thing you go on about.

Anyway I'm with you now. It's you I want. It's you I think about when I wake up in the morning with an erection; its you I think about for the rest of the day.

But I'm angry that you are behaving so childishly about that photo. It's just a bloody photo of a friend, Sarah. I don't want to be in a relationship were there's jealousy. I want you to trust me. Because you can. Don't ruin what we have by these petty thoughts. I beg you.

I had to get all this off my chest, because most of all we must be honest with each other in this relationship. That's the most important thing I think.

Anyway you silly cow. I love you. Lets put all this behind us.
Me
xxxx

I stared at it. Then I made the sound 'urgh' as loudly as I could.

'I've made *him* angry. I'm childish! Jealous!'

I picked up my mobile phone. I was shaking. I started to write the longest text in the world.

I can't believe you sent that. I told you I didn't want to think about it while I'm here. This job is a big deal for me Si! That fax was all about you. Think how I feel. I used to hear you shagging loudly in the room next to me. I know

you used to have hot sex with her and then I find a photo of her in your filofax. It's not just any old photo Si. She's in her pants with her bum in the air!!! So don't insult me by calling me jealous. Anyone would feel the same.
ME
PS. The reading went very well. Thank you.

I lay down again with the milk patties. Negative thoughts were multiplying at a terrifying rate.

I needed the medication that was Mother. I knew it would cost a small fortune but I didn't care. I reached for my phone and called my parents' number.

'Mum, what do you do when Dad really, really annoys you?'

'Oh, hello darling. Are you having a nice time?'

'Yes, oh well, no, kind of ... Mum, I'm really sunburnt.'

'Oh, darling, that was silly.'

'I know!' I moaned. 'Look, we have to keep this really brief because it'll bankrupt us both. But I've just had a foul fax from my Si. What should I do?'

'That doesn't sound like your Simon,' she said, obviously thinking that he was in the right and I in the wrong. 'I'll tell you what you do. Nothing. Don't respond in the heat of the moment, Sarah, for God's sake. Calm down, have a gin and tonic. And talk about whatever this is another time.'

My mum always knows best. I let her words register.

'Bollocks.'

'Oh, Sarah, you didn't.'

'Oh, Mum, I did.'
'Oh, darling, that was silly.'

♥ *eighteen* ♥

The next knock on my door had to be my burger. Or so I thought. But no, it was Rachel Bird standing before me in a cream evening dress with Maid Marian hair. She looked beautiful and oddly innocent. Sadly, she still had the mouth of a disgruntled builder and the will of a girder.

'You ARE coming!'

'I am not.'

'You bloody well are.'

'I bloody well am not.'

'You . . .'

'Rach. Please, I am not going to the party in a wall hanging.'

'No, you can't go in the SAME wall hanging.' She pointed at the huge holdall at her feet. 'So I brought you all the wall hangings we had for you to choose from.'

That was actually very sweet of her. So I smiled.

'Oh, hi, Erin,' I shouted to Erin as she walked down the corridor.

Erin stopped and hovered behind Rachel. She eyed the bathrobe I was wearing and the wet flannel over my head.

'Oh, Sarah, aren't you coming?' She sounded disappointed.

'No. Sorry, lovely. It will be full of people and if anyone accidentally touches my skin I'm liable to impale a martini glass in their neck. Which is incidentally what I'll do to Rachel here if she continues to harangue me.' I smiled sweetly at Rachel. But Rachel was staring open-mouthed at Erin.

'Rachel. Erin. Erin. Rachel. Rachel is Eamonn Nigels's girlfriend. I'm going to go back in my room now. So have a brilliant night. I want to hear all about it tomorrow.'

Erin smiled and held out her hand to shake Rachel's, clearly oblivious to the fact that they'd met before and discussed G-spots. Rachel linked her arm ominously through Erin's. 'Now then, darling, what are you going to wear?'

Erin blushed. I had a very bad feeling.

'Do you have anything a bit less *Little House on the Prairie*?'

Erin stood stock-still and continued to blush.

'For God's sake, chicken, you can't go in that.'

'Erin, do you want to come in and try the dress I was going to wear tonight?' I offered.

'It'll be massive on her.'

'Cheers, Rach. No, seriously Erin, try it on. It's a stretchy material. It would look amazing on you.'

Rachel marched Erin past me, into my hotel room and towards my wardrobe. She pulled out my black dress.

'Is it a Herve Leger?' Rachel gasped, yanking it off the hanger.

'Is it bugger. It's H&M.'

'Sarah's right, for once. That will be amazing on you! Now come here, sweetheart.'

Erin trundled meekly towards Rachel, who grabbed the end of her French pleat, pulled the toggle off and started to free her hair from the plait.

'Oh, thank God for that,' sighed Rachel when her hair had been released. Erin looked like she'd just put a finger in a live socket. It really suited her.

'There you go, Roller Girl,' laughed Rachel.

'Who's Roller Girl?'

I rolled my eyes at Rachel.

'A beautiful character from a film,' I managed to get in quickly before Rachel had the chance to inform her that Roller Girl was a 1970s porn star.

'I'll do your make-up in a sec, but put these on first.' Rachel handed Erin a pair of earrings. It was a sweet, if septic, gesture, as Rachel had to take them out of her own ears first. They were the biggest, sparkliest, dangliest earrings I'd ever seen. It would be like lugging the Oxford Street Christmas decorations around by your lobes.

'Dress! Now!' was Rachel's next instruction. Erin obediently began a shy change in the corner of the room. I wished I wasn't witnessing it. Rampant convent girl gives nice Christian girl a makeover. It felt like something I read in *Jackie* when I was eight. Those stories never ended well.

'Do you have a boyfriend, Erin?' asked Rachel. This was an embarrassing question for Erin because:

1 it was an embarrassing question for anyone
2 all she was wearing was a pair of very sensible
   knickers

Erin shook her head self-consciously. This sparked a look
in Rachel's eyes that would have terrified even Bruce Willis
in a vest.

'You need to put your light on, darling. If your light's not
on, you won't get a ride. Don't worry, darling, we'll find you
a fella in no time.'

Erin responded with a look that demonstrated she
intended to worry about the situation a great deal. But such
was Rachel's ability to bark orders in such quick succession
that you didn't have time to protest that Erin simply
nodded.

'Would you like a drink, Erin?' I asked sympathetically.
'Look on it as though it's medicine.'

She hesitated and then, to my surprise, nodded. I made
her and Rachel a gin and tonic from my mini-bar and when
I turned round I gasped. Erin looked stunning. She looked
so beautiful she would have made Cheryl Cole look rough.

'Go Gok,' I cooed to Rachel, who was giving Erin smok-
ier eyes than a pub patio.

'Finish that drink and we'll be off.'

Rachel stood with her arms folded as Erin swallowed and
then grimaced a few times.

'Come, Sarah, please come,' asked Erin when she'd drunk
as much as she could.

I did feel bad about this. I wouldn't normally have allowed a sweet young girl to be sullied by a sexual deviant with an old vendetta. But I had my own problems that night and I'm ashamed to say they were making me a bit mean.

'Sorry,' I said shaking my head to Erin.

'Will you take a photo of us?' asked Erin.

'Of course.' I took her camera from her. They stood together in front of me. 'Say, "Lesbian!"' I instructed. I read somewhere that the word 'lesbian' gives you the perfect photo face.

Rachel yelled the word. Erin just opened her mouth in surprise. Eventually I got some lovely ones of them both. I even took one on my evil camera as well.

'What will you do?' Erin asked when I'd finished.

'Nothing much,' I said sadly.

'Is something up with you?' asked Rachel softly.

'Nothing. I just had a bit of a fax/text row with Simon, that's all,' I said, handing Erin back her camera.

Rachel's face lit up like a new coin in the sunlight.

'Oh, well, you need to have sex quickly to make it up!'

'Brilliant, Rach, I'm in LA.'

'Come on, Erin,' said Rachel with a sly smirk. 'Let's leave Sarah to get on with some make-up phone sex.'

PHONE SEX!!!

♥ *nineteen* ♥

PHONE SEX! I'd never had phone sex for the simple reason that I knew I'd be CATASTROPHIC at it.

1 I went to a convent – I still giggle when I hear the word 'willy'
2 I'm rubbish at sex speak – I seem to have a problem with pretty much all sex words. For a start, what are you supposed to call your lady place?
   Pussy – too porn mag and unfair on kittens
   Fanny – sounds like I've got an old aunt down there
   Twat – sounds like I've got David Cameron down there

In light of these facts, I shouldn't have attempted phone sex for the first time that night. Especially with a man I had just had a fax/text row with. However, I had it in my head that instigating phone sex was just the olive branch I was looking for. It involved me stepping out of my comfort zone. And if there's one thing that Simon loved more than people looking at the positive it was people stepping out of their comfort zones. In fact, I was quite prepared for the stepping out of the comfort zone part to get him going more than the phone sex. So I sat there on my bed covered in milky flannels, psyching myself up for some telephone loving.

'Come on, Sarah, how hard can it be?' I sighed to myself. 'Oh, that's it!' I muttered. 'I need to use words like "hard" but I should probably say, "Hhhhhaaaaarrd."'

I started to feel nervous. But then I reminded myself that I was an adult and an actor and I had done sex, so how haaaaaard could it be? Very hard, hopefully. Tee hee.

'OK, let's do it,' I whispered as I dialled his number.

'Baby.'

'Hey,' he sounded quiet and drained.

'Sorry about, you know, all that stuff.'

'No, it wasn't you. It was me too.'

A pause. I used it to try to contact my harlot alter ego.

'What are you doing?' I attempted to say it sexily.

'Lying on the bed. Just played football.'

Not exactly D. H. Lawrence. I needed to try harder.

'Hmmm,' I cooed like the caramel bunny. 'Are you sweaty?'

'Nah, I've just had a shower.'

Oh, for God's sake, it was like attempting to seduce a Pot Noodle.

'So you're clean, because I'm feeling very dirty.' (I said it 'diiiirrrty'.)

'You are, as well!' He finally started to sound more

animated. 'I couldn't work out whether you were trying to talk sauce or you were practising to audition for a character who's got learning difficulties or is inbred or something.'

'Fuckster.'

'And what are you doing?' he said, clearly taking the piss out of my accent.

'Lying on my bed . . .' I considered saying, '. . . thinking about your cock,' but it sounded so rude. I blushed and bottled it.

'Hmmm. What are you wearing?'

'Um, nothing,' I said, peeling off the wet flannels.

'You look beautiful.'

I smiled. Then I looked down at my body. But my eyes met the acres of vivid red skin. Thankfully, I managed to stop myself from shrieking, 'I look like raw liver! You freak!'

'I might have to tie your hands up so I can pleasure you and you won't distract me.'

I glanced at my swollen, sunburnt wrists. I started to gurn. I hadn't thought this through.

'Hmmm. I've got some baby oil. I'm going to massage you.'

My mouth opened in agony at the thought. But I did very well. I managed to suppress actual screams of pain as he talked me through all the red places he was kneading, stroking and tickling. Even when he took my knickers off, which in reality felt as though someone was shaving layers of my skin off with a cheese slicer, I kept quiet. I blocked out his words and imagined that I was lying face-down on an ice rink instead. It wasn't very erotic. Phone sex was much more stressful than I'd thought. I suddenly felt exhausted.

'You're very quiet.'

Oh arse, I'd forgotten to do sexy groaning.

'You're not normally so quiet.'

I started to think of something wanton to say. But then I stopped.

'We've never had phone sex before.' My stomach lurched. 'You're getting me confused with Ruth!'

'Sare!'

'What?'

'I'm not getting you confused with . . .' – sigh – 'Sare! I've got an erection here.'

'What do you mean, I'm "not normally quiet"?'

'I meant when we normally do it,' he sighed.

'I'm not that noisy. But she was. I know she bloody was. Because I used to hear her!' I felt sick. Sounds of Ruth's screams and images of Simon and Ruth nakedly writhing exploded spectacularly in my head. For the briefest second I considered taking a deep breath or calming down. But the bad thoughts sodded that idea and I hung up. Then because I had no idea what else to do, I put on a wall hanging and the hoodie and I went to investigate the party.

♥ *twenty* ♥

I didn't actually go into the party. I was too embarrassed by the 'Carol Thatcher in the jungle' look I was sporting. Instead, I texted Rachel Bird and she said she'd get me a martini and I should meet her on the terrace outside. I needed to check that Erin hadn't been led astray by Rachel and wasn't about to go dogging with some lady boys.

It wasn't quite that bad. But as soon as I joined her and Erin I regretted leaving them alone together. Rachel was animated. Erin was swaying. I learnt that:

1 Rachel had got Erin drunk. She told her that the passion fruit martinis were non-alcoholic. Erin thought they were delicious and was by this point on her fifth

2 Rachel was teaching Erin how to pull. Rachel teaching anyone to pull would be a fearsome concept. But I had a nasty suspicion that Rachel wouldn't be satisfied until Erin's preacher father discovered his daughter on the altar with a feral man between her legs

'Nooooooo, noo, na, na, slower, that's it, now you're getting it.' Erin was being taught how to seductively drink a drink with a straw. 'That's it, work it. Remember the mantra: if your light's off, you won't get a ride. Good . . . good. That's it, keep it slow.'

'What if she doesn't get given a straw?' I asked. It was a valid point.

Rachel shook her head and rolled her eyes at me. So I shut up and watched Erin fellate a straw.

'Well, obviously, she will do lots of hair and neck fiddling like we went through earlier, and then she should do this.'

Rachel started circling her finger around the edge of her shiny lips. 'It's all about the lipgloss. Lots of lipgloss. So you circle the edge of your lips slowly, like this, and then just let the tip of your finger slip inside your mouth like this.' Rachel started sucking on her finger. Now, Rachel is a dirty blonde with a husky voice who has a Bachelor of Bedroom Arts. When she gently sucked on her finger she looked like Christina Aguilera doing a lipstick commercial. When little Erin had a go it looked like she'd got a ring stuck on her finger and she was trying to get it off.

'But the most important thing,' said Rachel, wiping her dribbly finger on my wall-hanging skirt, 'is to pretend that they are fascinating.'

'Ahhhh, Rach, you can't tell her that!' I choked. 'Thousands of years of patriarchal society and you give her "pretend they're fascinating"?'

'Well, what do you suggest?'

'Being yourself.'

'How long were you single, Sarah?'

'Bitch.'

'Never, under any circumstances, just be yourself,' she said to Erin, and gave me an angry headmistress look and started to say something scolding. She was silenced by a loud, high-pitched female voice.

'Are you the English girl?'

Rachel and I both spun round. The ingratiating voice belonged to a malnourished-looking woman in one of those tops that only Keira Knightley can wear because it's just a small bit of fabric draped over your boobs. She was looking at me.

'Yeah.'

'I'm Chelsea,' she screeched. I would have rather heard a symphony of knives on plates and nails down blackboards.

'I'm Basildon,' I said, and a little part of me died when I realized I had said a joke that bad out loud.

'Huh?'

'Really, really bad joke. Sorry.'

'Huh?' When she said, 'Huh?' it sounded like a tiny dog yapping, which was interesting because at that moment she decided to produce a small, rat-like creature out of her handbag and it started yapping. It had big ears and was wearing a green-and-pink stripy jumper.

'Oh, Cleopatra,' she said, kissing it. The dog continued to yap as she continued to smother the poor thing while repeating eloquent phrases like, 'You love mumsy, moo,' and

'Mumsy loves pattie, poo.' I suddenly understood why you are allowed to carry guns in America.

'I'll be seeing you a lot. You're coming to meet my pop for voice classes.'

Classes! Classes! As in plural. Miles Mavers didn't mention more than one session to me.

'Let's go back inside, Cleopatra,' she said to the dog, and without even acknowledging anyone with two legs, she stalked back to the party.

'Oh bye, Chelsea, lovely to meet you,' I shouted after her. No response.

'Swallow, just swallow,' Rachel was telling Erin, who was looking like she was about to retch. Erin obediently swallowed seven times, hesitated for a moment, then she started beaming again.

'So, where were we?'

'You were upsetting feminists everywhere.'

'Oh, that's right, the most important bit of all. Act fascinated, don't let your eyes deviate from them, do all that stuff with your hair and neck then your mouth and the straw. You'll be on your knees in the disabled loo within half an hour.'

I rolled my eyes again but Erin was still beaming.

'Come on, let's go back in and put it to the test.' She gestured to Erin to follow her but Erin just swayed slightly. I didn't like the situation at all. Erin had been kind to me and I wanted to get her away from Rach. But Rachel had also been kind to me and I didn't want to upset her.

'Rach, I should take Erin up to bed. She's wasted.' I turned to Erin and added quickly, 'That's no bad thing, sweetheart.'

I pulled Rachel away from Erin and out of earshot.

'Rach, she's really nice,' I said. 'Can't we just take her up to bed?'

Rachel looked at me and pretended to sulk.

'I'm just having a bit of fun.'

'Rach,' I paused here. 'Please.'

Rachel looked at me and raised her eyebrows.

Suddenly there was a big commotion by the balcony door. It looked like Leo Clement was walking through it surrounded by about six women on their knees. A closer inspection showed that the women were all petting and fondling a dog. A proper-sized dog.

'Oh, that's another good one,' said Rachel, viewing the scene. 'Play with his dog, if he's got a dog.'

I looked at Leo Clement. I tried to remove my eyes from Leo Clement. It was impossible. He was wearing a suit jacket over a pale blue T-shirt. The T-shirt brings out the blue of his eyes, I thought. Leo Clement is so handsome you've started thinking ridiculous things like that, I thought after. He had on those jeans he wore for the flight. Everything looked creased as though he'd just picked it off his bedroom floor and his hair was all over the place like it had recently been ruffled in a sweaty bed. He started walking towards us. I managed to finally look away. Talk to Leo Clement as though he's ugly, I told myself. Talk to him as though he is lovely, I tried again. UGLY! Sarah, listen! Talk to him as though he is ugly! I instructed myself. It was my only hope of not acting like a pillock.

'Hey,' said Leo Clement.

'How are you, ugly?'

I stood still in shock for a second. I wasn't supposed to tell him he was ugly! Luckily, he laughed. Erin looked at Rachel and demonstrated that she should start alluring-tactic number one: hair and neck fiddling. Erin caught on and began to yank an earring about while playing with her hair. If I didn't know the game I would have said she had nits.

'Boy,' Leo shouted, and the dog ran over to him. The women stood up and dispersed. His dog nuzzled up to me and began to sniff the bottom of my wall hanging. I never know what to do with dogs. They normally sniff my bum and when I start to play with them they just wander away so I feel like a plum.

'Oh, oh,' I said, feeling something moist on my toes. 'Oh.'

'He likes your toes, huh.'

'Hmmm. Must be the fungus.'

I spied Rachel Bird giving Erin a look that said 'under no circumstances be yourself'. Erin responded by grinning and getting faster with the neck fondling.

We all stood in silence for a moment, me guiltily enjoying the toe-licking. Luckily, a canapé lady appeared carrying a tray of something. Leo and I reached down for one.

'They're hot,' said the waitress. 'Spicy.'

I took a bite.

'Oooh yeah. You'll feel that on the loo tomorrow,' I panted.

It just came out. Rachel gave Erin another look but Erin's head was at a funny angle. Her ear was nearly on her shoulder. Leo took a step forward.

'I think it's caught in her hair. The earring.'

I moved to have a look too, but Rachel gestured for me to stay where I was. Rachel looked on proudly as Leo tenderly took hold of Erin's neck and inspected her ear.

'It's a mess. I don't want to pull it. Step into the light. Here.' He led the swaying Erin towards the outside light. I noticed how gentle he was for someone so strong. And he really did seem concerned about her hair. 'I might need to cut it.'

I gazed at them, thinking what a ridiculously beautiful couple they made, until Rachel barked at me.

'Sarah, go and get some scissors.'

'Why me? I've got half a mile of ethnic rug wrapped round my lower half,' I humphed.

Rachel ignored me and kept her eye on Erin and Leo. I removed my feet from the dog's tongue and started my geisha slow step to find some bloody scissors somewhere.

♥ *twenty-one* ♥

After we extricated Erin I took her up to her room and helped her get changed. Then I went to bed myself. I had a horrible night.

There is one thing in life that I am really good at. Sleeping. I am peculiarly proficient at it. I've spent my life embracing sleep and sleep has always responded by warmly snuggling me back. It's been a beautiful relationship. I can sleep anytime, anyplace, anywhere. I can snooze for five hours straight. I have an impressive sleeping CV. I fell asleep during my oldest friend's wedding. I fell asleep during a Geography GCSE. But that night, sleep buggered off without telling me.

I lay awake all night and I thought about my Simon and that photo in his Filofax of Ruth in her pants. I mulled over the feelings he must have had for her. They went out for an entire year. Was he desperately disappointed that she couldn't have children? Was I a consolation prize? What if I didn't want children or, God forbid, wasn't able to have them? My mind was having a right laugh with all these questions. Then I began to ruminate about them having sex together. Obviously, I'd never seen them having adult fun. But in my mind it was porn-star sex. She was ballerina bendy and blow-job-giver of the month.

The problem was that once I entertained these thoughts, it was like they put their feet up in my mind and settled in for good. Images of Simon and Ruth bonking away in Cirque du Soleil positions were hanging out in my mind and they didn't seem to have any intention of leaving.

Then, just for a bit of variety, I moved on to comparing myself to Ruth. I felt really fat in contrast to her. I admit I'm not obese. But I wobble and my arse is mahooosive. I knew that if I wasn't present and people were discussing me the conversation would go like this:

'Sarah. Who's she?'

'Oh, you know Sarah, actress, big girl. Built for comfort, not speed.'

But Ruth had, to quote anyone who's ever met her, 'a lovely figure'.

And I didn't think I was very good in bed. I couldn't even muster the confidence to say the word 'cock' in a phone sex situation.

So I lay there feeling crap about myself and very cross with Simon. But when I asked myself, 'Why are you cross with him, Sarah?' the only answer I came up with was that I was cross with him because he had an ex-girlfriend who was better looking than me. And even I knew that was a ridiculous thing to be cross with someone about. And realizing that I was ridiculous made me feel crapper and crosser.

And to top it all off, I thought, I bet she doesn't have these ridiculous thoughts.

I was stuck in my own head, going round and round a vicious crap-thought roundabout with no exits. I reckon I could have mustered a modicum of control over these thoughts in the daytime. But lying there unable to sleep that night, I didn't have a chance against them. It was as though the security guard in my mind had clocked off for the night and all these bad thoughts had broken in and were running wild.

At about four in the morning I realized what all this was. It was jealousy and it was horrible.

♥ *twenty-two* ♥

When Miles Mavers instructed me to come to his house for voice coaching at 8 a.m. I imagined his wife opening the door in her dressing gown, maybe letting the rat dog out for a poo in the garden at the same time. Then she would smile kindly and say, 'He's just getting up, he'll be down in a minute. Coffee?' Instead I found myself in one of the weirdest morning scenes I'd ever witnessed.

'DAD! SARAH'S HERE!' Chelsea caterwauled to her father. She was wearing a leotard and pointe shoes and she was as vocally torturous as she was at the party. It seemed that her father was upstairs. Now she could have gone upstairs and quietly told him that I was here, thus saving my delicate two-martini, one-gin and no-sleep head. She didn't. But it wasn't just Chelsea that was creating this cacophony of tonal terror. Chelsea also had the stereo on. The stereo was playing piano polka music. It sounded like a mad love-crossed French pianist was stabbing notes angrily with a stale baguette. It was eight o'clock in the morning.

'DAD! DAD! DAAAAAD!'

Then the dog appeared.

'Cleo, baby, bum booms, DAD! DAAAAAD!'

'Maybe I should come back later.'

'Sarah!' Miles Mavers jogged down the stairs before me in a shell suit. 'We've got a lot of work to do.'

'Morning.'

'Let's make you into a Yank.'

To Chelsea, he said, 'Morning, princess.' She hopped on pointe to give him a kiss.

'Morning, Daddy. Can I watch your lesson?'

'Of course, princess,' he beamed at her. 'Chelsea's an actress. A very good one,' he told me.

'Ah, are you? Lovely.'

Now I could have been wrong, but Chelsea looked about twenty-seven. I didn't understand why we were all talking to her as though she was four. It must have been the ballet gear.

'Would you mind getting me some water?' Miles Mavers appeared to be talking to me.

'I'll have one too,' said Chelsea.

'Um, where's the kitchen?'

Chelsea sighed and said, 'Last door to the right.'

These people are freaks, I thought. I walked to their kitchen, looking in all the rooms on the way. I entered the kitchen. It was huge and so was everything in it. I had never seen a fridge even half as big as the one in there. I was tempted to get in it and hide. I tripped over an exercise ball on the floor. Well, I was hardly expecting it. There was a fitness programme playing on a huge TV. The lady on the telly had abs like my dad's patio steps.

'AHHHH.'

I had trodden on a woman doing crunches.

'Sorry! Are you OK?'

'Four, five, six,' she panted, which I took to mean she wasn't mortally wounded. This was Mummy. Mummy's breasts and lips had been surgically altered. Perhaps I stared a little too long while deciding whether it had been for the better. I climbed over her to get to the sink. She bashed my shins with her hand when I obscured the TV. The pain brought tears of fresh sunburn pain to my eyes. I saw two empty and probably dirty glasses. I filled them quickly and headed back to the office.

'Perfect, princess, that's perfect.'

'Aa, ee, ii, oo, uu.'

'Perfect.'

Chelsea was saying her vowels in her own American accent.

'I just started off the vowels with Chelsea.'

'Hmmm. Here's the water.'

'Oh,' she exclaimed, taking a sip of it. 'Is it tap?'

'No, I peed in it!' I smiled sweetly at her.

'Uh, uh!' started Chelsea.

'Right, Miles, let's get cracking. What have you got for me?'

'Uh, uh,' repeated Chelsea.

'I didn't really pee in it,' I whispered to her.

'Daddy,' she started again.

'OK, are we doing vowels?'

Miles Mavers was speechless for a second.

'Yes. Vowels. Now, Chelsea, do your vowels again, princess.'

'Aa, ee, ii, oo, uu.'

'Now, Sarah, you try.'

'Aa, ee, ii, oo, uu.'

'No. Listen again. Chelsea, repeat the oo.'

'Oo.'

'Marve . . .'

I cut him off.

'Um, Miles, I start shooting scenes in two days.'

'Yes, Sarah, you do.'

'Well, what would really help me is if we could go over the scenes I'll be doing. I thought that's what this session was for.'

Fuckety fuck. I'd offended him. Oh well, in for a penny, or whatever that saying was.

'And would you mind if it's just the two of us in the sessions?' Fuckety gangbang of fuck, now there was a look of war in his eyes.

'If that's what you want. Chelsea, would you leave us to it?'

Chelsea attempted to stomp off but was thwarted by the pointe shoes and ended up doing quite a good Charlie Chaplin impression out of the door.

'She seems nice!' I said to Miles, and then I handed him the script.

♥ *twenty-three* ♥

I treated myself to a full-fat American brunch in the hotel restaurant after my first Miles Mavers lesson. The restaurant was light and made you feel as though you were on board a jolly ship, which was apt, because what with the sleepless night and the jet lag I had the sensation that I was on a stormy sea. I was sitting at a window table looking out towards the ocean. Before the sea there was a coast path and it looked like the whole of LA was in transit along it in every cardiovascular way possible. It was like that old Tampax ad where everyone's on rollerblades or running with dogs, whooping. It was nothing like Camden. About all you see in Camden at 9.30 on a Sunday morning is a disgruntled road-sweeper and a few gurners who haven't gone to bed trying to ponce fags off French people. I shook my head with pity as I looked at all the sweaty exercisers. Didn't they understand that Sunday mornings are for bacon sandwiches and the *Screws of the World* in bed?

'More coffee?' asked the pretty waitress. I stared at her for a moment in wonder. I'd only drunk half a cup. That was another thing you didn't get at home: waiters and waitresses being nice to you.

'Um, yes, please, thanks, amazing.'

'You're welcome!'

'Thank you.'

'You're welcome!'

'Whoah,' I said, because the 'you're welcome's came at such rapid fire.

'You from England?'

'Yeah.'

'My mother's brother lives in Scotland.'

'David?'

'Yeaaasss! Do you know him?'

'No, I'm joshing.'

She looked upset. So I added, 'Scotland's beautiful.'

'Your food will be ready shortly.'

'Thank you.'

'You're welcome!'

I was just thinking that I'd better cut down on expressions of thanks, when Erin approached my table.

'Hey!'

She was wearing an oversized Christian Union T-shirt over cycling shorts.

'Have you just been for a run?' I asked, amazed.

'No.'

'Thank God for that.'

'It was just a jog.'

'Do you want to join me for breakfast?'

'Thanks.'

'Hi there.' It was the waitress, appearing from nowhere. I've never known waitressing like it. I used to waitress in a small café near Hampstead Heath with Julia at the weekends. We were never nice to the customers. We found them to be an unfortunate distraction as we ate free food and caught up on gossip. And if we left them long enough they came to the counter to order so we didn't have to move.

'What's good?' Erin smiled at the waitress.

'Oh, I haven't been working here long, and I'm fasting.'

'Sure,' nodded Erin looking at her menu.

'Fasting? Is it a religious thing?' I asked, squinting at her. She was blonde and blue-eyed and didn't look like any of the other Ramadan fasters I'd met.

'No, it's just a fast,' she said, as though fasting was natural.

She worked in a restaurant! One of the, I mean, the only benefit of working in a restaurant is the free food. I started to suspect America was dropped at birth.

'Well, what do you eat?'

'Nothing. I make this drink with maple syrup and vinegar and water and I drink that.'

'Urgh,' I said, my mouth filling with hot saliva. 'Does it make you vom?'

'Huh?'

'How long do you do it for?'

'This is my eighth day.'

'Eighth day! How are you standing?'

'I feel great.'

I needed to lie down.

'Is there cream in the soup?' said Erin.

'Crème fraiche.'

'Is it low fat?'

'No.'

'And the asparagus, is it cooked in oil?'

'No, boiled.'

'Great. I'll have a green salad, no dressing, asparagus, no sauce and an egg-white omelette.'

'Blimey, Erin, are you sure you don't want a pint of vinegar/syrup juice?'

'No. It's good though. I've done that fast.'

'Coffee?' said the waitress.

'Sure.'

'I don't know what's wrong with me,' sighed Erin after the waitress had gone. 'I really want a bagel.'

'Get her back and order a bagel.'

'No!' she gasped. 'I have a wheat allergy.'

'Oh. I love bagels.'

'Was that your boyfriend I saw at the airport with you?'

'Hmmm.'

'He looked nice.'

'He is,' I said sadly.

'Are you OK?'

'Er, yeah, fine. Kind of. Although I had a terrible night's sleep and you'll probably think I'm mad but . . . sorry, you don't know anything about jealousy, do you?' Now, I didn't know Erin. She was very young but I liked her. I thought she was a good person. For some reason I wanted to confide the whole sorry Simon situation to her. 'You see, I had this weird sleepless night last night and, well, I've never been jealous before, but I think I've become jealous of his ex-girlfriend. I know it sounds ridiculous but I keep thinking he'd prefer to be with her and that their life was more exciting than ours and they only split up a couple of months before we got together, surely he can't be over her . . .'

I stopped because I realized that Erin wasn't even looking at me. She was staring at a man next to us who was reading a copy of the *LA Times*. Then suddenly she leapt up from the table, strode briefly off and returned holding a newspaper out for me. I took it. I didn't really understand why she was giving me a newspaper though.

'Thanks, Erin.' I smiled.

'Look,' she whispered.

It was the *LA Times*. I stared down at it. There was a headline saying, 'LA Water Board Announces Cuts'. I wasn't sure whether I was supposed to say 'Oh gosh, that's great,' or 'Oh dear.' But then I saw it. It was an advert. A small box on the corner of the page said:

Feelings of anger, resentment, jealousy? Silas Anderson leads a wonderful free workshop to help you to rid these feelings and be the person you want to be. Today. 2pm. LA Convention Centre. Petree Hall.

'Fuck me, that's awesome!' I whooped, but then I looked at Erin and she had waterlogged eyes. I took it that I wasn't supposed to be looking at the advert. I scanned the page again and it was then that I saw a smaller heading, which said 'On and Off Screen Chemistry', and there was a picture below it. I registered what the picture was of. Then I said, 'Shit,' and looked at her again.

'Oh, Erin.'

'This is the worst thing that's ever happened to me,' she whispered.

I looked at the paper and shook my head. It was a beautiful picture of Leo and Erin. They were standing on a balcony in the moonlight. Leo was holding her face attentively. She was beaming. Her head was cocked and so was his. It looked like they were seconds away from a tender kiss. If you could have Photoshopped out the unhinged, scissors-wielding lump in the background it could have been a poster.

Erin started gasping and sobbing, which in turn started captivating the other breakfast eaters.

'Come on, darling, let's get you back to the room,' I said, steering her towards the exit. Truthfully, I was gutted to be missing out on my breakfast, but she was proving to be a bit of a howler so I needed to get her away from people. No sooner had we left the restaurant than my phone rang. Simon? No.

'Sarah, it's Eamonn, have you got Erin with you?'

'Um, yeah, that's what the noise in the background is.'

'Oh, bollocks.'

'Well said.'

'Can I speak to her?'

'Erin, darling, it's Eamonn Nigels on the phone. Can you talk to him?'

Erin did try to compose herself but the result was a gasping, hiccupping sound and the sight of a little slug of snot that crept out of her right nostril.

'Hmmm,' said Eamonn. 'Best leave her for a while. Just tell her we'll issue a statement saying she had an earring caught in her hair. That was Rachel's idea. Good, isn't it?'

'Eamonn, it's the truth. Why else would I be charging towards them with the scissors?'

Eamonn laughed.

'So how come Leo is so famous? I'd never heard of him.'

'Leo's not that famous!' he stressed, as though I was stupid. 'Although give it time. He's a model who turned to acting, and he's good. No, it's Erin who's the biggest name in the film.'

'No! Really? Blimey, I would never have guessed.'

'She was in a big kids' show for years. We didn't have it in the UK. It was set in New York though, so she lived at home. She turned twenty-one last week and this is her first job away from home. Her dad's a celebrity preacher in New York. He has a show about happy families on a Christian TV channel. It's a bloody nightmare this happening really.'

'Oh.'

'Tell her that her dad's been trying to get her. He's flying in this afternoon.'

'OK.'

'And Sarah.'

'Hmmm.'

'I'm not blaming you.' He pauses.

'But.'

'But you go out with Rachel and Erin. I find Rachel being sick in the strelitzia this morning having set the burglar alarm off trying to get in, and Erin, a preacher's daughter, is on the front page of the *LA Times* in a sexy cinch.'

'Well, it's good you're not blaming me, Eamonn,' I sang sweetly.

'Goodbye, Sarah Sargeant. And if you could, try to keep out of mischief for the rest of the day.'

'Goodbye, Eamonn Nigels.'

♥ *twenty-four* ♥

I had to go. It was free and I'm a woman. The only thing I like more than a sale rail or two-for-the-price-of-one offer is a freebie. But the taxi there was $60. And when I asked a lady at the conference centre main desk about buses back to my hotel she laughed and shook her head and said, 'Jesus!' So it turned out to be a $120 round trip. And if there's one thing I hate spending money on, it's travel. I object to spending money that leaves me empty-handed.

The LA Convention Centre was huge. I think it might have been a planet, a planet with no natural light and an awful lot of emotionally dysfunctional people who tended to carry quite a lot of extra weight. Planet Girth, it could have been called. I fitted in nicely. There must have been at least two thousand people there. It was a very mixed age group, although there did seem to be a lot more women than men.

Yet again I was in my hooded-top-sarong/wall-hanging ensemble and although my skin colour would still have been described as vivid I was feeling much, much better. Also, I had the confidence of someone who looks crap but is in a strange place in a foreign country and won't bump into anyone she knows.

I walked slowly down the central aisle, keeping my eyes peeled for a free seat. I was just about to give up and stand at the side when a lady near the front suddenly sprang up from her seat and hissed, 'I don't have to stand for this,' to a red-faced man next to her. She stalked out of the conference centre followed by the embarrassed man and I slipped into one of their seats.

'She could have done with staying, if you ask me,' said a man's familiar voice as I sat down. 'Well, well, well. Of all the gin joints in all the town . . .'

'BRIAN!' I whooped. It was lovely Brian, the air steward from my flight over. He looked younger out of his uniform, but he had the same huge, beaming grin that couldn't help but make me smile.

'This has to be fate. Seeing you again. We have to be friends forever now.'

'Hello, lovely.'

'Sarah, darling, now what's happened to your lovely skin? You look like you've been boiled in a bag.'

'Ta.'

'Now, quickly, because when Silas gets up there I have to concentrate. Fill me in. Tell me what happened with Banana Man. Have you made up?'

'Nope. I've become a jealous freak. Hence me being here.'

I stopped then. It suddenly felt slightly strange meeting someone there. I didn't like to ask Brian which affliction out of resentment, jealousy and anger he was there for. As if telepathic, he leant towards me.

'Sarah, you have just uncovered a dirty, guilty secret, which no one knows about me.'

'Cool. Give it to me. I can take it.'

'I have a big, huge, twisted crush on Silas Anderson.'

'How big, huge and twisted?' I asked excitedly.

He thought for a moment.

'I made a slide show of Silas pictures and put it on YouTube.'

'That IS twisted.'

'I haven't finished.'

'Tell me!'

'It's to the music of Right Said Fred's "I'm Too Sexy".'

'NOOOOOO.'

'YES!'

'What? Is he really fit?'

'Ultimate fitness.'

Suddenly a piercing female scream came from the back of the auditorium and interrupted us. I spun round thinking that there might be a terrorist or a rodent in the conference centre. As I did I heard another and another. I looked back to Brian but he was on his feet already and yelling too. I jumped up and followed Brian's gaze to see a man with a Madonna in 'Vogue' microphone walk slowly onto the stage. The sound of screaming had reached Take That proportions.

Silas Anderson was attractive in a healthy, toned, all-

American, forty-year-old man way. He was smiling and nodding and looking exaggeratedly bashful and overwhelmed while making absolutely no gestures to calm the maniacal mob.

I was working out his score out of ten when something hard prodded me on my sunburnt cheek.

'Ah!' I screamed. The scream was futile. No one would have noticed if I had been stabbed. I clutched my cheek and looked to my right to see what had hit me. It was only Brian's elbow. He'd lifted up his T-shirt to above his nipples and was jiggling like he was on a Powerplate.

'AHHHH! I LOVE YOU, SILAS!' he hollered. I must have looked appalled because he shouted, 'Sarah, darling, you must never tell another living soul about this,' without taking his eyes from Silas.

It might have been as a result of Brian's nipples but Silas finally raised his hands to quieten the mob and began walking confidently around the stage, looking at us all. Brian and I sat down.

'Your secret's safe,' I assured him.

There were a few more whoops, which were subsequently silenced by shushes from the flock. When we were all silent, Silas Anderson roared, 'THIS COULD BE THE GREATEST TIME OF YOUR LIFE! THIS COULD BE THE GREATEST TIME OF YOUR LIFE!!!! THE GREATEST TIME OF YOUR LIFE. DO YOU WANT THAT? I SAID, DO YOU WANT THAT?'

'Yes!' the crowd shouted.

That'd be nice, I thought.

'IS THAT WHAT YOU WANT? DO YOU REALLY WANT THIS TO BE THE GREATEST TIME OF YOUR LIFE?? DO YOU? ARE YOU SURE?'

'YES!!!!!'

I did a little church mumble along with them that time.

'SO IF YOU REALLY WANT IT, ARE YOU GOING TO WORK FOR IT?'

'YES!!'

I did another mumble then. I've never been that fond of work.

'ARE YOU GOING TO MAKE THE CHANGES IN YOUR LIFE THAT COULD ALLOW THAT TO HAPPEN?'

'YES!!' I surprised myself by actually shouting that time. Brian nodded at me with pride.

'SO THAT YOU CAN MOVE FORWARD CONFIDENT THAT YOU WILL BE ABLE TO CONTROL FEELINGS OF ANGER, RESENTMENT AND FEAR WHEN THEY ARISE?'

'YES!!!!' And then I was panting. I couldn't help it. There was so much electricity in the room I thought I'd get a bill from EDF.

'ARE YOU SURE?'

'YES!!!!!!'

'Great, well, I'll be in LA holding weekend courses for the next four weeks and if you sign up today it will be only $500,' he says.

Everyone cheered and then he walked off the stage.

'Huh! Is that all?' I asked Brian.

'Yeah. They often do this as a taster so you fall in love with him and give them all your money.'

'Oh. Are you going to do it?'

'No, darling. I doubt I'll be here. I have done one of his courses though.'

'Any good?'

'Darling, I was fantasizing rather than concentrating. But he is rather brilliant. He's motivated some big names.'

'Should I do it though? Seriously, Brian. This photo thing is really doing my head in.'

'No. Save your money and I'll take you for lunch at Venice Beach and teach you all I know about the green-eyed monster.'

'Really?' I whooped.

Brian took my hand.

'Do you know I also wrote captions on my slideshow?'

'Oh God. What did they say?'

'Do you want it? Do you really want it? Do you really, really want it? Yes, yes, YES!'

I laughed.

'Tell no one, Sarah. No one. Ever.'

He led me away from the people who wanted my money and into a taxi outside.

♥ *twenty-five* ♥

Brian and I went to Venice Beach, which only turned out to be the place they filmed the Leonardo DiCaprio *Romeo and Juliet*. It felt a lot like Camden by the beach, with all the mad people and people trying to sell me drugs and the fact I had to keep an eye on my bag the whole time. We sat outside a café and ordered beers and burgers and, true to his word, Brian told me everything he'd learnt about jealousy on the course.

'You see, darling, you're insecure.'

'Oh great.'

'They told me that on the course and I didn't like it.'

'Insecure, jealous. I sound like a right laugh.'

'You're gorgeous in every way. Although can I say something to you, Sarah?'

'Anything you want.'

'It's about your clothes.'

'What? Why? Oh, it's a wall hanging from my friend's rented house. We thought it looked like a sarong.'

He shook his head in incredulity. 'Sarongs make me very glad to be a gay man.'

'It's because of my sunburn!'

'You've got a lovely figure. And all I've seen it in is a bloody wall hanging and a pair of pyjamas. No wonder you're insecure. So when the sunburn's healed and I see you again, I want to see cleavage, let the puppies out for some air, and a waist! Darling, I need to see your waist, you shouldn't be walking around like a sack of potatoes. You're in LA. In a movie. Dress like a movie star.'

I smiled at him. I was in LA. I wasn't quite a movie star. But I was the closest I'd ever been to it.

'So this whole insecure thing. You don't need it. So what if this bitch can touch her toes? Lordy! I bet she can't do a cartwheel as well as I can.'

Brian jumped up from the table, hurdled over the low fence and stood on the beach path. He stretched his arms up and closed his eyes for a moment. He nodded to himself a few times as though practising the cartwheel in his head. Then he did the tiniest cartwheel I've ever seen. It was a crawl with a kick. But he got up and flung his arms in the air and arched his back like a gymnast who's just landed without wobbling.

'Ten from the English judge,' I shouted as I clapped.

'See, I bet naked yoga woman isn't doing a Hollywood movie and hanging out with a handsome, athletic man . . .'

'Who's that then?'

'I think they told us to throw our insecurities in an imaginary bin or something,' Brian said as he sat down. 'You only feel jealous because you are insecure about yourself. You need to love Sarah Sargeant like everyone else does. OK? And I shall help.'

'Stop being so nice to me! I'm embarrassed.'

'No, darling. You're in LA. You should be saying, "I deserve everyone to be nice to me because I am the bollocks."'

'Hardly.'

'I AM THE BOLLOCKS! Come on, repeat after me. I AM THE BOLLOCKS.'

'Brian, shhhh, please, this is very embarrassing.'

'Repeat after me. I am the bollocks.'

'No. Brian!'

'I AM THE BOLLOCKS! Come on, say it. You'll feel great. I AM THE BOLLOCKS!' The tables around us turned to stare. I hung my head in my hands.

'Oh, save me, please.'

'I'll carry on until you do! My apologies, everyone.' He smiled at his audience. 'But my new friend Sarah here is the bollocks and she just doesn't realize it. Come on, poppet. Repeat after me.'

'Noooooo!'

'I AM THE BOLLOCKS!'

'I am the bollocks,' I whispered.

'YEAH! SHE IS THE BOLLOCKS!!!!!!' he roared.

The two people at the next table clapped. And I had to smile at my new lovely friend. Then I looked at the sea and smiled. I smiled when I thought of my other two lovely friends, Erin and Rachel. I smiled when I remembered that

I had a wonderful boyfriend in London. I smiled to think of the following day when I was going to shoot a scene in Hollywood. And I suddenly felt like the happiest girl in the world.

'That's better, Pop Tart,' Brian said when he saw my grin.

♥ *twenty-six* ♥

I was insecure. Brian was right. I Googled 'jealousy' when I got home and had it confirmed. The jealousy you feel alerts you to your own feelings of inadequacy, apparently. I saw a photo of Ruth in her pants. Her thighs were smooth like an aubergine. But I had cellulite. Someone looking at my thighs might think I'd been sitting on Lego for a long time. And I remembered Ruth's pornographic vocals and began to think I was dull in bed. Google suggested improving those areas of your life in which you feel inferior in order to rid yourself of jealous feelings. Which basically meant I needed to sort my bottom out and get more wanton. Hence, I did something unprecedented the following morning. I decided to go for a walk at 6 a.m. But not just any old walk. It would be a walk-slash-jog. Although I wasn't going to put too much pressure on myself to do the jogging bit. I thought I might even prac-tise saying the word 'cock' out loud as well.

I've always had a dysfunctional relationship with exercise, largely due to a lack of coordination. People laugh at me when I run. It looks like I'm trying to negotiate a pebbly beach in bare feet with a wasp up my T-shirt. But I felt safe leaving the hotel at 6.15 a.m. because no one would be around.

I sauntered past the concierge and out of the hotel. I stepped onto the beach path.

'Arrrgggggghhhh,' I screamed.

'Arrrgggggghhhh,' screamed a lady cantering along with a buggy, whom I had nearly killed by walking into.

'Bloody hell,' I said to myself, as I staggered to seat myself on a concrete bollard. I looked about me.

Not again! I thought the mad fitness people only came out on Sunday. But here they were again, on a weekday at 6 a.m.! The place was heaving with Lycra and swinging ponytails. It was like the Tour de France meets *Starlight Express* in a Jane Fonda workout video. It was terrifying. Camden at 6 a.m. on a weekday was empty save for a couple of people waiting for buses having their first fag of the day.

I stared at a group of women nearby. They were clinging onto benches and doing dips.

'Join us!' shouted one to me.

I shook my head.

'It's an easy morning,' they panted like they were giving birth.

Everywhere I looked there were diehard fitness fanatics. I felt like die-lard. They were really pushing themselves. I couldn't remember ever pushing myself like that. Actually, I could: the Last Man Standing Tequila Contest I did with Julia and two sisters from Devon.

'Sarah!'

Oh my Lordy Lord. It was Leo Clement, cantering like a stallion towards me. He was topless except for a rucksack. The dog was chasing him, his tongue lolling out of the side of his mouth.

'Leo!' I waved, expecting him to gallop past me. He didn't though. He stopped.

'I haven't seen you down here before,' he smiled.

'Have you not? That's probably cos I'm sooo quick,' I said, but I had to look down at my trainers because I knew if I looked at a topless Leo Clement I would blush, have a paroxysm and faint, in that order.

He laughed and flopped down on the seat next me. I was still looking down but I got a whiff of his fresh man sweat.

I looked up. It seemed a bit rude keeping my eyes on my rarely worn trainers. But I squinted my eyes so I could barely see him as a precaution.

'Sarah, do you want to meet and practise our scene this week?'

'I'd love to.'

'Cool. We could grab a bite as well,' he said casually. He stood up and started to bend over and touch his toes a few times. I stole a glimpse at his rippling back muscles.

'Oh, yeah, great,' I said, but there was a lot of moisture in my mouth suddenly.

Grabbing a bite with Leo Clement, the handsomest man on the planet, was a terrifying thought. I could barely speak in his presence, let alone eat. Leo sprinted off and I skipped back to the hotel. I planned my morning. Shower, twenty-six poos and then I would be ready to film my first Hollywood scene.

'Oh, excuse me, are you Miss Sargeant?' asked the suited man at the concierge desk.

'I am indeed,' I smiled.

'I have a message for you.'

'Oh, thanks.'

He held out an envelope. It was six feet away from me. I jogged towards it. The sum of my early morning exercise was a six-foot jog. But on a positive note, it was something to improve upon.

'Please, Simon, not today,' I muttered to myself as I ripped open the envelope.

I pulled out a sheet of paper. I stared at the few words scrawled in biro on the page. Then I slowly closed my eyes.

'Bad news?' the man asked when he saw my frowning face.

I looked up at his concerned expression and shrugged.

'Um, yes.'

'I'm sorry,' he said kindly.

'Shit happens,' I philosophized.

'It certainly does, yes,' he answered efficiently.

I looked back down at the piece of paper and shook my head.

Filming suspended. Backers pulled out. Call Eamonn ASAP.

♥ *twenty-seven* ♥

'Turn to the camera, please, Sarah.'

I turned to face the camera obligingly.

'Hold it up to your nose.'

I raised the imaginary bowl that was in my hands.

'Great. And sniff.'

I took a big, long, heavenly sniff.

'Now say the line.'

I eyeballed the camera with a dreamy smile.

'Pedigree Chum. Because they love it.'

'Cut. Thanks, Sarah,' the director said.

You can always tell if you're in with a chance by the way the director speaks to you after your commercial audition. If he or she says, 'Cut, and thanks,' without looking at you, like this chap did, then there's no way you'll get the job. If they like you, you know because they ask you whether you are in any other commercials at the moment. You see, Pedigree Chum wouldn't be happy if this director had cast me and shot the commercial, and they then found out that I was already the face of Winalot or Chappie.

'Thanks,' I smiled back.

I never get adverts. I've had a lot of auditions for them. It feels as though I've spent a significant portion of my life imagining that washing powder makes me moist or that I've got indigestion. But I never get the job. I can think of two reasons for this:

1 I don't have the sort of face that sells stuff. I have the sort of face that would put you off buying stuff. You look at some girls and you imagine that they eat Special K or use Nivea Visage, so therefore they would be suitable to sell these products. But if you look at me and ask yourself the question, 'What products does she look like she uses?' the answer would be sambuca or Biscuit Boosts or Cornish pasties. But even they would prefer models to endorse their products, not Sarah Sargeant

2 Every time I'm in a commercial audition I have to fight terrible urges. I find it very hard to focus and do what they tell me. I think it affects my performance. For instance, just now, when I had to sniff the dog food and smile, what I really wanted to do was to make loud choking noises and then pretend to retch

I walked out of the audition studio and back through the waiting room, past the twenty other Pedigree Chum suitors. Julia was waiting for me outside the building. Julia always met me after commercial auditions because they were generally in Soho, where she worked for a production company in the week. We would usually go to Caffè Nero. Julia took my suitcase from me while I followed her with the carry-along case. Carry-along cases always make me think of dejection. I must have looked like the tearful one at the end of *The Apprentice* whom Alan Sugar had just fired. However, I was still a big fan of carry-along cases.

'What did we do before carry-along cases?' I shouted to Julia. Not a particularly tactful question as she was struggling along with my big old-fashioned heavy case.

'Ooops, sorry,' I said to the swearing lady whose foot I'd just run over.

'Did they make you sniff it?' Julia said when we'd squeezed into the café with all my luggage.

'Hmmm,' I laughed sadly. 'From LA movie land straight to sniffing dog food. Can you believe it? I called my agent from the airport to tell him the news and have a good moan. He tried to cheer me up with the immortal phrase, "Well, get your skates on, there's a Pedigree Chum commercial at 12.30!"'

'Oh, bubba,' she said lovingly. 'What a wank.'

'Big wank,' I agreed.

'What now?'

'Waitressing, I suppose.'

'Least you can spend some time with Si.'

'Yeah.'

But the last time I saw Si I had been literally huffing about the Ruth photo. And the last time I had spoken to him I slammed the phone down because I thought he had an erection and was thinking about her. So although I wanted to see him, I didn't know what I would say to him. And I hadn't even told him I was coming back to England.

'What are you guys up to later?'

'Dunno.'

'We'll pop over.'

'Cool.'

'Well, actually, I can't speak for Carlos, but I'll come by definitely.'

'Wicked.'

'Right, I better get back to bloody work.'

'Thanks, Jules.'

I got up and resumed my *Apprentice* walk back to the tube. But I didn't feel particularly *Apprentice* any more. I wondered why. Then slowly something dawned on me. I had a free hand. I couldn't hear that cladder-cladder-bump sound behind me. I'd left my carry-along case in the café. Arse.

I raced back there. There was no sign of my bag. I asked the man at the counter. He shook his head and absent-mindedly pointed to the poster behind him, which said THIEVES OPERATE IN THIS AREA. WATCH YOUR BELONGINGS.

Bloody marvellous.

♥ *twenty-eight* ♥

I didn't tell Simon that I was coming back. I wanted it to be a surprise. There are two reasons for surprising people in such a way:

1 To see their *X Factor* winner look of unrestrained joy at seeing your face unexpectedly
2 To catch them doing something they shouldn't be

Never do as I did and do number 2 under the guise of number 1. Not telling Simon I was coming back was one of the worst things I did. It pretty much shattered our relationship. And although I tried to gather up all the pieces with a dustpan and brush, some were just too hard to reach. And it was never the same again.

Admittedly, I didn't do the best warm-up for Simon's surprise. I stomped along Camden High Street, holding a clenched fist where my carry-along case should have been, muttering the words 'bugger', 'bugger' and 'wank'.

I love Camden. But it's not for everyone. Many people rampantly loathe Camden. They are people who like peace and quiet, clean streets and shops like John Lewis. Not everyone finds it easy to embrace an area where you have pound shops and posh shops, ethnic tat shops and shops that sell every Rizla ever conceived. But it's the mix that I love. I particularly love the mix of mad people. The man who wears the fluorescent green Babygro and has two green wires coming out of his head for hair, or the lady with the dog called Adolf. (No one I know has ever actually seen the dog, but she shouts for it incessantly.) A lot of people buy pizza off the street in Camden. They deserve to be classed as mad, too. It was a blessing that I lived in Camden that day. No one found my 'bugger,' 'bugger' and 'wank' chant strange. It was Camden.

Having things that don't even belong to you stolen isn't the perfect preparation for a surprise either. This is because having things nicked is crap. It's a horrible feeling. I knew it was my fault for not keeping an eye on it. But I wished the world was nicer. And I wished I still had the film script that would have been a souvenir to show my children. My children that I wasn't planning on having for a few years! I was really hoping that Simon wouldn't start those negotiations again now I was back.

'Bugger, bugger, wank,' I repeated as I turned down my road.

My road was normally a peaceful enclave amidst the circus that is Camden. It wasn't that day. There was a massive lorry parked in the middle of our small street and lots of people were running around it shouting, one of whom I recognized as being the man from Flat 3. I stopped and took in the scene.

'Bugger, bugg . . .' I continued until I saw Simon, my Simon, crawling on his hands and knees on the pavement, shouting, underneath the lorry.

'How did he get it? Do you think he took any?' flapped the man from Flat 3.

'Hamish!' shouted Si.

Hamish was the man from Flat 3's dog. It looked like he'd taken something that belonged to Simon and run under the lorry with it. As I walked closer I heard the sound of cardboard being wrenched from a dog's mouth and suddenly Simon sprang from under the lorry proffering something in his hand. He looked flushed and sexy from his canine capering. I put my case down and stood and admired him.

'Got it! Sorry about . . .' Simon stopped when he saw me. I smiled.

'Sare!' he said. But he didn't smile back. 'Sare, what are you doing back?'

'The film got pulled,' I said, as I walked towards him for a hug.

'Why didn't you tell me?'

Still no smile.

'Because I wanted it to be a surprise.'

'Oh.'

'What was all that about? What's this?' I said, pulling a nearly shredded small box out of his hand. I stared at it.

Most of the text on the dog-eared packet was illegible except for one pristine word: Viagra.

'It's a packet of Viagra,' I whispered. I stared at the packet. I was confused at first, my face elegantly positioned in the 'manoeuvring a difficult stool' expression. We'd never used Viagra. It wasn't in the bathroom cupboard. Maybe it was in his wash bag. Maybe he used it with Ruth.

I looked up at his face and he looked . . . guilty. The penny plummeted. Neighbouring dogs don't rifle through your wash bag. You don't take Viagra on your own for a laugh. He had to be with someone. Ruth. The semi-naked photo. His lack of joy at my re-arrival. It could only mean one thing. I became Usain Bolt. I ran up the stairs two at a time.

'Babe, don't go in. Wait!' Simon cried behind me. 'It's not as bad as it looks.'

'It's not as bad as it looks'! That was at the top of the list of things boyfriends should never say, along with 'It's not you, it's me,' or 'I need some space.'

I stormed through our front door.

'You bitch!' I screamed.

'Babe! Whoah! Jesus! Sare!' screamed Si.

Like Usain through the finish line I stormed into the living room, panting. Si was with me in seconds. Instantly I felt like a right plonker.

Our living room looked like an erotic branch of Big Yellow Storage. Neatly stacked, from floor to ceiling, on every available inch save for a small area around the sofa and fridge, were boxes. And printed on each box was a picture of a little pink dancing willy with a smiley face and the words: 'Cockaconga, the herbal Viagra, guaranteed to give you a party in your pants all night.'

'I just had some trouble with storage.'

I placed my arms around him and said, 'I love you.' But I felt him flinch and he didn't say he loved me too.

And it all went downhill, like a tin tray on ice, from there.

♥ *twenty-nine* ♥

Simon didn't speak to me for ninety minutes after that. Not a 'Tea?' or a 'Show us your white bits, Sare,' or a 'Darling, you are so special. Few women would tolerate erectile aids about the place like you do.' He spent that time stacking boxes and grunting. I had a bath.

It was after this bath that we started our amazing row. I was clean, at least. The row was amazing, not because it was fun or featured pyrotechnics but because it was three fully formed rows in one. A Tiff Triple Bill. A Tiffle Bill. Otherwise known as a hideous afternoon of shouting the same things to each other over and over again until there was a knock on the door.

I tripped over as I left the bathroom. Not because I was drunk or attempting a dance move, but because there was a box of organic Viagra in my way. I responded in accordance with the proper trip etiquette guidelines. I shouted, 'Bugger!' and kicked the thing that tripped me up. At which point Simon forgot to say, 'Sorry, I didn't mean to leave that there, are you all right, babe?' and instead came out with a very hostile interpretation of the word 'careful'. One where he elongated the word and his register went up and up as he said it.

'Care-ful!'

It sounded like I was being told off, so I said, 'Sor-ry!' in a stroppy adolescent voice. To which Simon tutted. Now, I hate tutting. It's joint first with shushing on my list of most hated sounds made by humans.

'What's up with you, grumpy?' I asked, fully armed with the knowledge that the thing grumpy people hate most is being called grumpy.

'I'm not grumpy,' he muttered, then added, 'I'm just pissed off,' grumpily.

I didn't mean to laugh but a small, breathy *Beavis and Butt-head* 'huh, huh' sound escaped me.

'Yeah, it's hysterical, Sare,' he said flatly, without looking at me.

'This is nice, quality time together,' I sang as he used Olympic weightlifting force to pick up and put down a light box.

'Yeah, great.'

'And the decor's perfect in here now we've got all these Viagra boxes everywhere. Very feng shui.'

'It won't be for long,' he humphed.

'So, what made you want to branch into Viagra?'

'Jay said the stuff was amazing.'

I screwed up my face and took a pause to see whether Simon was having me on. He wasn't.

'You took business advice from Paranoid Jay?'

'What's wrong with that?'

I considered answering the question but changed my mind when I realized the answer would take too long. Paranoid Jay is an old childhood friend of Simon's. His heart's in the right place but his brain isn't anywhere near it. I'm not being hard on him when I say that Paranoid Jay couldn't organize an orgy in a brothel. Last time I saw him he told me he couldn't find his mum's car. So I answered with the question my mother always asks me when I've lost something: 'When was the last time you had it?' He said, 'About two weeks ago.'

'How much did you spend on it?'

'Fifty grand.'

'Say that again.'

'You heard.'

'This might be early onset senility, babe. You invested fifty grand on Paranoid Jay's advice!'

'Yes. What's up with your ears? Did they not pop yet?'

He was being a cock. So I told him.

'You're being a cock.'

'I'm being a cock, am I? I get accused of having an affair. Now I'm a cock.'

I half smiled. But only because he'd been huffing about the issue for nearly two hours and finally mentioned it.

'I'm insulted you'd think I was having an affair.'

There were many facets of wrongness to this Channel 5 low-budget-gratuitous-breast-showing-film-dialogue answer, the main one being that it wasn't a denial of the charge. The other was that he was claiming the wounded party role that was surely mine. I had found the photo. I was accommodating his bloody Viagra. I should be upset and wounded. And he was supposed to be nice to me, rather than jump on the insulted train.

'Well, I found a photo of your cellulite-free ex-bloody-girlfriend in your Filofax, so what was I supposed to think?'

He rolled his eyes!

'Maybe I should find an ex-boyfriend, oil him up and take some photos of him in his pants, see how you like that.'

'That would be tricky for you, Sare. You haven't had many boyfriends.' AND THEN HE SAID . . . 'I'm starting to see why.'

I glared at him. I didn't blink. I could feel the stinging nettle tingle of tears. I walked out of the lounge. I let three tears fall in the hallway and felt sorry for myself for about twenty seconds. But then a giant hogweed of emotion began to burn through me. It was anger. Wowzers. I wasn't usually an angry person.

'AT LEAST I DIDN'T SHAG EVERYTHING THAT MOVED!' I shouted, as I re-entered the lounge.

'I hardly shagged everything that moved, Sarah. Just Ruth, who was my girlfriend at the time. THAT'S WHAT PEOPLE DO.'

'YOU DON'T NEED TO WANKING WELL REMIND ME SIMON! I HEARD IT BLOODY EVERY NIGHT.'

Simon rolled his eyes again, which was infuriating.

'Have you got something wrong with your eyes?'

'No, it's just an involuntary response that happens when you start talking like a psycho nutter girlfriend.'

The way he said it was almost funny. Then the content registered.

'YOU COCK!' I screamed, which was frustratingly un-original. 'IT'S NOT FUNNY!' I added, which was also lame.

'Well, Sarah, your girlfriend thinking you're boffing some bird isn't funny either.'

'Si, you were holding a packet of Viagra! Think about it! If you'd found a photo of oily big dick bloke in my Filofax and then you came home and I was holding a packet of con-doms what would you think?'

I didn't let him answer. But I really should have shut up then.

'You still fancy Ruth. You still like her.'

'Is there anything else that I'm thinking that you want to tell me about? . . . No? That's nice. Well, I'll tell you what I actually do think, Sarah.'

'What?'

'You're jealous.'

'I'm not jealous,' I humphed. 'I'm insecure.'

'Oh, blinding.'

Our intercom buzzed.

'Is that the door?' said Simon.

'Oh yeah, it'll be Julia and Carlos,' I replied.

Simon looked at me and blinked.

'Why?'

'They wanted to come over,' I said casually.

'Did you tell them to come over?'

His hands were on his hips and he was biting his lip.

'Yeah.'

'Why?'

He was still biting his lip.

'What do you mean, "Why?" She's my best mate.'

'Yeah. But you could have asked me.'

'What?' I laughed. 'You wanted me to call you up and say, "Please may Julia and Carlos come over tonight?"'

'Something like that would have been nice. Yeah.'

'I probably would have mentioned something but I've been slightly distracted by the erection section in the flat here and the codswalloping great row we seem to be having!'

'Sare!'

'What?'

'Well, maybe I didn't want them to come over.'

'But . . . but . . . it's only Jules.'

'That's not the point. I was going to have a shower.'

'So go and have a sodding shower.'

'I'll look antisocial. It'll look like I don't want to see them.'

'You've just said you don't want to see them.'

'Sare, if I'd invited Jay over tonight and I hadn't told you and you were all scruffy, how would you feel?'

'Oh, yeah, I see your point.'

'THANK YOU.'

'Well. They've probably gone by now anyway because no one's let them in.'

'I'll go,' he said, walking into a pile of boxes, knocking them over and screaming, 'BOLLOCKS!'

Tonight was going to be a right laugh.

❦ *thirty* ❦

Carlos and Julia arrived. You could have cut the atmosphere with a plastic spoon. The only option was to get drunk. The only booze we had in the flat was Cockolada, a beverage with which Carlos was unfamiliar.

'Apri-cock,' he said, reading the flavour of the one he was holding.

'That's a nice one,' Julia chattered. 'Not as good as the Penis-Colada. But much better than the Tropic-Erotic. That's cack.'

'The Margar-willy-ita one's the best. Si, can I have a . . .' I stopped there because Si was ignoring me and throwing me a Tropic-Erotic. It was widely known that the Tropic-Erotic was the rankest flavour of them all. I knew, for sure, he'd gone off me then.

'Right,' said Si. 'Now you're here, you can work.'

'You what?' Julia asked.

'Brainstorming!'

'I love a good brainstorm,' said Julia sarcastically. 'Oh, I hope Big Nose didn't leave on our account?'

'What?' I said, alarmed. Big Nose was the name Julia and

I gave Ruth, Simon's ex-girlfriend. It is quite large, her nose.

'Ruth. She was leaving as we arrived.'

'Ruth, as in Si's . . .' I stared at her in disbelief.

'Yeah. Maybe I got it wrong. It looked like her. I thought I saw her walking away from here as we were parking,' Julia chattered. I looked at Simon. He shrugged and hurriedly started speaking again.

'If I say Viagra, what do you think of?'

'Flaccid willies,' I offered limply.

'A particularly disappointing night with a doctor,' ventured Julia. 'Long time before you, big boy,' she added, turning and smiling at Carlos.

'Right! That's what we want to change. We need to make Viagra fun!'

'Make Viagra fun,' repeated a baffled Carlos slowly.

'Carlos, mate, you're a DJ. Isn't there a song about the conga?'

'Yeah, that Black Lace song!' shrieked Julia. 'Carlos is always playing that one!'

Carlos looked momentarily pained. Julia started humming the song.

'Ah, that's it, Jules,' Si shouted excitedly.

Simon started to hum along loudly with Julia. Then he began to add sporadic words like 'der', 'la', and 'conga'. It made my panto Princess squawk sound like Katherine Jenkins.

'Right, what rhymes with conga?' asked Simon.

'Longer,' I said flatly.

'Oh! Oh! Oh!' He started panting. 'You beauty!

'Der, de der, something something longer, der, de der . . . it's not getting any longer! . . . That's great . . . Ah, bloody phone,' he said, pulling his mobile out of the back pocket of his jeans. Simon looked at the phone. His face dropped for a moment and his jaw tightened. Then he silenced it and put it back in his jeans. It was the briefest of disturbances and within seconds he had resumed his efforts of reworking the lyrics to the Black Lace wedding classic 'Do the Conga', while we sat watching him and sucking on our plastic willies.

'Der, de der, it's not getting any longer. Der, de der, have you tried the conga . . . Der, de der . . . his fella's getting longer . . . Oh! Oh! Oh! That's it! Der, de der, his fella's getting longer! It's Cockaconga night.'

'He's off on one,' I told the other two. 'Si. That's the landline phone.' I lurched towards it. 'Hello, the *Sex Factor*?' I sang into the receiver, because there's nothing I like more than answering the phone with a sweetly sung Sarah's Fisting Fun Palace, or Blow Job Friday Two for the Price of One, or whatever other sexually orientated nonsense springs into my head. I waited for broken English to ask me if I needed home insurance or wanted to come back to BT. Nothing. The other person didn't respond. 'Hello? Hello? Helloooooooo. Who are you? Can I help you?' I tried. The other person hung up.

'Hung up.'

'Do – whatsit? 1471.'

'Oh yeah.' I went back to the phone. 'It's a mobile number. I haven't got a pen. Shall I call them back?'

'No, leave it Sare,' Simon said quickly. Too quickly. I remembered the mobile call he had just silenced. I felt uneasy.

'Yeah, they'll call back if it's important,' Jules said.

'Yeah,' I agreed, with a fake smile.

'Listen, I've got it!' yelled Si. 'Listen.

'Boo, hoo, hoo, it's not getting any longer,

'Ooo, ooo, ooo, but have you tried the conga?

'Woo, hoo, hoo, his fella's getting stronger.

'Doo, doo, doo, it's Cockaconga night!'

We all sat quietly and stared at him. He looked excited. I had a very bad feeling.

'Time to get the video camera.'

'Oh no. Oh no!' I started.

'Let's make the viral ad.'

'The wha . . . ?'

'He likes to make these dreadful video ads for his products, which go on the Internet,' I whispered to Carlos.

'Oh no.'

'Quite.'

♥

Four Cockaladas and an hour and half of rehearsals later, we were bobbing our heads to the rhythm, preparing for our seventh take.

'Sare, Sare, Sare, are you sure that was the tune?' asked Si.
I nodded. Julia laughed.

'OK, babe, maybe just don't sing as loud as everyone else.'
Julia laughed again.

'Right, guys, I think we're ready for another take.'

There was a small flurry of activity as Simon sat down
and covered his lap with a Mexican poncho. Julia slid onto
the floor and wiggled into position. She was out of shot
on the floor. She positioned a cucumber underneath the
poncho. For the purposes of our viral ad the cucumber was
the willy, which would be dancing around under the poncho
by the end.

'Steady with that, Jules,' squeaked Si.

Carlos focused the camera on me. I got ready for my
'unhappy with my flaccid willy' face close-up.

'That's great, Sare, you look really miserable,' Si praised.
This was unsurprising. Any actress will verify that there are
some products you feel uncomfortable endorsing: stool
softeners, heavy-flow sanitary towels, feminine deodorants
for even the worst smells; you grasp the gist. I can confidently say that most actresses would have baulked at
becoming the face of erectile dysfunction. However, because
it was my boyfriend's business, I was sat there emoting at a
cucumber. I prayed my agent would never find out. Also I
knew, I just knew, that the product was a dud and the only
thing worse than being the face of Viagra would be being the
face of a Viagra swindle. Men across the land would hold me
personally responsible for their downward facing dogs.

I tried to block out my reservations. If I was going to act in a Viagra advert I might as well act well. Luckily it was a short commercial, so within about thirty seconds the cucumber was up and dancing and I was clutching the Cockaconga packet lovingly.

'Bloody brilliant,' shouted Si as he jumped up.

'Simon!' shouted Julia as he trod on her head.

Si planted an excited kiss on my head, and then snatched the packet from me.

'After dinner mint, anyone?' he offered.

'I didn't know we had chocolate,' I said innocently. Then I looked at Simon and I realized that he wasn't talking about chocolate at all. He was putting a Cockaconga tablet in his mouth and holding one out for Carlos.

'It's Cockaconga night!' giggled Julia to the tune of the conga.

I didn't giggle. I saw Julia and Carlos to the door and got ready for bed. Then I waited for Simon to go into the bathroom to brush his teeth. I extracted the iPhone from the back pocket of his jeans. I had always thought private detective work would be a glamorous second career. I changed my mind when my shaking hands let the smooth Apple surface slip from my fingers and onto my foot.

'Ah!'

'You all right, Sare?' Simon called through a mouthful of toothpaste.

'Yeah,' I acted back. 'Stubbed my toe.'

I picked up the phone. It was nothing like mine. My heart

was thrashing around in my chest so forcefully, I'm surprised seismic hazard services weren't alerted. I found his call history. The call he had silenced earlier in the evening was from Ruth. And it was her number the operator's automated voice had told me when I did 1471.

♥ *thirty-one* ♥

I knew that Cockaconga wouldn't work. It was obvious. There was an old saying: Paranoid Jay involved, disaster looming. Simon was starting to panic but I was so confused and terrified about the Ruth phone calls that I couldn't comfort him. I went to bed and lay turned away from him pretending to sleep for most of the night. I felt him get up in the early hours and say, 'Bloody hell, Jay, man,' and take another tablet to see if increasing the dosage worked. Then an hour or so after that he took a third one. Eventually, I must have slept because I woke groggily at 11.13 a.m. Simon was lying on his back, staring at the ceiling next to me. We were instantly on to the a.m. leg of our argument.

'Oh, tits, it's late,' I said sleepily.

'Hmmm,' he replied stonily.

'Mum and Dad'll be here just before twelve,' I said, but then I remembered that I hadn't mentioned the lunch with parents arrangement to Si.

'WHAT?' said Si, as though he was on a rocky boat on a stormy sea instead of lying a ruler's length away from my ear.

'Sorry,' I winced. 'I just forgot to tell you. We've been so busy rowing, there's been no time to compare schedules.'

'I can't believe you've done it again.'

'They're my mum and dad!'

'What about all this?' Simon gestured to the Viagra-crammed bedroom.

'It's not my fault you got yourself involved in the great Viagra swindle!'

I got out of bed. I was only wearing my pants. I stumbled about the room until I eventually found Simon's red hoodie. I put it on.

'Er, Sare.'

'Hmmm,' I said, turning around to look at him in the bed. He'd pulled the covers back. Something was certainly standing to attention.

'Oh, bloody hell. When did that happen?'

'About two hours ago.'

'Blimey.'

I couldn't take my eyes off it.

'My mum and dad'll be here in half an hour.'

'We didn't think this through.'

'Do you think if we have sex it'll go?' I asked.

I won't go into details. But dutifully I did my bit for the relief effort. When the quickie's aim was achieved, we lay back. There was still a giant gherkin on the skyline.

'Wow,' I said. I leant forward to see if I could push it down.

'Ow,' Simon said.

'Fuck.'

'Call Jules.'

I did as I was told.

'Jules.'

'OH MY GOD!!!!' she screamed.

'How is, um, Carlos, doing? Did he get a, you know . . . ?'

'I can't even push it down!'

'When did it come on?'

'Ages after he took it. But he couldn't go to work. He had that meeting with the dance producer at 9.30! He had to cancel.'

'My mum and dad are coming to take us out for lunch in twenty minutes. And Simon took three!'

My doorbell rang.

'Bugger! They're early. SI!'

Si had been trying on outfits. He was wearing jeans and his longest shirt. It wasn't long enough.

'Do you think jeans are better than trackie bums?'

'Definitely not the trackie bums. Trust me, darling,' I assured him. 'It looks like a gerbil absconded down there even when you haven't got a lob on.'

'Sare, you've got to let them in. I can't open the door to your mum with a stiffy.'

'Maybe we should tell them the truth.'

'Baby!'

'What?'

'Well, I don't really want you to draw attention to it.'

'Shit, Jules, what do we do?' I shouted into the phone

'What's she saying?' asked Simon keenly.

'Nothing, she's laughing. Bye, Jules.'

'Have you got an apron anywhere?'

'Only that one with the boobs on. And you don't need any additional stimulus today.'

'Hmmm.'

'Could we tape it down?'

'What about my pubic hair?'

'Oh yeah.'

The doorbell again.

'Just put a long coat on.'

'OK,' he said, nodding. 'Cool.'

Simon dived into the hallway cupboard. I ran downstairs to let them in.

'How long has it been up?' said my dad.

'Wher . . . ?'

'This erection,' he laughed.

My eyes widened until I realized he was talking about the scaffolding around my building.

'Oh, just a few days,' I answered, hoping it wasn't a metaphor for Simon's affliction.

'I hope it comes down soon.'

'Oh, me too, Dad, me too,' I said with emphasis that surprised them.

'Security risk. I'll come up and check your window locks while I'm here.'

My father doing DIY was scary at the best of times because he wandered around with a gin and tonic in one hand, a power tool in the other, screaming at Simon and me to 'hold things higher'. Adding Simon's erection and a flat full of boxes into that mix was unthinkable.

He clocked my reluctant face.

'For my peace of mind as well as yours, Sarah,' he said, striding upstairs.

'How are you, darling?' asked my mum, lagging behind. 'How's your little problem?' she whispered. My mum's whispers can be heard in Kent. By deaf people.

'Yes, Sarah, how are you and Simon?' shouted my dad from the top of the stairs. 'Oh, hello, Simon, coat on? You not stopping?'

I raced up the stairs to help Simon. The two men were embracing in our communal hallway. Simon was leaning forward at 45 degrees, not wanting to get too close.

'Hello, gorgeous,' Simon beamed at my mum. 'Right then, we're starving, shall we make a move?'

'I was going to check on your window locks, Simon,' my dad said, inching forward towards the front door.

'No need, Mike. Did it myself as soon as they put that bloody scaffolding up. We're watertight in there,' Simon said, brilliantly, before shutting the door with a click.

I stood smiling at my Si for effortlessly engineering us out of that nightmare. Until my dad's next comment registered. It made me shiver.

'Simon, we bumped into your old friend as we were parking. She looks like Selina Scott. What's her name again, Val? Blonde, nice figure. Ruth, wasn't it?'

'Dad!'

'What?'

'Nothing.' Simon had an erection and my father was talking about his ex-girlfriend. Far be it from me to point out this lapse in lunch etiquette.

'Er, yes, sir, that's right, Ruth,' Simon answered uncomfortably. A bit too uncomfortably if you ask me.

What was Ruth doing lurking around Camden all the time? She worked in the City and she lived in Chelsea. She hated Camden. I remember her saying that it was full of undesirables. I'd been amazed that someone under fifty used the word 'undesirables'.

'Right, let's be off,' said my mother with forced jollity.

We all traipsed down the stairs. My mum leant in my direction and, for the first time, achieved a very good whisper. She said something lovely to me.

'Ruth has put on weight.'

But then Simon stopped walking.

'I'm going to catch you up. I need to make a call. I completely forgot.'

'OK then, Simon, see you there,' said my dad cheerfully. But I didn't feel happy as I watched Si race back upstairs. It was very odd how he suddenly remembered that call when he heard that Ruth was in the vicinity.

He was having an affair.

❤ *thirty-two* ❤

'We will order in a second, we're just waiting for someone.' I smiled at the nervous, skinny Eastern European waitress. It must have been her first day. I could tell this because:

1 she was actually working
2 a burly Italian man was watching her every move waiting for a mistake

Poor thing. She'd get no tips and everyone would give her crap jobs all day.

'These are my long-distance glasses, Val. Where are my readers?'

'Mike,' my mother sighed. 'I don't know where your readers are. Maybe you left them in the car.'

'No, I had them on to deal with that bloody pay and display machine. 20p for four minutes. Sarah! 20p for four minutes! That's six pounds for two hours. I'd expect Selina Scott to be personally looking after it and giving it a wipe over in a bikini for that.'

'I like Piers Morgan,' my mother sighed as she was reaching into her bag. She produced a box of glasses.

'Not those ones.'

'Oh no, they're your bifocals. Oh, Mike, you and your bloody glasses.' She tutted.

Eventually she found the right pair and gave them to Dad. I stared at my mum and dad, amazed.

'Can't he look after his own glasses?' I asked.

My mother raised her eyes and suggested a gin and tonic.

'Oh yeah, shall we get garlic bread while we wait for Si?' I started to beckon the waitress over but stopped when I watched her struggling across the floor with a bulging bin bag.

My dad looked at me like I had suggested sacrificing a family member.

'What did I say?'

'He's on the Atkins,' whispered my mother.

'I thought you lost a pound on Paul McKenna.'

'He lost that pound but then he put on three.'

'You can't be on the Atkins. This is a pizza restaurant.'

My father nodded sadly. We were sitting by the kitchen and he had full view of the pizzas as they came bubbling out of the oven.

'How's it going?'

'He's been very grumpy. He can't drink, you see.'

'I can have a light beer.'

'No, Mike, you can't.'

'Val.'

'No, Mike.' It was Mum's firm voice. She used it when I wanted a pair of high-heeled shoes at the age of seven, a tattoo at thirteen; the list goes on. 'You told me not to let you.'

'You'd only be cheating yourself,' I told the children wisely.

'What's Simon doing? Chasing after Ruth?'

'Probably.'

He'd been twenty minutes. He must have bumped into her. Or arranged to meet her. With an erection! There was no way he could have been on the phone all this time. I had an image of them having a quickie behind KFC, which might have seemed a ridiculous thought if Simon hadn't then bounced through the door flushed as a teenager caught masturbating by his mother.

The waitress was instantly upon him, trying to take his coat. He shook his head and teetered over to us. His long, done-up parka was shortening his stride. He eyed the wood-burning oven. A look of anguish crossed his face. My mother started stroking the front of his coat. The look changed to alarm.

'Oh, what a nice coat, Simon. But you'll need to take it off, it's ever so warm in here.'

'Er, no, Val. I'm a bit chilly,' he said, sitting next to her.

'Oh, darling, you don't look it. You're starting to sweat. I hope you're not coming down with something.'

She pressed her hand against his forehead. Then his cheek.

'Oh, you poor poppet,' she said as though she was nursing a toddler.

My mother clasped his hands (which were on his lap and therefore very close to a certain member) in hers. Then she pressed her lips together and scrunched up her face.

'Are you feeling a little dickie?'

My hand went to my mouth. My stomach had started doing crunches of its own volition. Simon looked like his eyebrows might meet his hairline in a second.

'Oh yes, a little dickie,' I whispered.

And it felt good. I'd never done innuendo. But they're like alcoholic drinks. You can't just have one.

'Hmmm. Oh, Mum. He was up all night.'

And I knew it wasn't funny. But I couldn't stop.

'All his muscles are stiff. And, and, and . . .'

Bugger, I couldn't think of any more.

I looked around me for inspiration. But all I could see was the Italian man pointing towards Simon and telling the girl off for not taking his coat.

'Can I take your coat?' asked the waitress again.

'No, no,' said Si, eyeing me warily.

'Please let me take your coat,' she said desperately.

'No, love, I'm chilly, brrrr,' he said, the sweat dripping off him. 'But I think we should order.'

'Yes, a beer for me,' piped up my dad.

'Oh, Mike.'

'Lovely bit of wood, this,' I said, pressing my hands on the table.

♥ *thirty-three* ♥

Simon went out after that lunch. He didn't volunteer where he was going.

'I'm off out, Sare. Not sure what time I'll be back.'

To which I said, 'What? Off to see if Ruth'll help with that?' and I gestured my head to his loin area.

I didn't even want to say that. I wanted to say, 'Si! What's happening to us? Can we make it good again? Please. I love you.' But bitter words replaced them. He didn't respond. He just looked at me as if I was a totalled car that he'd spent a long time saving up for.

I spent that evening with two old friends: Google and cheap wine. They love each other, those two. Prior to this pursuit I was suspicious of Simon and Ruth and the nature of their current friendship. Post-Google and cheap wine, my suspicion was terrifyingly powerful, like Simon Cowell, or God, or Google itself.

I sat in my pyjamas cross-legged in bed and I typed in things like 'signs of infidelity', and received information like:

*If your partner is receiving regular cell phone calls from a
woman or he goes out unexplained at unusual times then
chances are he is cheating or considering doing so.*

*Does your partner silence certain calls or disappear from the
room to take them?*

Has his behaviour changed towards you?

Does he find fault and look for arguments with you?

*Does he like going out alone and protest when you suggest
accompanying him?*

*Does he feel threatened if you change your schedule or surprise
him in any way?*

Has he purchased products such as Viagra?

Then I placed the mouse on headings such as HOW TO CATCH
A CHEATER and I clicked.

*Do not confront him until you have proof! Proof is an email
exchange, a text message, a photograph, a credit card receipt, etc.
The only way to get proof is to purchase surveillance equipment
or hire a private investigator. Failing that you must do it all
yourself . . . Watch him but don't ever question him until you are
sure . . . Talk to mutual friends to see what they think.*

I called Julia.

'Jules, quickie: did Simon seem weird to you last night?'

'Honestly?'

'Course.'

'Yeah, what was with that phone call he ignored? And then one straight away to your landline that he didn't want you calling back. Spooky.'

'It was Ruth. I checked later.'

'Fuck. I'm sure I saw her last night. She was walking away from your building. I think she saw me and deliberately looked away.'

'My dad said he saw her today as well. What would you think if you were me?'

'Bubba, I don't know. How's he been with you?'

'Horrible. He seems pissed off I'm back.'

'Oh, babe.'

'What would you do?'

'Go through his phone and emails. Sniff his shirts for perfume. Demand sex all the time. If they're not up for it, they're getting it somewhere else. Can't think of anything else.'

'Thanks.'

And that was that. I became a sleuth. It wasn't a seamless Miss Marple start, though, on account of the jet lag and the wine and me falling asleep with the laptop before he came home.

♥ *thirty-four* ♥

When I woke up the next morning he wasn't there. He stayed
out all night, was my first thought. Rather than enforcing
my rights as an out-of-work actress and snoozing for an
hour and a half as is my normal habit, I quickly sat up on
the edge of the bed and reached for the nearest of Simon's
clothes that were strewn on the floor. I loved the abundance
of brilliant bummy clothes that having a boyfriend provided: outsized tracksuit trousers and T-shirts that hung or
lay on any available surface, ready to be thrown on. Before
Simon, I was always wrapped in a towel. It wasn't nearly so
comfortable and was a logistical nightmare if you needed
two hands to carry something. So that morning I was cosy
in head-to-toe Abercrombie as I fought a path into our
kitchen. When I say kitchen I mean kitchen/lounge/dining
room: the only room that isn't a bedroom or bathroom. It
was dark. I made out Simon's figure curled up on the sofa.
So he had come home and had decided he didn't want to get
into bed with me. I wondered whether this was because
he smelt of perfume. I bashed some boxes as I stumbled
towards him.

'Tea?' I asked, bending down to near his neck and trying silently to sniff it. He wafted me away like a wasp.

'What you doing? Going to suck my blood?'

'No,' I said defensively. 'I was going to give you a kiss good morning.' And I plonked a little cold kiss on his cheek. I couldn't smell anything untoward. I wandered over to the kettle. I flicked the switch and wondered how I could look in his wallet to check his receipts from the night before and check his phone for texts.

'How come you slept out here?' I asked, but, in accordance with the website's instructions, not in an accusatory way. Simon didn't answer. I turned to look at him. He'd started shaking his head as though he was in pain. I assumed it was the sight of my face that did it. I'm not at my best two minutes post-waking after a bottle of wine and some heavy-duty American infidelity websites.

'Babe, you've got to do something about your snoring.'

'Si,' I laughed. 'I don't snore!'

'No, Sare, you do snore. I got into bed next to you last night. It was like King of the Beasts.'

'Baby, no one's ever complained about my snoring. It can't be that bad,' I told him emphatically. The website had said that guilty parties start finding new faults in their partners. Simon had never mentioned my snoring before.

I put the teabags in the cups and started pouring the water. But a loud noise of workmen drilling outside made me jump.

'Ow, fuckit!!!' I screeched as the boiling water splashed over my hand. I jumped back and a box of Cockaconga landed on my foot.

'Shit, babe, are you OK?' The noise stopped and Simon started navigating boxes to get to my side.

'That bloody noise outside made me jump,' I muttered as I ran my hand under the tap.

'Er, Sare, that wasn't from outside. That was your snoring.'

'Huh?'

Simon held up the dictaphone I had used to help with my accent exercises. He pressed Play. There it was again. The sound of an industrial pneumatic drill cutting through concrete.

'Fuck,' I said. Well, I had to shout, actually, to be heard above the racket. 'Why didn't you say anything before?'

'I did. You were in denial,' he shouted back.

'Yeah, all right, you can stop it now,' I humphed.

'Sleeping with you is a bit of a nightmare.'

'Oh thanks, Si, rub it in. I've just burnt my hand.'

'And you like to sleep with one leg out like this and one arm out like this.' He demonstrated the position. It looked like he was doing a difficult ballet pose. 'And you take all the duvet as well. You clutch it to you so I can't get at it.'

'All right. Calm down, grumpy.'

'I'm not grumpy. I'm tired!'

I stared at him sadly.

'Come on, baby. It'll be all right. You're just not used

to sleeping with someone else,' he said. I gasped. Then I nodded.

'Oh, but you are. Ruth would only take up a corner of the bed . . .' I heard myself speaking in a horribly toxic voice. I remembered what Mum said about not speaking in the heat of the moment. But I couldn't stop myself. 'Why don't you go back to that bendy bitch then, if she's so wonderful? You don't need to sneak around. Just go back to her. She's probably outside now anyway. She seems to be hanging eerily about the flat at the moment. And you just popping out. Go on. Bugger off back to her. Do your sodding yoga, take photos of her in her pants, have crazy loud sex on 114 Viagras. Just please leave me alone.' I've never before sounded so hysterical. I was shrieking. I sounded like a psycho nutter woman. My awful words were flying round the room like bats.

I managed to stop there. I tried reversing out of that dangerous place but I got stuck in mud, changing gear.

He stared back.

'We can't do this,' he said slowly. 'I'm going to get dressed. I'll see you this evening. We'll talk then.'

He walked exhaustedly out of the room and then out of the flat. All I could think was:

1 he hadn't said where he was going
2 he hadn't denied the Ruth charges

So I put on my pair of rarely worn trainers and followed him.

I didn't know which way he'd gone but assumed it was in the direction of the Tube. I turned out of my road and there he was, standing on the corner, iPhone pressed to ear.

'Listen, babe, no! All right, I'll see what I can do . . .' he was saying. He most definitely said the word 'babe'. At least, I most definitely thought he said the word 'babe'. He saw me. 'Better go, speak later,' he said quickly and guiltily into the receiver.

'Sare, are you following me?'

'No,' I said. 'I'm just going to . . .' I had been going to say 'get milk' but I didn't have any money. 'Go for a run.'

'Good,' he said, unconvinced. 'You could do with some exercise.'

I had to jog until I was out of his sight. It was very uncomfortable and embarrassing as I didn't have a bra on and had to hold my breasts with my cupped hands. When I turned round he'd disappeared. So I wheezed my way back home.

♥ *thirty-five* ♥

I spent the rest of the morning recovering. The phone rang three times. I was sure it was Ruth but I couldn't be certain because she'd started to withhold her number.

'Hello,' I said tentatively into the receiver on the fourth ring. These calls were so unnerving I could no longer muster up sex references.

'Sare, you all right?'

'Jules, do I snore?'

Julia snorted.

'Yeah, like a bloody train.'

'Seriously?'

'Yeah, that's why I always have to get off my tits when I stay at yours. To sleep through it.'

'You never said.'

'Sare, I've told you like about a thousand times. You always go, "I don't snore."'

'You should have told me seriously.'

'Poor Simon. Has he realized it would be quieter to sleep with a digger? How's it going on that front?'

'Awful.'

'I've had an idea.'

'Go on.'

'Kill him with kindness.'

'Huh?'

'I spoke to Carlos. He was saying that if I started going all snoopy and accusatory, he'd probably end up having an affair. But if I was all lovely, he'd feel guilty and stop it.'

'Oh, interesting.'

'So do something nice. I would say cook. But I've tasted your cooking.'

'Jules, I can cook.'

'What's his favourite dinner?'

'Dunno. Chicken something.'

'Oooh! Boss! Fuck, gotta go. Ah! I'm painting my nails as well.'

I called Simon's mum and she told me that his favourite dish was roast chicken. So I went all the way to the big Sainsbury's and bought a chicken. But not just an ordinary chicken, oh no; an organic chicken, which is four pounds more expensive than an ordinary chicken. It was reared to classical music. I worried it would think it was slumming it coming back to mine, so I put on Classic FM.

I had always believed that spending hours concocting something that was going to be consumed in a few minutes was a pointless use of my time. However, I enjoyed the day I spent preparing Simon's dinner.

I didn't have a clue what to do with the cultured bird so I called my mum twice and Simon's mum twice. Simon's mum did overreact when I told her that I chopped up the potatoes and chucked them in the oven to make roast potatoes. She seemed to think that everyone knew you had to boil them first. But I blamed the title. They're roast potatoes. As I pointed out to her, I'm roasting a chicken. I didn't boil it first. She saw my point. Eventually.

And then I found myself waiting for my man to come home after a hard day at the office. It was so 1950s. I'd laid the table with a tablecloth (well, sheet), napkins (all right, toilet roll). And if he was able not to trip over all the crap that used to be on the table and was now on the floor along with hundreds of boxes of Viagra, then I believed we would have a very pleasant evening. I even put lipstick on to greet him. And I had made, wait for it (I found this quite disturbing myself) crudités to start with.

'Hello, baby, in here!' I sang when I heard Simon letting himself into the flat.

My little darling came in, slammed the door and started bashing around in the bedroom.

'I've rustled up a little dinner,' I shouted, pouring him a glass of wine and sitting at the table as though it had all been effortless instead of a whole day's worth of shopping, preparing and delving up a chicken's bottom.

'See you later, Sare,' he shouted, putting his head round the door.

'Wher . . .'

'What the fuck?' he said, walking into our multi-purpose living space and taking in the scene. He was wearing his football outfit. Undeniably sexy but UNBELIEVABLY inappropriate for dinner. Then he said, 'Have you got people coming over?' and bent down to do up his trainers.

'You never said you were playing football.'

'It's Wednesday.'

'But you said, "See you this evening." We were going to talk about stuff.'

'Aw, Sare, is this for me? Smells bloody amazing.'

'I made you your favourite dinner.'

'Oh fuck. Babe. Fuck.'

'Do you have to play?'

'Babe. I can't let the boys down.'

I tutted. Now, I know I'm not a big fan of tutting, but I was so disappointed it just came out. And he had never mentioned football.

Then he tutted!

I was so disappointed I couldn't even speak. So I tutted again. Then I sighed. Then he left. Then his phone rang. It sat buzzing on the kitchen surface. I rushed to grab it and chased after him.

'Si,' I shouted. 'Your phone, it's . . .' I looked down at the screen as I was moving. It was Ruth calling.

'Urgh. It's that bitch on the phone again!' I said as soon as I saw her name, and I stopped moving with a jolt.

What happened next is a matter of dispute between Simon and me. I can confidently say that it was the combination of the slippery iPhone bodywork and the loose grip I had on it that caused it to fly out of my hand at this moment. Simon, however, maintains that I hurled it directly at his head. This of course is ludicrous. I wouldn't have thrown anything at his head. Because I loved him.

Whatever, the outcome was that Simon ducked and the mobile ricocheted off the front door and landed in three pieces at his feet.

'SARAH, STOP BEING SO MENTAL!' he screamed at me.

'Well, at least you can't call your other girlfriend now,' I replied at the same volume. He turned his back on me and walked out of the door.

I did what any sane woman would. I drank a glass of wine very quickly while crying, then I called Julia to arrange to meet her at a club where Carlos was playing.

♥ *thirty-six* ♥

The next morning my mouth felt like I'd been licking a cow's bottom all night. Then I remembered. I wasn't far off it. I'd eaten a burger from a kebab shop. The definitive gauge of drunkenness is if a mank burger smells good on the way home. If it smells disgusting you are not too bladdered. If it smells tasty you are a disgrace. If you eat a dirty burger in that state you will be full of two things the following day:

1 remorse
2 smelly wind

And I'd done something to my neck. I suspected it was a move I tried to copy off a young girl in the club. I opened one eye. I was on the sofa, completely clothed, although I'd managed to take one boot off. Simon was smiling at me and holding his nose. He had a chicken leg in one hand and with the other he took my other boot off, then lifted my legs and sat under them on the sofa.

'I'm not going to come too close, babe, because you're a little bit stinky.'

I smiled.

'Was it a good night?'

'I don't know whether it was a good night. But it was definitely a night.'

'Sorry you went to all that trouble with the chicken, Sare.'

'It had giblets.'

I always do this when I'm hungover. Talk random and complete nonsensical gibberish.

'My mum makes gravy with hers.'

'Hmmm. She told me in graphic detail.'

In hindsight it was foolish to start a conversation about giblets when that hungover. I think Simon sensed that because he leant over and touched my cheek.

'What's happening to us?' I whispered sadly.

'I dunno. But I'm sorry.'

'I'm sorry too,' I said with a half smile. 'Have I been mental?'

'Yeah, a bit. But I've been a cock. Sorry. Sorry. Sorry. Sorry. Soz. Sorry.'

I nodded and smiled.

'I would say lots of "sorry"s too but I think it might make me a little bit dizzy.'

'I would kiss you now, Sare, but there are fumes emanating.'

He picked up a foot and moved his mouth towards it. 'There's nothing between me and Ruth.'

'But she keeps calling you! She's been hanging around!'

'I know. I know how it would look. But I've no idea why she's popped up. I was just so pissed off you thought I'd cheat on you. But I swear to you. I haven't spoken to her. She left a message the other night. She wants to meet up. I haven't called her back. I was going to talk to you about it. I won't see her if you don't want me to. But I was thinking that maybe you could come too. We could all go out for a drink. Then you'd know there was nothing to be worried about.'

'Maybe. My head won't stop going round in circles about the two of you.'

'Baby, I don't want to be with Ruth.'

'But you had all that amazing sex and she's got a great figure. Why don't you want to be with her?'

'Because I love you.'

'I love you too.'

'Baby. You know the hard skin on your feet?'

'Hmmm. Are you talking bollocks now?'

'No. She's not even the tiniest patch of that on you.'

I smiled.

'Thanks.'

'Oh God,' he sighed. 'I'm going to have to kiss you, aren't I, stinky chops?' He lifted up my top and kissed my belly. And because it was the nicest moment we'd had in a long time the phone had to ring. I reached behind me to pick it up.

'Sarah's Sex Pit?' Silence. Not again. 'Hellooooo, please talk to me.'

'Hello?' said a posh male voice I didn't recognize.

'Hello.'

'I'm not sure if I have the right number. I'm trying to get hold of a Sarah Sargeant.'

'Oh, that's me.'

'Hello, my name is Terence and, very embarrassingly, I seem to have picked up your carry-along case.'

'No way!'

'Yes. I don't suppose you have mine?'

'Oh, no, I'm sorry.'

'Darn.' I'd never heard anyone use the word 'darn'. I reckoned he was a Tory.

'Sorry.'

'It must have been stolen in Caffè Nero. I should have kept an eye.'

'Hmmm.'

'Now then, I'm in Liverpool at the moment.'

'Ah.'

'But I'll be back in London later today. Shall I drop it round to the address on the label?'

'That would be amazing. Are you sure?'

'No bother. I hope you'll be wearing more clothes than in that photo!' he exclaimed like it was a joke.

'What?' I said.

'Oh, I do apologize, I don't know what came over me.'

I had no idea what he was on about but Simon was smiling and all was good in the world.

♥ *thirty-seven* ♥

After that, Simon decided to go for a celebratory run. I didn't doubt his motives. The boil had been lanced. The poison sucked out. The abscess drained. So I ran a bath. I love a bath. Time to clean and contemplate.

'I'm off for a run now. Sare, will you let me in? I'm not taking a key, I'll only be half an hour!' Si shouted, banging on the bathroom door.

'OK, baby. Oh! Si! Hang about. You know those BT ads they used to have that went "It's good to talk"?'

'Yeah.'

'Who's the actor that did them?'

'Ah, yeah, short bloke, cockney. Whatsis chops. Fuck, dunno. Wait. John something. No, no, Bruce!'

'No,' I exclaimed. Then I thought for a moment. 'Maybe. Is it? Bruce something?'

'Ah, Sare, you're killing me. I'll see if it comes to me on my run.'

'Bye, baby.'

'Sare,' he said sexily.

'Hmmm.'

'Have you got any plans for the afternoon?'

'No.'

'Good. Shall we hang out in the bedroom?'

'Naked dancing?'

'Hmmm. Ohhh! Better go! Getting a semi.'

'Bye, gorge.'

I'm not actually with BT. I left them for someone cheaper. And I never liked those ads.

1   It was clear that BT didn't give a toss about your familial relationships. All they cared about was that you stayed on the phone for hours so their board of directors got new, conservatory-sized bonuses

2   I always thought that they were cruel to people who couldn't talk. Like going up to a blind person and saying, 'Oooh, I love looking at things.' Looking back, this was an over-sensitive reaction, I think caused by the fact that the ads started when my neighbour Robert was growing his own marijuana and making his own home brew

But as I lay there in bubbles I decided that they were on to something. Just that tiny little chat with Si and I felt different. Better, happier, freer, lighter. I lay back in the water and smiled. But I suddenly saw something. Something that shouldn't have been in the bath.

'ARRRRRRGGHHHHHH,' I screamed. I wasn't over-exaggerating.

'ARRRRRRGGGGHHHH.'

I stepped out of the bath. I started pacing. How long had it been here? Did Simon know it was there? My breath caught in my throat. I needed to calm down. I needed to breathe. But I couldn't. My heart was battering in my chest. I was panting. Tears were stabbing my eyes. This couldn't be happening. Not then. I didn't know what to do.

I bent over, lamenting the fact that I'd never got into yoga. I peered at it. It was a grey pubic hair. It didn't even seem to be the same type of hair as the others. It was long, thick and stringy. It looked like it should be on Keith Richards's head instead of my lady place.

'Right, you little bastard. You have to go.'

I pulled at it.

'Argh!'

It was still bloody there.

'Stubborn are you, Keith?'

I reached for the shaver. Now I understood why people went for the full Duncan Goodhew down below. It's because they were actually John Major grey down there. I started shaving. Keith went first. I couldn't bring myself to take the whole lady lawn off though. And I didn't want one of those little fanny goatees that look like you've got George Michael's chin for a minge.

'I know,' I gasped.

I was obviously thinking creatively because I had the fun and romantic idea of shaving my pubic hair into a little heart. It proved not to be my brightest idea. It was very hard.

Practically *Krypton Factor*. I did manage to complete it. However, I wasn't convinced that it looked like a heart. I think if I'd asked someone what it was they might have guessed correctly, but only after the more obvious answers of 'squirrel' and 'tractor' had been exhausted. Still, it was these little things that kept love alive. I got out of the bath and was drying off when I noticed Simon's football kit hanging over the radiator. I put on the football socks and nothing else and waited for him to get back from his run. He'd be all sweaty and panting. Goodie.

♥ *thirty-eight* ♥

True to his word and bang on time, Simon rang the front door buzzer half an hour later. I skipped to the intercom. I must say, I liked wearing the football socks. They made me feel playful and frisky, although they were quite acrylic and that probably wasn't good for my fungus. I pressed the button to let him in and then ran to our front door and stood behind it.

I composed myself for a moment. When I heard the footsteps reach the top of the hall steps, I opened the door a little bit and pushed my football-socked calf through the gap. It occurred to me as my leg was waving outside the door that it could be Terence and the carry-along case. I did some quick arithmetic. I allayed my fears. I was absolutely sure it was Simon. It had to be impossible to travel from Liverpool to London in an hour and a half. With a new confidence I began to rub my leg up and down in a gesture that clearly wasn't sexy but would probably make Simon laugh. Or so I thought. But I didn't hear anything. And I had been so sure that dry humping the door would get a titter.

'Helllloooo, sexy,' I said sultrily in my American accent.

I opened the door a little wider and squeezed half my body through. I was trying to be demure; first I showed him a whole leg and a tiny bit of my logo-ed lady place. But even that didn't get a laugh. So I squeezed my tummy and breast round and finally I revealed my grinning face.

'Oh, sorry, Sarah, I have a feeling that you were expecting someone else.'

'Shitbags! Shitbags! Sorry, Ruth. I'm so embarrassed.'

It was Ruth. Simon's ex-girlfriend! Yoga Woman! I closed the door quickly on her. I told the bad thoughts in my head to please bugger off. What was she doing here? I couldn't believe she'd just seen me naked. She was a super-sorted high-flying City girl and I knew she'd always suspected that I was mad. Although she didn't look as super-sorted as I remembered. She was wearing an anorak for a start, and Mum was right. She'd put on a bit of pudding. I grabbed a dressing gown and returned to let her in.

'Ruth. Sorry about that. I hope I haven't scarred you for life. Come on in.'

Ruth beat a slow path to the lounge. I followed her. She clocked the champagne glasses, well the one champagne glass, and one mug with 'Hello big boy' on the front.

'You've got a man!' She sounded amazed.

'Hmmm.'

It was awkward. I'd seen Ruth as a sexually rapacious threat to me. But I realized then how stupid that was. She obviously hadn't seen him for ages and had no idea that Simon and I were even going out together.

'Would you like a cup of tea?' I asked, willing her to say no.

'No. I was looking for Simon. Does he still live here?'

'Yeah.'

'Oh right, yeah, obviously,' she said, gesturing towards the cock-related products being stored in the living room. She suddenly turned back to me. 'Is he well?' Her tone was too casual to be casual. It dawned on me. She was still in love with him. Of course. She'd spent the last few months eating her body weight in chocolate and pining. Now she was back and she wanted him and I'd got him. And he loved me.

'Yes. Um. Yes, he's good.'

'Good. Right. I'd better go and come back another time.'

'OK,' I said, following her back to the front door. 'Maybe give him a call,' I suggested.

'I have been trying to get hold of him on the phone, but he's not responding. But it's important. I really need to speak to him face to face.'

'Well, he'll be around this week.'

She looked at me and I had no idea what was going on in her head. But she didn't look like the Ruth of old.

We both jumped, as there was a ferocious knock on the door. And Simon's voice, his beautiful deep, sexy voice says, 'Babe! Babe! It's Bob Hoskins!'

Of course! It was Bob Hoskins.

He knocked again. 'Let us in, babe, we've got to get on with that naked dancing. I want to practise some new moves!'

Ruth and I were standing behind the door. Neither of us made a move to open it. Ruth looked at me. Her eyes started to water. Then for some reason she looked at the football socks and said ever so quietly,

'You and Simon.'

I let Simon in. I didn't know what else to do. He looked gorgeous. He was sweating, smiling and carrying a Threshers bag.

'Hey bab . . .' he started, until I moved to one side so he could see Ruth. She'd started crying. But she wasn't making a noise. It was silent sobbing. It was pretty terrible.

'Ruth!' exclaimed Simon, but he looked at me. I pulled one of those polite expressions that you do when you haven't a clue what's going on but you know it's something major. Simon took a step towards Ruth but touched my hand in a reassuring way as he did.

Ruth raised her head from her hands and said some words that I misheard. It sounded like she said, 'I'm having your baby,' to Simon, to my boyfriend.

'What?' said Simon, so softly it was barely audible.

'I'm having your baby.' Ruth's reply wasn't soft and what she said was very audible. She undid her anorak. We all stared silently at her tummy. There was a bump. A very big bump with Simon's baby in it. I was amazed by the size of it. It seemed massive. I half expected her to go into labour there in the hall.

♥ *thirty-nine* ♥

Some conversations stay with you for months after they've happened. You revisit them in early sleepless hours and wonder who that person was, talking all that bollocks. Then you realize, in a cold sweat, it was you. And you buggered everything up. The next conversation I had with Simon was one of those.

Ruth had gone downstairs and was waiting for Simon to take her to his mum's house so they could discuss the situation. They couldn't speak in the flat because the sight of me in Simon's football socks was making Ruth hysterical. Really hysterical. I'd started to worry about the impact it was having on the baby. She closed the door behind her and Simon and I looked at each other.

If my life was a film, a refrain of violin music would have soared to indicate the magnitude of this moment and the actress playing me would have taken her man in her arms. She would have held him tenderly so he could quietly come to terms with the impending responsibility of fatherhood. But it wasn't a film. It was my life. So there was no music or embracing. And I was unable to stop the colonic-irrigation amounts of crap coming out of my mouth.

'Si!! How could this have happened?' was my first utterance. An utterance impressive only in that it achieved more levels of ridiculousness than a Limahl hairdo.

Unsurprisingly, Simon raised his eyes as though I was stupid.

'Ruth is the most sorted person I know. She keeps all her shoes in their boxes. She's hardly likely to say, "Bugger it, I'm not on the pill. You just whip it out before you come!"'

'Sare, keep your voice down,' he snapped. 'She's downstairs.'

'Sorry,' I whispered.

'She thought she couldn't have kids!' he spat at me.

I knew that but I'd forgotten it. And I'd just said 'whip it out before you come'! My mind wasn't even working at Monday-morning-just-after–the-alarm-went-off capacity, as I further demonstrated with my next question.

'Why didn't she tell you before? She can't just turn up like this and drop this bombshell.'

'Sare!' His vehemence made me jump. 'She's been trying to get in touch with me! But you didn't want me to talk to her and then you broke my phone!'

'Sorry,' I whispered and then we were both silent for some time.

Ruth's news had come smashing through the windscreen of my world. But it was still a miracle.

'Wow,' I said.

Now, I realize that 'wow' was a ridiculous thing to say under the circumstances and I hate the way tense situations bring out my limited vocabulary. But I didn't really know what else to say.

'Just give me some space, Sare.'

I didn't say anything. But I gasped. Everyone knows that if someone wants space, they want out. Simon wanted space. I stared at him.

'You don't mean that. Do you?'

'I do,' he shook his head. 'I need space, Sare. Quite a bit of space. From you and me. So I can work this out properly.'

This weird nasal laugh flew out of me. He closed his eyes like there was something terrible in front of him and he'd rather not look. My mouth actually dropped open. I didn't think that happened except in cartoons, but it does, apparently in response to something inconceivably awful.

'Sare, course I need space. I'm going to be a dad. Ruth's going to have my baby.'

As he said the word 'baby' I noticed a tiny, fleeting, 'I'm not firing blanks' smile at the corner of his mouth.

'Ruth's going to have my baby,' he repeated.

I tried to think of the baby. But it's hard to imagine a baby that is in a tummy. In my head it just looked like a twelve-week-scan printed photo, which looked a lot like a fingerprint smudge.

'You hate Ruth, Sare . . .'

'No, I don't,' I answered, surprised.

'Sweetheart, you do.'

'No.'

'Sare, you do. I won't be able to deal with all your jealous stuff at the moment. Not with this. It's best if we just leave it for now.'

'Leave it for now!'

He'd said 'I need space' and 'leave it for now'. I didn't know what was worse, the fact that he appeared to be dumping me or the fact that he seemed to have got the script from a trailing-behind fourth-year pupil.

'Babe. Look, it's not you. It's me.'

There was a soft knock on the door. I walked wearily to open it. The words 'space' and 'leave it' were throbbing in my head. A middle-aged man in a cravat stood before me. I'd never seen him before in my life.

'Sarah?'

'Hmmm.'

'Terence. There was a lady in quite a state downstairs. She let me in.'

'Oh.'

'Your case.' He picked up the carry-along case and handed it to me.

'Thanks,' I said quietly.

'I'll be off, then,' he said with a smile, and then for some unknown reason he winked at me. I closed the door and took a deep breath before I began to speak.

'Si, of course I don't hate her. I don't hate anyone. I may have said stuff, but that was when she was just your ex-girlfriend. Now she's the future mother of your child. It's all very different now.'

Oddly enough, that was exactly what I wanted to say and exactly what I should have said. But it came too late.

'It's really different now. I need to get my head around it. How will you feel when I'm in contact with Ruth all time? Think about it. You'd be a nightmare. It's for the best.'

He looked like he was about to kiss me but then he changed his mind. And he just walked out of the flat.

♥ *forty* ♥

I gave him space. Days passed. I lay on the sofa next to the landline phone clutching my mobile and willing him to call. I didn't cry. I didn't want to fall apart like a self-assembly chest of drawers as soon as it was given something heavy to deal with. I lay and I thought of him. I knew exactly how he would be feeling. And I knew above all that he would want to do the right thing, by Ruth and by his unborn baby. But however I thought about the situation from Simon's perspective I always came up with the same problem. And that problem was me.

He didn't call. On the fourth day my agent called the house.

'Hello,' I said. Please be Si, I thought. 'Sarah's house of pain.'

'Sarah. You all right?'

'Not really. Is that my lovely agent?'

'It certainly is. Sarah, what on earth's the matter? You sound like you're about to stick your head in an oven.'

Not the best aura to be cultivating to my acting agent. Come on, Sarah, act normal.

'I'm fine,' I said perkily. 'I was thinking . . .'

'Dangerous.'

'I was thinking about a role I think I'd be perfect for.'

'It wouldn't be Kiefer Sutherland's sex slave, would it?'

'Well, that goes without saying. But I was thinking that my range and talent could also stretch to playing George Clooney's masseuse.' I was doing the routine solely for effect. My heart wasn't in it. The George Clooney was an old one.

'Sarah, that's wonderful, I'll let his people know straight away.'

'Marvellous!'

'Now then, in the meantime, another commercial audition.'

I thought I'd better play my usual commercial guessing game as well.

'Oh, let me guess, the face of . . . Strepsils?'

'No.'

'Hmmm, but we're in the flu season. Beechams?'

'No.'

'Oh, Gaviscon?'

'No.'

'Oh, I'm normally good at this. Oh God.' It dawned on me what it was bound to be, based on my current luck. 'Imodium?'

'No.'

'Blimey, give up.'

'Crème de Menthe.'

'No bloody way!'

'Yes way.'

'Cool.'

As soon as I hung up I called Julia.

'Good afterno . . . oh, uh, sorry, good morning, IKI.'

'Jules, are you OK?'

'Uh, Sare,' she whispered. 'I am knackered.'

'You sound fucked, baby girl.'

'Stayed out till five. Carlos was playing.'

'Was it fun?'

'Was it fun?' She sighed. 'No. Not really. It was one of these Pacha parties and all the girls were young and gorgeous and dressed in bloody hot pants. I didn't want to leave Carlos there alone.'

'Oh.'

'Yeah, I'll have to sneak off to the loo for a power nap in a minute.'

'Don't forget to set the alarm on your phone.'

'Shit, yeah, that was embarrassing. Anyway, sorry to go on. How you doing?'

'Numb, really.'

'Have you heard from him?'

'No,' I sighed. 'It's been four days. How much space do I give him?'

'Oh, babe, I wish I knew.'

'Actually, Jules, I don't really want to talk about it, do you mind?'

'We'll talk about it tomorrow at the café.'

I suppressed a groan. Not only would I be back to my old waitressing job but also I would be talking about the fact that my boyfriend appeared to have left me for his pregnant ex-girlfriend. That'd be fun.

'Listen, guess what I've got an audition for later.'

'Oooh, cool.' Julia loved this game. 'Well, we're in the flu season so I would say either a nasal decongestant, or we've got Easter coming up so, oh, say it's Cadbury's Mini Eggs!'

'Good guesses. But totally wrong.'

'Tell me.'

'Crème de Menthe.'

'No bloody way.'

'I know! How mad is that?'

'Cool.'

'Anyway, it's in Soho, shall I meet you after?'

'Yeah, come to the office.'

'OK, I'll bring sandwiches, economy drive.'

'Great,' she said excitedly.

♥

'Great,' the director said flatly. 'Say your name to camera.'

'Sarah Sargeant,' I said professionally, and then because I just couldn't help it I added, 'MASSIVE FAN OF CRÈME DE MENTHE.'

'Good, good,' bleated the director uninterestedly.

'Why is that, Sarah?' asked a friendlier American voice. The voice belonged to a silver-haired, cuddly man in a suit. He looked like an elderly cowboy. He'd even got one of those ties that looks like it's made from a shoelace. He was sitting behind the director and next to a plate of chocolate biscuits.

'Hello. Oh, because my best friend and I completely became friends while drinking Crème de Menthe. Our mums drank it, so we carried on the tradition.' It was probably best not to mention that we were fourteen at the time.

'We have some great memories of times spent drinking Crème de Menthe.'

It was also probably best not to mention the main ones:

1   The time I tried to buy a bottle from Budgens and they called my mum
2   The time we made Crème de Menthe ice-lollies and Julia went to A and E

'We were trying to buy some last Christmas to reminisce but we couldn't find it anywhere.'

'That's why we're relaunching it.'

'Excellent. Well, I for one will definitely be buying a bottle!'

'Much obliged.'

'You're American?'

'Yes, indeed.'

'Oh, where are you from?'

'Los Angeles.'

'I thought so. I just got back from there.'

'Really? Were you working over there?'

'Well, yes, I was there to do the new Eamonn Nigels film. But the money got pulled at the last minute and I had to come back.'

'Now then, Sarah, if you could just say the line. We have to be getting on,' the director shouted over me.

'Sorry.'

I turned to the camera. Instantly the urge was upon me.

'Crème de Menthe. It's the bollocks,' my inner voice whispered.

Control it, Sarah, I thought, he's American. They hate swearing.

'Crème de Menthe. It's the bollocks,' my inner voice shouted.

'Any time you're ready, Sarah,' sighed the director.

'Crème de Menthe. It's the b-b-b-b . . .'

Wank! It was really obvious that I wanted to say bollocks.

'B-b-b . . .'

I wrestled. I wrangled. The director sniggered.

Finally, I wrenched the word 'best' out of my mouth and sighed with relief.

As I left the room the American man stood up.

'Sarah?'

'Yes.'

'For you,' he said and he handed me a bottle.

'No way! Really?'

'For you and your friend.'

'Oh, thank you so much,' I said sincerely, but his kind gesture made me want to cry. I hurried away, hugging the bottle of Crème de Menthe to my chest. My tears were constantly at the ready, and it was taking a lot of bullying to keep them back.

♥ *forty-one* ♥

I didn't hear from Simon. But I did hear from friends and family. I had to tell them what happened. Most responded with a slowly pronounced expletive: 'sh-i-i-i-t' or 'f-u-u-u-u-ck'. This was usually followed by a gem of psychological wisdom such as 'You need to cheer up,' or 'You need to move on.' When I told people that Julia had wangled my old wait-ressing job at the café back for me, the news was met with much excitement. The words 'It'll be good for you to get out of the house' were often quoted. Amazing, really, the pap people preach when you've just been dumped. I lived in a flat for a start, and the café was about a quarter of a mile away and contained sexually deviant Polish chefs who had decided to wear Borat mankinis on the day I returned.

Within the first twenty minutes Julia had put a plate of food under my nose and was asking me to identify the foreign body it contained.

'It's a hair.'

'Yes, I know it's a hair, Sare. But does it look pubic?'

'Oh,' I said, peering into the plate of beans on toast that Julia was holding. 'I see what you mean.'

'I can't take it to the table, can I?'

We both looked at the man on table four who was waiting for his breakfast.

'No, you'll have to get the pube out first,' I whispered.

'I'm not touching it! You do it.'

'I am in a very fragile emotional state.'

'Let me call Ruth.'

'And tell her about a pubic hair?'

'Sare, you know what I mean.'

'Yes, I do wanking well know what you mean and I wish you'd shut up about it.' I snatched the plate from her. I stalked to the kitchen and lobbed the food in the bin. I told the kitchen staff to make another meal. Then I calmly walked over to table four and pulled a very apologetic face.

'I am so sorry, sir. Julia over there dropped your breakfast in the kitchen but the chefs are preparing you another. Sorry for the wait.' Then I leant closer to him and whispered, 'She's not very good. We're looking for a replacement.' He seemed very happy and got back to his paper.

I walked back to the counter and Julia.

'Sarah,' started Julia.

'Sorry, I didn't mean to snap but I really, really don't want to talk about Ruth,' I sang shrilly.

'Fuck me. I wasn't going to mention that.' She was staring at me as though I was a stranger. 'What's with the nice waitress routine?' And she gestured towards Mr Beans.

'Oh,' I replied, suddenly realizing I'd just been a good waitress.

'Yeah,' she said seriously. 'Pack it in.'

'You know what I think it is?'

'No.'

'Well, in America you should see the waitresses.'

'Why?'

'They're all like, "How is your meal?" and "Can I get you anything else?" and "Would you like more coffee?" and "You have a nice day." They even offer you ketchup.'

'Sir!' she said, taking the piss. Then she shook her head in disgusted disbelief.

'They get good tips.'

'Like what?'

'Like you're supposed to leave them 20 per cent.' Now she was interested.

'Nah. They're tight, the Americans. When they come here they never leave us anything.'

I raised my eyebrows at her.

'You know what I think?'

'No.'

'I think you did that because you're not yourself.'

'Oh, Jules, please. I don't want to talk about it. And if I did, I wouldn't want to talk about it here.'

'I can't help it. You and Si are soulmates. He's being a dick. There's no way he'll be happy with Big Nose even if she is up the duff. The whole thing is awful. We need to work out what you're going to do.'

'Please, Jules, I don't want to talk about it!' The tears sprang into my eyes. I got a paper serviette to wipe them.

I couldn't look at her. So I took some deep breaths instead. I really didn't want to start crying because I feared it'd take me a fortnight to stop. It took me about two hours to recover from *The X Factor* as it was.

'Go and take a few minutes' break,' she said, pushing me towards the kitchen.

The Polish chefs weren't in there. They were outside smoking, so I did what I always did when the kitchen was empty: dived into the fridge to steal some cheese. But when I opened the fridge door I realized that I didn't feel like it today. I didn't feel like anything today. I never thought anything could put me off cheese. But Simon had. I went into the tiny staff room to check my phone instead.

'Argh!' I screamed as soon as I saw the screen.

'Argh!' I screamed again when a seventeen-stone Polish chef walked in there behind me, wearing nothing but a mankini.

'How boot a blow job?' he asked.

'Argh!' I screamed again and barged past him back into the restaurant. Tears had finally started to fall. But they were tears of relief and they were wonderful.

'I've got a text from Si!' I shrieked.

'Oh my God, what's it say?' said Julia at the same volume.

The man who was waiting for his beans rubbed his ears.

'I haven't opened it yet,' I screamed, laughing and crying and dabbing a serviette on my cheek. 'Oh, thank you, God!'

'Well, bloody well open it, Sare.'

'OK.'

I took a few deep, nervous breaths. Then I pressed the 'open' button and started to read. Julia leant over my shoulder.

Sare. That carry-along case was Ruth's. I'll pop round at some point and pick it up.

'Wanker,' said Jules, and it shocked me.
'He's not a wanker, Jules, I'm the wanker.'
Julia made a 'pah' sound.
'Not even one stinking kiss,' I said sadly.

♥ *forty-two* ♥

Ruth could have left me the carry-along case. Taking a boyfriend would have been enough for most. Not Ruth. She wanted luggage too.

'Anything else you fancy, Ruth?' I muttered as I unzipped the main compartment to unpack it. 'The fridge?'

Simon was going to 'pop round at some point and pick it up'. At some point! The chaotic series of events otherwise known as my life had taught me that the 'point' at which Simon would choose to appear would be the 'point' at which I had fallen asleep in a pizza after two bottles of red wine. And I was not having it. I was going to get dressed and put make-up on and take the carry-along case there myself. (Ideally finding some fox pee to wheel it through en route.)

I unpacked the clothes from my LA trip. Then I started to unzip the gazillions of side pockets in case I had left belongings in there as well. Just as well I did, because I found an unusually soiled pair of pants in the first one. The small bottles of bubble bath and shampoo I stole from the hotel were in the second. I didn't think I'd used any other side pockets but I checked just in case. There appeared to be something in one of them, so I tipped the contents onto the carpet. Out fell a small pile of papers and receipts and a partly used packet of pills. I picked up the pills. I'd never seen them before. A tiny trail of little yellow tablets snaked round the golden packet. The days of the week were printed in black next to each pill. It was a packet of contraceptive pills. It must have been Ruth's. I put it down and picked up the papers. The first was a receipt for a hotel in Paris. Simon and Ruth went to Paris for Ruth's birthday last year. It was her favourite city.

'Not a particularly original favourite city, is it? What's your second favourite, New York?' I grumbled.

I flicked through the other receipts. An A4 sheet of paper was folded amongst them. I unfurled it. A photograph fell out. I nearly gagged. It was of Ruth. At least I assumed it was Ruth. The picture wasn't of her face. It was of a naked body. There were nipples and pubic hair. Not much pubic hair, admittedly. She'd gone for the George Michael. I turned the photo over quickly and picked up the large sheet of paper. There was handwriting all over it. It wasn't Simon's handwriting. It must be Ruth's. I read:

> *Follow these instructions carefully*
> *1 Enter*
> *2 Take off all your clothes*
> *3 Pour yourself a glass of champagne*
> *4 Lie on the bed*

5 *On the bedside table is a blindfold. Put it on*
6 *Wait...*

It must be some little sex game she'd left for him. There was a piece of Blu-tack on the back of it. It would have been stuck to the door for him to find. At least I didn't discover this lot when I was on my jealousy jig in LA. This would have sent me over the edge with a weighed-down backpack. Although I didn't feel much better equipped at dealing with it then, I couldn't compete with this. With my heavy metal head-giving I was the antithesis of Ruth's exotic sex games. Perhaps that is what he wanted. Great sex and a baby.

I wondered whether to leave the stuff in the bag or throw it away. The pill was no good to her now she was pregnant.

I choked. Ruth was pregnant! Ruth was on the pill! Why was Ruth on the pill if she couldn't have children? And if she was on the pill then how did she get pregnant? I sat staring at the pill packet pulling my very unattractive thinking face. Why would Ruth have been on the pill? The more I thought, the more confused I got. She might have taken the pill to regulate her periods or stop her getting spots or something. However, if she got pregnant while on the pill it showed she was super fertile rather than infertile. It didn't make any sense.

I picked up the pill packet. I had to tell Simon about this.

❤ *forty-three* ❤

'Sarah!' It was Simon's mum, Bonnie, who answered the door. She was whispering.

'Hello, Bonnie. I'm here to talk to Simon.'

'Oh, love,' she said sadly. 'Give us a second, will you?'

I stood on the doorstep and nodded. She closed the door on me. She was fastidiously careful not to make any noise. Everything was wrong. Normally when I was there she would say, 'Sarah, it's so lovely to see you. Come in. Take your shoes off though, love, I've just done the carpets. Now, have you eaten?' And even if I had I said no because she was really good at cooking. Suddenly I felt like the ex-wife.

A few moments later Simon came to the door. He looked tired.

'Ruth's in there, isn't she?'

'Yes.'

'Here's her case.'

'Thanks.'

'I won't be long but I just wondered if I could speak to you.'

'Er, all right then,' he sighed.

'Don't go into orgasm about it.'

He gave me a look that indicated he wasn't comfortable with me making comments about orgasms on his doorstep.

'Come upstairs,' he whispered. Then he did the finger-over-the-mouth 'shhhh' sign. I obviously wasn't myself because it didn't make me feel violent. I trailed behind him up the stairs. He opened the bathroom door. I hovered tentatively on the threshold. I didn't want to enter the bathroom. I couldn't possibly have a seminal conversation in Simon's mum's bathroom. My main problems with Simon's mum's bathroom were:

1 It was coral. Not a bad colour, admittedly. One or two items of coral could be an aesthetic treat in a blue room or white room. Being in a room decorated entirely in coral is like being suffocated in a giant pumpkin

2 I don't know what the stipulated guidelines are for different-shaped fluffy mats on bathroom floors. Whatever they are, Simon's mum's exceeded them. There was one by the bath, one by the door, one round the bottom of the sink, but the one that really scared me was the one shaped to go round the bottom of the loo (in coral). Every time you stepped on these mats the tassels moved, so that when you left the bathroom and looked back, the room looked violated. I don't like violating bathrooms so I spent a

lot of my time on my hands and knees before I left her bathroom. It's best not to get me started.

3 It was so clean it wasn't right. It was so clean I didn't even want to wash my hands there let alone do dirty bodily waste practices. 'Hold it in at Simon's mum's house' was always my motto

'Do we have to go in the bathroom?' I whispered. Apparently we did, because he didn't answer but just walked in and turned on the shower and the radio.

'I'm flattered but I don't think now's the time for us to shower together.'

He nearly smiled.

'I don't want her to hear us. That's all.'

'No, we don't want to upset Ruth.' I hadn't wanted that utterance to sound bitter and sarcastic but it did. Si looked shocked. He opened his mouth but I spoke first.

'Sorry. I didn't mean to sound like that. I am really trying to understand and give you space. I just, um . . .'

He wasn't even looking at me. He had just propped his bum against the towel rail and was staring at the floor. I sat myself on the loo and started playing with the lady in the big petticoat on top of the toilet roll. I pulled her out and turned her upside down, admiring her big phallic pointy thing.

'The lady with the massive penis,' I mused. I looked at Simon. He half smiled and then he let his face drop completely and started shaking his head. My phone started ringing. I stopped it quickly.

'It's a nightmare, Sare.'

'Come on, babe. What happened to Mr Positive?'

He shrugged.

'She's really depressed . . .'

My phone again. It was Eamonn calling. I ignored it.

'Do you want to get that?'

'No, no, sorry. Go on. Why is she depressed?'

'It can happen when someone gets pregnant and they didn't think they could. She's hysterical. She thinks something will happen to the baby. She thinks I'll leave her.'

'Are you with her?'

He shook his head. Then he shrugged. Then he said, 'I don't know.' So that was very clear. Eamonn was calling again. I turned my phone off this time.

'Listen,' I started. Then I sighed. 'I found this. In Ruth's carry-along case.'

I held out the pill packet.

'What's that?'

'It's the pill.'

He looked blankly at it.

'The pill, pill.'

Another vacant stare. Then his phone started ringing. He looked at it.

'It's Eamonn.'

'Oh, he was just calling me.'

'Hello,' Simon answered. He put one finger in his ear and squinted. 'What? Er, yes, sir, I am with her. I'll pass her over.' Simon offered me the handset. 'It's a bad line.' I put it to my ear.

'Er, Eamonn, can I call you back?' I shouted above the crackle and the shower. 'What? Eamonn! I can't . . . Something about your back?'

'WE'RE BACK ON!!' I heard him say faintly.

'What?' I shrieked and I started moving around in order to try to find some better reception. He sounded less like a robot if I stood by the bathroom door.

'THE FILM'S BACK ON! WE NEED YOU OUT HERE!'

'Ahhhh!' I screamed. 'Oh my God!'

I noticed that Simon was shaking his head and looking at me in the same way that my first boyfriend did when I accidentally spilt Crème de Menthe on his mother's bed sheet while he was groping me. I remembered the 'sshhh' sign and Ruth and the fact that I was in a bathroom having a crucial conversation.

'And you've got an extra scene. The writer loves your work. We'll courier it over to you!'

I started to scream again but stopped because Simon looked like he would strangle me had it been legal.

'Eamonn, I'll call you back,' I said, hanging up and giving the phone back to Simon. 'The film's back on,' I told him.

'I gathered,' he said sarcastically.

He handed me back the pill packet.

'Si, it's the contraceptive pill.'

'You what?'

'Did you know she was on the pill?'

He squinted at me.

'What?'

'Did you know Ruth was taking the contraceptive pill?'

It was like talking to a foreign child.

'I don't . . .'

'Did you know she was on the pill?' I asked slowly.

'What are you trying to say?'

'Um.'

I hate hard questions. The fact was I didn't actually know what I was trying to say.

'I just thought it was a bit fishy and you should know.'

He stared at me and shook his head.

'You know, if she couldn't have children then why was she taking this, and if she was taking this then how did she get pregnant?'

I finished speaking and realized that he'd turned the shower off.

'I can't believe you, Sarah! The girl didn't think she could have children and now she's having my baby. She's not play-ing games,' he hissed.

Then he turned the radio off and opened the bathroom door. He waited for me to walk ahead of him.

'Thanks for bringing the case back,' he said, opening the front door. And before I knew it I was walking down the driveway with a clear impression that that hadn't gone very well.

❤ *forty-four* ❤

I thought my new scene might add an extra layer to my character. I imagined a scene where Taylor, my character, went to a local hospice and donated some of her stripping money, or she saved a child from being run over. But as I carefully opened the envelope that had been sent to me, I realized that it would be better if she had a scene with her handicapped brother whose medical bills she stripped to pay for. That would give the Academy a semi.

'I would like to thank the Academy . . .' I said out loud.

I pulled out the contents of the envelope. But it was just one page with a tiny section highlighted.

INT – LUCKY BAR – NIGHT
Sleazy Los Angeles Strip Bar
TAYLOR (late 20s, rough and world weary but with a heart)
strips for a small crowd of unconventional looking men. The
tune 'She's A Maniac' from Flashdance *plays loudly. The men*
shout and leer. When the routine ends she works the crowd with a
beer glass for tips.
Close up on Vince as he stares at Taylor.

I picked up my phone.

'EAMONN!!!!'

'Sarah! How's my favourite actress?'

'Eamonn, is this a piss take?'

'What's that?'

'This extra scene malarkey.'

'No, no, no, no. It'll be discreetly done.'

'Eamonn,' I laughed. 'Stop now. I'm not completely gullible.'

'It adds a layer of grit to your character. I think we'll go with it.'

'Eamonn!'

'Now, Rachel has booked you some one-on-one classes with an ex-stripper.'

'Eamonn, stop it. I know you're joshing.'

I glanced back at my front door, expecting a television personality with a microphone to appear and say, 'We had you going there.'

'Now then, because of the scheduling you've got the first lesson on the day you get back and every day for a week. I thought that was extreme but Rachel said she'd seen you dance and it was necessary.' Eamonn started to guffaw. It dawned on me that Ant and Dec weren't going appear.

'Are you serious?'

'Yes, Sarah, for goodness' sake. The writer, Joel, was really taken with you. He wanted your character to be rounded.'

'Well, she's certainly that! Eamonn,' I hissed, 'I feel like showing you my bottom so that you know what a terrible mistake you're making for your film.'

'Darling, you're a real woman. You'll be wonderful.'

I took no consolation in his words. Every woman knows that the phrases 'You look well,' and 'You're a real woman,' mean 'You should think about WeightWatchers.'

'Eamonn,' I gasped. 'You don't want nipples, do you? I can't show my nipples! My dad will watch it!'

'No, darling,' he laughed. 'No nipples.'

'But Eam . . .'

'Oh, Sarah, sorry, got to go. I've got another call.'

If I had to think of two things I was terrible at, without hesitation they would be:

1 looking good naked
2 dancing

I walked into my bedroom and stripped down to my knickers. Then I turned on the radio and I started to move to the music. After about twenty seconds I stopped. I looked like a blancmange in an earthquake. This was now classified as a crisis.

❤ *forty-five* ❤

I wasn't looking forward to the return flight. I kept thinking about the pigeons and Simon and the fact that as soon as I arrived in LA I would get whisked away to a stripping lesson. And I was missing Erin. There's something very comforting about the presence of someone more terrified than you in the seat next to you. The lady next to me on this flight was anything but scared. She was choc-ice cool. She was dressed in head-to-toe black except for whore-red lipstick. And she was wearing shades because night flights are dazzling. She looked like she'd just escaped from the set of that Robert Palmer video. She had a stack of magazines and I really wanted to borrow one.

'Um, excuse me,' I asked, leaning towards her.

She jumped. She was wearing shades – how was I supposed to know she was asleep? We'd only just boarded.

'Sorry, I didn't mean to disturb you, but I was wondering whether I could borrow a magazine.'

'I need them for work.'

'Blimey! What do you do? Make papier mâché animals?' I asked.

She gave me a look that said, 'Don't be ridiculous. I am very important.'

'Oh, never mind. Sorry I disturbed you.'

'I've finished with this one.' She held up a magazine called *Nads*. It featured a teenage girl in her knickers on the front cover.

'Oh, I couldn't possibly look at your *Nads*!'

Not a flicker. My best jokes were wasted on Americans. She placed the magazine back on her pile.

'I'm a publicist,' she said with a sigh.

'Oh, right.'

'You?'

'I'm sort of an actress, waitress person.'

'Oh, are you resting?'

Normally when I was asked this question I bowed my head and mumbled, 'Hmmm, er, yes, when aren't I?' But not then.

'No, actually I'm doing a film.'

Instant interest from publicist lady. She even lifted up her shades.

'Really? What film? Anything I'd have heard of?'

'The new Eamonn Nigels film.'

Kerching! She took her shades off completely.

'With Leo Clement?'

'Yeah, I have a scene with him.'

'The sex scene?' she gasped, showing too much surprise.

'It's a rape scene. It's not hot monkey sex,' I said curtly, like a professional.

'Sure.'

'Are you friends with Leo?'

'I'm his publicist.'

'Oh. Hi.' I didn't mention the fact that up till a few weeks ago I'd never heard of him. 'Sarah Sargeant.'

'Good name. Do you have a publicist?'

'God, no! You have to go through about seven pages on Google before you get to me. Even then it's my Facebook page,' I blurted. Then I quickly added, 'Not that I've Googled myself.'

'I'm Palmer,' she said, stretching out a hand. 'Pleased to meet you, Sarah Sargeant.' She was called Palmer. Brilliant. 'Take my card.'

She held out a shiny black business card. I took it. I put it in my bag and fiercely suppressed the urge to whoop. A publicist had given me her card! I'd be the face of the Pound Shop and doing a reality TV show called *Sarah Sargeant Stateside* before you had time to say, 'Rehab clinic in Arizona.' I watched as Palmer refused a glass of champagne and took a glass of orange juice from a tray that was proffered to her. Then she put her shades back on and reclined in her seat. I deduced the conversation was over. The same tray was offered to me.

'Oooh, champagne please, BRIAN!'

'Sarah, my chosen sister. How are you, petal?'

'A mess!'

'Did my brilliant photography not work?'

'Oh, Brian. You've no idea.'

'I don't believe it! Are things not going well with Banana Man?'

I shook my head. 'You could say that.'

'Was he having an affair with the yoga bunny after all?' he asked incredulously.

'No.'

'Thank God for that.'

'But she was carrying his baby.'

Poor Brian nearly dropped his tray of complimentary glasses of champagne.

'Right,' he squinted at me seriously. 'We'll start with this champagne and some macadamia nuts. Here you go. Now get that down you. Then we'll have a nice chat, there's no problem you can't get round, remember!'

I started to protest.

'We'll give you a nice dinner, then you need a good weepy film, then a gin and tonic, perhaps a savoury snack, then you need a comedy, possibly with another gin and tonic. It'll be all right, darling.'

'Thank you. I wish you could be manufactured into pill form and got on the NHS.'

'Darling, you need to moisturize. You're flaking. I'll get you some face cream and bring you another glass of bubbly.'

'Ah, Brian, you're not to get me drunk!' I suddenly remembered. 'I'm being picked up from the airport and taken to a stripping lesson.'

He raised his eyebrows and smiled. Then he kissed me on the top of the head.

'Do you know the secret of stripping?' Brian asked, taking a tube of something made by Clarins out of his pocket and squirting it onto my finger.

'Have you done a bit of stripping in your time?'

'For the lucky few.' He smiled and did a move that looked like it came from a Britney video.

'Tell me the secret. I need help.'

'It's just confidence. You are the sexiest person in the world! It's great. Oh, and head up and shoulders back. Oh, and lick your lips a lot. And the hips, use the hips.'

I got a vision in my head of me doing all those things. It looked like I was having some sort of seizure.

'What about getting Simon back? Any ideas how I do that?'

He thought for a moment.

'What does Cheryl Cole tell us to do?'

'Huh?'

'"Fight for This Love".'

Cheryl and Brian are right. I may have wanted to kill both of them for putting that tune in my head but they had a point. I had to fight for my love.

♥ *forty-six* ♥

Why, oh why did I let Rachel pick me up from the airport? I could have been in a nice yellow cab asking a jovial immigrant where he was from and if he'd been busy today. But no! I'd meekly accepted Rachel's offer of a lift, so there I was in the passenger seat with a pulse higher than a priest on poppers.

I had my eyes closed. That way I couldn't see the red lights she went through and the moments she forgot that Americans drive on a different side of the road. Voluntary blindness didn't entirely solve my problem though. Even with eyelids locked the experience was ghastly, as I could still hear the swearing of the incandescent drivers around us. In fact, the jury was out as to whether having my eyes closed was any less scary. At least before, I knew why people were hurling expletives at Rachel. Now I could only imagine.

'ARRRRRRGGGGHHHHH!'

'Sarah! Shut up! You're distracting me.'

'Rachel! Slow down! You're terrifying me!'

'I don't want us to be late.'

'It's a stripping lesson. I'm not in labour!'

'I know. I found you a great stripping teacher, by the way. You should thank me. I got you a big woman. I didn't want you to be intimidated by the perfect physiques of some of the younger ones.'

Bless her.

'SLOW DOWN!'

'Oh, for God's sake, Sarah, live a little.'

'Actually, Rach,' I humphed, 'it was my intention to live a bit longer, but then you picked me up from the airport and I'm starting to feel that perhaps that goal might now be scuppered.'

I clenched my eyes tighter and increased the intensity of my prayers for it to be over.

'So, I bet you're looking forward to meeting Dolph Wax.'

'When am I likely to meet Dolph Wax?'

'He's in the film. Did Eamonn not tell you?'

'No.'

'Yeah, he is one of the new backers. He's playing the private investigator.'

'What?' I choked. 'Dolph Wax as in the bloke who starred in *Absolute Destruction* and its twenty-seven sequels who looks like Barry Manilow?'

'Yep, that's the one.'

'Jeez. What does Eamonn say about that?'

'It wouldn't be fit to print.'

'I bet. What? So that poor talented bloke got sacked to make way for Dolph "I only make films with an average of fifty-nine violent deaths per minute" Wax?'

'Yep.'

'How's it going with Eamonn, by the way?'

'Ish,' she yawned. 'What about you and Si?'

'Oh,' I sighed. 'Bit of a nightmare. Actually, full-on nightmare. You could call it the *Nightmare on Camden High Street*. Uncut. With bonus scenes and behind-the-scenes footage. We split up. His ex-girlfriend appeared and she was carrying his baby. And he wants space.' As I said the word 'space' I did the rabbit-ear-inverted-comma-sign. I hate the rabbit ear sign but sometimes I do it for words I loathe. On that day, as I did the rabbit-ear sign I inadvertently opened my eyes. When I opened my eyes I noticed that Rachel Bird – the driver of the car – had her eyes closed.

'RAAAACCCCHHH!'

It looked like she'd just dozed off behind the wheel. I heard that yoga was supposed to relax you. But this was extreme. I felt the car sharply swerve. We started to plough into the oncoming traffic. Horns tooted. I dived over to the wheel and steered us too sharply the other way. I heard the screeching brakes of a car behind. Rachel came to with a shudder, made a noise like she was having a Brazilian then yanked the wheel from me. I wish I could say that my life flashed in front of my eyes, but it didn't. I just thought, 'I don't want to die! I haven't sorted things out with Simon! If there's a post-mortem my blood will be 94 per cent champagne! It's all Brian's fault!'

The odd thing was, we got back on track and continued the journey to the stripping class, and neither of us mentioned the incident. It almost seemed as though we had imagined nearly dying. We were both silent. I can't speak for Rachel, but my heart was hammering like an Ikea showroom employee. A car slowed down to drive level with us and the driver shouted in our direction.

'What's the time?' He was very aggressive.

'Oh, um,' I looked at my phone. No new message from Simon. 'Eleven thirty,' I screamed back at him. The rude man put his finger up at me.

'It's not my fault he's late,' I said to Rachel when he'd driven away.

'He wasn't asking, "What's the time?", Sarah,' she smirked. 'He was saying, "Learn to drive." Because of that, you know, blip back there.'

That blip!? Rachel Bird had just crashed out behind the wheel of a vehicle that was dramatically exceeding the speed limit. And:

1   she didn't smell of booze
2   she didn't smoke dope/take heroin/believe in Paul McKenna hypnosis CDs
3   it was only 11.30 in the morning

Something wasn't right. But I was bloody glad that I was in the car with her and not making small talk in the back of a yellow cab.

♥ *forty-seven* ♥

I became aware of my lack of rhythm when I was fourteen. I bought a drum kit and formed a band with some of the girls from the convent. The band was called The Revenge of the Stoned Flower Children. We specialized in The Cure covers. We practised in my bedroom. I didn't understand my role as drummer. I would drum along to the tune. The rest of the band would scream, 'No, Sarah, you set the tempo. We do the tune bit. Let's try "Boys Don't Cry" AGAIN, shall we?'

Like all things I'm rubbish at, what I lacked in flair, skill and competence, I made up in rampant enthusiasm. I would bash away at the drums until I got bored. Then I would say, 'Can we smoke out of the window now?'

I'd had years to get used to the fact that I look like I'm being electrocuted when I dance. However, Sunflower Oil, my stripping teacher, had only had an hour. And I think she found it stressful.

'Now take your top off.'

'No!' I shrieked.

'Don't stop moving though,' yelled Sunflower Oil. 'You were nearly in time then,' she added sadly.

I think Sunflower Oil was her stage name. Although, she was a big girl; she might have considered Lard or Lurpak as alternatives. She was really into stripping. You know how when little girls love ballet, they do ballet steps even when they're in a petrol station or in the kitchen? Well, Sunflower was like that. Even when she was talking to you she'd be playing with the boa round her neck and jiggling her breasts while looking at herself in the mirror. She gave me a stripping demonstration when I arrived. It was terrifying. I'd never seen such gigantic breasts, let alone seen them spin in different directions. It was impressive and technically flawless but I'd only just met her and I had just nearly died in a car crash and I'd eaten far too much on the flight.

Rachel Bird snorted as I attempted to straddle a chair.

'You get up and do this then. It's not that easy,' I hissed.

'I will in a second.'

'That's a good idea. Let's both get up there and join her.'

Oh please, God, I thought, not those breasts again.

'Right, have a little rest, Sarah. We'll put the song on again in a moment and we'll both join you. It'll be fun.'

'I think we might need to redefine the word "fun",' I muttered as I flopped onto the chair. Sunflower did a hip-wiggling stomp over to me.

'Are you feeling empowered yet?'

'Um. I'm starting to,' I squeaked.

'It'll be wonderful. We've got a lot of sessions booked.'

'Great.'

'We'll work out a sizzling routine.' She smiled. Then she

dramatically turned around and bent forward so that her bottom was in my face.

I pulled Rachel a face to indicate that I thought Sunflower was nice and everything but she was also clearly a mentalist. Rachel just kicked off her shoes and joined us in the middle of the room. Sunflower moved her pose down onto the floor and started vampily crawling to the stereo.

'Let's do it again. This time, Sarah, I want you to think of a special man.'

Poor Sunflower Oil. After she'd pressed Play on the CD and turned round she was faced with me sitting on a chair with my bottom lip quivering.

'Er, Sarah's not really doing men at the moment, Sunflower,' volunteered Rachel.

'Oh, Baby Oil, what's the matter?' cried Sunflower, running over to me and pressing my head into her pillowy breasts. I tried to explain the Simon situation and the fact that if your boyfriend leaves you, you feel like:

1 eating toast/mashed potato/pizza
2 drinking Pinot Grigio/Sauvignon/Chenin Blanc
3 lying in bed listening to a purposely made playlist entitled 'Pain'

You didn't get an urge to fly halfway across the world and take your clothes off for a worldwide distribution film. The only person who would contemplate that was Jordan. A fact that in itself indicated danger.

'But at least Jordan can dance and looks good naked,' I wailed.

Sunflower looked pained. I don't think she'd ever heard of Jordan.

'Baby Oil. You are a beautiful young woman.'

'I'm thirty!'

'Darling, I'm forty-six and I'm a beautiful young woman.'

'Hmmm,' I smiled.

'And we're going to do this routine and it will be brilliant. Do you know why?'

'No.'

'Because if you give up, if you don't give it your all, you will feel worse. You will be really depressed then. You will feel so shit you'll never get out of bed again. Do you hear me? Never! So you go back to your hotel and call him or SMS him or get a contract killer on to him or whatever you need to do. Then you come back tomorrow and I don't want any of this "I can't dance, I'm overweight," because we are going to work that cute little toosh of yours off. And you will do this routine in this film and it will be the best routine that anyone has ever seen in any film. Am I making myself clear?'

'Yes,' I squeaked.

'Good,' she said, and then she smiled and hugged me again. 'And it's OK. We've all been there.'

❤ *forty-eight* ❤

Having decided to do a Cheryl, I was faced with a conundrum. How do you fight for a man's love? It's not easy, especially when you're an eleven-hour flight away, there's an eight-hour time difference and he has a pregnant ex-girlfriend and wants space. Still, I tried to look on the positive side. I had a mobile phone.

Rachel came to my hotel that evening and introduced me to the most lethal cocktail of them all. The vodka martini. There is nothing in it that isn't hard liquor. Not even a squeeze of lime or dash of cranberry. Just an olive that she calls dinner. It was after the first of these liver-busters that I typed

Hey, thinking of you . . . x

and showed the phone to Rachel.
'Should I text it?'
'Sarah! Don't be a freak!'
'What? Will I be a psycho stalker if I send a text?'
'No! It's just a stupid text. You have to ask a question.'
'Why?'

246

'Oh, Sarah, this is playschool. You have to ask a question. That way, he will respond. He's a man. Men respond to questions. They don't respond to statements. They're not like us. We'd respond to a fart in a bath.'

'Oh,' I said, recalling all the texts I'd previously sent. 'So what question do I ask?'

'Hmmm. Well, that's tricky.'

'This is very important, Rachel, I need you to think very hard. And don't fall asleep.'

'I'm not going to . . . Right. Let's think what we want from this text. It needs to be – ' and she counted each point off on her fingers – 'One: short – no more than two sentences. Never ever go into two page texts! Two: a question – as covered – so he responds. Three: spontaneous – it has to look like you've dashed it off, not spent two hours writing it with your mate. A typo would help here. Four: witty – but not too witty. You don't want him to think you're funnier than him. Men are the funny sex, remember! Five: sweet and sexy – you somehow have to straddle the line between virgin and Madonna in "Like a Virgin". As I said, it's tricky. Six: not desperate – you need him to think that you are having lots of fun without him! But not too much. He must feel that you would be having more fun if he were there . . .'

'Blimey. Right. How about . . . how's it going? Thinking of you . . . x'

'Nah. "Thinking of you" is needy. "Wondering how you are . . ." is not. And you need to make him think you're busy and fulfilled without him, remember!'

'LA madder than ever. Wondering how you are . . .'

'It's not funny though.'

'Hmmm. What about LA is mental mental chicken oriental. Wondering how you are.'

'Is that supposed to be funny?'

'No, but it rhymes.'

'Where on the list does it say it must rhyme?'

'How about LA, madder than . . . Hmmm, what's mad?'

'Frogs?'

'LA madder than frogs!' I scoffed.

'Hmmm.'

'Meercats are quite mad and cute.'

'Meercats! LA is madder than meercats!'

'We're losing it.'

'Hmmm.'

'LA is madder than a meercat on acid.'

'Frog on acid.'

'LA is madder than a box of frogs on acid.'

'Looks like you're trying too hard.'

'I think we should move away from cute animals on drugs. I'm trying to cultivate an aura of a responsible and fun stepmother.'

'True. Maybe we should give a reason why LA is mad.'

'Dolph Bloody Wax is in the film! Wondering how you are . . .'

'Hmmm. I'm not sure.'

'Me neither.'

'It's not bad though.'

'Yeah. It grows on you. It's definitely a possibility.'

'Write it down.'

'How about Pick me! Pick me! She's a freak! I love you . . . x'

'Are you going to take this seriously?'

'Sorry. What about Wondering how you are, you'll be pleased to know I'm giving the sunbathing a miss this time.'

'Dreadful.'

'The more I think about it, the Dolph Wax thing is good. It's juicy info. Dolph Wax is a blokey action-type actor. So it makes sense that I send it to Si.'

'Hmmm.'

'But is it too impersonal?'

'No, you want it to be quite impersonal so you don't look too desperate.'

'OK.'

I typed it and showed it to Rachel for approval.

'Do you want to put a typo in to make it look spontaneous?'

'What do you reckon?'

'Well, you could just make one little mistake, like you could miss the "e" out of "wondering". But what I think is good is when you make it look like you didn't check your predictive words. So one word will be completely wrong but it's obvious you were using predictive and were so not desperate that you didn't check.'

'Oooh, genius!'

I set about finding out what other words my predictive

suggests. Eventually I found that the 'you' could also be 'wot' or 'wou'.

'OK. What's better? Dolph Bloody Wax is in the film! Wondering how wot are . . . or Dolph Bloody Wax is in the film! Wondering how wou are . . .'

'How wou are, definitely.'

'Right, here goes.'

I sent the text and then left the phone in the centre of the table. Rachel ordered two martinis. I went to the loo. When I got back my phone was flashing.

'Oh my God!' I grabbed the phone. One new message.

'Oh, wank,' I said sadly when I saw it was a number I didn't recognize. I opened it and read.

Hey Sarah. Welcome back to sunny California. Do you want to practise our scene? Leo.

'Bollocks,' I muttered.

'Nice text,' said Rachel, with one eyebrow raised.

♥ *forty-nine* ♥

I didn't respond to Leo's text and Simon didn't respond to mine. To be honest I didn't give Leo's a thought. I was too busy imagining Simon opening a text from me, reading it and then either:

1   shaking his head and saying, 'I wish she'd fuck off.'
2   thinking, she'll get over me eventually and then deleting it
3   saying, 'Ruth, baby, look at this, Sarah sent a text from LA. Oh, darling, you've got something round your mouth, let me get it off with my tongue.' And Ruth leaning over as she stroked his thigh and saying, 'Humph, she can't even spell.'

And I'd asked a question too. I would have preferred a

fine thank you, bog off now

to nothing. I'd been demoted from someone he slept with to someone he didn't even think was worth typing a couple of letters into an iPhone for.

After twenty-four hours of waiting I sent another.

Shoot my first scene in two days. FUUUUCK! How you doing?

Suffice to say, I didn't run that one by Rachel. I didn't get a reply to that either. I sat in my class with Miles Mavers the next day with the phone clasped in my hands for the whole lesson.

'Sarah, Sarah!'

'Yes, Miles?'

I had to raise my voice slightly. Tinkerbell was outside practising her tap.

'I don't know what to say.'

He was sitting behind his big dark wood desk shaking his head at me. It felt like that time I was refused a bank loan to pay off my student loan and the man in the Halifax laughed at me.

'Is it not getting any better?'

'No.'

'Oh.'

'Sarah, I'm worried.'

'Oh.'

'We need to go back to basics, as I said before.'

I sighed and looked out of the window. A sprinkler danced across his lawn.

'I don't understand your reluctance to do that, Sarah.'

'Well, I just don't think there's enough time. I shoot my first scene tomorrow.'

'Uh, huh.'

'If you take apart my accent now, I think it'll throw me.'

'You're an English girl playing an American. I think you should do whatever it takes,' he said. And then he sat there nodding at me with his eyebrows raised.

I didn't know what to say. My instinct said it would mess up my performance. My instinct told me that I only had seventeen lines to say in this film and he should teach me how to say them. I wouldn't be improvising in American, MI6 weren't sending me undercover to infiltrate a drugs gang, all I needed to do was sound like an American when I said those lines, three of which were two 'yes's and a 'hmmm'.

'I have been doing this a long time,' he added.

'Oh God, sorry Miles, of course you have.'

We looked at each other and listened to the sound of tap shoes on the wooden floor. They stopped outside the door.

'Daddy,' she screeched, knocking twice.

'Come in, Chelsea,' boomed Miles Mavers.

Chelsea opened the door a few inches.

'Leo Clement is here to see you.'

'Thanks, Chelsea, we won't be much longer,' he said, putting his hands together and stretching so that his fingers cracked. I hate that sound so I scrunched my face up.

Chelsea closed the door and Miles Mavers looked at me again.

'Look, Miles, as I'm shooting the Ned scene tomorrow can we just go over that in the morning? Then the next day we can discuss going back to basics. Is that OK?'

'Your call,' he said, with his eyebrows raised.

I stood up and started to collect my bits of script from Miles's desk.

'Oh, leave those here, save you bringing them in every time.'

I nodded. I had another copy at the hotel.

'Thanks, Miles. See you tomorrow.'

I didn't actually want to walk out of Miles's office. I would have put make-up on if I'd known Leo had the session after me. I looked rough as a badger's bottom. I was wearing pyjama bottoms, a vest top, and a blanket I'd stolen from the aeroplane as a shawl. And I had bed hair, in a ponytail that I'd done without a mirror. I wondered whether Miles Mavers would mind if I escaped through his garden. I didn't like to ask. So all I could do was plaster on a smile. It felt very uncomfortable on my face.

I walked into the hallway but it was deserted. I darted to the front door and had just opened it when . . .

'Sarah!'

I spun round and there was Leo wandering from the direction of the kitchen. He was holding a sandwich and Tinkerbell was tapping along behind him. He got offered sandwiches there. I had to fetch the water.

Leo was wearing shorts, a sweatshirt and a black woolly hat. Obviously you'd never need a woolly hat in California, what with it being a tropical climate. But he wore it well. It was sexy, too sexy to look at, so I looked at the ground. I'd met a man who was too sexy for his hat.

'Hi, Leo. How are you?'

'Good. How was England?'

Ghastly. Probably the most miserable time of my life.

'Great, thanks.'

'Sarah, I was wondering if you wanted to hook up.'

'Huh?'

'To rehearse our scene.'

Chelsea started noisily doing the time step or Time Warp or something next to him. We both looked at her.

'Oh, sorry, Chelsea. You're great.' She beamed and stopped tapping. Then Leo turned to me. 'Chelsea reads with me in my sessions with Miles.'

Cow.

'Lovely.'

'Did you get my text?'

'Yes, yes, I did, sorry I didn't get back to you. I've just been jet-lagged to buggery the last few days.'

'No worries. But if you wanted to practise one day . . .'

I smiled.

'Leo, I'd love to.'

♥ *fifty* ♥

Things that reminded me of the man I'd lost:

Bananas, chicken, wetsuits, cameras, football kits, Bobby Davro (it's staggering how often he pops up when you're forlorn), bathrooms, comfortable tracksuit trousers, Viagra, the Internet, songs with the word 'love' in them, charities, people doing exercise, couples kissing, couples not kissing, old couples, young couples, couples of indeterminate age, couples who look happy, couples who clearly hate each other, women on their own, mad old alone women, Threshers, children, schools, buggies, toys, pregnant people, phones, men, going to bed, waking up and thinking.

So it was getting better. The nights were the hardest. I was glad of the time difference so I could Skype Jules.

'He hasn't texted back!'

'How many have you sent?'

'Three!'

I sent the third twenty-four hours after the last. It said

I wish you'd reply. Please. I'm feeling really low. X

Rachel would have killed me if she'd found out.

'Oh.'

'What should I do?!'

'Give him space. I thought he wanted space.'

'I can't give him space!'

'Jesus, Sare, you're going mad.'

'Thanks, Jules.'

'OK. He's ignored the texts.'

'Ah, rub it in, why don't you! I know he's ignored the texts.'

'Sarah, I'm trying to think. Stop the wailing.'

'OK.'

'Right, there is something we could do. But I'm not sure if you're in the right mental state.'

'What mental state is that?'

'Well, like, sane.'

'Jules, I'm sane.'

'Well, do things like calm down, breathe, talk about something other than Simon and a text message, and I might agree with you.'

'OK. Look, I'm breathing. Lovely breaths. Now then, what is this thing we could do?'

'Fuck me, I wish I hadn't said anything.'

'Well, you did. So hand it over.'

'OK. Well, we could make him a little bit jealous.'

'Oooh. Hardcore.'

'Yes, that's what scares me.'

'Jules, I'll be fine with it. It's me.'

'Exactly.'

'So what do I do?'

'Just, oh God, I can't believe I'm encouraging this.'

'It'll be fine. Tell me.'

'OK. A while back, I was a bit worried about Carlos and a club promoter. I'm not proud, but I used and abused Facebook to make him wonder if I was as loyal as he thought. Anyway, it worked.'

'Ah, poo,' I said sadly.

I hated Facebook. I called it Sit on My Facebook. I liked it when I first joined. I spent six days stalking all the people I'd ever met or snogged. I uploaded the only flattering photo ever taken of me for my profile picture. I tried my best to accrue more friends than my nine-year-old nephew. And then the seventh day happened. On the seventh day, I had twenty-two facebook updates. 'Oooh, you must be popular,' someone of my mother's generation might cry. But as anyone under the age of thirty-five will recognize, out of these twenty-two updates, seventeen were people tagging me in photos. Not just any photos. Photos I didn't know were being taken at the time. Photos that I was blissfully unaware existed. Photos where I had between one and all of these characteristics:

1 A yellow period spot on my chin
2 A heartfelt smile giving me an obese man's belly where most people have a neck
3 A stunned expression as though someone had sharply inserted something unexpectedly up my rectum

4   A perfect one-chin-only smile but the presence of a
     nearly vomiting rugby player making a swearing sign
     behind me
5   A deliberately unattractive and comedic face while
     everyone else in the photo looks like they're part of an
     elite models' party

The other five messages on the seventh day were from
people I barely remembered meeting asking me to join
pointless groups. Matey you met once wants you to join a
pub group nowhere near you. Do you accept? Er, no.

I made a pact then and there that I would only go on
Facebook to un-tag everything.

'Well, that's the only advice I can think of. If you're going
to be fussy, I'll fuck off.'

'Well, tell me exactly what you did before you go.'

'OK,' she yawned. 'I got Nikki's cousin, you know Daryl,
to go on and write flirty posts that everyone could see. And
then I went through my old photos and got Nikki to upload
all the ones where I looked gorgeous and was in the vicinity
of a hot male.'

'OK, how can I do that?'

'You must know some handsome actors who can write
messages on there.'

'Dunno.'

'Look, I'll see if Carlos has got any tasty friends and then
I'll see if we've got some photos to put up. I promise, I'm on
to it. Now, go, before I get the sack.'

'OK. Thanks, Jules.'

When we hung up the Skype connection, I went onto Facebook. I clicked on Simon's profile. I looked at all his photos fifteen times while listening to Lily Allen's 'Littlest Things' on repeat. And that was how I spent the night before shooting my first Hollywood scene.

❤ *fifty-one* ❤

'Bye, Ned,' I said and it sounded English. And I was standing in the wrong place. I was supposed to be standing on a different mark. I wouldn't be in the bloody shot.

'Sorry!' I said, putting up my hand.

'OK, get ready to go again,' boomed a weary voice.

'Sorry,' I repeated, for about the thousandth time.

'And action!'

'Bye, Ned.' That sounded as though I was from Turkey. I tried not to wince. I kept walking to the mark on the right. But then I remembered that I didn't have my handbag. I needed my handbag for continuity. They couldn't use the shot if I didn't have my handbag.

'I don't have my handbag!' I cried. 'I'm so, so sorry.'

'OK, hold it there.'

'Are you all right, Sarah?' It was Eamonn Nigels. He was speaking through one of those speech funnel things.

'No, I'm not OK! I don't know how to speak any more. I say a line. But then I hear it in my head and I know it's all wrong. I can't relax. I can barely breathe. And I really need the loo.' But of course I didn't say that. I put my thumb up in the air instead. I could see Miles Mavers on one of those upright seaside chairs behind Eamonn. He was mouthing something. I think it was the vowel sound 'o'. I was surprised he didn't bring his daughter, Anna-I'd-love-to-see-your-head-in-a-Pavlova.

OK, Sarah, you can do this, I told myself. It was five lines. I had to leave the strip club, have a joke with Ned on the door and then get in the pick-up truck and start the engine. The stupid thing was that I knew it was easy, but the combination of walking and talking and trying to remember which side of the car I entered and how to bloody speak in an American accent had made me so tense. I had loads of good stuff prepared for that scene, too. I was going to give Ned the finger when he insulted my driving and do this little dance, because in my back-story I quite fancy Ned. Suddenly I couldn't even look at Ned. That was the worst thing. I knew I could do it. But I was so bloody worried about it all that I'd gone to pieces. It was heartbreaking.

A lady approached me to touch up my make-up. I was wearing Sunflower Oil's body weight in make-up because I was supposed to have just been working at the club. I looked like Marilyn Manson's muse. That lady had probably powdered Angelina Jolie's nose. Everyone there was a bona fide Hollywood person. I was Sarah Sargeant from outside Croydon. And I'd been found out. I didn't think I could do it. A career in waitressing suddenly didn't look so bad.

'Sarah,' it was Eamonn Nigels, in person, not on a loud speaker. 'Are you all right, darling?'

The director had come all the way over to talk to me because I was so crap. Everyone was looking.

'Oh, I've lost it, Eamonn,' I whispered.

'What's worrying you?'

'Everything.'

'Would you like an Eamonn hug?'

I smiled because Eamonn Nigels hugs are the best.

'No, I think that make-up lady would have a coronary.'

'Hollywood's intimidating for the first time. All these people around. But you have a right to be here. The buzz was all about you and Erin after that read-through. I mean it Sarah.'

'But my accent's shite. My vowels are all wrong.'

'Your accent?'

'Mmm.'

'Your accent's great. Let's do it again in rehearsal. We've got plenty of time. This is the last shoot today.'

'Yeah, but that means everyone wants to go home.'

Eamonn looked at me seriously.

'Hold it together, please, Sarah.'

I was embarrassing him. He brought me into his film. I was the only English actress. I wasn't nearly as experienced as everyone else.

He clocked the panic on my face.

'Try and do it as terribly as you can.'

'What?'

'Sarah, you're so worried about not letting yourself and me and everyone down that you can't let go. Just say, "To hell

with you all." Allow yourself to make mistakes. It's all OK.'
And then he hugged me. I started to murmur objections.
'Fuck the make-up woman,' he said.

♥ *fifty-two* ♥

'Now then, do you agree we need to go back to basics?' Miles said the next morning.

'I don't care what we do, Miles, I just want to be able to speak again.'

I was so tired. Another sleepless night. Not a word from Simon. My first experience on a Hollywood film set kept being played in my mind. It was basically me going, 'Sorry!' over and over again. Eamonn hoped that by telling me to be bad I would be good. Oops. He won't do that again. You should have seen his face when I showed him just how bad I could be. I just wanted to cry. At the very end we managed to get a take. I even did the finger and the little dance to Ned. But it was still rubbish.

I had lost the cockiness I had before and Miles Mavers was acting like a very ungracious winner. He was smug.

'You see, Sarah, you don't just paste an accent onto your lines.' He laughed at the concept. Then he got up and walked to the corner of his desk and perched there. His thighs in the shell suit shorts spread over the mahogany. Miles Mavers was the sort of person who knew that he was attractive and young-looking. No one else saw it though. 'You need to learn to speak again.'

'Yes.'

'So.' He leant further towards me. His thighs spread more. I could hear the shell suit material stretching. He caught his scrotum in the fabric. He jumped off the desk and made a quick adjustment.

'Chelsea will join us later, to read with you.' He waited for me to protest. But I was too tired.

He started me off with some vowel exercises. I repeated them conscientiously. I was mid-flow when his mobile phone rang.

'I'll take this outside. You carry on,' he said, and opened the patio doors to take the call in the garden. I didn't know why he bothered as I could hear every word he was saying.

'Yar . . . yar . . . uh huh. Not great,' he laughed. 'Yar . . . yar.' I stopped my vowel exercises and started to imitate him. 'Yar, yar, uh huh,' I said to myself in a deep whisper. 'Yar, yar.' But I stopped taking the Miles Mavers Mickey when I heard this sentence:

'Well, if it doesn't improve, she'll have to be recast.'

Maybe he said something else? No, I definitely didn't imagine it. I couldn't have misheard him. He was a voice coach, for God's sake. He knew how to speak. And I knew he was right. If I didn't improve, they would have to recast me. He must have been on the phone to Eamonn Nigels. I couldn't catch my breath. I felt like invisible hands were strangling me.

Miles walked back in the room.

'So, where were we?'

I couldn't look at him. I honestly felt I couldn't breathe. I thought I was dying. I'd never felt anything like it before.

'Sarah? Are you OK?'

I shook my head.

'You don't look well. Is there someone I can call to pick you up?'

I shook my head again.

'I have to go.' I gasped the words. I didn't even wait for him to answer. I stumbled out of the house. I couldn't breathe! I thought about calling Rachel Bird. I thought about calling Simon. I really wanted to hear his voice. It was getting worse. I felt everything was slipping away and I couldn't catch it. My relationship. My career. And I didn't know what I'd done wrong. I'd tried so hard. I was crying. I was standing outside Miles Mavers's house gasping and crying. I heard the rat dog yap. I had to get back to the hotel and call my mum. I walked slowly and tried to breathe. Breathe. I didn't know what was happening but it had to be something very bad.

My phone. My phone was ringing. 'Oh Simon, please be you,' I sobbed. 'Please.' It wasn't him. It was Rachel Bird.

'Sarah! Eamonn wants you come for dinner tonight.'

And I knew what was going to happen. He was going to tell me I'd been recast. He'd just got off the phone to Miles Mavers.

'Sarah, are you there?'

'Rachel . . .' I gulped.

'Sarah, what's the matter?'

'Rachel, I c-c-c . . .'

'Sarah, what are you doing?'

'I c-c-c-can't breathe.'

'What?'

'I know I sound hysterical. But I can't breathe!'

Rachel was silent for a moment.

'Yes, you can,' she said calmly.

'No, Rachel, I can't. I feel like I'm being strangled.'

'That's what it feels like.'

'Ah, ah, it's getting worse.'

'Listen to me. You can breathe. You are breathing.'

'No, no, I'm not.'

'It's anxiety.'

'Rachel, I'm serious. It's really bad.'

'Ah, Sarah. That's how it feels. The first one is terrifying.'
She listened to my sobs and gasps for a few seconds.

'You're having a panic attack. Tell me where you are. I'll
come and get you.'

I was getting sacked from the film, my boyfriend didn't
want me and now I had an anxiety problem.

'I'm a mentalist,' I said quietly and I slumped down on
the kerb.

♥ *fifty-three* ♥

'Wow, look at you!' I said to Rachel later that night. She'd just got out of the rooftop swimming pool to greet me. She was wearing a bikini. There were fairy lights in the plants around the deck area. It was all a bit James Bond.

'You've got an amazing figure. I would give anything to have a body like yours,' I said, staring like a man.

'I've lost weight, actually.'

'You don't have any cellulite at all.'

'You have to work for it, Sarah. You don't get it by eating burgers.'

'Oh yeah. You've got really nice boobs as well. I wish I had nice boobs. Mine fly under my armpits when I don't have a bra on.'

'They're not bad are they?' she smiled. 'But they're not real. And I think I've got trouble with this one. It's hurting. I can barely sleep at the moment.'

'Go to the doctor.'

'Yeah, yeah, I should. How are you feeling?'

'Battered.'

That was the only way to describe it.

'Have lots of wine tonight and knock yourself out.

You're not shooting tomorrow and we can see Sunflower late afternoon.'

'Hmmm.'

I didn't think I'd have a job tomorrow. I'd be on a plane home to pain. I wondered whether they flew you home in Economy when you were sacked from a Hollywood movie. I wondered how I'd cope with the humiliation. What would I say to people?

'Sarah!' It was Eamonn Nigels.

'Eamonn,' I said, walking towards him. Then I lowered my voice so that Rachel didn't hear. 'Look, I know why you invited me over.'

Eamonn looked uncomfortable.

'What? Sarah. Damn it. I need to take this call. Blast,' he said, looking at his iPhone.

'Will you do those gins, darling?' he shouted to Rachel without looking at her.

I saw her jaw tighten.

'Yes, darling,' she sang sarcastically.

'How are things?' I whispered when he'd gone.

'I don't think I exist any more. I'm just some muppet who makes Eamonn drinks and lies in bed next to him at night.' She walked over to the outside kitchen area and started to pour three massive gins. 'I started stripping for him last night.'

'Did he like it?'

'He fell asleep.'

'Oh.'

'Don't laugh!'

'Sorry.'

'Oh, bloody laugh if you want.'

'Rach.'

'What?'

'Thank you so much for today. I thought I was going to die. I don't know what I'd have done if I hadn't spoken to you.'

'Sarah, it's cool.'

'Have you ever had one?'

'About a thousand.'

'No.'

'Well, maybe not a thousand. And I haven't had one for ages. But I got loads at school.'

'At the convent?'

'Yeah.'

'But you were the girl everyone wanted to be!'

'Was I?'

'Totally.' I couldn't bring myself to tell her that I used to spend hours in front of the mirror copying how she rolled her socks down and tied her jumper around her waist.

'Funny old world,' she said and clinked my glass.

'Ladies, I am so sorry.' It was Eamonn again, taking his gin and joining it to our glasses. 'To the Brits in LA.'

'The Brits in LA!'

Lovely as all this was, I wished he'd get down to it and tell me.

'Eamonn, I know why you asked me here tonight. I just want to say that I understand.'

Eamonn looked very uncomfortable.

'It's OK. I understand,' I assured him.

'Look Sarah, I don't think we should . . .'

'No, please, we have to discuss things, Eamonn.'

'Sarah,' he sighed. 'OK, let's have a little chat in my office.'

We got into his office. He closed the door. I was still breathing. Just.

'Sarah.'

'Go on. It's OK,' I said as soon as he'd closed the door and faced me. 'Let's get this over with.'

'I just don't know what's the matter with her.'

'Who?'

'Rachel.'

'Uh?'

'Well, that's why I invited you. I thought it would be nice for Rachel. She barely talks to me at the moment. She's always tired and she sleeps a lot. I don't think she's enjoying it out here.'

'Uh.'

'I thought you were going to start doing some relationship counselling out there.'

'Me?'

'Yes.'

'Me?' I repeated. 'I couldn't offer relationship advice to a pair of socks.'

'Sarah, what on earth is all this about?'

'I thought you were going to sack me from the film.'

'Sarah, why on EARTH would I sack you from the film?'

'Because I can't act and I sound as though I'm from Tooting Bec.'

'Sarah, for God's sake, you are great! I loved the stuff you did in that Ned scene. That little dance was genius. The accent's great.'

'Oh.'

There was a knock on the door. It was Rachel.

'Sarah, your phone's ringing. Do you want to take it?'

'Yes!' I screamed, racing to the door and grabbing it from her. It was a withheld number. Oh please, please, please be Simon.

'Hello.'

'Sarah, Miles Mavers. 8 a.m. tomorrow?'

'OK. See you then.'

'Sorry. I thought it might be Simon,' Rachel whispered when I'd hung up.

'No. Just bloody Miles Mavers.'

'Miles Mavers? What does he want?' overheard Eamonn.

'Oh,' I tutted. 'It's just about my early morning voice class.'

'Really?'

'Every morning at 8 a.m.'

'I didn't know you'd asked for them.'

'I didn't ask for them. He told me I needed them. Although I wouldn't call them voice lessons. More like an hour of humiliation by Miles Mavers in sportswear.'

'He told you you needed voice lessons.' Eamonn's voice was rising.

'Yes.'

'He told you that you needed voice lessons.' I'd never seen Eamonn cross.

'Yes,' I squeaked.

'He told you . . .'

'Eamonn, what's the matter?'

'He's only here to work with Leo. Leo hasn't done much acting and he has a habit of swallowing his words. He had no right to approach you. You don't need coaching. Your accent is perfect. I wouldn't have cast you if it wasn't. And even if you needed them, I wouldn't give you lessons while you're working! You would have had them weeks ago.'

Eamonn was furious.

'The cunt!'

I leant back. I'd never even heard Eamonn say 'fuck', let alone 'cunt'. Eamonn was a bloody and bugger man. I took it from Rachel's face that it was a first for her too.

'What is that man playing at?' He drained his glass and strode back to the bar.

♥ *fifty-four* ♥

Eamonn Nigels was a Scorpio. Miles Mavers was about to feel the sting in his tail. Eamonn had instructed me to go to my early morning voice class and keep my phone on.

I pressed the doorbell. I heard a tinny rendition of that famous song from Swan Lake. Mummy answered the door. Not in her dressing gown letting a dog out for the toilet; far from it. She was wearing a lilac fitness ensemble: tight shorts and a leotard over the top. There was something incredibly masculine about her. Not quite like that shot-putter who was disqualified from the Olympics for being a man, but not far off. She made a grunt-like sound and then turned around. Her leotard went into a thong at the back. I don't think I'd ever seen such a tight bottom. She might well have been touching cloth. I watched her bottom cheeks as they headed towards the kitchen: not a wobble. She left me alone in the hallway. That was no good. If Eamonn called me it would have no impact. I wondered what he'd do. He had been incandescent the night before. Rachel and I managed to calm him down with three gins and a bottle of red wine. Their chef, yes, their chef, made an amazing three-course dinner. When I left they were snuggled together in an arm-chair feeding each other Stilton and grapes. I was very happy for them, although I do hope the Stilton goes to Rachel's thighs. I was able to sleep then, knowing that I still had a job. However, I dreamt that Simon flew over to LA and told me that he loved me.

'Sarah!'

Oh no. Oh please, God, no. I didn't think I could do it. Miles Mavers was wearing cycling shorts. On the top he had a T-shirt with the logo 'I gave up drinking, smoking and sex. The worst fifteen minutes of my life' across the front. He'd tucked the T-shirt into his cycling shorts.

'I'd love a glass of water.' Why did this man think that I was put on the earth to personally irrigate him? 'Bottled water!' he quickly added.

I went to the kitchen. His jury's-out-on-the-gender wife was on the floor again. I went to the fridge and opened it. Blimey. It was crammed with food. Mainly 'fat free', 'calorie free' foods. I was sure if I touched anything I would be buried under an avalanche of nutritionally bereft sustenance and it would take four days for the emergency services to find me. Luckily the water was in a side compartment.

'Ah,' I cried. Something had hit me on the bottom. I looked behind me to see Mummy's trainer-ed foot squidging my bum.

'Don't move' she panted.

I couldn't frigging move; I was wedged in by the fridge door and her spread-eagled body.

'I gotta do fifteen.'

I waited for her to do fifteen crunches with her legs akimbo, then I grabbed a glass and left the kitchen, taking the bottle with me. As I walked to the office, my phone started to vibrate in my pocket. Miles was standing in his study doing pelvic rotations. I tried not to look as I dispensed him his water. Even though I knew it was Eamonn calling I was still disappointed not to see Simon's name.

'Oh, sorry Miles, it's Eamonn Nigels. I'd better take it.' I acted very apologetic and watched his reaction. He didn't seem so cocky now. He'd stopped circling his groin and nervously picked up a paper clip.

'Hi, Eamonn. Thanks sooo much for last night. I had a lovely evening. What . . . oh no, I'm not at the hotel . . . no . . . I'm at Miles Mavers's house . . . I'm having a voice session . . . no, no, God no, I didn't ask him . . . he told me I needed help . . . haha . . . yes . . . we all need help, true very true . . . oh, OK . . . let me just check with Miles.'

'Miles, I am so sorry, the writer has written me another scene, apparently! Eamonn wants to make sure I get it personally. Do you mind if he pops round? He won't disturb the class. I won't let him. We've got work to do.'

'No . . . n-no.' He was clearly shitting it. He was cleaning his nails with a paper clip and you don't do that in public unless you're distracted.

'OK, Eamonn. See you shortly,' I sang. I fixed my eyes on Miles in his ruffled state and smiled. 'Ah, Eamonn is such a nice man.'

I hated to admit it but I was enjoying this. Blimey. Eamonn must have called from just outside because at that moment Swan Lake was piped around the house.

'DADDY!!' we heard. The windows hadn't shattered, which was surprising.

'DADDY!! EAMONN NIGELS IS HERE. DADDY!'

'Wonderful projection,' I said to Miles.

He didn't respond.

'Shall I let him in?' I asked. I was clearly too late because Twinkle Toes entered at that moment, dressed as before but with lipstick.

'Daddy, Eamonn Nigels is here to see you.'

'Actually, Chelsea, I'm here to see Sarah.' He looked at me and held out his arms. 'There she is, my little star!' I thought I was going to start giggling but luckily he hugged me so I composed myself in his armpit. 'Now then, the writer has written more for you. Can you believe it, Miles? The writer has heard her once and wants to write a new scene for her.' Eamonn started shaking his head and looking at me in disbelieving wonder. I didn't know what to do. So I hit him and said, 'Oh, go on with you!'

'Now then, why are you here so early?'

'Voice classes,' I said innocently.

Eamonn's tone changed.

'Sarah. I don't think you need voice classes.'

Miles's face fell like a plane with a pigeon in the engine.

'I am the director. I think your accent and performance

are fantastic and I don't want anyone except me to give you assistance.'

He paused, then he eyeballed Miles and said, 'Is that clear?'

Miles didn't respond. Eamonn carried on.

'Chelsea, would you leave the room?' He didn't look at her though. He was still pointedly staring at Miles. Chelsea did a brisk arabesque, stubbed her foot on a floorboard and then scuttled away.

'One other thing, Miles.'

'Eamonn.'

'If you do try to interfere with my actresses, don't be so obtuse in future as to email me your daughter's CV repeatedly while you're doing it.'

Miles opened his mouth.

'I know. I'm a father too. There's nothing we wouldn't do for our kids. But I made my decision when I cast Sarah and NOT your daughter for this role. And that is the *final* decision.'

Miles looked very humbled. I started to feel sorry for him.

'We'll show ourselves out.'

I held my breath until the front door was closed behind us.

'Wow. You are the bollocks. "Don't be so obtuse."'

Eamonn put his arm around me, I was sure for the benefit of eyes at windows.

'Did she really audition for my part?'

'Yes, could you imagine anything more deafening?' He did a Chelsea screech. 'Bye, Ned!' I had to laugh.

'Now then, where am I taking you for breakfast?'

♥ *fifty-five* ♥

'Wowzers, you lost weight on that fast! I mean, you were tiny before but now I'd be worried about you falling down a drain.'

'Yeah, eighteen pounds.' She bared her Simon Cowell-white teeth proudly.

'Sit at that great table by the window. I'll get your coffee.'

Already-good service suddenly became fit for Gordon Ramsay when you were with a successful film director in LA.

'I'll come and take your order in a moment.'

Just once, in LA, it would have been nice to be served by a lardy waitress. Or even just someone who enjoyed food. Or even just someone who ate food. There's something heavenly about an obese waitress. One who says, 'Do you want a fried slice with that?' Obviously, you don't let on that you are a fried bread fiend when faced with that question. You don't reply. You falter and say, 'Um . . .' And then the obese waitress says, 'Oh, go on! You're a waif. Have two. Get some meat on your bones!' It's got to be wrong when you want to persuade the server to sup rather than the other way round.

'Coffee,' she said, pouring. 'Are you ready to order?'

Blimey! When she said 'in a moment' she meant 'in a moment'. When Julia and I were at the café and we said, 'We'll be back to take your order in a moment,' we usually only remembered about that table when we were on the bus on the way home.

We ordered. No fried slices were offered. I turned to Eamonn.

'I'm feeling bad.'

'Well, I'm not surprised after that appalling experience with Miles Mavers.'

'No, it's nothing to do with that. I feel bad because last night the subject changed to our ambitious voice coach and I didn't give you much sympathy about the Rachel situation.'

'Ah.'

'Tell me.'

'She's just not herself at the moment.' He shook his head sadly.

'In what way?'

'Well, she's lost her get up and go.'

'Eamonn, she does yoga every day, she comes to stripping with me. She never stops!'

'She never used to stop. But when she's at home she's always asleep. Haven't you noticed?'

'Well . . .' I paused. I didn't want to tell Eamonn about the near-death experience because I didn't want to worry him.

'Sarah?'

'We nearly had a crash the other day because she sort of dozed off.'

'She what? Sarah! Why didn't you tell me?'

'Eamonn, I'm hardly likely to call you and say your bird nearly totalled her hire car.'

'Well, perhaps she's ill.'

We were quiet for a few moments.

'She might be anaemic,' I suggested eventually. 'I think that makes you tired.'

'She might well be anaemic. She does look a little pale,' said Eamonn, ridiculously. Rachel Bird could never have been described as pale. Orange, yes. The colour of a crab in a tanning-booth, yes. The only way in which you could have used the word 'pale' in conjunction with Rachel Bird would have been to say that she made Peter Andre look pale.

I had another theory. Rachel Bird could be depressed. She was sleeping because she didn't want to face the world. She was used to being someone in her own right. Admittedly, that someone was a sexually depraved ex-convent girl. But she'd become Eamonn Nigels's lady friend. And she'd moved all the way to LA to be with him and he was ignoring her. But how could I say all this to Eamonn? 'You've made your bird miserable!' And what did I say to Rachel? 'Oh, cheer up, you lazy cow!'

'Hmmm.'

'Will you talk to her about it? Encourage her to go to the doctor's.'

'Yeah, she was saying something about her implant hurting as well.'

I suddenly felt my mobile phone vibrate in my back pocket.

'Eamonn!' I gasped. 'You have to pray this is Simon calling. He loves me! He's left Ruth but Ruth is cool about it because she's met a fabulously hung landscape gardener. OK?'

'Er, of course.'

'Arghhh! It's an English number. Hello?'

'How's my favourite client?'

'Oh, Geoff,' I said miserably. 'It's you.'

'Well, that's no way for my favourite client to speak to me.'

'Sorry. But you're not my boyfriend.'

'Oh, well, I'll be off then. I won't mention the incredibly well-paid commercial you have just been cast in. Bye!'

'AH! AH! What? Geoff!'

'The face of Crème de Menthe, no less.'

'NO?'

'Yes!'

'OH MY GOD!!!!!'

'Now then, I'm going to tell you how much they're paying. But I need to know you're sitting down and you're not holding any glassware.'

'Why, is it dreadful?'

'No, no. I don't think seventy-five thousand pounds is dreadful.'

'H-h-h-how much?' I whispered.

'Just over, actually. It's a worldwide campaign. And, Sarah, I don't know what you did, but they love you. I'm slightly worried they might have you confused with another actress.'

'Seventy-five thousand pounds.'

'That's right. Just over.'

'Seventy-five thousand pounds.' I was crying. I spotted the starving waitress heading our way with the breakfasts. 'I'd better go, Geoff!'

It was almost supernatural. Obviously, I'd imagined getting a commercial job before. But I'd always thought I'd be the face of an Egg McMuffin or a Whopper and I'd be paid seven hundred and fifty pounds, which wasn't even a smudge on my overdraft. But now, not only was I going to be the face of Crème de Menthe, my all-time favourite spirit, a spirit I felt shaped me as an individual, but I was being given such a large sum of money it was making me feel faint. It was thrilling and terrifying in equal measure. It was a bit like going to bed with a man who has a massive penis.

'Here's your omelette. Oh!' she said, clocking my face. 'Is everything OK?'

'She's just won a lucrative commercial. She's a bit over-whelmed,' Eamonn laughed as an explanation while I blew my nose on the serviette.

'No way!' sighed the waitress.

'I know! It's mental, mental chicken oriental!' I sobbed.

'Wow. I just asked the universe to get me a commercial job!'

'R-i-i-i-ght.'

She was wacky. I wondered whether it was a symptom or cause of the vinegar diet. It would have been wrong to ask.

'Oh my God. I just read *The Secret*. And that's what I asked! I just asked the universe to get me a commercial job. It feels really meant to be that I should witness your news today!'

'Er, I don't suppose you have any English mustard?' asked Eamonn.

'What is this thing? *The Secret*?'

'It's a book. You basically ask for what you want and then you believe it and it happens.'

'Do you think it would help me get my ex-boyfriend back?'

'Yeeeaaas!'

'Even if he's with his ex-girlfriend who is carrying his baby?'

She scrunched her face.

'It's worth a try.'

'Er, the English mustard?'

She scurried away. I gloated that even perfect waitresses forget mustard. When she reappeared, she left a jar of English mustard by Eamonn and a book called *The Secret* next to me.

❤ *fifty-six* ❤

Ask the universe for what you want and the universe will give it to you! Piece of piss! I wished I'd thought of that and written a book about it.

'Right then, Universe, world-type thing. If you're not too busy, please could you make Simon love me again?' I whispered.

Job done. I stared at my reflection. My reflection stared back. Neither of us looked impressed by the view. I didn't know how you're expected to feel having just tried to cadge stuff off the universe, and you can call me demanding, but I at least expected a tingle. As it was, I felt nothing. I could probably have mustered a more emotional response if I'd just asked the bloke at the Halifax when a cheque would be cleared. Although I wouldn't need to be doing that after this commercial. Blimey. It hadn't sunk in. I was still cowering in the corner at the sight of the big willy.

I decided it wasn't dramatic enough to talk to the universe in the ladies' loo under fluorescent light having just had a pee. So I washed my hands and then, rather than heading up to my room, I walked out of the hotel and onto the beach.

It was overcast and drizzly and there was such a nip in the air that I could see my breath. Not really. It was boiling. I wandered across the sand trying to find a suitably thespian position to entreat the cosmos. I decided that one of the raised wooden lifeguard lookouts would be perfect. Very *Baywatch*. I would stand looking out to sea like C. J. I made my way up the walkway and turned and faced the sea.

'Helloooo! Great Universe! Wonderful as you are, I was wondering . . .'

I stopped there. I doubted the universe was moved by flattery. I don't think it really has self-esteem issues. The book said I needed to be firm and clear. I prepared to go again. I definitely felt more dramatic up there, addressing Creation from my lifeguard lookout pulpit.

'OK, Universe. Please, please. I don't want Simon to be with Ruth, I want him to be with me. ARGGGHHH!'

A very tanned homeless man had just grabbed my ankle. He didn't look happy. I'd woken him up. I felt bad. I hate people waking me up.

'Sorry, sorry,' I muttered, running away.

I plonked myself on the sand and started to flick through the book. I stared at a chapter I hadn't seen. The book said that you can't say anything negative when you ask for stuff because the universe won't hear the negative. It will think you want what you don't want. For example, 'I don't want Simon to be with Ruth,' will be heard as, 'I want Simon to be with Ruth.'

'Tittie wank,' I sighed. 'Right. That'll be take three. Universe, please ignore all previous efforts.'

I closed my eyes. I relaxed. I focused. I sat listening to the breeze and my breath and I waited until it felt right to speak.

'Universe,' I said simply. 'Simon and I are soulmates. Please bring him back to me.'

I imagined my words floating on the wind. I hoped they'd bump into fate and she would sort it all out. I sat for a while with my eyes closed, feeling the sun on my cheeks.

When I finally opened them again a surfer was walking up the beach in my direction. He was lit brilliantly from behind by the sun. His powerful legs were striding through the wash. His long hair was wet. Water sparkled on his wet-suit like diamante. He could have been a Greek god rising from the sea having slain creatures in the underworld, carrying his surfboard like a shield. He looked a lot like the male version of Catwoman.

'That would be Catman, Sarah,' I muttered.

He'd obviously just dropped into LA to show men how being a man should be done. Once out of the wash, he threw the surfboard down onto the wet sand, reached behind him and unzipped his wet suit. He leant forward and slowly unpeeled it from his torso and arms. As I was staring, I realized two things:

1 My mouth was stuck open like I was taking a bite of a hot dog
2 The man I was gawping at was Leo Clement

I responded as most hot-blooded women would. I said the words, 'Fuck me,' to myself and texted a friend. I picked up my mobile.

> Talk about sight-seeing! Leo Clement is down on the beach in a half-pulled-up wetsuit! Drool! Blimey! Rippling wet muscles . . . think I need the kiss of life!

As I was scrolling through the numbers to get to Rachel's I pondered on whether the universe sent me Leo then as temptation. I had asked for Simon and the cheeky bugger sent me a Leo sideshow to test my resolve.

'Well, Mr Universe, pretty as this man is, he's nothing compared to my Si.'

This got me thinking about my Si in a half-pulled-up wetsuit. I imagined Si doing that peeling-off-the-wetsuit routine with the sun behind him. I smiled. But then my face dropped suddenly. I grabbed my mobile. Oh please, God, please tell me I didn't. But of course I did. I'd sent that text to Simon.

❤ *fifty-seven* ❤

My stripping lessons weren't going very well. I couldn't dance. My instinct wasn't to wiggle bare bits; it was to cover them up with my hands. And I had been given a pair of shoes that were so high I suspected it was an attempt at murder.

'Baby Oil. I know you're trying, sweetie. But you need to try harder,' Sunflower said, kissing me on the cheek as I left one afternoon.

'Don't worry, Sunny, I'll put her through her paces later,' sang Rachel.

I gave her a look that indicated that evenings are for drinking martinis and finding ways of making Simon love me again. But it wasn't my most effective look because she answered with the words 'I need a pee. Won't be a sec,' and ran off.

I followed her into the locker room and took the other cubicle. I made the common but disappointing error of not checking whether there was loo roll before the pee. I waved my fingers under the next cubicle where Rachel was.

'Rach, have you got any bog roll in there? I don't want to do the wiggle.'

No answer. But I hadn't heard her leave the loos.

'Rach? Are you in there?'

Rachel made a groan.

'Are you all right?'

Another groan. Followed by a retch. Followed by the dulcet tune of vomit down a toilet bowl.

'Rach? Listen, I know you're having a little chunder, but can you whack me under some loo roll?'

I waited for a while. Then I heard 'Urgh. Sare,' and the biggest retch yet. I had a good wiggle.

'Oh, bubba, you poor thing. I'll get you some water.'

I left my cubicle and got my bottle of water out of my bag and slid it under Rachel's door.

'Thanks,' she moaned. I heard her take a swig. Then ten seconds later she scored the retch hat trick.

'Nasty. What did you eat?'

'Nothing,' she groaned.

'Well, Rach, you really should do the eating thing . . .' I quickly quietened my wittering. Tired all the time, not herself, voming in the daytime. What sort of nutter was I, thinking that she was anaemic?

'Rachel, is there something you're not telling me?'

'Urgh.'

'Are you due a period or anything?'

Rachel opened the cubicle door. She was slumped on the floor and staring up at me.

'Are you pregnant?' I whispered.

She didn't answer because she had to dry retch a bit down

the loo. I held her hair back because that's what girls do. When she'd finished she shook her head.

'But we haven't had sex for ages.'

'Have you done a test?'

She shook her head sadly.

'Shall we get one?'

She shrugged.

'I don't know what's wrong with me,' she groaned.

'You're up the duff, love.'

She looked like she would attack me if she didn't have to stick her head in the toilet one last time.

'Come on, sweetie, let's go to the chemist and get you a test.'

She started shaking her head.

'What's up?'

'I'm not peeing on a stick for twenty-five bucks. I'll go to a doctor.'

'Fair enough.'

Then she looked at me. And Rachel Bird, strong, mad, always sorted Rachel Bird looked weak and tired and scared. I hugged her. We were there a while.

'Will you come with me?' she whispered.

'Course.'

❤ *fifty-eight* ❤

The doctor's waiting room was the absolute polar opposite to the multicultural mayhem of mine in Camden. It looked like an upmarket Chinese restaurant. It was subtly lit. There was a huge aquarium along one wall. Copies of magazines that you wanted to read were neatly stacked in subject-related piles on a wooden table. There was a children's area that made the Early Learning Centre look Buddhist. And there was only the male receptionist, who looked like he was reading a script, us, a man whom Rachel suspected was a pervert and a mother with a little boy there. So it was very quiet. At my doctor's, there would have been one old copy of *Fabulous* and a dog-eared Iceland catalogue to fight over, nothing for a child to play with except a free booklet on cystitis, and it would have been noisy. Screaming children, punctuated by 'Pack it in!' and slaps from mothers and an elderly Italian man trying to chat up the teenage reception-ist. Eamonn Nigels must have had the Hilton of health insurance. Poor Rachel had to fill in a three-hour written exam on a clipboard and write an eye-watering cheque before we even sat down. I thought it was worth it though. They were very comfy seats.

A ridiculously attractive lady in a pressed white coat opened a door.

'Mr Washington?' she smiled. Her teeth were mozzarella-white.

'Oh my God, even the doctors here look like models!' I whispered excitedly to Rach.

We watched the middle-aged man race into the consulting room behind her.

'Bet there's nothing wrong with him. Probably just wants her to stick her finger up his arse.'

I was pleased to see that impending motherhood hadn't softened Rachel. I smiled at the small boy playing on the floor with some primary-coloured bricks.

'Hello,' I cooed. 'Aaah, is that a smile for me?' I said just as I realized that, of course, it wasn't. No. The small boy was in fact starting to cry. Even with my experience of making small children cry I didn't know what to do. Should I carry on smiling or leave well alone? I decided to keep smiling. He'd warm to me eventually. I mustn't be frightened of him. He was only two.

'Sorry,' I mouthed to his mother as she picked him up.

'I won't ask you to babysit,' whispered Rachel.

'How you feeling?'

'Weird.'

'Mummy.'

'Fuck right off,' she said beautifully. But then a tiny smile landed on her mouth and, although she tried, she couldn't get rid of it. I smiled too.

'So, let's talk about Simon – what now?'

My smile swiftly disappeared.

'I just don't know,' I sighed.

'Can't believe you sent that text.'

'Yeah, all right. I'm only taking constructive criticism at the moment.'

'OK. How do we get him back?'

'Dunno.'

'Let's write him another text.'

'No, the texts aren't working. He never responds to them.'

'Wanker.'

'Wanker,' I said, louder than I had meant to.

'Wanker,' said the little boy.

He does like me after all!

'Wanker, wanker, wanker,' I said in a voice like Yogi Bear.

'Wan . . .' started the little boy until his mummy turned his head away from me.

'I didn't think they knew what "wanker" meant here.'

'It's LA, Sarah, they love Hugh Grant.'

'Rachel?'

Another lady, late thirties, great figure, expensive shoes. Nothing like Britain.

'Leave that poor child alone while I'm gone,' Rachel joked as she got up. I grinned and nodded. But I wished I found it funny. I was crap with kids. And everyone was having them. You get to thirty, and bam: babies. I needed to get over my baby phobia. If Simon and I were to have a future his baby had to like me. I would have played with the little boy again but his mother had moved him from my sight and was now reading him a story. I picked up the *Hollywood Reporter* instead, and found myself engrossed in an article about Dolph Wax's spiritualist. Eventually Rachel opened the door and reappeared. I looked at her in anticipation.

'No baby,' she said sadly, coming over.

'Oh.'

'Yeah, I feel quite disappointed.'

'Oh, Rach, I'm sorry.'

'Nah, don't be. They think I might be anaemic.'

'Oh.'

'Let's go and have a martini.'

'Cool.'

'The thought of a teetotal nine months was giving me the fear.'

♥ *fifty-nine* ♥

'We can't have a fifth.'

'Why?'

'Because it's only eight o'clock and we're wankered!' I said, pulling her raised arm down so the waiter wouldn't come over.

'So?'

'I'm a professional actress.'

'Are you shooting a scene tomorrow?'

'No.'

'You don't ever shoot scenes, darling. Are you sure you're in this film?'

'Yes.'

'How many scenes are you in?'

'Four.'

'Ah, bless.'

'Oh, sod it. Let's have another.'

'Huh!' Rachel gasped. 'I've got it!'

'What?'

'We'll practise your striptease.'

'No, we bloody won't.'

'Sare, I love you, but . . . oh my God, I do quite love you.'
She did an involuntary shudder, then welled up! She lunged
towards me. 'I'm so glad you're here.'

'Me too, ya nutter. But I'm not practising my stripping.'

'Oh yeah, what was I saying? Oh yeah, your stripping.
Sarah, now listen to me, you have to practise.'

'Why?'

'Because you're not exactly Kylie up there.'

'Bitch.'

'Darling, you're not even Madge.'

'Oh.'

'Sweetheart, you're barely Bouncer.'

'Who the wank is Bouncer?'

'The dog.'

'Oooh, my phone vibrated.'

'OK. OK. Ruth, blah blah, gardener with a massive dick,'
she sang. 'Now, what does it say?'

'Oh, it's from Leo.'

'Lovely.'

'Hmmm.'

'Well, what's he saying?'

'He wants to meet to practise our scene.'

'What happens in this scene?'

'We have sex and then he kills me.'

'Sarah, you're really not the brightest, are you? Why don't
you stop pining for Simon and take your mind off things by
practising that scene. A lot! Text him now. Say yes.'

I did what I was told but my hands were shaky. I was even

more terrified of practising my scene with Leo than I was of actually shooting the scene with Leo. In a practice environment was I supposed to use tongues? Did you allow breast touching? And if the answer to those questions was yes, was that being unfaithful to Si? And if the answer was yes then I didn't want to do it. It was fine to do it with a crew and a director there because that was my job. But if we did it on our own, then it became extra-curricular. And what if, and this was the awful question, what if we did practise and I enjoyed it? What if I spent an afternoon snogging Leo Clement and I enjoyed it? Where did that leave me and Si? You see, I didn't trust myself not to enjoy it. Leo was gorgeous. And there was something about his lips and his eyes and his broadness that told me it would be lovely to kiss him. And if I kissed him and enjoyed it I knew that I would be wracked with guilt and bad things would happen to me.

'When are you going to meet him for shag practice?'

'Don't call it that.'

'Shag practice.'

'Tomorrow afternoon.'

'What are you going to wear?'

'It's a rehearsal! What does it matter?' I exclaimed, having already thought of that question and panicked.

'Come on, get up, Bouncer, and practise your strip routine. There's no one around.'

We were on the hotel bar terrace. I looked around. It was deserted.

'No.'

'Woof.'

'All right. But I'm just doing the moves.'

I stood in front of Rachel Bird. That was tricky enough after four martinis. I started a very lacklustre routine.

'Sarah! Look like you enjoy it, at least a little bit.'

'My character doesn't enjoy her job.'

'Clearly. But if she did it like that she wouldn't have a job!'

'Am I that bad?'

'Truthfully?'

'Yes.'

'You're worse.'

'Bugger.'

'Pretend I'm Si.'

'No,' I said sadly. 'That's cruel.'

'Come on. I'm Si.' She sat back in her chair like a bloke. 'Rach, stop being a freak.'

'Come on, Sare,' she said gruffly, doing a terrible impression of my Si.

I blame the four neat vodka drinks I had drunk to wash down my four-olive dinner. But I stood in front of her trying to imagine what Simon looked like. His face didn't appear for ages. I couldn't have forgotten what he looked like.

Suddenly he was there in my mind. And it was lovely. He was smiling. Which was nice because I was sure in real life he wouldn't be smiling at me. He'd probably be sticking pins in a doll of me while discussing school catchment areas with Ruth. But in my imagination he was smiling at me in a saucy way.

'Getting a bit of a semi, babe,' he said.

I smiled.

'It'll be a bloody maxi after you've seen my hot stripping routine.'

(I was speaking in my head – Rachel would never have let me live it down otherwise.)

Simon laughed and pretended to adjust his four-foot penis in his pants. I started my opening breast jiggle.

'Cor, wiggle those Bobbie Davroes!'

(Simon had called breasts Bobby Davroes since he was about sixteen.)

I wiggled and rocked my boobs about, then I moved towards him/Rachel and started maniacally pretending to slap him round the head with them.

'Steady on there, Sare, you'll have an eye out,' he laughed.

Leaving his head alone, I did an over-acted Sunflower Oil hip-stomping wiggle around my stage/small area between bar tables. Then I pretended to take off a stocking while making a come face. I stomped back to Simon with the stocking and placed it round his neck.

'Babe, you wanna do something about that athlete's foot.'

I took the other stocking off and teased it over his penis, which was now six feet long. Then I got on the floor for my downward dog move where I pumped my bottom up and down in his direction. It was my least favourite move as I looked like a pillock and it was agony. But on that evening it was the most fun I'd had in ages.

'Hit me with those ping-pong balls!' Simon cried.

I started to make ping-pong-ball-out-of-fanny noises even though I had no idea what these are.

Simon was saying something but I couldn't hear him.

'What?' I said, stopping still with my bottom in the air. Then I realized that I couldn't hear Simon because his voice was in my head. So the male voice I heard couldn't belong to Simon. It must belong to someone real. It was bound to be a waiter or the manager.

'Sarah! Meet Erin's dad! Pastor Schneider,' cried Rachel with glee.

'Wha . . . ?' I gasped, spinning round and getting up and then stumbling over again elegantly.

'Sarah!' smiled Erin.

'Erin!' I rushed forward and gave her a hug. Mr Schneider didn't look impressed.

'Mr Schneider, I'm Sarah.' I held out my hand. 'Pleased to meet you. Excuse me there, I was practising a, er, routine for the film.'

He looked nothing like I imagined. He didn't look like a vicar. Well, not like the English vicars I've seen who tend to be described with terms like 'morbidly obese' and 'pasty'. Erin's dad looked coiffed. He had clearly just dyed his hair because there was a brown smear around his hairline. He'd got a better tan than Jay-Z and he was wearing a polo shirt. If I hadn't known who he was I would have said he was a sexually deviant golf pro. He ignored my hand, looked at Rachel as though he couldn't quite place her and then turned to Erin.

'We'll be late.'

Erin looked mortified by his rudeness.

'We've got a prayer meeting. See you later,' she whispered, and skipped off to catch him up.

'Well, Sarah!' Rachel gushed. 'You have very nearly got it!'

'What?'

'This stripping lark!'

'But I was taking the piss!'

'Right, now that's sorted, let's work out what you're going to wear for shag practice!'

♥ *sixty* ♥

I like summer. But I hate the wardrobe. I, Sarah Sargeant, am a winter wardrobe woman. I love a winter wardrobe. It gives you the confidence of three mulled wines on a Boots Shapers sandwich. I love my hold-you-in tights that I estimate take off two arse inches. I feel contentment when the cellulite on my arms is safely ensconced under a jumper and coat. I can relax when I wrap a scarf around my neck and hide my double chins. I step confidently in boots knowing they hide my Wayne Rooney calves. In winter, I can wear high heels to make me look thinner. But summer. Summer! Where do I put my cellulity arms? Do I let the dough folds flap freely in a vest top or do I cover them up with a sweat-ringed shirt? And what do I do with my arse? Do I let it lollop around under a flimsy bit of floral material? Because if I do, summer dictates I should team said unflattering floral skirt with flat sandals. I repeat: flat sandals! Do I wear flat sandals and shuffle dumpily around as the imitation leather blisters and scabs my feet? The only good thing about summer is that you get to wear sunglasses. A pair of sunglasses never makes you look fat. You see, in England, I can get away with winter clothes in the summer. I can go out in July in a polo neck and tights, sweat a bit, but say, 'Oh, it was freezing when I left the house.' And people will nod and understand. But there, in LA where it was constantly hotter than a Pop Tart, I could not.

So what was I supposed to wear to meet Leo for our rehearsal on the beach? I couldn't cope with the question. All I could do was put my head back under the covers and scream, 'Leo! Beach! Gah!' repeatedly. Deciding what to wear when you are meeting The Most Handsome Man In The Universe™ was Pythagorean in its difficulty already, without adding the fact I was meeting him on a blinking beach! I picked up my phone. The only answer was perjury. I had to text him and tell him I was ill. The clock on my phone said I was meeting him in twelve minutes!

'BUGGER!'

That scuppered that plan. I didn't mind telling a whopper. But I went to a convent. I didn't want him to think I was rude. I had to meet him. I got out of bed. I looked at my reflection.

'NO!'

I pulled off the floral skirt and vest top. But then I caught sight of me in a bikini in the mirror.

'WHY DIDN'T YOU DIET???' I shouted at my reflection. 'You were always planning to diet, weren't you? And then you just got a bit distracted by food. Now look at you. With your beach meetings and stripping scenes! THAT'LL TEACH YOU!'

I pulled on a maxi-dress.

'No, you'll trip over the bloody thing and then your boobs'll fall out, and YOU LOOK LIKE LORRAINE KELLY!!' I took the maxi-dress off again. It was like Britney backstage. I was starting to sweat. I suddenly understood why people in LA got into prescription drugs.

'Seven minutes!' I panted.

I was flushed. It looked like I'd been masturbating. The clock moved in front of me. Six minutes!

'Gah! Sort it out, Sarah. You dick,' I hollered.

'Right, breathe.' I breathed. 'It doesn't matter. He's ugly. And you have got a seamless plan to stop you enjoying the kissing. You worked it all out when you woke up dehydrated this morning, remember? Now breathe and put some bloody clothes on because you only have five minutes. I SAID, BREATHE!'

I picked up my old tatty, were-briefly-in-fashion-when-I-was-seventeen-and-never-came-round-again, cut-off above the knee jeans. I put on a white shirt that I had slept in once. I sat on the bed to put on my flesh-cutter sandals. I heard a crunch under my bottom. I pulled out my broken sunglasses and said the word, 'Bollocks!' with feeling.

❤ *sixty-one* ❤

Leo Clement didn't worry about what to wear that day. Leo Clement didn't contemplate sending a text with the words

sore throat and swollen glands

in it. He just threw on a pair of surfing shorts. That is because Leo was a professional. Although it had to be said he didn't do up the surfing shorts quite tight enough. They were sitting very low.

We practised our lines repeatedly. To the point where even I, who am a major shareholder in Self-Deprecation, was able to say that the scene was sounding 'not bad'. There had been no talk of practising the physical stuff. No lip-to-lip contact. His muscular, slightly surfing-calloused, tanned hand hadn't gently brushed my breast. I hadn't felt those thigh muscles, smooth and hard like stale ciabattas, tense against me. Although my mouth had spent a lot of time open in the hot dog position.

'We don't have to if you don't feel comfortable.'

He had been speaking. That was the thing with Leo; he was perfect to look at and seemed like a very nice young man, as my mum would say. But he talked like he was tired and had just done a skunk bong and I normally switched off after the first 'Hey,' and just watched his lips move.

'Sorry. I was miles away.'

'Oh, well, I was wondering . . .'

Such beautiful lips, the colour of nearly ripe cherries. Pay attention, Sarah, I thought. I was acting like an Italian man. Giovanni, pack it in.

'If you wanted to do the, er, you know, if you feel comfortable.'

I suspected he was talking about the naughty bits. He was gesturing to me and then to him uncomfortably in a way that implied he wanted to practise the rude stuff.

'Oh!' I started to gesticulate to him and also to me and then I did an abstract swirly command, which I hoped indicated getting jiggy with it. Then I added the words, 'The, er, bits with the, er?' to make it clearer.

'Yeah.'

Blimey.

'Oh. OK,' I squeaked.

'Cool,' he nodded seriously.

'If you do. For practice. I mean, I'm cool if you're cool.' In hindsight, a ludicrous thing to say because in no sense of the word could I be described as cool. I was breezeblock-size bricking it about kissing that man.

Leo leant towards me.

'Are you ready?'

Shit. Fuck. No. My plan. What was my plan? I remembered.

Only my plan didn't sound like much fun all of a sudden. In fact my brilliant plan suddenly held as much appeal as a vegan diet. Next time I woke at 4 a.m. to drink two pints of water from the bathroom tap in quick succession and decided while I was at it to come up with a plan I should remember to come up with a Plan B.

'Yeah,' I nod to Leo.

I got my mouth ready in the snake kisser position. I'm not proud. But this was my plan. If I had to kiss Leo, then I was going to make sure it was terrible. I had decided that I would only be being unfaithful to Simon if I kissed him like Sarah Sargeant. So I wouldn't kiss him like I would normally. Not that I would ever have got the chance to kiss Leo Clement in real life, I mean possibly, maybe, if I had been single and I somehow managed to snog him, say, in a night-club in the very early hours, when he was on a stag weekend and there were no other women in a five-mile radius and he'd been living in an Indian ashram for the preceding nine-teen years. Anyway, I vowed to snog him in the manner of my character, Taylor, who wasn't very good at kissing. Bless her. She kissed like a snake. Lips shut for the most part, like kiss-ing a bum hole. Although lots of people liked that, so I didn't want to make it too pleasant. I would very occasion-ally dart my tense tongue out but only if absolutely necessary. Because I mustn't enjoy it. I mustn't get carried away.

'So, I join you here, and then I thought I might touch your face like this.'

I watched his hand move towards my cheek. Then I felt his coarse fingers on my skin. He moved his head so that it was level with mine. And he kept it there. And he just looked at me. He was simply holding my face and looking at me. He didn't move in for one of my amazing snake kisses. We simply stared at each other. I got the far better deal in this looking-at-each-other business. His lips were slightly parted. And I decided that his eyes were very kind. Blue, piercing and all the other wanky words you use to describe gorgeous men's eyes. But, more than any of them, kind. Mind you, I am a terrible judge of character; I used to think Tony Blair was quite a nice man.

My lips were slightly parted as well, which was bad because they should have been tightly closed for a snake kiss. We were still staring at each other. It had been ages already. I wanted to shut my eyes. But then I wanted to savour it too. Because it was sexy. All right. Very sexy. Don't tell Simon, but this man had taken sexy to a rooftop bar at sunset and bought her a drink. Actually, no, she bought him a drink and said, 'I take my hat off to you.' Our breathing had reached the same rhythm. Every time we breathed out together it felt as though we were melting into each other. Eventually, he leant in further and my parted lips moved to welcome his. We did some small kisses as we got to know each other's fleshy bottom lips. When we kissed it even sounded right. Perfect little 'mchau' sounds.

Shitit!!!!! I suddenly remembered the snake kiss. I pursed my lips shut quickly. Leo was surprised. He stopped and looked at me again. Then he used his finger and thumb to trace my lips, which was very sneaky because it meant I had to relax them. I couldn't very well let him do that if my mouth was pursed shut like a sphincter. Once my mouth was relaxed again he started to kiss me as before. And I put my hand in his hair. It felt a bit odd at first, like fondling a girl's head. I thought of Katy Perry because I liked it. We kissed and then we stopped kissing and just pressed our cheeks together and breathed in each other's ear. Then we carried on kissing. Suddenly Leo's hand went down to my boob and it all changed. He'd gone for a boob grope. The cheeky fecker. What was his name, Russell Brand? I pulled away suddenly. I was panting a bit, which was embarrassing.

'No,' I said breathlessly.

'Oh, but it says in the script . . .' he started.

And it was then that I remembered the film we were rehearsing for.

sixty-two

She's definitely a maniac!

You'll be brilliant today! Just remember to keep thinking about Simon!

You go girl!

Rachel! (Had to put an exclamation mark after my name because for some reason I've started putting bloody exclamation marks after everything else!!!!)

PS. I'd have asked you to be godmother.

I held Rachel's note in my shaking hand.

'Are you decent?' shouted Eamonn, knocking on my dressing room door.

'That's debatable.'

'How you feeling about this? Do you want a drink?' he said, opening the door a fraction and peeking in.

'What you got?

'I have brought along my special lady-about-to-take-her-clothes-off hip flask.' Eamonn walked in and took a silver hip flask from his back pocket.

'What's in it?'

'Whisky.'

I scrunched my face up.

'Pah. I hate whisky.'

Eamonn put the flask back in his pocket.

'Wait! That doesn't mean I won't drink it!'

He handed it back to me and I took a swig.

'Ew!'

It sounded like an army was marching past my dressing room. Eamonn huffed, then walked to the door and opened it.

'The ego has landed. Look at this wanker,' he sighed.

'Who?' I giggled, because Eamonn just shouldn't say words like 'wanker' or 'dickhead' or 'knob'. He was too old.

'Dolph "I have a responsibility to my fans, Eamonn, I can't say that line – where's my lawyer?" Wax.'

'Oh my God, is he there!' I screamed, jumping up. 'Where is he?'

'Somewhere in the middle of that coterie,' Eamonn said, pointing to a cluster of briskly marching people in smart clothes.

'Who the fuck are they?'

'Oh, the hairdresser, the chef, the lawyer, the bloke who beats the bongo drums so Dolph can find his inner child every time I want to shoot a scene!'

'Oh, that sounds like fun.'

'Yes, Sarah, it's a hoot,' Eamonn said fiercely, taking out his hip flask again and having a swig. 'Maybe we should all join him. I could do with finding my inner child.'

'The thing is, Eamonn, I'm not very good with children.'

'You surprise me, Sarah, I thought you'd be very good with children,' he said, and I think he meant it.

'Ah, Eamonn, thanks.'

'You being such a big kid yourself.'

'Should have known that was coming.'

'Come and meet the extras.' He took my hand and led me out of my dressing area and into the studio.

'This is Sarah Sargeant. The actress who'll be playing Taylor and dancing for you.'

I smiled weakly at what looked like the cast of *One Flew Over the Cuckoo's Nest*. They all clapped politely. I did a mock curtsey.

'Now, that's Darren, in the wheelchair there.'

'Hi, Darren,' I said, taking in the twenty-seven-stone man in a specially made wheelchair. He had a head like a joint of lamb. I had to put my stocking around Darren's head later. I reminded myself that the action should be titillation rather than strangulation.

'Hello. I have a bad leg. Just thought I'd warn you in case you wanted to climb on me.'

'Oh,' I scoffed. 'I won't be climbing on you. Or I hadn't planned to. But I'll try not to get too carried away!'

'OK, we'll mark it through with the music. We may have to do this quite a few times. Bear with us. There'll be a lot of action. People moving to and from the bar and a fight we've plotted. You'll have a few cameras, so just do your thing in that area and we'll move round you.'

'OK.'

What did you do at work today, Sarah? Oh, I took all my clothes off in front of about a hundred men. Lovely, darling.

I took some very deep breaths. A costume lady came and looked up my dress to check that my flesh-coloured body-suit was in place to protect people from pubes.

'How are your nipples?' she whispered.

I groped myself to check that the Nicorette-like patches were still over them.

'I think they're still there, thank you.'

'Atta girl.'

'Sadly, Sarah . . .' shouted Eamonn. I couldn't see him. I couldn't see much because there was a massive light in my eyes and lots of dry ice stuff. 'You will need to take your clothes off for these practices.'

'OK!'

'Oh, Sarah, darling. I understand you have some rhythm problems. Don't worry about keeping in time with the music. We sort that out in the edit. OK?'

♥

I did get carried away!

'Do you think I should press his head into my breasts?' I said these words. I was vampily straddling the wheelchair with my dress riding up.

'Try it.'

I grabbed Darren by the head and then I shook my boobs

in front of his face. It was my inner Madonna coming out. Terrifying!

'Great, keep it!' shouted Eamonn.

'Ahhhh,' cried Darren.

'Oh shit, did I get your bad leg?'

'My neck.'

'Oh, sorry.'

'I've got torticollis.'

It sounded like something you have with a dip. I stared blankly down at Darren's head.

'Ahhhh.'

He didn't look happy. His head was at a 45-degree angle. I clambered gently off him.

'Sorry.'

'I need my neck brace.'

'Um, Eamonn. I think I've killed Darren.'

'OK, everyone relax,' shouted Eamonn. Someone wheeled Darren off to find his neck brace. I looked sheepish and put my dressing gown on. Eamonn approached.

'Eamonn, I'm so sorry,' I whispered.

Eamonn didn't respond. He was looking past me and not saying anything. I froze. Eamonn would never work with me again and Darren would probably sue me.

'Eamonn.'

He ignored me again.

'Eamonn! I'm really, really sorry.'

'I'm trying not to laugh, Sarah.'

'Oh, OK.'

Darren was wheeled back on. They'd somehow managed to put the neck brace on even with his head at that angle, which must have been tricky.

'It's actually going to look great,' whispered Eamonn, studying Darren.

'You are such a bastard.'

'Right, we'll go again. Without the breasts in Darren's face. Sarah, if you could arrange not to injure any cast members this time that would be most appreciated. We'll go for a take this time. One thing, Sarah: you're going dangerously close to that cable there when you do that crawl around the floor at the end of the routine. I don't want you to trip when you stand up. I'd like to limit the amount of neck braces being worn in the studio if we possibly can. Have a look now where it is.'

I looked at the cable.

'Eamonn, I've got it.' And then I tutted. 'I'm a professional.'

'And AAAACTION!'

I heard the opening beats. I started bobbing my head and prowling around the stage. I made eye contact with the uglier members of the audience. I'd picked them out earlier. I knew what I was like around good-looking people. I had discovered that the key to me doing the striptease is to:

1   pretend it's a piss take
2   pretend Simon is there, making me smile
3   pretend I am a fully dressed eighties power rocker and

318

disguise all mistakes with an eighties power rock
move or an eighties power rock pout

Ooops, little stumble. Make it a shimmy. 'Nothing's Gonna
Stop Us Now'. It was fun. Perhaps I did feel the empower-
ment that Sunflower had talked about. Although it was
more like the time I drank four WKD and came home and
danced in my lounge to Heart FM.

I summoned my Si when I had to start touching myself
as though no one was looking. Not that I do touch myself
like that when no one is looking. I'm hardly going to put on
heels and wipe my hands over my boobs with a facial expression as though a dog has just bitten my foot.

'Oh yes, she's a maniac!' Si piped up. I blew him a kiss.
I teased my dress up but wobbled on my heels. Nothing a bit
of heartfelt power ballad swaying couldn't get me out of.

'Pissed again.'

I gave him a sexy growl.

'Time to get on the floor and pop those ping-pong balls
out, babe.'

I turned round and attempted to do a downward dog
sexily. Then I pumped up and down.

'Shit, babe, that landed in Jay's beer. Did I not tell you he
was coming round?'

The boys cheered as told. I put my bum on the floor and
swung round. I took a stocking off and crawled over to
Darren. I eyeballed him. He looked in pain. I couldn't take
my stocking off and put it around a neck brace! Taylor

would look like she was mocking the afflicted if she did that. Sorry, Darren. He tensed as I approached. So I was very gentle. More cheers when the stocking went around his neck without a need to call Casualty. Then I went back into the centre to whip it all off and start hotting it up. I was stomping and taking all my clothes off. I did my crawl around the floor. I managed to avoid the wire. I'd done it! I'd bloody done it! It was the homeward stretch. Now all I needed to do was patrol the men for cash.

There were only a few plasters, a pair of shoes and my knickers between me and my birthday suit. I stuck my beer glass in front of the men. If they didn't give me money I pretended to get riled. I picked a ten-dollar note out of the glass and kissed it. Then I moved on to the next person with it in my mouth, hoping he'd match it. But the next punter was Leo Clement in a black wig. I needed to hold eye contact with him. Suddenly I was back on the beach kissing him. I thought about Simon. And at that point I could have screamed at Simon. I tried to get back into the scene. Leo clearly wasn't giving me any money, so I did a dramatic pissed-off stomp away. Brilliantly Beyoncé. I was at the end. Thank you, God. I turned and gave Leo one last glare before the music stopped. I picked up my back foot. It didn't move. However my front foot had already carried on. I tried to grab hold of something. Which was unfortunately Darren's bad leg. He screamed. I shouted, 'Fuuuuck!' And before I knew it, I had landed spread-eagled across the stage, beer glass shattered and money everywhere.

As I put my head in my hands I heard Eamonn saying, 'Smashing, that was smashing.' I looked up as Darren was wheeled away and Eamonn started to convulse above me.

♥ *sixty-three* ♥

There were positives and negatives. On the negative side: I had sprained my ankle.

However, on the positive side: I had been given prescription drugs by a personal physician. So I think the positive won. I felt like Marilyn.

There was a knock on my door.

'How's the ankle?'

'Swollen, but I'm floating, so hey.' I held the ice in place on the ankle and turned around to see which runner I was talking to now. Cor blimey. It wasn't a runner. It was Dolph Bloody Wax, star, as you doubtless already know, of those subtle philosophical masterpieces of modern cinema, the *Absolute Destruction* series. He plays a character called Baptiste Fury who kills everyone before saving a baby to violin music, bonking its mother and then buggering off to do more butchering in the sequel. Thought I'd better explain in case you had it confused with something French.

'Swollen.'

'I haven't laughed like that in years. And it's good to laugh.'

I could have broke me leg!

'Oh yes, there's nothing like a good laugh.'

'It's a medicine. A tonic. In this industry, if you don't laugh . . .'

'You take prescription drugs?'

He gave me a sharp look; I feared I had touched a nerve. So I smiled, which made him smile.

'Oh, a joke. You're funny.'

'I'm a hoot.'

'Did you hear I'm having a party for us all?'

'No.'

'Next Friday. I just wanted us all to get to know each other away from the mechanics of film. Time to really interact, swap experiences. This is a journey. We're struggling to achieve our aim but . . .' He stopped here for effect. I waited and wondered what chicken nugget of wisdom Dolph would impart now.

'We are human.' He said this with a nod and a smile.

Brilliant, Dolph. I wasn't sure, but you cleared that up for me.

'We are human, Dolph,' I repeated emphatically.

'Yar, we are all human and we need to stop and refresh ourselves on the way.' Dolph had started laughing. So I figured that was a little attempt at humour.

'Ha, yes, very, very true. We are indeed all human.'

He suddenly stopped laughing.

'You get it,' he said seriously.

'Yes, I do. Oh gosh, I get it.'

'And I love your accent.'

'Thanks.'

'Great accent.'

'Thanks. I'll tell my mum.'

'I like you.' As he said this he did a disco-move finger-point in my direction. This was great. Floaty painkillers and a truly mad Hollywood Star. I thought of Simon. He would have found Dolph Wax hysterical. That was the first time I'd thought of Simon today. Except doing the striptease for him. But I hadn't done my usual forty-five thoughts a second along the lines of, 'Oh, I miss him, oh, I buggered it up, oh, I want him to call.' I decided to think about him lots for the rest of the day. I didn't want him to think I was going off him.

'Sar . . . Oh, hi, Dolph.' It was Leo Clement. Dolph took Leo's hand and shook it. Leo was minus the wig but still in the costume. Black tight jeans, cowboy boots, black leather jacket. It was quite Kurt Cobain. But clean. And sexy. Obviously. Just once, for the novelty, it would be nice to see Leo look crap.

Blimey, Dolph had still got hold of Leo's hand. It was getting on for a fifteen-second hand clasp. When he eventually stopped that he put a hand on Leo's back, but he wasn't doing masculine back-clapping; he was just patting it. Actually, it was more of a stroke than a pat.

'Sarah, how's your leg?' asked Leo, extricating himself from the man embrace and coming over to me.

'Um,' I wanted to say something witty. Actually, forget

witty, anything would have done. But I couldn't think of any words, because me and Leo on the beach was coming back to me. 'Um, good, thanks.'

'See you at the party, you two!' shouted Dolph as he left. Leo sighed.

'I think you have an admirer.'

'What?'

'Dolph. I think he likes you.' Because I hadn't progressed much from the playground I sang 'I think he likes you' as though I was seven.

'Huh?'

'I think Dolph likes you. Likes you, likes you.' It probably goes without saying but I did the seven-year-old sing for 'likes you, likes you'.

'I wouldn't say that around here,' whispered Leo.

'Why?' I whisper back.

'Because according to his publicist, who is somewhere round here, he is a straight Hollywood actor.'

'Ah, a straight Hollywood actor,' I nod. 'One of those straight Hollywood actors who likes boys.'

'Hmmm. Will you protect me at the party?'

Oh dear. The party was on the night after Leo and I filmed our sexy scene and I was really hoping to avoid Leo from then on. It was just too obvious that I thought he was beautiful and that kissing him was one of the most sensual things I had ever done. And I wanted to be beyond that. I wanted to be his dumpy English friend. I didn't want to be like all the other girls he met. I didn't want to stare at him with my gob open like an accident-prone loon. I wanted to be shaken-martini cool around him so that we could be friends and have a laugh. But that was completely out of the question because when I was around Leo I was about as cool as PVC-clad bollock.

'Don't worry, Leo. I'll protect you,' I said.

And he smiled. And I smiled. And we held the look and then our breathing started to get in synch again.

I looked away quickly and started thinking about Simon.

♥ *sixty-four* ♥

That afternoon I had hours to kill. I was at a clinic waiting for Rachel to finish having more anaemia tests done. As it's impossible to have happy thoughts in hospitals, I let my mind get on the crap-thought roundabout. And of course I thought about Simon.

I tried to imagine what he was doing. I guessed he was racing around trying to shift his Viagra product. I bet he'd already bought a baby Tottenham Hotspur outfit. I could see him touching her tummy and whispering stories and jokes to the bump. I thought about them in bed at night, her and her bump taking up just a tiny corner as she slept silently like an impregnated angel.

I wondered if he was happy with his choice. And whether he thought of me and, if he did, in what context. I suspected that if he ever spoke of me my name would be preceded by the word 'nightmare' and closely followed by the word 'nutter'. I wondered whether he'd been back to the flat and taken his stuff. And if he had, would there be a note waiting for me? And what would it say?

And I wondered whether I'd be happy again soon. I'd never had the highest self-esteem but now it felt as though it was underneath the sole of my bandaged foot.

They really do things properly in the States. I thought they'd just give Rachel a prescription and she'd be off. But we must have been in that surgery for hours and hours.

I dozed off and woke to see Rachel and a doctor walking towards me. They didn't say anything. I must have sensed they were coming. Rachel looked wired. Her eyes were open really wide and there was a far-away look there that I couldn't place.

I was disappointed that the male doctor didn't look like George Clooney. He more resembled the villain from *The Simpsons*. He was wiry and slightly hunched like he was about to walk into an olde worlde low-ceilinged tearoom.

'Are you Rachel's friend?'

'Yes,' I said, getting up. 'Yes, I am.'

'Would you mind joining us in here for a moment?'

'No, no, of course not.' As we walked I took Rachel's hand like the nuns used to make us do at school. I'm not sure exactly why I did this but it suddenly felt very wrong to sing 'Anaemia' to the tune of 'Insomnia' as I had been doing all morning.

'Now then,' said Mr Burns. 'It is anaemia as we thought.'

Rachel sighed and I started doing some bad singing.

'However, as is often the case, the anaemia is brought on by an underlying health problem. And in your case, we have to be relieved that it has brought it to our attention. Because we have to act quickly.'

What's this, the bloody trailer? Get to the point, doctor.

'We are looking at breast cancer, as feared.'

Oh no. Not that point. Don't get to that point ever, doctor. Why didn't he say something else?

'My personal method of attacking this would be a mastectomy as soon as possible. It will immediately be followed by chemotherapy. The key here is to stop it spreading to the lymph nodes, if it hasn't already, and therefore round the body. I understand this is a huge shock but, on a positive, you are in a very good place.'

I glanced at Rachel; she was staring at Mr Burns. He did a slow, doctorly sympathetic head-nod thing. It was deathly quiet in there, until I started breathing through my nose and twitching. I felt like punching something. She was thirty-two. Not that I wanted it to happen to anyone older. But she was only thirty-two. And she did yoga every day. It was just wrong.

'Fuck,' I said. 'Sorry, sorry, I didn't mean to say that out loud.'

Rachel started to laugh.

'My friend Sarah, she knows exactly what to say in any situation. Yes. Fuck. Fuck. Fuck. Fuck. Fuck . . .'

I think Mr Burns was a bit worried that Rachel wouldn't stop saying 'fuck', but he managed to stop the 'fuck's by saying, 'I quite agree.'

'Fuck,' said Rachel again, but it was just the one.

'Like I said, you're in a good place,' nodded Mr Burns.

Rachel sat blinking at him.

'Well, team tumour, let's fight this fucker,' I said.

I still cringe to think I said it.

♥ *sixty-five* ♥

Rachel didn't call Eamonn or her mum and she didn't cry. But she did howl, out of rage. Rachel was furious. I have never seen anything like it. It was anger that could have powered the national grid.

She didn't want to go home. She wanted to go shopping. So we went to a posh clothing shop. I can't remember the name of the place or where it was. It reminded me of Fenwick, except that in Fenwick I might have been able to afford one or two things. Those prices detonated any budget I'd ever had in my life. Rachel strode through the store roughly handling designer clothes, muttering, 'My stupid body, my stupid body, I so looked after it, and what does it go and do?' over and over again.

'Rach, do you want to go somewhere and talk?' I asked quietly, as I unwrapped a leather belt that she'd coiled round her fist.

'No, no. I want to buy you a present!'

'Rach, you don't need to buy me a present.'

'Let me!'

'No.'

'I'm going to buy you a dress to wear for Dolph's party.'

'But Rach . . .'

'I've got cancer, don't argue with me.'

'Oh, I see how it'll be.'

'Yep, and you'd better get used to it.'

'I'll do anything you want except that stripping routine again.'

'Great, because I don't want sympathy, OK?' She stopped and swallowed before she continued. 'Please. No sympathy. We can have the occasional hug. But that's it. No poor Rach. OK? Got it? No bloody sympathy.'

'Like I was going to give you sympathy. You're going to beat the bitch.' I have no idea where the hip-hop talk came from. 'You have the cancer. It is a wanker. We gonna beat it. Like an egg in an omelette,' I rapped dreadfully. It was so hard to know what to say. 'We gonna beat it. Like an egg in an omelette. Bloody genius that.'

'Try that on. And that.'

'Rach!'

'Do it now!'

She threw two beautiful dresses at me. One was navy silk and long with a halter neck and a low back, and the other was a deep red, shorter, with little straps and a cinched-in waist.

A young shop assistant approached.

'How are you doing?' she said in a particularly high register. 'Can I help you guys?'

'Yes,' barked Rachel. 'I've got cancer and my friend here . . .'

'Oh, I'm sorry,' the woman gushed.

'I'm not sorry. I'm angry!' she barked at her.

'Oh.'

'We're fine, thank you,' I said to the terrified girl.

'Call if you need me,' she whispered and then she scampered away to find some jumpers to fold.

I looked down at the dresses and caught sight of one of the price tags. It had four figures on it!

'Rach!'

'I've got cancer,' she shrugged.

'Stop that, Lance!' That was my new name for her, after Lance Armstrong.

I did as I was told and walked into the changing rooms. I stripped down to my Primark underwear and I put the navy dress on. When I walked out of the changing room, Rachel was sitting before me in a big armchair with her head in her hands. I watched her for a few seconds.

'In a really unsympathetic way, I was just wondering if you're OK,' I said softly.

'In a really not-wallowing-in-it sort of way, I don't bloody know,' she answered, still with her face in her hands.

'Would you like a really unsympathetic cuddle?'

'Yes, although gentle on this boob because it's agony.' She looked up. 'Sarah! Oh my God. I have to buy you that. You look . . . like . . . beautiful.'

She stood up. I opened my arms and we hugged gently. We were there for a long time. I thought I heard Rachel say, 'Thank you,' into my hair but I didn't say anything and I didn't hear her speak again. Then a song came on the sound system and it sounded like the singer was singing, 'Fuck the pain away,' which made us laugh. So I said in a funny voice, 'I won't be doing that, no.' And then she said, 'Thank you,' again, and her voice sounded so choked that I just carried on hugging her.

'Come on, let's pay for the dress and then I want to take you to the bookstore,' she said eventually.

'Book shop. Why?'

'I want to buy you a book called *Get the Love of Your Life Back*.'

♥ *sixty-six* ♥

That day changed everything really. I started doing different things. Odd things.

The first one happened the next day. I walked to the Santa Monica LA post office with a parcel under my arm. It was a bright, airy, calm building, nothing like the post office in Camden where they once had a queue out of the door and onto Camden High Street. I thought that was impressive, because it's as big as HMV inside and it wasn't even Christmas. I liked to annoy other queuers there by guessing which of the cashiers would come free next and saying, 'Cashier number seven, please,' before the automated response system. Easily pleased.

The problem with sending a package through the post is that the recipient equates a package with pleasant things. They think, 'Oooh goodie, a parcel. Someone is thinking of me and has bought me a present,' and then they tear it open and cry, 'Oh, they shouldn't have! How kind, it's lovely.' Only in this instance I suspected the receiver would open it and their face would drop and then they'd sadly say, 'Oh bollocks.'

Not that I was completely cruel. My package did come with a warning. Once the package had been pulled out of the jiffy bag there was a handwritten sign on a Post-It saying, I AM SORRY FOR THIS. I AM A DICK. BUT I HAD TO DO IT, which I considered pithy under the circumstances. The package was for Simon. My Simon. Funny how hard it was to stop calling him my Simon. He wasn't my Simon. He was Ruth's. And by sending that parcel I was letting him go. I hoped. Contained in that parcel were all the Simon-related bits and pieces I owned, and a note. So, wrapped in bubble wrap I held

1 the newspaper advertisement for the 'how to stop being a crazy freak' workshop
2 the sleeve of the book *The Secret*. I thought it would be too expensive to send the whole lot and I wasn't sure if the starving waitress wanted it back
3 the sleeve of the book *Get the Love of Your Life Back*
4 Ruth's packet of contraceptive pills
5 the naked photo of Ruth and the 'come in lie down with your legs akimbo' note, complete with Blu-tack on the back

And my note.

Dear Si,

Above all, I'm sorry. So sorry. Sorry not to have been the person you or I hoped I was in our relationship. I was a mad

woman. If it is any consolation I was a mad woman because I wanted to be the right woman for you so much.

I think you're amazing. You're like sunshine in Wales or a ray of light when the bulb's gone. There's no one else like you and I thank you for the years I've had you as my mate. Because right now I really miss you as my mate. But I hope you're happy. I hope Ruth's happy. I hope the foetus is healthy. I mean that.

Anyway, what I want to say is good luck. I wish you well. And I'm going to fuck off now.

I'm going to stop sending you texts, which incidentally take three hours to write and work out where to put the mistakes in. I'm going to stop making myself amenable to small children in the hope that I will one day make a good step-mum. (Not that I intend to be cruel to them, but I'll stop homing in on them and doing my Yogi Bear impression.) I'm going to stop spending money and time on working out how to repair things. Because I can't. I accept your decision. I want to move on from all this. I wish you well and I hope more than anything that one day we can be friends.

If you're wondering why I'm doing this now, it's because Rachel Bird's got cancer, although please keep that to yourself because no one else knows. It's breast cancer. And even after she'd been given this terrible prognosis she wanted to take me shopping. She wanted to buy me a beautiful dress to make me look nice even though I wasn't feeling great. And she wanted to buy me a book called GET THE LOVE OF YOUR LIFE BACK which as you can probably tell by the cover is an unbelievably priced pile of tosh. And I felt glad that she had something to take her mind off with on the one hand but on the other hand ashamed that it was my refusal to let go of a bloke who clearly wasn't interested in me.

But if you want to take slight consolation, Rachel and I have become really close and I don't think we'd have done that if you hadn't dumped me so brutally (joke!!!). No, if we hadn't spent many hours and martinis plotting ways in which to make you love me. Duh! Women!

So, that's it. Apologies on top of more apologies.

Take good care of yourself, Gusset, because you're very, very special.

SS.

x

'Next, please,' smiled the cashier.

♥ sixty-seven ♥

It was very quiet on set. Normally there were about a hundred people walking around with a walkie-talkie, a cable or a purpose. However, Eamonn wanted a smaller crew for that 'delicate' scene. The crew might have been small and sensitive but I was still tense. I was so tense I made Gordon Brown look like he was on opium. At least it was essentially a rape scene, so I wouldn't be relaxed at all. Leo looked nervous too. Handsomer than Brad Pitt in *Thelma and Louise*, but nervous. We were sitting side-by-side, waiting for Eamonn to instruct us in our first take.

'Do you have to wear protective underwear too?' I asked Leo. I had meant it to break the ice but a make-up girl giggled, so perhaps it sounded a little more suggestive than I meant. Actually, from the way she was laughing I might as well have said, 'Hi, I'm Sarah, I don't have a gag reflex.'

'I have a sort . . .' He started cupping his right hand as though it was holding his imaginary penis. The make-up girl and I didn't blink. 'A sorta . . .' He moved the cupped hand back and forth as he searched for the right word. 'A sorta

. . . it's sorta like a sock on my penis.'

Now, I was pretty sure that Leo was plumbed with a penis, but now he'd confirmed that, I felt a little warm. He confirmed that he had one, simulated its girth and told us there was a sock on it. I glanced at the make-up girl. She was blushing. I think we would both have liked a quiet, uninterrupted moment to process that information.

'Well, well, well. How are you two doing?' said Eamonn, clapping his hands and joining us under the gazebo-style tent that was behind the bush where we'd be filming. It was 8 p.m. and very dark already. It was a little chilly so I had a puffer jacket over my costume.

We both nodded and mumbled 'mmm's.

'It'll be fine. Now that you know your positions, we'll just start shooting. Try to forget the cameras are rolling. I find in these scenes the good stuff happens on early takes, if not in rehearsals. So we'll just keep repeating it with the cameras rolling until we've got enough. I'm not entirely sure what I want from this yet to be honest, so I'll direct as we go. I saw the rushes of the strip bar scene and we got a terrific moment between the two of you, just before Sarah, er, crashed to the floor and hospitalized an extra.' He laughed.

'Bastard.'

'It's very powerful, that look. Anyway, don't think of it as a rape scene. It's consensual sex but it's the disgust you feel after you've slept with her that makes you murder her . . .'

'Oh, ta very much.'

'In the film, he feels disgust that he allowed himself to

sleep with this stripper and that's when you kill her. Clinically, cleanly, quickly. She liked you; she fell head over heels for you. Literally.'

'That's right, Eamonn, you wring that joke out for all it's worth.'

'Sarah, that story's going in my memoirs.'

'Oh,' I said, rather pleased I'd get a mention in his memoirs.

'So, have fun,' he said.

We took our positions. I took off my puffer and hid myself in the hedge. I felt strange. I didn't think these strange feelings were particularly professional. I, Sarah Sargeant, was looking forward to kissing Leo again. Normally before you're about to do a scene you try to get into the head of your character. You try to lose your own thoughts and become someone else. But at the moment I didn't actually have a clue what my character was thinking. I just wanted Leo to do that thing where he cupped my cheek and we looked at each other and breathed together. I suddenly gasped. He'd be cupping my cheek with the same hand that just cupped his penis! You see, that was where my imagination currently was. And it was definitely not where it should have been. What was wrong with me? I went to a convent. It occurred to me that this might have been my sexual peak. Perhaps I'd just, that second, entered my sexual peak. I took consolation that the make-up woman had as well. If it was my sexual peak I might as well enjoy it. If the last four years were anything to go by, it'd probably be the only bit of action I'd get while I was in it.

'So, let's put you in your positions and have a crack,' said Eamonn. 'I mean a bash.'

The scene started on me. I was sitting in a hedge spying on a house, as you do, when Leo appeared by my side. You see, it was a psychological thriller. I knew I was being stalked, but I thought it was by the man who lived in this house. Hence me sitting in the hedge. However, he wasn't stalking me. He was stalking four other women. But not me. Leo's character was stalking me. So he follows me to this hedge, seduces me and then murders me. Erin then finds my body. She was the other stalker man's daughter and she ends up working it all out and being the hero.

A few shots were taken of me looking at the house and feigning boredom. Then the cameras shifted so we could move on to Leo's entrance.

Leo quietly came into shot. I thought it was the stalker. I grabbed my gun. Yes! I had a gun! But luckily I didn't hold it for long because I hate firearms. I saw that it was Leo, whom I recognized from the stripping club. I looked scared.

'I know,' whispered Leo, in a way that didn't make me suspect him to be a murderer. 'I'm here to help you.'

I hesitated for a long time. Then I put the gun down. Then I smiled. Then we both started looking at the house. Then slowly, ever so slowly, Leo stopped looking at the house and started looking at me. I didn't know why. A house would have been prettier. But slowly I turned my head and met Leo's eyes. Now it was the fun part. We looked at each other. We held the gaze. I was doing 'I want you to shag me' breathing already and I wasn't sure it was acting. His hand was on my cheek. It was like the beach again. He touched my lips with his thumb. It was rougher than we had done it before but I wasn't complaining. He moved me towards him. My dress rode up. I know, I wouldn't hide out in a hedge in a dress either, but this was Hollywood. We were kissing. It was much more urgent than the beach. He was touching my breast already. Leo Clement was touching my nipple and we were being filmed. I groaned. That bit was acting. Sort of. I hoped my parents would never see this film. Leo was really good. It was like he was possessed. He manoeuvred himself on top of me and pretended to line things up down there. Then he pressed down on me. I thought I felt a semi! Leo Clement or his character had got a semi. I could feel it against the top of my leg. He was squashing me now. It was full-on frottage. I tried to take things slower and push him off me a bit but he held me down and did a very good impression of an orgasm. I smiled dreamily at him and played with his hair. But he forced my hand down and picked up the gun.

'Cut.'

Leo touched my face. I looked at him. We held the gaze. What were we doing? This was the film again.

'Did I hurt you?' he whispered.

I shook my head. I covered myself and stood up. I needed to be away from this man.

Was it a semi? And if it was, is that normal? I mean, when Keira Knightley is having a bit of James McAvoy in *Atonement* has he got a raging stiffy? I'd never thought about it before. I'd never had to. There had been something to be said for playing comedy maids and bit-part shop assistants. Genitals never came into 'Your tea, ma'am,' or 'That'll be three pound ten.'

'Bloody brilliant!' shouted Eamonn. 'Bloody, bloody brilliant.'

♥ *sixty-eight* ♥

Dolph Wax only lived on Mulholland Drive. I had to make the taxi driver stop and take a photo of me next to a road sign. That one would end up on Facebook. Well, Dolph said he lived there, but I think he might have been having us on and really it was a modern art museum. His house didn't have normal things that homes have, like a sofa and a telly and an area near the front door with a pile of shoes. He didn't have much in there at all. Although maybe he'd hidden everything because he thought we'd nick it, which was actually a sensible idea on his part because I would definitely have taken a souvenir to give to Julia. The few things he did have were unnickable and odd. He had armchairs but they were so high you needed a leg-up to get into them and they were made out of plastic. A chair made out of plastic in your living room? The electric chair would be more suitable for idle reclining and watching Dave.

He had paintings on the walls. But the paintings were of stripes. And in Dolph's house, walls looked like walls but they were actually cupboards. But the strangest bit of interior design was the room that had just one table in it. One table but no chairs. I saw it and said, 'You didn't tell us to bring our own chairs, Dolph.'

I always thought that I'd be tongue-tied and embarrassed meeting an A-list Hollywood star. But I wasn't around Dolph. That could have been because I thought the *Absolute Destruction* series was about as good for the world as genocide. Dolph didn't seem to mind when I said that about the table though. He just looked and me and told me I was funny again. Apparently the table belonged to James Dean and no one was allowed to touch it.

'Live fast, die young. But keep your hands off the furniture,' I said. And Dolph didn't mind when I said that, either. But that was because he didn't notice. He was too busy looking at Leo's bottom. I know this because I was also looking at Leo's bottom. Giovanni needed to be sedated. But I defy anyone not to have been looking at Leo's bottom too. Because Leo Clement was wearing a suit. But it was more than a suit. The trousers were tightish – hence Dolph and I gazing when Leo bent down to look under the table – the shirt was white against his surfer's tan, and he was wearing a thin black tie and, best of all, a waistcoat. I love a man in a waistcoat. He had been wearing a jacket but he'd taken it off and now he'd rolled his shirtsleeves up. And his shoes were cream. I know! Cream shoes. Bless him!

'Leo, I'd like to show you my library.'

Leo's eyes darted towards me. Dolph had been showing both Leo and I around his house while the other guests were outside. Obviously I was not allowed to see the library.

A knowing smile crept across Leo's lips. I smiled and raised my eyebrows in response.

'This way, Leo, you'll like it,' Dolph said firmly and extended his arm for Leo to follow him. I pretended to be riveted by a stripe painting as they left the room. Then I quickly looked in my bag to check my phone. No news from Rachel. She and Eamonn weren't there. They were having a quiet night in under the pretext of going to a fundraiser because Eamonn said he'd rather eat his own liver than spend leisure time with Dolph-Drive-Any-Director-Demented-Wax. But Rachel was planning to tell Eamonn tonight.

'Sarah, come and see the library!' Leo appeared in the library doorway. He was pulling a face like Benny Hill when he was being chased and it's a close-up.

'Do you need me to save you?' I whispered.

'Please.' He mouthed the word but as he did his face lit up. He looked so gorgeous that of course I'd go and see the library with him. I'd go and see a dirty cotton bud with him. I wondered whether it was like this for men? When us women say, 'Why is he going out with her; she has no personality?' is the man just so enraptured that the beautiful woman could burp and he would dance? Because that was me at that moment.

Leo put his hand on my arm. I hopped into the room because it still hurt to walk on my bad ankle. I was wearing the navy dress, so his skin touched mine. Dolph was standing in the library. It was not a library in the sense of a room with lots of books in it. The library looked like all the other bare rooms. It had four white walls, although one of them had a few hardbacks lying flatly on a few shelves. You'd find more books in a branch of Iceland. And I could forgive Dolph for the plastic chairs in the other room if he'd had a chair with all the comfort of a bed hidden there in the library. But he didn't. He did have a chair in there though, to give him credit. Of course he did, because people like to sit down comfortably with a book. Only in Dolph's house you had to recline with a nice book on a stool. A stool? I considered popping a DFS catalogue through his letterbox.

Dolph was standing next to the stool looking petulant and holding out a large, heavy, what looked to be beautifully illustrated book called *The Art of Zen*. He ignored me and looked at Leo.

'It's for you,' he said. The corners of his mouth were folding tensely in on themselves. I noted that Dolph was probably a snake kisser.

'Dolph, man, I can't take that from you.'

'I want you to have it.' His voice was starting to rise.

'Dolph.'

'I like you, Leo. I want to give you this book.'

I considered volunteering to take the book, as it looked very nice. But I didn't. I didn't think that was what Dolph had in mind. Leo opened his mouth and shook his head for a moment.

'There's nothing weird here,' said Dolph, managing brilliantly to contest his own words.

'But, I won't read it. I don't read, man. I mean, I do read, sometimes. But you keep it.'

Dolph's neck muscles tensed like he was lifting a piano. He looked as though he was going to say something absolutely destructive but instead he stalked out of the badly stocked library, muttering, 'I need to see to my guests.'

'I can't believe he wanted to give his Zen book away. I'd be keeping that one if I were Dolph,' I said when Dolph had gone. I didn't get any response out of Leo because he was smiling at me with his head cocked to one side.

'I like your dress,' he said and he walked towards me and put his hands around my back. He eased his thumbs underneath the silk of my low-backed dress so that they were touching the fleshy bits above my fleshier bottom.

'You look beautiful.'

Hang about! That so was not true. It's not even in the same catchment area as truth. I know what beauty looks like and it's not I. Was I in a dream? Leo Clement is gorgeous. He's fifty-seven thousand out of ten. I'm a six. Probably a five and half now, because girls seem to be getting much prettier and younger. I think I have been a seven out of ten once, but that was only after an unprecedented British sunny spell and a bad bout of some sort of dysentery. And it didn't last once I put the weight back on.

'Nutter.'

'Sarah Sargeant, can I kiss you, please?' he asked.

'Huh, hmmm, er,' I managed to say before he puts his lips on mine.

It was just a single soft on-the-mouth kiss though. No tongue, because he took my hand and led me back into the dining room with no chairs.

'Come and have a look at this,' he said and he got down on his knees and looked at the underneath of the table.

'Nutter,' I said again, and I hoisted my dress up and crawled down on the floor. Leo was lying under the James Dean table.

'Come on, lie next to me.'

I lay down on the carpet facing the underside of the table. There was writing on the bottom of the table. Someone had carved something into the wood.

'Wow. What's it say?'

'It says,' started Leo, and he put his arm behind me so I could lean on his shoulder. 'It says, "Dream as if you'll live forever. Live as if you'll die today."'

'I hope James Dean wrote that and not Dolph.'

We lay there and looked at it. I thought about Rachel and felt sad. However, I knew wholeheartedly that Rachel would very much approve of me being under James Dean's table with Leo Clement in the blue dress she bought for me. And I knew for sure that she would want me to kiss him. So I did. I reached over and kissed him.

'I love kissing you,' he murmured.

'Leo?' a female voice called into the room. We stopped kissing. Leo put his finger lightly over my lips to stop me making any noise. I would have kissed the finger had he not accidentally kicked my bad ankle at the same time. I yelped.

'Hello, hello?' The lady's voice got nearer, then Palmer the publicist's impeccably well made-up face appeared under the table. 'Oh!' She seemed surprised to see us under there. 'Leo, I'm leaving,' she said slowly, while looking at me.

We listened to her footsteps as she left. Then Leo placed his lips on top of mine again.

We kissed a lot. We kissed until he manoeuvred me on top of him and I banged my head and we started laughing. That was when we became aware of a set of feet next to us in the dining room.

We both stopped giggling to hear Dolph Wax's unmistakable tones saying, 'I'd like you both to leave now, please.'

♥ *sixty-nine* ♥

Leo Clement took me to his ramshackle house on the beach. In Malibu. I couldn't tell you where, though, because we snogged all the way there. It was as though we wore braces, and they had got caught and we were frantically trying to extricate ourselves before a teacher caught us. Although I enjoyed it much more than the time that happened to me as a teenager.

'Whisky?' Leo said, smiling, when we got there.

I nodded. It seemed apt. Whisky was clearly the drink of choice before embarking on sex acts.

'Come outside,' he said. I started to hop towards the glass doors but Leo grabbed me by the legs and threw me over his shoulder.

'Stop it! I'll break your back!' I screamed.

He walked us out onto his deck area. Me hanging upside down in a fireman's lift, bashing him on the back. He placed me gently in his big swinging seat then disappeared back inside. I looked about me. There were steps down to the beach. I could hear the waves. They sounded like traffic. The dog curled himself up at my feet. It all reminded me of the bit at the end of *Beaches*, but I didn't want to think about that. I hoped Rachel was OK. I hoped she'd told Eamonn and he was cuddling her in her sleep.

Leo emerged, threw me a hooded top and then sat down next to me. I put my arms and head through the hoodie and when my head popped out Leo's face was there, smiling, ready to kiss me. He put his arm around me and we leant back and looked out into the blackness and listened to the sea.

'Best place in the world,' he said.

'Hmmm. You might be right.'

That was quite enough conversation. We started to kiss again. My lips were already red and swollen. His hands slid down to my bottom. He was picking me up again. I asked God not to give him a hernia. He was still kissing me. Oh my God, he was carrying me to his bedroom. Sex. We were going to do sex. Of course we were, that's why I was bloody there. I was about to have sex with Leo Clement!

He turned a light on in a big room. I saw a huge bed with a painting of the sea and a surfer above it. He laid me care-fully on the bed and kissed me tenderly. Then he stood above me. I looked up as he undid his waistcoat and pulled off his tie and unbuttoned his shirt. And I know that that image will be with me as a fantasy for life. It was such a close-up view of his chest that I was breathing like I'd just run ten metres, which is very heavily. He sat me up and pulled the hoodie over my head. Then, without me noticing, he untied the halter-neck bow and we were doing topless kissing. By that point I was breathing like I'd just run fifty metres. I was liable to get a stitch. He stood up. I hid my breasts with a hand because I went to a convent. He undid his trousers. He stepped out of them. He looked down at me. He was wearing a pair of tight grey shortie pants. There was a maxi in them. Shit, one hundred metres! There was a real danger of me passing out. Then he looked at me in my pants. I was still holding my hands across my boobs. He carefully unpeeled them and started to caress my breasts. I'd just run a mile. Now he was kissing me everywhere. Oh, blimey, he was getting lower. Cunnilingus! My pants were coming off. I hoped Keith Richards hadn't grown back. But then I remembered the heart/squirrel/tractor. It had grown out disastrously down there. It was Simon's heart. Suddenly, the track in my head changed from Marvin Gaye's 'Let's Get it On' to Britney Spears's 'Toxic'.

'Um. Leo.'

He didn't stop.

'Leo,' I whispered and then I bashed him on the head.

'Uh.' He looked up. He was all flushed and sexy and he was in between my legs. It would have been wrong to ask him if I could take a photo.

'I'm so sorry. I can't do this,' I whispered.

'Hey,' he said kindly, and he came up to my eye level and flopped on the bed next to me.

'I'm so sorry.'

'Hey,' he said, smoothing my hair back.

'I'm such a knob.' And then I thought sadly about that

maxi going to waste. Maybe I could do it. I looked at Leo's face. But I didn't even want to do kissing any more. I felt like I'd run a marathon and I wanted to go to bed.

'Did I rush things?'

'No,' I shook my head. 'I thought I wanted to. And I've loved all our kissing.'

He nodded and stroked my cheek.

'We can take things slow. I like you, Sarah.'

'I've just split up with someone and I didn't want to and my head is all confused.'

'Baby,' he whispered and he kissed me on the nose and smiled a sad little smile. He wrenched the duvet from beneath us and wrapped it round us. Then he cuddled me and it was lovely but I wished it was Simon. Bloody Simon. Ruined everything.

'Leo?'

'Hmmm.'

'If it's any consolation I think the sex would have been amazing.'

♥ *seventy* ♥

I woke the next morning to the sound of a mobile phone. Simon! I started flapping my arm about to reach it on my bedside table. Where had the table gone?

'Ow,' said a man's voice. It was Leo. I remembered I was at Leo's. I felt as though someone had punched me in the lips. I needed to break wind.

Leo jumped out of bed. It was his phone.

'Palmer!' he yawned. 'Shit! I overslept. OK I'm on my way. Tell them I'll be there in twenty. Sorry.'

Leo sat on the bed.

'Shit. That was my publicist. I'm late for an interview.' He stroked my bare back. 'How are you doing, pretty?'

'OK.'

'Was it bad with this guy?'

'Hmmm. He went back to his ex-girlfriend.'

'Fuck-tard.'

I smiled. Leo jumped up and put last night's creased clothes on.

'Sarah, help yourself to anything. Take a shower. Have a

walk along the beach. I might be a while. Do you need money for a cab to get you back to the hotel?'

I shook my head.

'Leo, thank you. Thank you for being so lovely. And I'm sorry for you know . . .'

'No, I'm sorry. I rushed things.'

I had a day without any stripping, filming or voice classes. I was free. I wished he'd hurry up and get out of the room so I could break wind though.

By the time I heard the door slam, I didn't need to fart. It was always the way. I lay for a while and contemplated my crapness. I couldn't have sex with Leo Clement. If I couldn't have sex with Leo Clement then there was no chance of me ever having sex again.

I stood up and started to locate my clothes. I found the bathroom. It was old-fashioned. A bath with legs stood in the middle surrounded by surfing magazines. I went to the loo. I was a little bit constipated. It must have been from trying to control the earlier flatulence, so I picked up a surfing magazine and settled in for the long haul. When I was done I pulled the old-fashioned chain. It took a few flushes to work. I looked down at the toilet to check I didn't need to use the toilet brush. But the, um, the, er, the poo was still there and it was MASSIVE.

I stared down for a moment, appalled and impressed in equal measures. I flushed the chain again. But it didn't move. I tried to remember what I ate yesterday as I waited for the cistern to fill. Another burger. I pulled the chain again.

It was still there. I seemed to have done an unflushable poo. I couldn't leave it there. Leo would think I had the bowels of an overweight long-distance lorry driver. I picked up another surfing magazine and looked at it while listening for the sound that the cistern was full and ready to flush again. Flush number four. It was still wanking well there. No! No! Flush Number five. Not budged a millimetre. What was I supposed to do?

'Julia!'

'Hey, bubba. How are you? How was the sex scene?'

'Very long story. I'll tell you later on Skype, this is costing us both a fortune. Listen, sounds weird, but you know when you do a massive poo?'

'Uh huh.'

'What if it doesn't flush?'

'Urgh.'

'Sorry.'

'Keep flushing.'

'I am,' I said, peering at the poo and flushing again.

'Has it gone?'

'Nope!'

'OK, I'll tell you what you have to do.'

'OK.'

'Where are you?'

'Leo Clement's house.'

'Oh, bloody hell, I've been meaning to tell you. Leo Clement writes a column in this magazine that Carlos reads.'

'Leo Clement writes a column? No way. What's the magazine called?'

'*Nads.*'

'Nice.'

'Yeah, it's hysterical, it's just him kissing and telling basically.'

I froze.

'WHAT?'

'Oh. My. God. Did you shag him?'

'No, no!'

'Did you nosh him off?'

'Jules! No! But there was nakedness.'

She laughed.

'It's not in the slightest bit funny. I couldn't shag him because I was frigid and now I've done an unflushable poo in his loo and he writes about his sex life in a lads' mag! JULIA, I MEAN IT. STOP LAUGHING!'

'Sorry, Sare.'

'Jules! If you don't stop laughing now I will never forgive you. This is serious. You have to help me get this cocking great turd out of his loo!'

'OK. OK. Go to the kitchen and see if he's got any plastic bags.'

'Oh no! Oh please, no.'

'If it doesn't flush that's what you have to do.'

'Have you ever done it?'

'No! My poos flush. What you eating?'

'I think it's the burgers, or it could have been the macrobiotic canapés last night.'

I go to the kitchen. I open some drawers. I am relieved to know that even successful models have a drawer in their kitchen full of empty carriers.

'Got one.'

'OK, put your hand inside it and get the poo.'

'OK.'

'Put the phone down and do it. You don't want that falling in there. I'll stay on the line.'

I gave it one last flush to be sure. Oh God. I had to fish it out. I reached in and held my breath. I took it out.

'Urgh, the bag's covered in toilet water! Jules!'

'Put it in the sink to give it a dry off,' she shouted through the phone. 'Then wrap it in more plastic bags. I'm going now. But Skype me ASAP.'

'Cheers, Jules.'

I tossed the bag in the sink. I was OK. Cool. Sorted. I walked back into the kitchen and nearly cleared all the plastic bags out of his drawer. Blimey. Leo had got a herb garden on his kitchen windowsill. I looked around his beach house. It was cosy. I located a pencil and the back of an envelope. I started to write Leo a note.

Dear Leo,

What was I supposed to say? Sorry I was a complete cock. Give me a few months and I'd love to try shagging you again as long as you don't mention it in *Nads*. By the way, I did a massive poo in your loo.

*I hope the interview went well. I'm just heading back to the
hotel. See you soon. Thank you for being so understanding about
last night.*
     Sarah

Kiss or no kiss? I decided on no kiss. I didn't think my
lips could take any more pressure.

I left the note on his kitchen surface. I grabbed the plastic bags. I went to the bathroom and collected the poo. My
phone. I'd left it on the kitchen table. Just as well it rang or
I would have left it here. Then Simon would have called
and Leo would have answered it. Although he might have
called him a fuck-tard and that wouldn't have been so bad.
Except Simon wouldn't have called you, Sarah, you fool. And
it wasn't him on the phone. It was Rachel Bird. I put the poo
down on the counter by the note and answered it.

'Hey, Rach.'

'Where are you?'

'Malibu.'

'Ahhhh. Oh my God. With Leo. Was it wonderful?'

'Um, no, it was all awful. How are you doing though?'

'I didn't tell him.'

'Ah.'

'Have you got time for a chat?'

'Course,' I said, going into Leo's room and checking I
hadn't left anything.

'I'm going to leave Eamonn.'

'Noooooooooo, no, Rachel, please don't say that,' I said, quickly closing Leo's front door behind me.

Rachel started sobbing.

'It's for the best.'

'Rachel, he wants to . . .'

'Are you still there, Sarah?'

I turned around to look at Leo's house. The door was closed. I had left the poo on his table.

'Sarah?'

♥ *seventy-one* ♥

I decided to wait for Leo to come home so I could collect the carrier bag. However it was the hottest day I had experienced in California and I didn't have any sun cream on. The only place where I could escape the sun was the large hedge in his gravelly driveway. I estimate that I sat in that hedge for about four hours.

The battery had died on my phone, although I'd managed to persuade Rachel Bird not to leave Eamonn, so it was worth it. But I was worried that Simon had left a message. The whole experience was foolish and frustrating. So I made the sound 'urgh' as loudly as I could.

'Hello,' said a voice. I peeked out of the hedge. It was a deliveryman. I hoped he wasn't planning on murdering me in the hedge.

'Hello.'

'What are you doing in there?'

'I'm just waiting for Leo.'

'In a hedge?'

'It's the only place in the shade.'

'Where you from?'

'England.'

He looked at me for a long time and then walked back down the path, taking the parcel with him.

'Bye,' I shouted, trying to be friendly.

I sat back in my hedge. I tried to get comfy. What was this bloody interview for? NASA? I heard a car pull up. Finally. I started to crawl out of my hedge. I was just in doggie position when I heard the words, 'Don't move, ma'am.'

I looked up. There was an American police car in front of me. The policeman who was talking to me didn't look very friendly though, and he made Tony Soprano look petit.

'Hello,' I squeaked. It was a very uncomfortable position for me because my knees were in the gravelly ground. Another one got out of the car. He was younger. He looked a bit like the policeman stripper that I got for Julia on her eighteenth birthday. He looked cross too. I started to move because it was hurting my knees. Stripper cop got out a gun!

'Don't move, ma'am!'

It was awful. If he shot me, I'd never get the poo.

'I think my knees are bleeding.'

'What are you doing in a hedge, ma'am?'

'I was just trying to keep out of the sun. I'm waiting for the man who lives here.'

'Where are you from?'

'England.'

'Cup of tea,' said Stripper Cop with the gun in a terrible English accent.

'Hmmm.' I tried to smile.

'Show me your passport.'

I was in a fecking hedge!

'I don't have it with me.'

'Where are you staying?'

'A hotel. Called Shutters.'

Stripper Cop did a wolf whistle.

'Yes, it's very nice there. I recommend it.'

'There is a gun pointed at you. So get up slowly.'

'Ow, thank you.'

'We'll drive you back to your hotel.'

'Nooo.'

'You're dealing with the law, lady.'

'I know but I really need to get something from his house.'

'What's that, lady?'

A poo! A bloody great bag of poo!

'Just a girly thing I left there.'

I heard a car on gravel. Please, please God, be Leo, I prayed, not a swat team. Thank you, God. It was Leo, driving an old estate car with a surfboard on the top. He got out. He was wearing a half-pulled-up wetsuit.

'Officers.'

'Do you know this lady?'

'Yes.'

The dog trundled over to the hedge I'd just been sitting in and had a long pee. I had thought the ground felt damp there.

'What is her name?'

'Sarah Sargeant.'

'Where is she staying?'

'That hotel, Shutters, on the beach.'

Tony Soprano nodded slowly.

'What's the problem?'

'We had a call to say that there was a suspect English lady screaming in a hedge outside your house.'

'She's a friend of mine.'

'Sorry to trouble you then.'

They drove off. I looked at Leo.

'I just left something inside. I thought I'd wait for you.'

'Sorry, Sarah. I went surfing. Let me have a quick shower and I'll drive you back.'

♥ *seventy-two* ♥

I was still holding the bag when I got back to the hotel. I felt like Gillian McKeith.

Leo walked me from the car. His arm was around my waist and I was leaning into him, trying to keep my weight off my bad foot. One of my knees was bleeding after the doggy position in the gravel with the policemen. So I had hoiked my dress up to my knees to stop blood getting on the fabric. Leo was carrying last night's shoes for me. I was holding the carrier. We entered the hotel like this. There have been walks of shame in my life before. But this was the daddy.

There was a party going on in the foyer. Lots of people were gathered together, whooping. I kept my head pressed into Leo's chest, not wanting to see anyone.

'Sarah!' It was Erin and her dad and lots of other people. I didn't have a free hand so I waved my little bag of doo-doo at her.

'Do you want me to leave you here or help you upstairs?' Leo whispered in my ear.

'Do you mind helping me upstairs?'

'No, no . . .'

Erin broke free from her group and approached us as we were trying to sidle our way to the lift.

'It was my father's birthday yesterday. All my family came to celebrate. They're just leaving now for New York. Meet them.'

We turned and smiled at the strangers she was talking about.

'Lovely to meet you all,' I said.

Leo nodded.

Erin did the rounds and introduced them all to us individually. I swapped hands with the poo so I could shake their hands, which were being proffered, and started murmuring 'pleased to meet you's.

'Well, lovely to meet you all. And happy birthday for yesterday, Mr Schneider,' I said when I thought it wasn't rude to leave.

'Oh, Sarah!' cried Erin.

'Yes, lovely?'

'Would one of you mind taking a photo of all of us?'

'No,' said Leo.

'Course not,' I added.

'Here, Sarah, you take it, you've got the same camera.'

I took the camera that Erin gave me. They gathered into an awkward-looking huddle. Leo offered to take the carrier from me to free up my hands. I declined.

'OK. Everyone say, "Lesbian!"' I shouted. The response was a chapel hush. They'd be sorry.

'Oh, OK, then. Everyone say, "Cheese!"'

They all said, 'Cheese!' and looked disturbed. I took one photo to prove my point. Then I tried to arrange them in a quirky school-sports-picture arrangement. I was mid telling Erin's granddad that he should really go behind Erin as he was two feet taller when I saw something. It was a familiar figure moving at speed through the foyer of my hotel. I couldn't be sure. But it looked like my Si.

'I'm so sorry, excuse me . . .' I said to Erin's party without taking my eyes off the figure, who was nearly out of the hotel doors. I started to run after him.

'Argh!' I screamed. I'd forgotten about my bad ankle.

'Sarah,' Leo cried as he rushed to my side.

But I hopped away from him.

'I think I saw someone,' I murmured as I left everyone behind. It must have been a frightening sight; me, braless breasts bobbing, unwashed in last night's clothes, hopping through a luxury hotel foyer. But I didn't care. I reached the double doors. And I saw him. It was Simon. My Simon. He was just about to get into a yellow taxi.

'Simon!' I shouted. Now I have the voice force of a frigate at my disposal normally, but that 'Simon', that all-important 'Simon' barely reached gnat power. He didn't hear me. Or if he did, he didn't turn around.

'Simon!' I tried again. His hand was already on the taxi door. 'SIMON!' I watched him open the door. I couldn't let him go.

'SIMON!' I screamed and this time I charged towards the

cab. Again I forgot that I had a sprained ankle, only this time I ended up sprawled on the pavement. It was a disaster. I made the sound 'urgh' as loud as I could. And Simon looked. He didn't smile. He didn't tell the cab driver to go. He just cast his eyes upon me on the ground.

'What are you doing here?' I shouted. A valid question.

'I had some work stuff over here.'

'Can we go for coffee?'

Simon looked at me on the ground in last night's dress with grazed knees and it was a look of absolute contempt.

'What?' I said.

'Nothing, Sare, I'll leave you to it.'

'Si! *You* left *me* to be with Ruth.'

'The baby's not mine.'

'What?'

'Well, it could be mine. Although I doubt it. But Ruth was seeing her boss at work as well, so it could be his. That photo and sex game note, that wasn't anything to do with me. There'll have to be a paternity test when he or she arrives.'

'Oh, Si, I'm sorry.'

'Yeah.' He nodded. 'And she could have kids. She just didn't want kids with me.'

'Oh.'

'I was just going to tell you, that's all. I shouldn't have come.'

'No, no, please, Si, please, let's talk, have a coffee.'

Then Simon's body language and tone changed completely and he said, 'I'll see you around, Sarah Sargeant,' and got into the taxi.

I turned around and Leo Clement was walking towards me. He'd obviously just appeared.

'Leo, please could you help me up?' I said urgently.

Leo escorted me to the escalator and then he left. I was relieved because I had a plan. I was going to get rid of the bag of poo and change my clothes, then I was going to the airport. I didn't have a clue whether Simon would be there. But I needed to at least try.

Once I was out of the lift I saw a bin. I thought about kissing it. I didn't.

'You are a beautiful thing,' I said to it, and lobbed the bag in there.

'Sarah, what are you doing?'

It was Rachel Bird. She was leaning against my hotel room door. She was wearing a baseball cap and shorts and she was sitting on top of a very big bag. I stared at her. Her eyes looked red and blotchy.

'Oh, you didn't,' I said softly.

'I did,' she replied.

'Oh, Rach.'

'Can I stay with you?'

'Of course.'

'Can we order burgers and martinis?'

'Well, I've discovered the problem with eating burg . . .' I started, but then I looked at her sad little face and I changed my mind. 'Yep, we'll have whatever you want.'

♥ seventy-three ♥

So I never went to the airport. It wasn't that I didn't want to. But Rachel had come to me at one of the hardest points in her life and I couldn't leave when she needed me.

So we had a burger and a martini and we talked. Then I showered all my body, bar one bandaged ankle, and when I had finished Rachel was sound asleep. Based on past behaviour I would have sat on the bed next to her and mulled over the Simon situation before Skype-ing Julia. However, I did neither of those things. I left Rachel a note, a glass of water and a key on the bedside table and I hopped out of the room. I went next door and knocked.

Erin answered.

'Sarah, hey.'

'Hello, Erin, I don't suppose you're free? I never bought you that milkshake and I was feeling bad.'

'Oh, no, we're just off to a prayer meeting.'

'Oh.'

'Come.'

And I was about to say, 'Oh no, that's not really for me,' but instead I said, 'OK, although I will have to hop.' Perhaps it was strange that I chose to hop to a prayer meeting rather than chase after the man I loved. The truth was, I was scared. I wanted to do the best by Rachel. But I didn't know what the best was. All I knew was that it didn't involve me having a big dramatic scene with Simon.

So I hopped the two blocks alongside Erin and her father to the community centre-type place where they held one of their many prayer meetings. I couldn't help move chairs in a circle so I arranged a bunch of tulips in a vase that Erin had brought and placed them in the centre of the circle.

A couple in their late thirties were the first to arrive. He was a giant of a man with a donkey-like large chin and she was rounded and kind-looking, a bit like Mrs Tiggywinkle. They smiled at me and shook my hand before they sat down. Erin and her dad greeted them warmly. Then an older woman walked slowly in with the aid of a stick. She didn't look well and she collapsed into the first seat she came to.

By the time Mr Schneider began there were seven of us in total.

'Good afternoon and welcome. We come together today to pray with and for each other. We offer up our prayers to God in the knowledge that the big man is always listening. And we get strength and joy from one another. Now, let's start with you two,' he said, pointing at Donkey Man and Tiggywinkle.

The poor couple explained how they'd been trying for a baby for ages before Mr Schneider said a prayer that we all repeated. Then the older lady spoke. Her name was Flo. She had cancer and wanted us to pray that she lasted six months so that she would see her favourite grandson get married. I asked them to pray for my friend as she'd just been diagnosed with cancer. And I asked them to pray that I was the best friend I could be to her in this time.

All in all it was probably the most depressing afternoon of my life. At the end of the session I stood up to thank Mr Schneider.

'I'm sorry about your friend.'

'Yeah, it's a bit rubbish, but I'm sure she'll fight it,' I replied.

Flo had joined us in the conversation and immediately responded to my remark.

'Don't give her lots of positive talk, she won't like that.'

'Sorry?'

'It's infuriating when people say, "Oh, you'll fight it." You want to scream, "I might not, I'm not Lance Armstrong."'

'Oh,' I said. My mind was scanning all the insensitive things I'd already said to Rach. The 'Let's fight this fucker,' and 'Come on, Lance,' comments. 'Um, what should I say?'

'Well, don't trivialize it either.'

'Right,' I said. The bloody ridiculous omelette rap was on a loop in my mind. 'Well, thank you, Flo.'

I hopped away feeling dreadful.

'Sarah,' it was Mr Schneider following me. 'Sarah, just be there for your friend. Tell her you care. I'm sure you're being a great friend to her.'

'Oh, no, honestly, you don't understand. I'm doing everything wrong. I called her Lance bloody Armstrong and I've been making awful jokes, I mean my jokes are largely based on knob gags anyway, sorry, Father.'

'I'm sure you're doing fine.' He smiled. 'And keep the knob gags.'

And I smiled because it really pleased me that a man of the cloth had said 'knob gags'.

♥ *seventy-four* ♥

When I returned to the room Rachel was still lying on her back with my First Class eye mask on, snoring lightly. I wrote her a little note and left it by the bed. It simply said:

> *Rachel, I don't know how best to help you through this. But I am going to do whatever I can and whatever you need. I'm not going anywhere. So use me to cry, to moan, to rail, to boss around, to talk to about anything. If I say the wrong thing let me know. Because everything I do comes out of love for you.*
>
> *Xxx*

And then I turned on my computer and braced myself for *Nads.com*. Hmmm. What the *National Geographic* is to natural science, *Nads* is to boobs. The holding page showed two teenage girls wearing nothing but diamante pants. They were both grinning, probably in agony as the diamante pants couldn't be much fun, especially when you sat down. One of the girls was helpfully holding the other's breasts, obviously to protect her modesty because she was shy. The contents page promised to show me 'sizzling pics' of someone called Eva naked, a strip by someone called Emma, saucy pics of Sandra, a section called 'Bank Holiday Boobs' and another called 'Best of Breast'. I suspect it was the diversity of commentary that set *Nads* apart from other literature on the market. I clicked on Eva. She did have truly amazing boobies. They were massive and she seemed to spend most of her time lying on the floor in just her shoes, touching them, which was good news for *Nads*. Eva was very lucky, though, because although she had mammoth mammaries, nothing else on her body was big. She had a tiny little waist and the tight bottom of a prepubescent boy. Even her bloody hands were wee. I could increase the size of my boobs. I had done it before. It involved eating a lot of peanut butter on toast late at night. The only problem was that every other body part grew too.

I went back to the homepage. I scanned it closely but I didn't see Leo's name anywhere, although there was a section called 'JizBiz' and something was telling me that I really, really, really, really, really didn't want to click on that.

'I can't do it,' I said aloud.

'What?'

'Hey, bubba. I thought you were sleeping. Can I get you anything?'

'No,' she reached out to the bedside table and picked up her phone. She looked at it and blinked sleepily.

'Has he called?'

'Hmmm,' she said quietly.

'I'll make you a cup of tea.'

'Are you looking at porn?'

'What? No. Did you know that Leo Clement has a column?'

She smiled.

'I would say that Leo Clement has a phenomenal column.'

Flashback of those tight grey short pants and the maxi.

'He's got a column in a magazine called *Nads*.'

'Classy. Let's have a read.'

'OK.' I handed her the computer.

'Wow, she's got nice breasts,' she sighed sadly.

'Look. I think Leo's stuff might be there, under "JizBiz".'

She clicked on the icon and I turned back to make the tea.

'Oh, you have to buy the magazine to read the column, it says.'

When the cups were ready I turned round and I said something I had been thinking since Rachel arrived.

'Rach, I'm going to tell Eamonn for you. I'll explain it all so you don't have to. It doesn't mean that you have to get back with him. It just means he'll be able to understand.'

She looked at me. I didn't know what she'd say. I was fully expecting a 'Bugger off, Sare, it's got nothing to do with you.' But instead she just looked at me and nodded.

'Thank you,' she said. And then she lay down again and closed her eyes.

♥ *seventy-five* ♥

Like a sleuth, I tracked Eamonn down through a tight-knit group of personal assistants and I learnt he was at the Chateau Marmont Hotel. Now the Chateau Marmont hotel is famously where the Hollywood hellraisers hang out, so if I didn't find Mickey Rourke and Courtney Love snorting coke off each other's bottoms in the reception I planned to demand my cab fare back. And it was on Sunset Boulevard. Sunset Boulevard as in the musical we did at drama school. Well, the musical that the rest of the year did except me, on account of it being a musical. This Hollywood history was useful because it distracted my mind from the job in hand. Leo called me as I was on that journey. I didn't answer.

I hopped into the hotel. It was very dark. I squinted. I wished they'd turn some lights on so I could see the hell-raisers. I kept my eyes peeled for them as I jerkily made my way through a lounge area. But I didn't see anyone of note and I tripped over a rug. I paid more attention as I negoti-ated my way out into a large patio area with a canopy over it. The patio was furnished with sofas and rugs. The first person I saw was Dolph Wax sitting in the centre of the large sofa. It appeared he didn't know what to do on comfortable seating. He looked unsure whether to lie back or lean forward, so he'd opted for a mid-sit-up position that hinted at torture. He was flanked on one side by a middle-aged lady who made Margaret from *The Apprentice* look fun-loving. I wondered who she was; possibly the lawyer or the bongo player. To his other side was a large man in a suit who was holding a walkie-talkie. I assumed he was a bodyguard. I noticed that when Dolph saw me the muscles in his neck tensed like he was having trouble with the piano again. Eamonn registered Dolph's expression and turned his head to locate the object of his displeasure. There was another man with him but I could only see the back of his head. Eamonn looked very tired. But he smiled at me and gestured me towards them.

'Sarah, you out on the tiles?'

'Oh, no, I came to find you, actually.'

'Oh, of course, well, we're finished here. Dolph wanted to discuss the merits of adding a scene where Dolph interviews Leo,' Eamonn told me. 'But I think we've just come to the conclusion that it would be repetitious, what with the other scene we've already shot where Leo is interrogated by the police officers,' said Eamonn, scarcely disguising his exasperation. The other man whose face I could now see nodded in agreement.

'Sarah, have you met Joel properly? This is Joel. The writer.'

I took in the man who was responsible for me stripping

on camera. I tried to smile back. I really did. Then I turned my attention towards Dolph.

'Oh, hello, Dolph, thank you so much for the party last night. It was great,' I say, because my mum would have wanted me to and also because it was the truth. As far as parties went, that one was probably up there in my top five.

'Hmmm,' Dolph responded. His mum obviously didn't teach him manners.

'Sorry about the, er, you know, the end bit,' I added to fill in the silence.

'Well, if that'll be all,' said Eamonn, obviously noticing some tension, 'I have a meeting now with Sarah. Thanks for dropping by, Dolph, it's always great when actors are so passionate about their roles.' They all stood up. It took Dolph three tries to pull himself up. The walkie-talkie man strode ahead.

'I'll see you out, Dolph,' said Eamonn.

They all filed out except Joel. I had imagined the writer to be morbidly obese, with a pacemaker and a penchant for porn. I didn't think he'd be young and slim and good-looking. I stared at him.

'Would you like a drink?' he asked.

'Er, no, thank you.'

'Not some champagne?'

'I hope you're not celebrating a new lesbian scene you've written for Taylor.'

'No, I'm celebrating meeting you properly.'

'Oh, thanks. Nice to meet you, too. I have actually imagined myself meeting you once or twice.'

'Oh?'

'Yes. Normally I'm holding a sharp implement, though, and you're cowering,' I said with glee. And then I laughed. It was my *Beavis and Butt-head* laugh. There was a small silence while I realized that not only had I threatened violence to a successful Hollywood writer, I had also laughed like a socially inept cartoon character. Unsurprisingly, this man, Joel, the writer, picked up his jacket, mumbled a curt good-bye and had departed within seconds. I watched him walk away and vowed to make myself more amenable to people who might be able to help my career in the future.

'I really didn't need that today,' sighed Eamonn when he reached me. 'Shall we have a drink?'

'I'm all right, thanks.'

'Yes, you're right, I shouldn't let Dolph Wax and my girl-friend leaving me drive me to the bar.'

We both sat down. Eamonn sighed and then looked at me.

'I can understand that I was neglecting her with this film as it is. But –' He stopped and put his head in his hands. 'I didn't think it was this bad. For her just to leave. Nothing but a short note. I want to ask you something, Sarah. And I'd like you to be honest with me.'

'OK.'

'Has she met someone else?'

'Eamonn, no, it's nothing like that. In fact it's nothing to do with you at all.'

'Why? What?'

'Eamonn, I'm so sorry to tell you this, but she's got breast cancer.'

'What?'

'It is quite bad, I think. The doctor's scheduled her a mastectomy and then she'll need treatment. She left you because she didn't want you to worry. She wanted you to be able to focus on your film. She knows how much it means to you. She doesn't want to be ill and be a burden.'

Eamonn said nothing.

'She won't be a burden.' But it caught in his throat. 'She won't be a . . .' He tried to say the words again but had to stop because he was choking on them. I stood up and walked towards him. 'I can't believe she thinks she'd be a . . .'

'Hey,' I whispered, and I squatted down and put my arms around him as he cried into his hands on the chair.

'I'm supposed to be flying to New York later. Shall I cancel and come with you to see her?'

'It's up to you. But Rachel really wants you to do the film. That's why she's done this. She'll hate you changing plans because of her. Go to New York and then come and see her when you get back. I'll look after her while you're gone.'

❤ *seventy-six* ❤

I did my best to look after Rachel. I didn't really know what to do or how to be or the words to say. But I knew that she needed to be fed, martini-ed, and administered really rude jokes on a fairly regular basis. That was the syllabus and I stuck to it. I would definitely have flunked an OFSTED report and I could have done with Jamie Oliver to help with the meals.

'Oooh, this looks delicious,' she would say flatly when I served her broccoli in bed. 'Such variety, Sarah. How do you do it?'

'I feel uncomfortable when you praise me about my cooking, Rach,' I would shrug bashfully. 'It's a gift.'

'How did you cook it?' she would ask, scrunching her nose up and pretending to appreciate the aroma.

'Well, I marinated it for four weeks and then flipped it around in the wok with some garlic and chilli, some home-grown herbs and a few other secret ingredients.'

'Funny, it looks as though you steamed it over the kettle.'

'Oh, that hurts!' I would gasp, having spent the previous

twenty minutes steaming broccoli over a kettle in an ornamental bowl.

'How many Michelin stars do you have?'

Talking bollocks was Rachel's broccoli avoidance tactic. It had to be counteracted.

'Here comes the aeroplane!' I would then suddenly and maniacally scream before stumbling around the room with the fork of broccoli, making aeroplane noises, until I got to her mouth.

'Oh, is that your phone?' she would say, granting herself a few moments' respite because I would always check to see if it was Simon. It never was Simon. Leo was the only person who tended to call me. Not that I answered his calls.

'I bloody hate broccoli. Do I have to?' she would sigh.

This was always a tricky question. Of course she didn't have to. I hadn't taken up tyranny. I wasn't studying *The Idiot's Guide to Stalinism*. I had simply read online that broccoli could reverse cancer.

'Is it really good for me?'

'If you believe online doctors, it's amazing, but, you know, it could be a load of old bollocks . . .'

I would feel uncomfortable but she would open her mouth and grant the first sprig entry. Then she would slowly chew the rest. And this was what Rachel was doing on the third day of this, our Odd Couple life, when there was a knock at the door. She was laboriously chewing broccoli with a 'could it ever get any worse' look in her eyes. I was bent over the kettle peering at a minuscule lump of wet spinach and wondering how to market it.

'Oh man, this will be amazing,' I said, having decided to go for the hard sell. 'Oh, was that the door?'

Assuming it was hotel staff, I left the wilting spinach and skipped towards the door. I was wearing my pyjama bottoms with a hooded top but I wasn't worried, as the hotel personnel were used to Worzel Gummidge in room 117 by now.

Only it wasn't a hotel employee. It was Eamonn Nigels, wearing a suit and looking embarrassed. He was flanked by two men in white jackets and bow ties. They were elderly men who held violins up to their warm, wise faces. I smiled at them. I love old men with instruments.

'No, no.' Eamonn turned to them and shushed. 'Good God, no. That's not her.'

'Oh, Eamonn,' I started gushing. 'You shouldn't have.'

'Sarah, is, er, Rachel here?'

'Well, she says she can't see anyone . . .' Suddenly I was thrown out of the way. Rachel bounded towards Eamonn. I noticed she'd applied lipgloss and a bit of blusher.

'Eamonn,' she gasped.

'Rachel. I want to be with you . . .' Eamonn started, but then he realized that I was there.

They both looked at me. I could understand why they wanted me to go because I'd already started crying. I knew I should go, but it was so beautiful and I'd got such a good seat.

'Sorry, let me put some shoes on and I'll leave you to it,' I said.

I had trouble finding my second flip-flop. And then my phone started ringing. Obviously I wanted to enhance Rachel and Eamonn's romantic moment, but it could have been Simon. I grabbed my phone, decided to forget about the other shoe and as a last-minute decision I picked up the laptop too, in case I was stranded for ages. Eventually I squeezed past them all and left the room. As soon as I was out of the way, I heard the violin start playing. When I was far down the corridor I turned back. I saw Eamonn down on one knee.

seventy-seven

'You said you didn't shag him. You said you didn't shag him.' It was Julia, unusually, calling on the mobile.

'Are you pissed?'

'You said you didn't shag him. You said you didn't shag him.'

'Jules. I've just been ousted from my room with one shoe and now I've got you on the phone and you're talking bollocks! What you on about?'

'You shagged Leo Clement. Why didn't you tell me, bitch face?'

'Jules. I never shagged Leo Clement,' I hissed. 'And I'm in the foyer of my bloody hotel. So I'm not going to shout and protest at you like I would normally.'

'That's not what he says.'

'What?'

'That's not what he says in *Nads* magazine.'

'What?'

'He says he shagged you. Well, I presume it's you. Blue dress, English and you won't like the other comment.'

'Please don't tell me his column is called "JizBiz"?'

'"JizBiz", yeah, it is! What's he like?'

'Oh God.'

I'd already got my laptop on my lap. I thought about typing the *Nads* address but then I remembered that the 'JizBiz' column wasn't online.

'Jules, Jules, you can't get it online. You have to read it to me.'

Julia coughed and then began.

> *A good week amigos. I hope you had as much luck as me. I met my cheerleader on Tuesday. Mamma mia. She had a new uniform and she wanted to practise her routine for me. You have to humour these teenagers. I told her to jump higher and bend over more. I couldn't resist it.*

'Jules, this is foul. Tell me you're making it up!'

'Nah! Holding it in my hand. Have to say, Sare, there's a picture of him in here. And, wow. Wow. W-o-w. Anyway, there's more, babe. Do you want to get a drink?'

'It's eleven in the morning here.'

'Your call.' She coughed.

> *She's a grade A cutie. But my best moment was an English girl. Not my usual type. Built for comfort not speed. But funny. You know, more dottie than hottie, but it made a change ...*

'Oh my God! Jules! Jules?'

My phone went dead. I caught sight of my face in one of

the foyer mirrors. I looked like I'd done a sicky burp.

'I don't bloody believe it,' I spat.

'Bad news?' a woman I have never met before asked me.

'You could say that,' I replied to the stranger.

She sat next to me even though there were about forty other free seats in the foyer. She was about my age and she looked, and I didn't say this often in LA, quite nice. I didn't really want to make any new friends at the moment but there was something comforting about her plainness. She wasn't the usual LA type. Her skin was a bit dry. She had some acne scars on her cheek and she too looked like she was built for comfort not speed. She could almost have been English.

'Have you ever heard of a magazine called *Nads*?'

'Oh, yeah, it's an English magazine. It's big.'

'No, I'm big, apparently.'

'No, you're not. You look great.'

Clearly I didn't look great. I was unclean and unbalanced but I appreciated her effort.

'According to Leo Cockhead Clement I am.'

The stupid thing is, I am the first person to say that I am not the slimmest. But it's not very nice to hear it from a man who has seen you naked. I wished I'd left that poo on his table.

'Urgh!'

'What's happened?'

'Do you know a bloke called Leo Clement?'

Perhaps I shouldn't speak about it, I thought. Then I remembered that Leo Clement had been happy to speak about it. In a lads' mag!

'Well, I know the name . . .'

'Well, in the magazine *Nads* he talks about me! How I'm fat and he shagged me,' I panted.

'Oh.'

'Wanker.'

'What's your name? I'm Carol.'

'Hey, Carol. Sorry about all this. I'm Sarah. Wanker. Not you, Carol. Leo Big Cock there.'

'Did he have a . . . ?' She glanced down at her lap and that was when I really started to like her, because I would have asked the same question.

'Yes, no, I don't know! I didn't shag him!'

Eamonn walked out of the lift carrying Rachel.

'Don't put your back out, Eamonn!' I called.

'Sarah, look!' Rachel shrieked and held up her hand. A diamond the size of a Brazil nut sparkled on her ring finger.

'Fuck me. Fraggle Rock.' I watched them as they giggled their way out of the door.

'Was that Eamonn Nigels?' asked Carol.

'Hmmm.'

'How do you know him?'

'Oh, I'm in a film he's doing.'

'Wow.'

'Are you an actress?'

'God, no, nothing so interesting.'

'Sarah!' It was Rachel on her own legs running towards me.

'Congratulations!' We fell into a big messy loud screechy hug.

'Oooh, careful of my boob.'

'Sorry.'

'Will you be my bridesmaid? Please. Eamonn wants you to be one too! Please.'

I didn't like to tell her that it would be my third time.

'Of course.'

'Ah! We're going to do it soon, before I go in. I'll call you tomorrow to plan!'

She shrieked off to join Eamonn.

♥ *seventy-eight* ♥

Eamonn arranged for Rachel to see the best doctors in LA. I finished shooting all my scenes. My six-week adventure was over and I should have flown back to England. However, Eamonn asked me to stay on if I could, to keep Rachel company. I said yes. I moved into their mansion and Rachel asked me to help plan her wedding.

'Me?'

'Yes, do you mind?'

'Like . . . be a wedding planner?'

'Yes.'

'Can that be my title?' I asked keenly.

'Er, we can call you whatever you want.'

'Wedding planner,' I sighed. 'Like whatsit in that film.'

'What?'

'You know, Jenny from the block, in that film.'

'J.Lo.'

'Yes, what was the name of that film?'

'*The Wedding Planner*, Sarah.'

'Oh. Deep title. You'd never guess what that's about. Right! When do we start looking at napkins and stuff?'

'We need someone to marry us.'

'Erin's dad!'

Rachel raised her eyebrows.

'Honestly, Rach, he'd be great. I went to a prayer meeting of his. He said "knob gags". He'd be perfect for you!'

'We need to find a place to have it first.'

'Oh. Probably wise.'

'Hmmm.'

'Where are you thinking?'

'Devon.'

Little tingles of bliss danced through me. I love Devon. I think it might be my spiritual home. We used to go on our annual family holidays to a place called Salcombe. It was the highlight of my childhood year. I didn't even mind the endless hours on the M4 and M5 when my father listened to his 'Become Fluent in German in a Week' cassettes. I knew that Devon was worth the wait. I would sit in the back with my head pressed to the window, watching the rain caterpillar across the pane, hopefully pointing out Little Chefs. I did get a little carsick when we came off the motorway and the roads got so windy that driving a quarter of a mile took forty-five minutes. But I'd always perk up at the first sight of the sea. California is nice and heated but it's not a nicotine patch on Devon. I even loved carrying forty-five bags to the beach and then sitting in the rain eating sandwiches in a cagoule and sun cream.

'Oh my God, you're going to get married in Devon,' I cried, and there were tears in my eyes.

'Sarah, pull yourself together and look at these.' She threw me a selection of brochures.

'Oh,' I sighed in pleasure at the shiny pictures. 'Uh, oh,' I groaned as I leafed through photos of bobbing fishing boats and coloured cottages. 'Oh, Rachel, it'll be so wonderful. Can I just have a little weep of happiness?'

'Off you go,' she smiled.

And I did. I cried little tears at the romance and the wonder and at the memories of home and childhood. But the fact that the last time I went to Devon was with Simon was mingled into the tears as well. It was a few years ago when we were just friends. We were poor and in need of a holiday. He borrowed a tent from Paranoid Jay and I borrowed my mum's car and off we went. I showed him my childhood haunts; we ate crab sandwiches on pontoons with our feet dangling in the sea, drank lager in ancient pub beer gardens and told each other ghost stories as the rain attacked the tent each night. As I remembered how much fun it had been, there was one loud thought in my mind. You really ballsed that up, Sarah.

Eamonn Nigels walked in as I was blowing my nose. He leant down, closed his eyes and kissed Rachel. The kiss looked like it meant the world.

'Sarah, darling, what the bloody hell's up with you?' he asked with an affectionate half smile.

'Oh, Devon, it's all so beautiful.'

'Meet our wedding planner, darling.'

'Oh, good God,' said Eamonn with feeling. 'This is the

one I like,' he continued, reaching over me and picking up a brochure I hadn't yet got to.

'Darling, it would bankrupt you,' Rachel said, shaking her head.

'It's there to be spent,' replied Eamonn firmly.

'Baby, it's so expensive.'

'Stunning,' he said, gazing at the picture of a beautiful white Georgian house set on a hill overlooking the sea. It was surrounded by huge trees and lush green plants.

'Devon, I'm in Devon,' I sang tearfully to the tune of 'Heaven, I'm in heaven' as I looked over his shoulder.

'It is amazing,' agreed Rachel. 'I've been there. I think it might actually be the most beautiful place I've ever been to. But Eamonn, I can't let you spend all that money.'

'You can,' he said with a glint in his eye. 'So I took the liberty of booking it today.'

Well, that was me. I was off. Rachel started crying. Even Eamonn wiped a tear. Rachel and Eamonn smooched while I flicked through the brochure.

'They do everything there. We have the whole place for guests to come for the weekend. All our professional, er, wedding planner has to do is help you choose the menu and do the seating plan. I like a carnage table plan myself. You know, mistresses next to wives, all the ex-husbands together, disgraced Tory peer next to a vicar and a journalist from the *Daily Mail*. That sort of thing. You're the perfect woman for the job, Sarah Sargeant. Oh, I should give you these.' He went into his man bag, fished out a pile of envelopes and dropped them into my lap.

'What are these?' I asked, taking an embossed card out of one and reading aloud. It was a reply slip. They had already sent out invitations asking people to keep the date free. 'Woody Allen would love to come. Poor bloke, fancy being called Woody Allen. People would be so disappointed when you booked a table at a restaurant and then you turned up and you weren't the famous film director,' I said, laying the card to one side and moving on to another.

'Not if you are the famous film director, Sarah,' Eamonn pointed out.

I looked at him.

'Woody Allen as in Woody Allen is coming to your wedding?'

'Yes, we go back a long way.'

'Eamonn, I have to say "fuck".'

'On you go.'

'Fuck me!'

We all laughed but the sight of the next card craftily pinched the look of glee from my face.

It was Simon's writing. Simon Gussett, Ruth Addinel and little Anna would be pleased to come to the wedding.

'You all right, Sarah?' Rachel asked.

'Yeah,' I said, but I wasn't. My eyes had filled with tears and I couldn't see.

'Oh, Sarah, yes. Ruth had the, er, the baby.'

'But I didn't think it, she, was his,' I said quietly. 'I didn't think they were together.'

'She is Simon's,' said Eamonn, gently putting a hand on my shoulder 'I'm so sorry, Sarah, it must be hard for you. I had a long chat to him yesterday. There was a . . . what do you call it? Paternity test. And she is his and they have decided to be a family, Sarah. They're all doing well.'

I put the reply slip back in the envelope and vowed to place those three as far as possible away from me on my table plan.

♥ *seventy-nine* ♥

The next day, after Eamonn had gone to the studio, as usual, I took Rachel in her tea and toast and broccoli spears with Philadelphia on top.

'How's the bride to be?' I asked as I did every day.

Every morning Rachel had come back with the same one-word answer: 'Fighting!' But that morning she looked like all the energy had been siphoned out of her in the night. She slowly propped herself up in bed. Her hair was bedraggled and her eyes looked punched from lack of sleep.

'Not feeling great, Sarah, to be honest.'

'Hey,' I said, carrying the tray to her bed and propping a pillow behind her head to make her comfortable. She dropped her head against it and groaned.

'No sleep,' she said. 'Just my breast killing and my mind going round and round.'

'Were you on the crap-thought roundabout, unable to get off?'

'Yeah. Big time. Bloody thing.'

'Can I do anything?'

'No,' she smiled. 'No, no, there's nothing anyone can do.

It's out of our hands, I guess. But I just want time, Sarah, more time. I don't want this to be it. Illness and death. I mean if it is, then you know me, I'll make of it what I can. But I just want days. Loads of them ahead of me. I still daydream. Of Eamonn and me setting up a proper home together and me learning Thai cooking. And you and I, Sarah, I want us to go New York shopping in the sales. I want to see you win an Oscar and help you dress to receive it. I want to become a yoga teacher. I want to go into schools and teach kids yoga. I want to be a good wife to Eamonn. I want to grow old and elegant and dress like a French woman. I don't want this to be it. At thirty-two.'

'It won't be, Rach. Don't stop daydreaming. We are so going to New York and you and I will be sitting in Paris when we're in our sixties and the French women will be giving you French evils because you look so elegant and sophisticated and we'll drink pink champagne in the morning.'

'Oh, Sarah, I keep beating myself up. I've been so obsessed by crap for most of my life. About my figure and men and bollocks. Talk about being a knobhead. I never thought I'd say knobhead. See how you're affecting me? I wish someone had tapped me on the shoulder when I was in my teens and said, "It's short this life thing, don't sweat the small stuff." Sorry. I'll shut up.'

'No, don't. To quote a bit of Bob Hoskins, "It's good to talk."'

'Oh, right, one thing I've been meaning to ask you . . .'

'What's that?'

'Do you see this, here,' she said, pointing a finger to her cheek.

'Your cheek.'

'Yes, Sarah, wonderful. It's my cheek. But this is where I get a hair. A bloody pubic hair grows out of my cheek, right here, and it needs to be plucked. And I just want to ask you, if I do get ill, whether you'll pluck that little bastard for me?'

'Of course.'

'Thank you. Now, though, one positive . . . see what you're doing to me with all this arsing positive? One positive thing that came out of last night is I decided to ask Erin's dad to marry us. What do you think?'

'I think he and Erin would be thrilled.'

'You don't think it's weird that he caught me having sex with another man in his church six years ago?'

'I can't say I don't think it's weird, Rach, and I shall have to try very hard not to remember that fact during the ceremony, because it will make me snort. Aside from that, I think he's the perfect man to marry you. Do you want me to ask him?'

'No, I thought I would. I thought I'd go along to that prayer meeting and maybe ask him there.'

♥ *eighty* ♥

Rachel was so nervous going to the prayer meeting that I held her hand as we walked in.

'Freaky, this,' she whispered. 'Crazy bloody freaky. They did my head in at the convent with all that God shit. Sorry, God,' she quickly added. 'I've spent my whole life thinking it was all a load of old bollocks. And now I'm doing this. It's not really right, is it? It's like when you go to bed with a guy and he does his thing and then lies down and is nearly asleep and then he says, "Oh sorry, did you want me to make you come?"'

I had to stop walking.

'What are you on about?'

'Oh, dunno. Just that's it's a bit late me being here, really.'

'That has nothing to do with a bloke not making you come.'

'I had a boyfriend who would do that. I was thinking about him today. Cock.'

We were in the lobby area outside the meeting room. On the notice board at our eye level a sign proclaimed JESUS IS COMING. We glanced at it at the same time.

'Even he's coming,' Rachel said.

'Duck!' I cried and crouched down as though I was going to be sprayed with celestial semen. We laughed raucously. I was about to suggest that we go home as we weren't in the right mood for quiet contemplation when Mr Schneider walked through the doors, clapped his eyes on me first and then Rachel. He opened his arms and walked towards Rachel.

'Rachel, it is wonderful that you've joined us,' he spoke slowly. Mr Schneider is the only man I've ever met who seems totally to mean everything he says. No wonder his daughter is such a good actress. 'Now then, Sarah,' he said, turning to me. 'We have been praying for your friend. Many words have been said to the big man. I do hope your friend is feeling better.'

Rachel took my hand. I think she knew it was her.

'Um, Mr Schneider, you know, um, I'm getting married. Do you think you would be able to marry us?'

'It would be an honour.'

'But, but, it's soon because of a, well, it has to be, it's in ten days.'

'The fourth?'

'Yes, yes, you're good. It's the fourth.'

'I am free.'

'It's, um, in England.'

'Oh.'

'But we'll pay for everything. For you and Erin, if you don't mind.'

'We'd be honoured.'

'Oh, thank you.'

'Come through,' he said, opening the double doors for Rachel like a gentleman. 'And you, too, Sarah.' I walked past him, and he winked. 'God bless Sarah Sargeant.'

'God bless Mr Schneider,' I sang back to him.

We walked in. The chairs were in a circle like the last time. The flowers in the middle were sunflowers. It was much busier than before. Everybody else was already seated. I spotted the tall Donkey Man and his wife.

'Oh, my goodness!' Erin squealed when she saw us.

We were the last to arrive and Erin helped us to the only two available seats, which weren't together. I wished I'd been able to sit next to Rachel because I think she found the hour hard. Mr Schneider had decided that we should use the session to focus on the good that can come from hardship.

'Seeing the good in the bad' was his tagline. I wished it hadn't been. Rachel had cancer. It was pretty hard to think of a positive. Everyone had to go round and say what they wanted to pray for and then say how their current hardship could be seen as a blessing. It was my turn before Rachel.

'Sarah, do you want to share? You know no one has to share here. The big man will hear silent prayers too.'

'Oh.' I thought about not speaking, but for some reason these words came out of my mouth: 'I lost a man I loved to another woman. And I've been very unhappy.'

Everyone said, 'Oh.'

'Hmmm,' I agreed. 'I thought we were like a done deal,

together forever. But, if I had to think of a positive I'd say at least he's happy now. He has a baby with her and he really wanted a baby. So he got what he wanted. And that's good. And I'm glad he's happy. I really am glad he's happy.'

'Rachel?' Mr Schneider said kindly. 'Is there anything you'd like to share?'

'No,' she said quietly, and hung her head so no one could see her eyes. 'If you don't mind. I don't think I'm ready. No. Sorry.'

But what was she supposed to say? Er, get to meet a lot of doctors. Scars are in this year. Never liked that breast anyway.

♥ *eighty-one* ♥

Rachel, Eamonn and I flew back to Heathrow five days later. My LA experience was over. After nearly quitting the film, spraining my ankle, making an enemy of an international superstar and being called fat in a lads' mag, I couldn't imagine being invited back soon. I was dreading seeing myself in the film almost as much as I was dreading seeing Simon at the wedding. But they were backburner fears. I was so pre-occupied with making sure that Rachel was comfortable and as happy as she could be that I didn't have much time to think about myself.

Brian was on our flight.

'What diet have you been on?' he asked as soon as he saw me.

'The bread and booze. How to put on a stone in a week one. I'm bloody brilliant at it.'

'No, Sarah Sargeant, I mean it, you've lost weight, treacle.'

'Have I?'

'What do you mean, "Have I?" You're a woman. Haven't you been trying?'

'No. Haven't really been thinking about it. I did think my

jeans were baggy but then I can't remember the last time I washed them so I thought that was probably why.'

'Lovely, darling,' he said, putting a glass of champagne on my little table.

I didn't take it as a compliment. My friend had cancer. That's why I'd lost weight. I would have much rather he'd said, 'Has Sarah Sargeant been deep-frying the Melton Mowbrays?' and Rachel had been well.

'I'm a wedding planner.'

'Well, yes, a perfect job for you, with your organizational skills,' he deadpanned.

Eamonn in the seat across the aisle pretended to choke. Brian tootled off and I resumed poring over my seating plan. I'd put Erin next to Woody Allen because I thought she could become his latest muse. I'd put Leo Clement next to Erin's dad and a lesbian fashion designer on a table where the average age was about seventy-six so he couldn't get up to any jizbiz. Leo had not stopped calling me. A fact I found weirder than The Krankies. Perhaps he thought tabloid humiliation got me going? Not that I cared what he thought. I was never going to speak to him again.

'What's that, angel?' Brian said as he dropped off some macadamia nuts.

'The table plan for the . . .' As I looked at Brian's warm, smiling face, I stopped speaking. I gasped. I was experiencing a moment of brilliance. They always surprise me. 'Are you working next weekend?'

'No.'

'Are you in England?'

'Yes, I'm back in Blighty. They're forecasting torrential rain.'

'Do you want to be my guest at Rachel's wedding in Devon?'

'Oh, like in that film, *My Best Friend's Wedding*! I can be your dashing, sophisticated gay male escort.'

'Would you?'

'I'd love to!'

'Oooh,' I squealed.

And that was that. I had a date. The invitation said *Dress code: whatever makes you feel wonderful* so Brian and I discussed his outfit whenever he topped my champagne glass up, which was frequently.

'Hmmm. I did feel wonderful when I went to a Super-heroes party dressed as Wonder Woman.'

'Rachel probably wouldn't mind . . . if you wanted to . . .'

He thought for a moment.

'No,' he said sadly. 'I lost the blue satin pants. It's nothing without those.'

'Well, just wear whatever you feel comfortable in.'

'I could wear a pilot's uniform. And I could pick you up like Richard Gere at the end of that film. Although I think I've done something to my back moving a heavy piece of hand luggage to the overhead lockers.'

And so it went on. Thousands of miles were covered as we discussed the issue. Eventually Brian decided he wanted to wear a red suit. And although I thought it sounded a little

Graham Norton, his enthusiasm blazed so brightly it would have been wrong to douse it in a fire blanket and suggest something else.

We spent at least ninety minutes trying to find him a handsome millionaire to sit next to because I would be placed on the top table and not be able to keep him company. Eventually, I had ANOTHER moment of genius.

'You can go next to Dominic. A gay theatre director. Dashing. Did cast me as the Beanstalk in *Jack and the Beanstalk* . . . but we can overlook that,' I said, rubbing out Dominic's date's name and replacing it with Brian. I then put Dominic's date on the oldies' table with Leo Clement.

'Who's this? What have you written?' He bent down, squinted and read the tiny writing next to Simon and Ruth's names: *to be moved if there is anywhere further away from the top table or behind a pillar if poss.*

'That's Simon,' I told him quietly.

'As in Banana Man?'

'Hmmm, him and Yoga Woman and their baby girl will be there.'

'Oh, popsicle.'

'It'll be fine,' I said.

Brian looked as though he didn't believe me.

'Fine?'

'Fine like getting a garden fork and stabbing it repeatedly on my foot. That sort of fine,' I clarified.

'Your really hot gay escort will have a packet of Kleenex in the pocket of his red suit should you need.'

'Thanks.'

I wished Simon and family had declined their invitation to the wedding. It wasn't that I didn't want to see them. It had to happen at some point. I just didn't want to see them on a happy day, that was all. I knew it was going to be emotional for me. Therefore it would have been better to meet them on a day of national mourning or after a natural disaster. Any event where people were openly howling in pain and grief would have done.

♥ *eighty-two* ♥

The heat under my simmering fears was about to get whacked up to high. We all got a taxi from the airport. Rachel and Eamonn dropped me off first. It was my first time away from them for days. Suddenly there was nothing to distract me from thinking about myself.

There was no note from Si. I searched and searched for one. I wanted some words. I was frantic for them. I don't even know what I wanted the words to say. But I wanted letters on a page that would make it all better. Words that would draw a line under Simon and me. Words that would say the pain is over. Off you go. You can move on now. Even though I've always hated the expression 'move on'. Generally when people have said, 'Oooh, you need to move on,' I've moved quickly away from the person who said that awful phrase towards the nearest bar. But I so wanted a note from him that would let me move on. I wanted the alphabet to be formulated in a way that would give me closure.

And I intensely disliked the word 'closure', too. I'd always thought it was a term made up by people from California to sell books. But as I went through the bin in case he'd written a letter and changed his mind, I wished I'd bought one of those books.

But there was no note. I even checked the bathroom. Nothing. Just floor space where the Cockaconga had been and some blue furry hummus and what might once have been a tomato in the fridge. It wasn't the ending I wanted. It didn't even feel like an ending at all. It felt like a DVD you'd buy from a Chinese lady with a big carrier bag, where the picture was fine and the movie was brilliant but it cut out before the end. And you were left staring at the screen, not knowing what to do with yourself. I did pretty much what I would have done had that happened. I just made myself a cup of black tea, as there was no milk, and went to bed.

I was pleased it was only for one night. Eamonn and Rachel picked me up the following morning to travel to Devon. I thought about Simon for most of the M4 and M5. And I was still thinking about Simon when we turned off the motorway and got stuck behind a tractor going at eighteen miles per hour. But when I thought about him, he wasn't my Si. The old Simon. The Simon who had gone to Devon with me. The Simon who massaged my feet. The Simon who took the mickey out of my blow jobs. He was a new Simon I didn't know. Daddy Simon. Ruth's other half. Someone who doubtless spoke about school catchment areas and weaning and wore a white piece of vomit-covered muslin over his shoulder. Someone who went to bed with a girl called Ruth and woke in the night to cuddle his beautiful baby. Someone who knew his future and knew who the main characters in it were. He had his happy ever after. But where was my bloody happy ending?

'You've got to find it for yourself,' I whispered aloud. Eamonn had The Rolling Stones up as high as the little black knob would let him. So no one heard me.

'Where's my happy ending?' I whispered again. But then Rachel turned around in the passenger seat and put her hand on my knee.

'Not long now. You all right back there, Sarah?' she shouted. She was smiling.

And I felt bad.

eighty-three

Rather than have traditional hen and stag dos, Eamonn and Rachel decided to have a boys' dinner and a girls' dinner the night before the wedding. Rachel didn't want a big exhausting evening where she was supposed to lick squirty cream off a stripper's bottom. She wanted something simple, somewhere she could slip away easily to bed. Therefore the girls' night was at the Georgian house where all the guests were housed and the wedding was to take place. The boys had a coach take them to a local fish restaurant.

Erin and I spent the few hours before the hen dinner decorating the dining room for Rachel. We had made place mats with photocopied pictures of Rachel looking stunning. We'd blown up various embarrassing pictures of Rachel and Blu-tacked them onto the walls. I had some great ones of her from the convent. And I'd taken one of her arse-end-on in a downward dog. We'd put that one on the door with the words IT'S RACHEL'S HEN DINNER – BOTTOMS UP! beneath it. We arranged candles and pink balloons throughout the room.

'We've done a good job,' said Erin, standing by the door and surveying the scene. Her hair was in a ponytail and she was wearing dungarees. She definitely did look like one of the Waltons. ''Night, John Boy!' I wanted to say, but didn't. I was wearing the jeans that still hadn't been in the wash and a jumper with a hole under the arm and a cardigan over the top. I had forgotten how cold England was. My hair was down and unbrushed. I was unshowered, because I'd got up late and there'd been a hundred things to do. If people saw me they were probably stopping themselves saying, 'Here's 70p, treat yourself to a cup of tea.'

'I think that's it! Oh! Bugger. I bought a book for us all to sign. It's up in my room, Erin, give me a second, I'll run up and get it.' I walked past her and just had my hand on the big bronze door handle when I felt it move. I pulled the door back to see who was trying to get in.

'Oh, uh, Sarah, sorry.'

It was Ruth. She stood before me. She looked pretty but tired. But I wasn't really looking at her face because suspended against her front was a small, ugly, hairy creature. It had wide red cheeks and lots of soft black hair sticking up. It was as if someone had created a mini Simon for a *Lord of The Rings* film. It was little Anna. She was unimaginably gorgeous.

'This is Anna,' said Ruth. But I couldn't speak back. I couldn't do anything but look at Anna. She was the coolest thing I'd ever seen. This was the closure I had been looking for. This was everything I needed to know. She was part of Simon. She was a little bundle of his genes and his energy and she was at the very start of her journey in the world.

'I was trying to find a quiet spot to sit and feed her.'

I really needed to do some speaking. But I was rendered mute by this crazy-haired thing.

'Come in, we're nearly finished. It'll be quiet in here if you need to feed her,' said Erin, walking towards us. She looked at Anna and cooed, 'She's adorable.' But Anna was looking at me.

'Yes, sorry, Ruth, come in,' I eventually achieved.

'Thanks.'

She strode in, little Anna bobbing up and down on her front. 'How are you, Sarah?' she asked, putting her bag down on the floor and sitting herself on one of the dining-room chairs.

'Fine. You?'

'Not bad,' she said, taking Anna out of the baby carrier and resting her on her lap. Anna was wearing a little baby-blue-and-white stripy Babygro. It looked part convict, part Baby Gap. 'Oh, that's my phone, could you . . .' Ruth stopped there but she seemed to be offering Anna to me.

'Um, should I take her?' I asked, and I manoeuvred my arms around the soft bundle that was little Anna and took her weight. I held her away from me at first, but then I brought her to my chest. How can I describe her? She was beyond amazing. She was like a priceless miracle that I wanted to protect forever. I know it sounds trite and wanky but I felt like I'd just met this little person and I already loved her entirely. I would probably never see her again but

I knew that if she needed anything at all during the next sixty years I would do it. Whatever it was. This was little Anna. Wow.

I looked down at her. I thought I was imagining it at first. I thought it might be the acid flashback. But she smiled at me. She opened her mouth and showed me her gums and it wasn't a grimace of pain or the start of a bawl. She smiled at me. I realize that it could have been a touch of wind as she was quite small to be smiling. But I like to think it was a smile. And I tried to smile back but no matter what I did that smile insisted on becoming a tear filled grimace. I pulled out a chair and sat down with her, cradling her in my arms. The only baby I hadn't made cry, made me cry. I'd met my match here.

'Sarah, are you all right with her?'

'Hmmm,' I mumbled. I didn't want Ruth to see me cry. This one was between me and Anna.

'Here, I'll take her,' Ruth said, walking towards me and taking Anna from my arms.

'She's beautiful,' I said, and swallowed.

'She takes after her dad.'

I nodded and smiled and looked at my lap.

'Least she didn't get my big nose.'

'You haven't got a big nose,' I lied.

There was a pause. I felt calm. Slightly emotionally battered, but calmer about this whole situation than I ever had. Simon and Ruth had made this awesome smiley, hairy little thing in a Babygro. I couldn't be jealous of this. I could walk away now. It was right that they were all together. Wow. It was going to be OK.

'Um,' started Ruth. 'I'm sorry, Sarah, about . . .'

I made one of those 'don't worry about it' gestures that you do if you've just spent 20p on someone and they're trying to give it to you. It struck us both as ridiculous so we both laughed.

'It's OK. I'm glad you're all happy.'

'Yeah,' said Ruth, but she didn't look happy as she said it.

'Right then, I'd better go and get sorted for this hen's dinner . . .'

'He's not happy, Sarah.'

'What?'

'Simon's not happy.'

'Oh, er, Ruth . . .'

'I mean, he's worried about business. That Viagra thing has hardly sold at all. But he's not happy with me either. Don't think he is. We want to all be together but it's not a big love job.'

I felt my hand clench. Not because I wanted to wallop her but because I didn't want to hear why Simon wasn't her perfect man. My breathing quickened slightly. I had to speak.

'Ruth . . . I don't think we should have this conversation, so I'm just going to say one thing and then I'll bugger off.'

She looked a bit taken aback, as though she thought I *would* wallop her. So I unclenched my fist. 'Simon is one of the kindest, funniest, most special, most emotionally intelligent, positive, pretty bloody gorgeous people on the planet. Don't lose him. I can say this because I did lose him. But I lost him to valid winners.' I looked at Ruth and Anna. 'Don't lose him, Ruth, because you'll regret it. There's not a day gone by since Si and I split up when I haven't looked in the mirror and said, "Sarah, you knobhead! What have you done?" But it's good that you're a family. Learn from my mistakes, Ruth. Make it work, because you won't find a better bloke than Si.'

Ruth's mouth was slightly open as I left her. And she appeared ruffled for the short time she was at the hen dinner later on. I knew she wanted to talk to me and I am ashamed to say I avoided her all night. But a conversation along the lines of, 'Sarah, I nicked your boyfriend but he's not up to much,' was not on my list of priorities for the evening. I didn't want to get dragged down into a mire of Simon and Ruth trouble. So I didn't. I sat next to Rachel. I met her family and Eamonn's family and a host of attractive women who were married to film directors. And after dinner I organized an English-versus-Yanks game of charades in the drawing room while we had our coffee and liqueurs. When I went to bed that night in Rachel's room, she turned to me before she put out the lamp and said, 'Thank you, Sarah, that was perfect.' And I knew she wouldn't have said that had I spent part of the night crying in a corner with Ruth. So I vowed to adopt Simon and Ruth avoidance tactics the next day. Although I was hoping for another little cuddle with Anna. And that's who I was thinking about when I passed out.

eighty-four

'SARAH!!!!' It was Eamonn's voice. He was banging loudly on the door. I unstuck one eye and focused it on the bedside clock. It was 7.14 a.m.

'He can't see me before the wedding,' Rachel grunted.

'Jesus, Eamonn,' I whispered when I got to the door. 'You can't introduce me to the mad Irish side of your family one night and then shout at me the following morning. That's abuse. I'll be on to Equity about you.'

'Have a look at this,' he said, hurling something at me. It was a cheaply manufactured celebrity gossip mag.

'The *National Enquirer*. Cool. Thanks,' I said, staring at a photo of Angelina Jolie with a circle around some armpit sweat and wondering why Eamonn chose this morning to be a paperboy. Must be pre-wedding jitters.

'Have a look at it.'

I started flicking through it.

'I really need a cup of tea,' I moaned.

'It's on the next page.'

'What?' I said, raising my head from an article entitled 'Plastic Surgery Shockers' and looking at him. There was something in his expression telling me that I really didn't want to see what was on the next page. 'Wha, wha, what's on the next page, Eamonn?'

'Look at it.'

'Nooooooo,' I squeaked. But then I thought to myself, what can be on there? The only embarrassing thing I've done in ages is an unfortunate incident involving a toilet and a hedge but there's no way there could be an article about that in the *National Enquirer*. So I turned the page.

'Oh.'

'Yes. Oh.'

The headline was

I DIDN'T SHAG HIM SAYS ENGLISH STAR.

I admit the use of the word 'star' was quite nice and would normally have me cha-cha-cha-ing towards a bottle of something fizzy. But in this case all I could do was groan. Because there was a photo of me below the headline. The main problems with the photo were:

1 I had no make-up on. Actually, that's a lie. I did have quite a lot of black eyeliner on, but it was from the night before, and it was halfway down my cheek
2 I was staring down at my laptop on my lap. And it didn't look as though I had the general neck-to-chin ratio. Instead it looked like I had an obese man's belly where my neck should have been

3   I was pulling the 'difficult stool' expression. I didn't look the brightest. I looked like someone from a limited gene pool who had a reputation for forming relationships with chickens

I read the article.

English actress outraged by sexual slurs. Sarah Sargeant, 34,

'Thirty-four!!!!?'

discovers that Leo Clement has made salacious remarks about her in an English publication called Nads. *This begs the question: Is Leo Clement the ladies' man he purports to be and is Palmer Newsome giving publicists a bad name? Carol Bronchstein investigates.*

'Oh. Carol,' I said sadly.
'Is that who you spoke to?'
'Yeah, but I thought she was nice.'
'Oh, Sarah.'
'Cow.'
'Yes, well.'
'I met her in the foyer because you were proposing to your bird,' I said to him. 'So, technically, it's all your fault.'
I stared sadly at the photo. The *National Enquirer* had been kind enough to offer an alternative image of me. Now, one would hope they'd have used an acting shot so the

reader might think that this one was just unflattering. But no. They'd used a still from the YouTube Cockaconga viral ad.

I read the article. It turns out that Carol was stalking Leo and Palmer the publicist. She claimed that Palmer wrote Leo's column. The week he was supposedly having a three-some in his hot-tub in Malibu he was actually surfing in Lanzarote.

'That was nice of them to include my quote, "Leo Clement is a star star star star head,"' I muttered.

'Eamonn, is that my phone? I better take it in case it's wedding stuff. Hang on a sec.' I ran back into the room quickly and snatched it from the bedside table. 'Hello?'

'Sarah, Sarah, Sarah.'

'Is that my favourite agent? Blimey. Calling me on a Saturday at this time. Is this like star treatment?'

'Hmmm.'

'What's up? You sound like you're going to put your head in an oven.'

'Next time you go moonlighting, please could you tell me?'

'What are you on about? I haven't been moonlighting.'

'Sarah, I've had Crème de Menthe on my phone today screaming at me.'

'Why? What have you done?'

'I omitted to tell them that their beloved actress, face of the newly re-branded Crème de Menthe, is also the face of a herbal-based Viagra product. And Sarah, if you were the face of an exotic perfume or make of jewellery I don't think Crème de Menthe would mind, but as it is, you're the face of a product that cures erectile dysfunction! And Crème de Menthe doesn't want to be associated with erectile dysfunction! So the commercial is, unsurprisingly, off.'

'Oh,' I said sadly. 'But. But. It's only a little Internet thing.'

'Yes, but that little Internet thing has had over two million hits.'

'What? Has it? Shit. I'm sorry.'

'Yes, so am I.'

I hung up.

'They don't want me in the commercial now either,' I said to Eamonn. He pulled a kind face and then gave me a hug.

'You'll be all right, Sarah Sargeant. Just a case of a little too much communication, I think,' he said, releasing me. 'See you later. Look after my bride.'

I'd never work again because I call fellow actors ****heads. I'd lost a lucrative commercial. It was a lot to process. I couldn't go back to sleep. I put on Rachel's Ugg boots and a cardigan and went for a wander.

I had been hoping to secure a cup of tea. But there were already guests in the breakfast room and I felt it wise to avoid people. So I snuck outside the front door and skipped along a path. The air was fresh and crisp and nothing like Camden or LA. I followed the wooded path until I came to a bench where the trees cleared in front so you could see the sea. It was beautiful.

I would have sung 'Devon, I'm in Devon' but I was somewhat distracted. I was about to see Leo at the wedding and
I had called him a cockhead in a gossip magazine. I would
have to put him on my list of people to avoid. If it kept
getting longer I'd probably be advised to eat in my room.
And I had gone and lost my lucrative commercial for a
lifeforming liquor. That wasn't just rubbish. It was four-
week-old rubbish during a bin-man strike. But although it
was stinking and putrid, it gave me an idea. I quickly took
my phone from my pocket and dialled the number of the
hotel I had been staying at in LA.

'Hello, could you put me through to the beach restaurant? Thank you. Hello, there's a pretty waitress who
works there. She's got dark hair and she went on a fast with
vinegar . . . oh, yes . . . that's the one . . . I don't suppose
she's there, or I could have her number? Brilliant, could I
speak to her? Hello, this is Sarah Sargeant, you lent me your
The Secret book . . . Oh no, he's still with her. But listen, I'm
not doing that commercial any more. So you should get in
contact with the director. Why not? Well, you've nothing to
lose. Cool.' We swapped numbers and I was just forwarding
her the information she needed when I heard something. It
was the crunch of gravel and a familiar voice coming
towards me. I needed to hide. I darted from the path and
scampered up the wooded hill. I leant behind a tree, quietly
catching my breath, and listened.

'Jay! Mate! Calm down. Tell me slowly . . . How many?
How many? . . . Jay, mate, chill. No, no, no . . . Don't have a

joint! . . . Uh huh.' It was Simon. 'Show me the money!' He whooped. It made me smile. 'So what happened? Did you put an ad in somewhere? . . . The national what? Oh, *National Enquirer*! What, my Sarah? Like a scarecrow . . . ah . . . Bless her, eh, Sarah Sargeant.' I waited for him to follow my name with a 'what a nutter', but it didn't come. He left it at that. He said my name warmly. He just said my name warmly and it meant so much.

More gravel crunching as he walked away. I started to negotiate my way down the hill and back to the path. But I had to freeze again.

'Mate!' Simon shouted. 'Mate!' More gravel crunching. I think he was running.

'Hey.' It was only Leo Clement.

'You don't know where I'd find a newsagent's around here?'

'Oh, no. But you could ask at reception, they might tell you.'

'Cheers.'

'What are you looking for?'

'The whatsit? The *National Enquirer*.'

'Come with me,' Leo laughed. 'I've got a pile.'

I leant forward to see their backs walking down the path.

'Do you do weights?' I heard Simon ask.

'No. I surf,' he answered before they were out of earshot.

I remembered Leo Clement in the half-pulled-up wetsuit and the way he held my face with his rough hands before he kissed me. And I realized something. Leo Clement! If he wasn't really a ladies' man, then what was all that about with me? Could it have been true? Could he have really liked me? I would see him later at the wedding. My stomach started to feel as though it was hosting an episode of *Strictly Come Dancing*.

♥ eighty-five ♥

Rachel and I got ready together in our room. After the make-up and hair ladies had gone we stood together in front of the full-length mirror.

'Oh, Sarah, did you give the lady the CD of the song we're walking in to?'

'What, "I Still Haven't Found What I'm Looking For"?'

'Sarah!'

'Oh, what, you mean "Road To Hell"?'

'Sarah! I'm serious, have you . . .'

'What? "Fifty Ways to Leave Your Lover"?'

'I'm not listening. I know you've got it.'

'Yeah, I took "Love Is a Battlefield" down this morning and gave it to the lady.'

'I have to ignore this because I feel it'll go on. Have you seen Eamonn?'

'Yes, and he looks dashing.'

'This is it,' she said, looking at her reflection in the mirror. 'I'm getting married.'

Rachel was wearing a long cream dress. Nothing like the

toilet-roll lady though. It had a sleeveless bodice top and flowed down gently to the floor. The bodice was covered in vintage lace, which also framed the hem of the skirt. She looked elegant and understated. Her hair was down and slightly curled and there was a tiara-like crown of fresh flowers on her head.

'You look absolutely stunning.'

'We both do,' Rachel said, smiling at me in the mirror.

Tooled up with the knowledge that Leo wasn't a wanker as previously believed, I had made a special effort getting ready. I was wearing the blue dress that I wore the night we smooched for hours. It felt like it was Leo's dress. Rachel and I had looked for something different but nothing else came close. So we had it dry-cleaned and repaired a small tear that I had made in Leo Clement's hedge that day. Rachel insisted I had my make-up done by her make-up artist. So I had smoky eyes, although I knew it would be down my cheek in half an hour.

'Do you think once you've called a bloke a cockhead in an international publication you're still in with a chance?'

'Not entirely sure. Although if you look like you do today, I'd say that you could call his mum a bitch and you'd be fine.'

'Maybe I'll get Erin's dad to hold a special vigil.'

There was a knock on our door.

'Is my little girl ready?' It was Rachel's dad to escort her downstairs for the ceremony.

'Oh shit. I'm really doing it,' she gasped.

'Hmmm. Marrying an amazing man in a beautiful place. Cool, eh?'

'Do you think it's a good idea? You know, at the moment?' she whispered.

I was going to say, 'Don't be such a knobhead,' but I didn't. I stopped myself.

'Yes,' I said instead, and she smiled.

♥ *eighty-six* ♥

I love a wedding! It's an orgy of love. A feast for the soul. A riot of goodwill. If I had my way I would go to a wedding every Saturday when *The X Factor* wasn't on.

Eamonn and Rachel's wedding ceremony was so wonderful, however, that I would have happily given up *X Factor* forever just to have been present at it. Erin's dad was the perfect man to wed them. Although he did shock Rachel when he said, 'I met Rachel some years ago when she visited my church in New York.'

The crowd murmured 'ahs' and Rachel's gran said loudly, 'She went to a convent, she's very religious.' Rachel turned round to me and made an 'eek' face while I sucked in my cheeks. Then I looked at Erin. Her eyes widened and her mouth opened and I saw the exact moment when she realized where she'd met Rachel before.

'I was struck by her spirit and lust . . . for life. I had the pleasure of meeting Eamonn more recently when he cast my daughter in his latest film. I cannot explain how happy I am to be here in this beautiful place in England to join these two in matrimony. Life has shown them both some challenges but in their love they are united to face these together, and it is this we celebrate today. Please stand and sing our first song. One of my personal favourites. "All You Need Is Love".'

It wasn't the normal embarrassed mumbling of a high hymn that no one had heard of. Everyone belted out the words. I turned behind me to look at the gathered guests. But the only person I saw was Leo Clement. He was wearing the waistcoat, white shoes outfit he'd worn before. He was standing next to Brian, who waved. Leo looked up from his hymnbook and smiled and seemed to be singing to me. 'All You Need Is Love'. But it made me think about Simon suddenly. Was love all you needed? Probably not. Simon and I had loved each other, and it had still gone tits up.

'Now, I have been married for twenty-seven years and I counsel married couples in New York. And the problem is always the same between them. They stop talking. So I want to remind Eamonn and Rachel, even though you may think that Rachel needs no reminding on this score. Keep talking. If she looks great, tell her, if you feel full of love, tell him, if he's being a dork, you should mention that too. Keep telling each other how you feel. It can be harder than you think. Now, I think we should have our next song. "Nothing's Gonna Stop Us Now".'

And we all belted out that power ballad as though soft rock depended on it.

After the ceremony there were champagne and photographs on the lawn outside. I had cried on and off throughout the entire ceremony so decided to slip away to apply cosmetic first-aid to my smoky eyes. I was nearly at the door of the main house when a hand reached out and touched my arm.

'Sarah Sargeant!'

'Yes . . .' I said to a large man who looked familiar. He was a big man in an expensive but crumpled suit. He had a bushy brown beard.

'Peter Jackson,' he said. I knew his name from the table plan. But I couldn't remember where or if I'd met him before. Then the sun rose in my mind.

'Oh my God,' I said before I could stop myself. 'Like *the* Peter Jackson, as in *Lord of the Rings*?'

'Yes. Now, Eamonn and I go back a long way. He happened to show me some rushes. I have to say, great work.' He looked at me seriously. 'Great, great work. We'll be seeing a lot more of you, Sarah, I feel. Are you English?'

'Yes,' I said. 'From Croydon.' Why I added that, I will never know.

'I had no idea.'

'Really?' I squeaked.

'Really,' he nodded.

Oh, don't cry, Sarah, I said to myself, please, please, for once in your life don't cry when nice things happen.

'Oh, thank you, ah, ah, ah. Excuse me, emotional day,' I mouthed and had to walk away towards the ladies. It didn't seem real. Peter Jackson thought I was good in the film. He'd sought me out to tell me.

'Sarah,' I heard my name again. Oh, please be Woody Allen, I thought. But actually it was better. It was Leo.

'Hi,' I said.

'Hey.'

'Hey,' I repeated back. Our eyes were locked.

My hand involuntarily travelled to my hair and started fiddling with it.

'I'm sorry.'

'You're sorry! Leo, I am ridiculously sorry. I called you a cockhead!'

'Oh, I thought the stars stood for shithead.'

'I love the term "shithead",' I sighed, because I do.

'So, I'm a cockhead.' He smiled. It didn't sound right when said in an American accent.

'I didn't mean it. I mean I did at the time. But only cos of what you said in your column.'

'I didn't even know I had a column.'

Oh, I did, Leo, I did.

'You must have hated me!'

'No!'

I'd started rubbing my lip with my finger.

'Well, a little bit, yes.' Now I was circling the rim of my glass with my finger! Giovanni wasn't behaving at all! 'That was why I ignored your calls and . . .'

A bell was rung from somewhere and a well-spoken

English man shouted, 'Would you all gather on the steps for a group photograph?'

This was just as well, as my finger was nearly in my mouth.

'I just need to pop in here for a sec, Leo, I'll see you later.'

He leant down and kissed me on the cheek. He lingered with his mouth against my skin. I closed my eyes. It was so intimate.

'Are we friends again?' he whispered in my ear.

How did Michael Flatley get inside my tummy?

'Hmmm,' I whimpered back. And I knew we were going to kiss properly again later, in a National Trust house in Devon by the sea, and I couldn't wait.

♥ *eighty-seven* ♥

By the end of the dinner I still hadn't seen Ruth or Simon. Such was the singular achievement of passing excellence that was my table planning. If truth be told, my table planning had been pretty stupefying all round, especially as I wrote Peter Jackson twice and completely forgot to seat Marcus, Eamonn's son. But no one got upset because it was a wedding and everyone was wankered on free champagne. Heaven.

The dinner was delicious. The speeches were brilliant, although watching the entire output of *The Sopranos* might have been shorter. Everyone seemed to be standing up and having a word. Marcus as the best man was very funny and very moving and by the end of his speech my smoky eyes made me look like the Joker from *Batman*. Then Eamonn stood up and did a speech where he said that Rachel completed him. *Jerry Maguire* is one of my all-time favourite films. I was Batman then.

'Excuse me.' It was Rachel tapping her cheese knife on a glass. 'I know that the bride doesn't normally make a speech, but there is just one special "thank you" I wanted to make.'

The crowd hushed and Rachel stood up.

'Um, where do I start? I suppose a little back-story. I must tell you that I've never had a close girlfriend before. I feel I've gone through life meeting wonderful women and letting their friendships lapse because I was too busy to maintain them. Now I find myself staring death in the face. Please, I'm not being morbid when I say that. I want you to know that I am staring it in the face with the look of Lara Croft and an Uzi and I won't let it stand a chance. But still, I am aware of its presence now more than ever.

'So, I just want to say a few words about my wonderful friend Sarah here. Sarah is one of those people who looks for the positive. It used to do my head in. She would say, "I'm overweight but on a positive note I make those thinner than me feel good." She would say, "My boyfriend's left me for another woman. I'm devastated, but somehow at some point some good will come out of all this." Sorry, Simon, wherever you are; at least we can all laugh about it now.

'When I was diagnosed I told Sarah that I didn't want sympathy. I didn't want to get wet and wallow, a fact which I sometimes regretted when Sarah was exercising her repertoire of truly dreadful jokes.'

Everyone laughed a bit too knowingly if you ask me.

'Well, now, I'm going to look on the positive and in the process probably get a bit wet. Because here I am, the day of my wedding, and I have a husband.' She stops and smiles after she says the word 'husband'. 'Not just any husband, but the best man in the world. A man that I love in a way

I could never have imagined loving anyone. He wants to marry me two days before I have a breast removed; he loves me unconditionally and is willing to stand by me through this ordeal. But I also have a great girlfriend. And she is Sarah here. So I stand here today, in front of all of you wonderful people, and although there's an illness attacking my body, which makes me tired and angry and cry out in pain, I actually feel richer than I ever have before.

'And I just want to say thank you to Sarah, who has been with me every step of the way. At every doctor's appointment, she was at my side and holding my hand. A day hasn't gone by when she hasn't called and said, "I'm coming round to make you tea and broccoli." She even told Eamonn when I didn't feel I could. She has helped me organize today. I used her strength when I didn't have any of my own. And when I should feel that life has dealt me a rough card I actually feel very, very lucky. So I'd like you please all to stand and toast Sarah. To Sarah. She's a goddess.'

I couldn't see because tears were sliding down my face.

♥

The tables were pulled back and the band started. Eamonn and Rachel did their first dance to 'We Go Together', the song from the end of *Grease*. Eamonn looked quite happy for a man with two left feet and sixty pairs of eyes upon him. I stood whooping between Dominic and Brian in his red suit.

I might have a second career as a matchmaker because they were getting on very well.

'Drink?' said Dominic to Brian when the song ended.

'Love one, thanks, Dom.'

'Beanstalk?'

'Yes, please, you bugger.'

Dominic walked away.

'Hallelujah!' cried Brian, squeezing my waist. 'Great guy. There's a bit of Silas Anderson about him. Commanding and powerful.'

I rolled my eyes.

'He thinks you're a superstar!'

'Me?'

'Said you were a bloody amazing actress.'

'Did he?'

'Oh, darling, don't cry. He did mention that you sing like you're being strangled. Now then, introduce me to Banana Man while I can still stand.'

'I haven't seen him myself,' I said, looking about me.

'Is he the one with that cute baby? And the miserable-looking blonde?'

'Shhhh. She's all right.'

'They were at the dinner. Maybe they're putting the baby to bed.'

'Hmmm.'

'Ding dong, darling, look who's coming over . . .'

I knew who it was before I looked around. I knew he was talking about Leo Clement.

'Sarah,' Leo said when he got to me. 'Do you want to dance?'

'Oh . . .' I said, wondering whether I was drunk enough. 'Yeah, although I don't really do what most people would call dancing.'

He smiled and put his hand on my back and eased his fingers slightly inside the fabric of my dress. Brian nodded approval and then pretended to faint at Leo's beauty. The singer was having a go at 'Angels'. A nightmare to dance to. I stood nervously until Leo pulled me to him. I didn't know what to do with my hands. So I rested them on his shoulders. I could feel the muscles under his shirt. Our faces were close. I didn't want to say a word to him. I just did some little shuffling steps and swayed my hips and smiled at him.

'I'm a shithead,' he said.

'Cockhead,' I corrected him.

'Cockhead,' he repeated, but he still didn't have it right.

'I'm also a fan of knobhead. Although, that would have been too lightweight under the circumstances.'

'Will you teach me English slang, Sarah Sargeant?'

'I certainly will, Leo Clement. You'll be learning from a master.'

'That guy, the boyfriend, ex-boyfriend, is that . . . ?'

'It's cool now. He's here with his lady and baby.'

'Not that cutie?'

'Yeah, little Anna. How cute is she?'

I felt him tighten his grip on me and I melted into his chest.

'What are your plans now?'

'Oh, well, no idea, actually. Owing to that beautiful story in the *National Enquirer* I lost a commercial that would have meant I didn't need to work for years. So I really don't know. I want to be there for Rachel. But I think they might want some time together, just the two of them.'

'Would you like to spend some time in Malibu?'

'Oh . . .'

'Whenever you want . . .'

'Yes, um, yes, I guess, yes.'

He kissed my head.

'I don't have a spare room, though, I'm very sorry.'

'Oh,' I blushed.

'I can teach you to surf.'

I laughed at the thought of me on a surfboard. Then quickly stopped laughing at the thought of me in a wetsuit.

'Maybe I'll just sit on the beach and hold your towel.'

'Sarah.' It was Rachel tapping me on the shoulder. 'Sorry, Leo. Sare, my lovely, will you give me a hand having a pee?'

'Sure.'

I gave a mock curtsey to thank Leo for his dance and linked arms with Rachel and headed to the loos. We walked straight into Simon, Ruth and Anna, who were in the hall. Rachel cooed her way to Anna, whom Ruth was holding. I hung back, aware of Simon and not knowing what to do or say.

'Sarah,' he nodded at me.

'Hi,' I said. He looked tired. He didn't look like Simon. He looked older and as though he had the weight of the world on his shoulders. He didn't seem to have his oomph. I wanted to cheer him up. 'Did you like your free advertising?'

'Oh.' He smiled! 'Yeah, a blinder, thank you!'

'Pleasure.'

'Right, we're off now,' said Ruth uncomfortably.

'Why are you going so early?' asked Rachel.

'Anna and I need to, er, get back to London,' she stammered.

'Oh, well, thank you for coming.'

I took a step forward and smiled at little Anna and she gave me another big gummy grin back.

'You are the coolest,' I told her, because she was.

'Yeeaasss!' Si said, his face finally lighting up as he picked Anna up. 'That's what Daddy calls you, isn't it? You are the coolest.' He kissed her head and Anna gurgled.

I watched them. It was the garden fork in the foot moment.

'She is so the image of you.' I didn't mean to say it aloud. It was just what I was thinking. My voice cracked slightly as I said it and my pained tone surprised everyone, including myself.

'We'd better get you to the loo,' I said quickly to Rach, and we walked away.

I held the skirt of Rachel's dress over her head while she peed. As she was shrouded in vintage lace, Rachel spoke to me.

'He so knows he made the wrong choice.'

'Don't say that. They'll be all right.'

'Man, there was so horrible energy between them.'

'Rach, stop it.'

'Still, you're all smoochy smoochy with Leo!'

'Hmmm,' I said, remembering. But I didn't smile. I didn't like seeing Si down. Si down was like California in the fog, or *The X Factor* in black and white, or alcohol-free wine. It was horrible.

We went back to the party. Dominic and Brian were dancing. I made a subtle thumbs-up to Brian. Simon was talking to Eamonn and Rachel moved to join them. I didn't. I hung back and Leo approached me.

'Have you seen the boat house?' he asked.

'No,' I smiled.

'Do you want to see the boat house?'

'Hmmm. I should change my shoes though . . .'

'OK. I'll get some champagne, you do your feet.'

'But Leo, we have to be back later for the burlesque show!'

'I wouldn't want to miss that either,' he said with an eyebrow raised. Rachel had asked Sunflower Oil to perform. I didn't like to tell Leo that she must have been getting on for sixteen stone.

I dashed up to my room and found Rachel's Ugg boots. I stepped out of my heels and put them on. As I was leaving the room I stumbled on something. A folded note. I picked it up, thinking it was news about breakfast, one of my favourite subjects. I read as I walked. It wasn't about breakfast. And by the time I had finished reading I had stopped walking and was slumped in an armchair on the landing.

Sarah, it's Ruth.

I owe you a big sorry. Huge, in fact. I wonder whether it's the biggest sorry I've ever said.

You see, I took your Simon. And I didn't really think much of it. I didn't really think much of you. I'd always thought you were a bit of a mess, to be honest. And when I found out you were seeing Simon I didn't think it could be serious. But it seems it was. I think he really loves you, Sarah. I don't think he's ever loved me. We were both blinded by our love for little Anna, we thought some of that love might rub off on us. But it didn't.

So I'm leaving Simon. Obviously he will still see Anna often. I need to let him go and find his happiness. He told me you were going out with someone. But you're not, and the way you spoke about him last night leads me to think you still love him. So I feel I need to step aside so you two can sort things out. I completely support the two of you. But most of all, I'm sorry. And I think you are a remarkable person. Truly remarkable.

Ruth

I looked down at my Ugg boots. I was supposed to be going to the boat house to do snogging with Leo Clement. How could I go to the boat house now? It felt as though Ruth had crashed like an asteroid into my life and then buggered off and left me with lots of rubble. I didn't know what to think or what to do.

Leo ran up the stairs two at time and as soon as he

reached the top he spotted me, curled up, looking suicidal.

'Sarah, what happened?'

'Oh,' I tutted. 'I got a letter.' I weakly lifted it in my hand as proof. 'It's sort of taken the stuffing out of me.'

'Sorry,' he said, and stood before me looking both concerned and delicious.

'No, I'm sorry.'

I sprang from my seat. I scrunched the letter into a ball and lobbed it at the rubbish bin that was about six feet away. I missed badly so had to scamper to pick it up and drop it in there. I knew if I didn't my mother's voice would be in my head all evening saying, 'What would happen if everyone did that?'

We walked down the stairs together.

And it felt right. I had no idea what was in store with Leo. The future was a clear space waiting to be written. We hadn't ballsed it up yet. I couldn't say the same for Simon. The future with Simon would be a big messy space crammed with past hurts. He had broken me more than anyone before. It had taken a long time to rebuild myself. But the work was done now. And the construction felt stronger than it had been before. I didn't want to risk it being bulldozed again.

At the bottom of the stairs I took Leo's hand. We skipped through the front door and into the mild night.

'It's a beautiful night,' I cried and I held out my arms and twirled as I looked up at the stars. Leo grabbed me mid-twiddle and picked me up and threw me over his shoulder.

'Honestly, put me down. You'll hurt yourself,' I shrieked, bashing him on the back. But he strode on. We passed the bench where I had sat that morning. There was a figure silhouetted on the seat. And I knew it was blinking, bloody Simon even before he turned round. He watched us. Leo hadn't noticed the figure. But I had stopped squealing. It suddenly felt all wrong.

I made the sound 'urgh' as loudly as I possibly could. 'Leo, can you put me down, please?' I added.

'Sure,' he said, obliging.

'Leo.'

I looked at this incredibly beautiful man who had some sort of curse making him bat so far below his best. 'Leo, that bloke on the bench was the guy, you know the boyfriend person, and the letter was about him. It was from the girl he was with. She thinks he still loves me. And, urgh! I don't know what to do. I want to go to the boat house, but it feels a bit . . .'

'Wow. It was a pretty big deal with this guy.'

'Well, I don't know. We only went out for a few months, and I behaved like a loon and he left me for another woman. But I just hated him not being in my life.'

'Sounds like love.'

'Hmmm. Feels more like sadism.'

'Well, I guess you should go and talk to him.' He pursed his lips, smiled, then shrugged. 'I'll go inside and have a vodka. And I shall bid you farewell and I guess we'll stop this train of ours here.'

'Yeah,' I sighed sadly.

'But I liked being with you, Sarah Sargeant. From the moment I saw you being escorted through LAX by the police I thought you were something.'

He turned and walked away. I waited until he would be back in the house. Then I made the 'urgh' sound louder than ever before and marched back to Simon on the bench.

'Urgh' is the sound I made when I saw him. 'Urgh' is the noise I made again when his lips parted and his eyes widened and he stared at me all innocently.

'Urgh' is the sound I made when I started slapping him in the chest.

And I made the final 'urgh' sound as I flung myself onto the bench next to him.

'Hi, Sarah Sargeant,' he said casually.

'Bugger off,' I replied gruffly.

'Having a nice wedding?'

'I was.'

'I was just enjoying the peaceful night when this mad woman started attacking me.'

'Good.'

Simon laughed. So I told him to 'bog off'.

'Shall we go inside and dance?' he asked.

I sighed. I loved dancing with Simon. He completely understood my lack of rhythm and would join me in jumping around and miming the lyrics. I felt as if I'd danced with him recently. But I couldn't have, as I hadn't seen him.

'Oh,' I said, realizing why that was. 'I had to do this

stripping scene in the film. It was mortifying, as you can imagine. But the only way I could do it was to imagine you were there, taking the mickey, going, "Show us your Bobby Davroes!"'

It suddenly felt like a very pathetic thing to tell him. And I wished I hadn't. But he smiled. And I smiled back. It was a sad smile.

'Maybe we should do it for real.'

'What are you saying?'

'I'm saying that I know I screwed up completely, in every way. But you're the one for me. I can't really do not being with you. It's all a bit shit, Sare. There's not much sunshine when Sarah Sargeant isn't around.'

'But . . . Si . . . you just left me.'

'I know, and you might not be able to forgive me. All I know is that I missed my mate. And I flew out to you but I saw you with that guy.'

'I wasn't even with him. I couldn't even do bloody shagging, because I was thinking of you . . . you bastard.'

'And all these blokes on Facebook kept asking you out. I thought I should leave you to it.'

'Oh,' I said. Julia had got carried away with getting strange men to ask me out on my Facebook page.

'Do you think you could give us another chance?'

I didn't answer. I looked out into the darkness.

I used to be in a wonderful relationship with a bloke called Simon. We were supposed to live happily ever after. But we didn't. Our wonderful relationship followed the other oft-trod path.

It went tits up.

❤

And after all that, is it possible to go back a second time and make it work?

I don't know.

I really don't know.

But I'm going to try.

'Go on then, you bugger,' I say.

My chin twitches like I'm about to cry. I blink back tears because I want to look at him. He's here, with his little face and his dark hair. And those blue eyes that are like mine. It's like looking in a mirror in a way. He's so much a part of who I am. He feels like where I'm from.

'I love you, Simon Gussett,' I say, and I've never been so sure of anything in my life. He smiles. A tear appears on his cheek.

'I love you, Sarah Sargeant.'

Our faces are very close. He reaches forward to kiss me softly on the lips. I let my tears fall. They touch his. Then he pulls away a fraction.

'Show us your Bobby Davroes,' he says with a wink.

Acknowledgements

I owe some rather massive thank yous to some rather wonderful people. The first being my dad. If there was an award for Dad Most Well Versed in Chick Lit it would be yours, Dad. Thank you so much for tirelessly reading and listening and giving advice to me. You are amazing. As is your glamorous sidekick, Mum. I love you both so much. Thank you! A big, big thank you is undoubtedly also owed to Paul, the man who has the challenging role of putting up with me on a day-to-day basis. Thank you for spoiling me rotten, taking me to wonderful places and for flying me First Class and not minding when I got drunk on champagne and whooped at everything. Also thank you to the beautiful Caroline Devlin, oooh you are such a joy to know! Thanks too to Simon and Avia Hawksworth, Brent Gaffan and Carol Incontro for the Californian adventures. And, as ever, big thanks to my legendary friends, Simon Paul Sutton and Julia Veidt. I would also like to mention two wonderfully positive and inspiring ladies, Jan Roberts and Amanda Barr.

Acknowledgements

Now then, at the risk of it all going a bit end-of-*Jerry Maguire*, I want to thank Rowan Lawton, my agent, and the best agent in the world. I'm such a big fan of yours, Rowan.

I am so lucky to have such wonderful publishers. Endless thanks to all the amazing people that make up the Macmillan women's fiction team: most importantly my editor, Jenny Geras; but also Jeremy Trevathan, Imogen Taylor and Thalia Suzuma; the genius marketing ladies, Becky, Amy and Naomi and the gorgeous Helen in publicity; also the brilliant Eli Dryden and Jennie Condell.

Last but not least, thank you to all who bought my first book and made it possible for me to write a second. I've been blown away by the kindness and support of friends, family and readers, from my proud sister Gail Roberts standing in W H Smith and telling everyone to buy it – that wasn't embarrassing at all! – to my twelve-year-old nephew starting a fan club on Facebook, to receiving emails from lovely people I'd never met. Thank you.

extracts reading groups events
books competitions books new reading groups
discounts extracts extracts discounts
competitions new events
books
events extracts reading groups
new books
interviews reading groups
events extracts events
discounts events
new books events interviews
events new books
discounts extracts discounts extracts
www.panmacmillan.com
extracts events reading groups books
competitions books extracts new